JOE BUFF

TIDAL RIP

HarperTorch
An Imprint of HarperCollins*Publishers*

This is a work of fiction. Names, characters, places, and incidents are products of the author's imagination or are used fictitiously and are not to be construed as real. Any resemblance to actual events, locales, organizations, or persons, living or dead, is entirely coincidental.

HARPERTORCH
An Imprint of HarperCollins*Publishers*
10 East 53rd Street
New York, New York 10022-5299

First HarperTorch paperback printing: November 2004
First William Morrow hardcover printing: November 2003

HarperCollins ®, HarperTorch™, and ❧™ are trademarks of Harper-Collins Publishers Inc.

Printed in the United States of America

Visit HarperTorch on the World Wide Web at www.harpercollins.com

10 9 8 7 6 5 4 3 2 1

If you won't dare to think the unthinkable now, then someday you might be forced to live through it for real.

*No land force can act decisively
unless accompanied by a maritime superiority.*
—**George Washington**

Battleships are cheaper than battles.
—**Theodore Roosevelt**

*We assume that peace is the "normal" pattern of relations
among states. . . .
No idea could be more dangerous.*
—**Henry Kissinger,**
in ***Nuclear Weapons and Foreign Policy***

ACKNOWLEDGMENTS

The research and professional assistance that form the nonfiction technical underpinnings of *Tidal Rip* are a direct outgrowth and continuation of those for *Crush Depth, Thunder in the Deep,* and *Deep Sound Channel*. First I want to thank my formal manuscript readers: Cáptain Melville Lyman, U.S. Navy (ret.), commanding officer of several SSBN strategic missile submarines, and now director for special weapons safety and surety at the Johns Hopkins Applied Physics Laboratory; Commander Jonathan Powis, Royal Navy, who was navigator on the fast-attack submarine HMS *Conqueror* during the Falklands crisis, and who subsequently commanded three different British submarines; Lieutenant Commander Jules Verne Steinhauer, USNR (ret.), diesel-boat veteran, and naval aviation submarine liaison in the early Cold War; retired Senior Chief Bill Begin, veteran of many "boomer" strategic deterrent patrols; and Peter Petersen, who served in the German Navy's *U-518* in World War II. I also want to thank two Navy SEALs, Warrant Officer Bill Pozzi and Commander Jim Ostach, for their feedback, support, and friendship.

A number of other navy people gave valuable guidance: George Graveson, Jim Hay, and Ray Woolrich, all retired U.S. Navy captains, former submarine skippers, and active in the Naval Submarine League; Ralph Slane, vice-president of the New York Council of the Navy League of the United States, and docent of the *Intrepid* Museum; Ann Hassinger, research librarian at the U.S. Naval Institute; Richard Rosenblatt, M.D., formerly a medical consultant to the U.S. Navy; and Commander Rick Dau, USN (ret.), operations director of the Naval Submarine League.

Additional submariners and military contractors deserve acknowledgment. They are too many to name here, but standing out in my mind are pivotal conversations with Commander (now Captain) Mike Connor, at the time CO of USS *Seawolf,* and with the late Captain Ned Beach, USN (ret.), brilliant writer and one of the greatest submariners of all time. I also want to thank, for the guided tours of their fine submarines, the officers and men of USS *Alexandria,* USS *Connecticut,* USS *Dallas,* USS *Hartford,* USS *Memphis,* USS *Salt Lake City,* USS *Seawolf,* USS *Springfield,* USS *Topeka,* and the modern German diesel submarine *U-15.* I owe "deep" appreciation to everyone aboard the USS *Miami,* SSN 755, for four wonderful days on and under the sea.

Similar thanks go to the instructors and students of the New London Submarine School and the Coronado BUD/SEAL training facilities, and to all the people who demonstrated their weapons, equipment, attack vessels, and aircraft at the amphibious warfare bases in Coronado and Norfolk. Appreciation also goes to the men and women of the aircraft carrier USS *Constellation,* the Aegis guided-missile cruiser USS *Vella Gulf,* the fleet-replenishment oiler USNS *Pecos,* the deep submergence rescue vehicle *Avalon,* and its chartered tender the *Kellie Chouest.*

The Current Strategy Forum, and publications, of the Naval War College were similarly invaluable. The opportunity to fly out to the amphibious warfare helicopter carrier USS *Iwo Jima* during New York City's Fleet Week 2002, and then join with her sailors and marines in rendering honors as the ship passed Ground Zero, the former site of the World

Trade Center, was one of the most powerfully emotional experiences of my life.

First among the publishing professionals who deserve acknowledgment is my wife, Sheila Buff, a nonfiction author with more than two dozen titles in health and wellness and nutrition, nature loving, and bird-watching. Then comes my literary agent, John Talbot, who lets me know exactly what he likes or doesn't like in no uncertain terms. Equally crucial is my editor at William Morrow, Mike Shohl, always enthusiastic, accessible, and inspiring through his keen insights on how to improve my manuscript drafts.

NOTES FROM THE AUTHOR

Recent geopolitical events have served to remind us all of important old lessons: The world is a volatile, dangerous place. Victory in one war can unpredictably heighten global tension and instability, creating power vacuums to be filled by ambitious new terrorists and tyrants, triggering more armed strife. International coalitions ebb and flow, but the proliferation of weapons of mass destruction raises the stakes of diplomacy to a frightening degree. Profound changes are taking place in the threats to America and our allies. These perilous trends require decisive action. Yet solutions are impossible without properly trained personnel, equipment, war-fighting doctrine, and national will.

Since their inception, in every era, submarines rank among the most sophisticated weapons systems, and the most impressive benchmarks of technology and engineering, achieved by the human race. Stunning feats of courage by their crews, of sacrifice and endurance, loom large on the pages of history. Special Forces commandos, dating in concept to the Second World War, tremendously leverage the power of main-line formations. In the strange new world the twenty-first century is turning out to be, joint operations beneath, upon, and launched from the sea will stay crucial to influencing events on land around the globe.

The tools and techniques of modern warfare are constantly advancing. Development will continue, rendered more urgent by the War on Terror and the pent-up spreading of nuclear arms. Breakthrough sonar systems enable a quantum leap in submarine capability to stealthily search for ultraquiet hostile targets. Advanced SEAL Delivery System minisubs, transported by larger host vessels, covertly deploy combat swimmers to the forward coastline area. Remote-controlled Unmanned Undersea Vehicles and Unmanned Aerial Vehicles, with mission-configured sensor packages—some of them even armed—turn their parent nuclear subs into veritable undersea aircraft carriers, invisibly lurking beneath the waves.

The world's oceans are the world's highways for the transport of goods and the conduct of commerce. The oceans are also barriers to wholesale invasion by enemy troops, yet they provide efficient routes of access to spy on those enemies and aid our friends. Mastery of undersea warfare is therefore vital, for whoever controls the ocean's depths controls its surface—and thus controls much of the world. Seapower, strongly employed, is key to protecting peaceful societies everywhere.

To some questions about the future of national defense, valid answers will be critical to preserve democracy and freedom: Which gaps in our security posture, or blind spots in our thinking, could be exploited in the years to come by a shrewd, aggressive emerging Evil Empire or Axis of Conspiracy? From what unforeseen quarter might the next bloody surprise attack fall? What sacrifices and feats of courage will America and our allies need to prevail in the almost inevitable, eventual Next Big War? Perhaps the only certainty is that heroic submariners and SEALs will play an indispensable part in deterring that war, or in winning it.

JOE BUFF
May 31, 2003
Dutchess County, New York

TIDAL RIP

PROLOGUE

In mid-2011, Boer-led reactionaries seized control of the government in South Africa in the midst of social chaos and restored apartheid. In response to a UN trade embargo, the Boer regime began sinking U.S. and British merchant ships. Coalition forces mobilized, with only Germany holding back. Troops and tanks drained from the rest of Western Europe and North America, and a joint task force set sail for Africa—into a giant, coordinated trap.

Then there was another coup, this one in Berlin, and Kaiser Wilhelm's great-grandson was crowned, the Hohenzollern throne restored after almost a century. Ultranationalists, exploiting American unpreparedness for such all-out war, would give Germany her "place in the sun" at last. A secret military-industrial conspiracy had planned it all for years, brutal opportunists who hated the mediocrity and homogenization of the European Union as much as they resented what to them· seemed like America's smug self-infatuation. Big off-the-books loans from Swiss and German money-center banks, collateralized by booty that would be plundered from the losers, funded the stealthy *buildup. The kaiser was to serve as the German shadow oligarchy's figurehead, made to legitimize their New Order. Coercion by the noose won over citizens who had not been swayed by patriotism or the sheer onrush of events.*

This Berlin-Boer Axis had covertly built small tactical atomic weapons, the great equalizers in what would otherwise have been a most uneven fight—and once again America's CIA was clueless. South Africa, during "old" apartheid, had a successful nuclear arms program, canceled around 1990 under international pressure. Preparing for new apartheid, and working in secret with German support, the conspirators assembled many new fission devices: compact, energy-efficient, very low-signature dual-laser isotope-separation techniques let them purify uranium ore into weapons grade in total privacy.

The new Axis, seeking a global empire all their own, used these low-yield A-bombs to ambush the Allied naval task force under way, then destroyed Warsaw and Tripoli. France, in shock, surrendered at once, and continental Europe was overrun. Germany won a strong beachhead in North Africa, while the South African army drove hard toward them to link up. The battered Allied task force put ashore near the Congo Basin, in a last-ditch attempt to hold the Germans and well-equipped Boers apart. In both Europe and Africa the fascist conquest trapped countless Allied civilians: traveling businesspeople, vacationing families, student groups on summer tours. Americans and Brits were herded into internment camps near major Axis factories and transport nodes, as hostages and human shields. It was unthinkable for the Allies to retaliate against Axis tactical nuclear weapons used primarily at sea by launching ICBMs with hydrogen bombs into the heart of Western Europe. The U.S. and UK were handcuffed, forced to fight on Axis terms on ground of Axis choosing: the midocean, using A-bomb-tipped cruise missiles and torpedoes. Information warfare hacking of the Global Positioning System satellite signals, and ingenious jamming of smart-bomb homing sensors, made the Allies' *vaunted precision-guided high-explosive munitions much less precise. Advanced radar methods in the FM radio band—pioneered by Russia—removed the invisibility of America's finest stealth aircraft.*

Thoroughly relentless, Germany grabbed nuclear subs from the French, and advanced diesel subs that Germany herself had exported to other countries—these ultraquiet diesels with fuel-cell air-independent propulsion needn't surface or even raise a snorkel for weeks or months at a time. Some were shared with the Boers, whose conventional heavy-armaments industry—a world leader under old apartheid—had been revived openly during the heightened global military tensions of the early twenty-first century. A financially supine Russia, supposedly neutral yet long a believer in the practicality of limited tactical nuclear war, sold weapons as well as oil and natural gas to the Axis for hard cash. Most of the rest of the world stayed on the sidelines, biding their time out of fear or greed or both.

American supply convoys to starving Great Britain are being decimated by the modern U-boat threat, in another bloody Battle of the Atlantic. The UK has suffered stoically through one of the harshest winters on record—food, fuel, and medical supplies are running critically low. Tens of thousands of merchant seamen died in the Second World War, and the casualty lists grow very long this time too.

Now, nine months into the war, in early spring of 2012, America is smarting from serious setbacks in the Indian Ocean theater. The vital Central Africa pocket—composed of surviving U.S./coalition forces and friendly local African troops—is in danger of complete envelopment by the Axis. With cargo vessels being sunk much faster than they can be replaced, resupply across the shipping lanes is becoming harder and harder. Yet if the pocket and the UK fall, the Axis onslaught will overwhelm all of two continents. At the same time, Axis agents are making serious trouble in Latin America, exploiting continued local political instability and economic distress; a whole new front could threaten U.S. security and strategic material resources from due south. Brazil, like South Africa, had a nuclear weapons program in the 1980s—its current status isn't known by American intelligence.

If the situation deteriorates much further, and Allied forces become too overstretched, the U.S. will have no choice but to recognize Axis territorial gains. With so many atom bombs set off at sea by both sides, and the oil slicks from many wrecked ships, oceanic environmental damage has already been severe. Presented with everything short of outright invasion, and nuclear weapons not used against the United States homeland quite yet, the U.S. may be forced to sue for an armistice: a de facto Axis victory. A new Evil Empire would threaten the world, and a new Iron Curtain would fall.

America and Great Britain each own one state-of-the-art ceramic-hulled fast-attack sub—such as USS Challenger, *capable of tremendous depths—but the Axis own such vessels too. With Germany's latest, the* Admiral von Scheer, *representing a whole new level of antiship power and stealth, the U.S. is on the defensive everywhere, and democracy has never been more threatened. In this terrible new war, with the midocean's surface a killing zone, America's last, best hope for enduring freedom lies with a special breed of fearless undersea warriors. . . .*

In the not too distant future

The air was cold and dank and smelled of diesel oil. Ozone laced with the stench of dead fish was pungent. Wearing his full dress uniform, including clumsy ceremonial sword, Korvettenkapitan Ernst Beck stood morosely on the concrete pier amid the modern underground U-boat pens, above the Arctic Circle. Noise echoed from all around him in the vast but sealed-off space, from cranes and pumps and power tools and forced ventilation ducts. Beck could almost feel the weight of thousands of meters of solid granite press down on him from above, from the steep and snow-clad mountain, up a long and very deep fjord, into whose sheltering massiveness this complex of pens had been blasted and cut.

While he killed time patiently waiting for his captain, Beck—whose rank equaled lieutenant commander in the U.S. or Royal navies—thought the recent construction work here looked skillfully done and well planned. He knew it was mostly completed by Norway, an active member of NATO, before Norway was overrun and occupied when Beck's country, resurgent Imperial Germany, went to war. In fact, if Beck paid careful enough attention when he breathed, the air still smelled slightly sour, from the curing of fresh-poured cement. The lighting, from floodlights and bare fluorescents, was glaring and harsh. From near and far many voices yelled to one another, orders or questions and answers projected above the machinery din. Beck's crewmen were crisp and professional; the yard workers in their own proud way sounded tough and intentionally vulgar.

As he glanced up for a moment at the lowering, hard gray ceiling of the pens—barely higher than the sail, the conning tower, of his stark black nuclear submarine—Ernst Beck also felt the weight of the burden of many cares. In the dock beside him loomed the big new vessel, the mighty undersea warship on which he would serve as executive officer, with all the responsibilities that entailed. A family man with a devoted wife and sturdy young twin sons, good Catholic in the traditional Bavarian way, and trapped in a tactical nuclear war he believed to be morally wrong, Beck knew he was lucky to still be alive. He also felt secretly guilty, that he could smile and make love with his wife and drink beer when so many others were dead and utterly gone, friends and colleagues some of them, vaporized or crushed and drowned or felled by acute radiation sickness. Yet ironically, Beck also was glad. He knew he was lucky indeed after his recent misadventures in battle: to have this fine ship, to get this important assignment, even to be allowed to go to sea once more at all. . . .

Again Beck felt that gnawing in his innermost self, and

fought against another combat flashback. *Not now, of all times, with my captain due any moment and our warship about to put to sea.* But still the flashback came, the same way the awful nightmares never ceased.

The screams of torpedo engine sounds, and of terrified, agonized men. The murderous crack and rumble and the body-wrenching shock force, like thunderclaps mixed with an earthquake, as nuclear torpedoes went off near and far. The acrid smell of fear in the control room, and the smell of choking smoke, then the worse smell of burning corpses mixed with urine and vomit and shit ... Running breathlessly, and hoarsely shouting orders above the crackle of the flames. Climbing the steep steel ladder in desperation with a dying master chief draped on his shoulders—Beck's best friend. Trying to think straight and give leadership while truly scared and exhausted beyond enduring.

Beck shook his head. There was nothing glamorous about tactical nuclear war at sea. It tore at the heart and battered the mind, and left the human soul in shredded fragments. These broken shards of Ernst Beck's soul ripped at him from inside sometimes, a feeling in his stomach like broken glass. The intergenerational Germanic craving for empire, even at the risk of national self-immolation, seemed incurable, unquenchable. Decades could pass, and the disease was reborn, like a flare-up of a stubborn case of malaria ... or the dreaded return of a once-cured cancer that this time might be terminal.

For escape, Beck turned to gaze admiringly at his ship, his submarine—his new home and his new life. She'd been christened the SMS *Admiral von Scheer,* to honor the commander of the German fleet at the Battle of Jutland in World War I—a battle the Germans called Skagerrak, and which to this day they insisted they'd won. The British saw it differently, but the Brits were on the point of starvation now, and maybe on the point of surrender, in part thanks to Beck's previous war-fighting handiwork. Beck had already helped sink a million tons of Allied shipping, and killed God knows how many people in the process, and he was a hero. He now wore the prestigious Knight's Cross around his neck.

But Ernst Beck didn't feel like a hero.

Blessedly, he was distracted when he saw a young, skinny figure clamber up through the *von Scheer*'s forward hatch. Beck recognized Werner Haffner, the sonar officer, a lieutenant junior grade from Kiel—a historic German port and naval base on the Baltic Sea.

Haffner was high-strung but capable. Unlike most of the *von Scheer*'s crew, Haffner had been with Beck *before,* on his previous mission, the one from which so few men came back. The crew of the *von Scheer,* who all reported to Beck directly or indirectly, were still largely unknown quantities to him. Though they, like Beck himself, had for years trained secretly aboard not-so-neutral Russia's nuclear submarine fleet—for a hefty fee, of course—the bulk of *von Scheer*'s crew were as untested in actual combat as their brand-new ship. This worried Beck, who would somehow have to turn them into one cohesive unit through the unforgiving medium of war itself.

"Sorry, sir," Haffner said.

"You're lucky our captain is running even later than you," Beck responded as sternly as he could. "Fix your uniform, and try not to trip over your sword again." But Beck smiled. He liked Werner Haffner, and felt better having the leutnant zur see standing there next to him. Seeing Haffner reminded Beck that surviving was possible.

One of *von Scheer*'s senior chiefs approached Beck on the pier. The oberbootsmann wore work clothes, gray coveralls and steel-toed boots. He looked harried but in control. The chief braced to a cocky, all-knowing attention. "We're ready to take on the fuel for the Mach eight missiles, Einzvo. The dockyard handling parties are getting in position now to transfer the liquid hydrogen."

"Carry on." Since Beck was executive officer—erster wach-offizier in German, first watch officer—he was often addressed in that navy slang, the acronym 1WO pronounced phonetically "einzvo."

Beck glanced toward the after part of his ship. The two

dozen thick, pressure-proof hatches for the cruise missiles were all tightly closed. Most of those hatches covered internal silos that each held several supersonic antiship cruise missiles, nuclear armed. These missiles were of Russian design, export-model Modified Shipwrecks. They did Mach 2.5, fast enough. Some of the silos held cargo instead, including crated tactical atomic warheads that Beck assumed were meant for delivery to the Boers in distant South Africa. The Boers made their own warheads, using native uranium ore, but they might be running low on weapons-grade material because of recent heavy use in the Indian Ocean battle theater.

And one of the *von Scheer*'s silos held two German-designed top-secret liquid-hydrogen-powered ground-hugging cruise missiles that actually did Mach 8. Nothing the Allies had could stop them, even if they knew they were inbound. One such missile, nuclear tipped, was enough to destroy an American supercarrier with almost absolute certainty. Beck hoped that on this next mission the *von Scheer* would account for two.

The Mach 8 missiles were in very short supply, thanks to interference from the Allies. For all Beck knew, the two he held on board were the last ones Germany had, and it would take a year to retool and manufacture more. Who could tell where the war might stand by then?

The loudspeakers in the dock area announced the commencement of fueling operations. The tinny-sounding voice concluded, "All unnecessary personnel leave the area." Beck listened to the words echo and die away against the oppressive concrete walls enclosing him and his men and his ship.

Beck ordered *von Scheer*'s hatches shut and dogged. But since his captain was still due from the base admiral's office with final mission orders any moment, Beck and Haffner stayed on the pier, as the ship's reception committee.

Beck's captain was a jolly, roly-poly man, emotionally expressive, candid and frank. Beck found this a refreshing change from his previous commanding officer, an austere and distant man, arrogant and unlikable; it had been hard for

Beck, the son of a dairy farmer, to work for such an aristocratic snob. Beck looked forward to his new captain's arrival
now, so they could get under way, and Beck could draw some
comfort from this captain's ample personal warmth. Obedience to someone he admired fulfilled Beck. He dearly loved
the sea, and loved being a submariner—the intimate sense of
community among the crew, hiding together submerged far
down underwater, to Beck was nurturing despite the risks. It
helped make up for the loneliness, the homesickness, each
time he went on deployment and left his wife and sons behind.
Besides, the sooner this war was over with and won, the
sooner Beck's family and the whole world would be safe. Safe
from constant danger and hunger and want. Safe from drifting
atomic fallout and all its harmful effects. Safe from the dread
of uncontrolled escalation to major nuclear fighting on land.

Beck caught himself, his mind wandering again, and felt
conflicted. Such doubts and fears, even unspoken, were unpatriotic. Beck was a man who'd been decorated by the figurehead kaiser himself. Beck forced his thoughts to focus on
specific tasks of the present. . . .

The liquid hydrogen would be pumped into the cryogenic
storage tanks inside the *von Scheer*'s hull through a special
fitting in the side of the hull near the stern. Beck saw the
thick insulated transfer hose was already in place. Several of
Beck's crewmen, supervised by the senior chief, stood on
the after hull or on the pier. They worked ropes that helped
support the weight of the hose as it bridged the gap from the
edge of the pier, over the frigid dirty water in the dock, and
up to the hull's refueling port.

All is in order. . . .

*And except for the type of fuel, and what weapons that
fuel is meant for, this could be a scene off one of our diesel
U-boats in World War II.*

Beck watched idly from a distance as technicians in protective suits worked controls at the base's fueling station, beyond the far end of the pier. Quickly, exposed pipes and
valves began to cake with frost: moisture from the air in the

pens, instantly freezing on contact with the chilled fittings. One man went to turn a large main valve wheel, to admit the super-cold liquid hydrogen into the hose to the *von Scheer*.

Beck saw a sudden blur of frantic motion. Someone shouted, but the words were lost in a roar of glaring, angry, bright red flames.

Beck flinched involuntarily against the radiant heat as men rushed to douse a fire by the refueling station. Other men dashed for more hoses. A special team in silver reflective flame entry suits moved in with their foam applicators.

Beck knew immediately that something was terribly wrong. The fire grew hotter and brighter, and as he watched, the visible front of the flames engulfed a wider and wider area. Beck's heart pounded hard—the men were being driven back, and their firefighting hoses were burning through. Beck heard more garbled shouting and screaming. He bellowed orders of his own, but the *von Scheer*'s crew were already racing to disconnect the fueling hose.

The heat in the enclosed space of the pens began to mount frighteningly. Burning rubber, lubricants, paint, even clothing gave off sooty, choking clouds of thick black smoke. The smoke mixed surreally with the fluffy billowing white of searing live steam from fast-combusting hydrogen. Beck watched in disbelief as someone in the distance collapsed, his whole body on fire.

Beck desperately wanted to help, but the scene was almost the length of two soccer fields away and there was nothing he could do. The *von Scheer*'s hatches stayed sealed up— Beck dared not try to have one opened lest he endanger his ship catastrophically. Beck turned to Werner Haffner, standing there mesmerized. He shouted, "Come on!"

Both men ran to the far end of the pier, beyond the *von Scheer*'s bow—away from the fire. They were confronted by the huge steel interlocking blast doors leading out to the fjord; the way was barred completely.

Beck glanced back in abject terror. Hungry flames like living things were leaping to more and more cartons and crates of provisions, feeding hungrily on hydraulic fluid in cranes, or licking seductively at oiled machinery.

Steam lashed Beck's skin and throat. Smoke hurt his lungs. His eyes stung blindingly. Roaring and crackling punished his ears. He felt unbearable heat on his face, felt heat right through his uniform. The fire was out of control.

Beck tore off his sword belt and urged Haffner to do so as well. *There's only one thing left.*

Beck shoved Haffner into the water in the dock and jumped in after him. Both men went far down before they could fight their way upward for air—from below, Beck saw eerie red and orange glows flicker and glint off the water. At last his drenched head broke the surface.

The water was salty and bitterly cold. Beck coughed as it went up his nose. His eyes burned even more, from the salt, but at least he and Haffner were protected from some of the heat. The air this low was more breathable. Beck felt his woolen uniform begin to soak through, chilling him—in the wintry fjord, just outside, floated many big chunks of ice. Then the cold hit with full force. Through his sodden white dress gloves Beck's fingers ached with a throbbing pain. His breathing came in uncontrollable, overrapid gasps. His clothing grew heavy from the weight of added water, and he knew his attempts to swim were getting clumsier. He began to fear hypothermia as much as he feared the fire.

Beck saw Haffner also struggling to keep afloat. Neither man wore a life jacket. Beck summoned the last of his strength. He grabbed the lieutenant and together they worked their way to the first of the big rubber fenders that cushioned the *von Scheer* against the pier. There were no steps or handholds for them to climb onto the fender. Its top was much too high for Beck to reach. Beck floated like an insignificant speck next to his ship. He looked longingly up at her massive hull: immense and round and smooth, inhuman, uncaring, and slimy from immersion in seawater during the latest shakedown cruise. It was impossible to get up that way without help.

Beck's fingers were completely numb from the cold, and

he'd lost most of the feeling in his groin and in his neck. His eardrums hurt as he heard a dull thud, then a sharp bang, from the direction of the fire. Above him a layer of smoke and steam grew thicker, reaching lower and lower each second. Beck wondered if he'd drown first, or asphyxiate. He and Haffner huddled their freezing bodies together for warmth, their arms hooked through fittings in the fender to keep their heads from going under. At the same time, in mind-twisting contradiction, the exposed top of Beck's head and the tips of his ears suffered more and more heat. In the distance men continued to shout or scream unintelligibly.

Beck waited for the end, for a final blast of liquid hydrogen flash-boiling into gas and detonating inside the U-boat pens like a hyperbaric bomb.

But the pitch of the fire sounds altered, becoming more defensive and subdued. The loudest roaring now was the blasting of water from firefighting nozzles. The shouting Beck heard was much more confident, not panicky . . . even triumphant.

The noise and heat began to diminish.

The roaring changed pitch yet again. Ventilators on full power drew fresh air in from outside and the smoke was expelled. At last crewmen appeared on the forward part of *von Scheer*'s hull. They lowered a rescue team on ropes, and these men pulled Beck and Haffner out of the oily, stinking water.

Someone put a thick wool blanket around Beck's shoulders and gave him a glass of medicinal brandy. He gulped it gratefully, but shook off any offers of further help. Now he was very angry, angry that something had gone wrong that might have harmed his beautiful ship. Angry at himself, for being caught so useless. Then he saw dead bodies on the pier, some of them charred, and wounded men, some with serious burns. Now Beck was even angrier, because in the crisis he'd run for his life while others bravely battled the fire. The fact that there was nothing he could have done did little to ease his mind.

The ship's medical corpsman came out of a hatch, with spare sets of winter coveralls and seaboots and towels.

"Get out of those wet things immediately, sir," the corpsman told Beck. Beck and Haffner stripped and dried themselves, putting on fresh clothes right there atop the hull. An assistant corpsman climbed out of the hatch and helped Beck don a thick orange parka for added warmth. Beck felt better physically, and the brandy and the anger he was feeling restored his mental strength. He had a thousand things to look into.

"How many of the crew are hurt?" Beck demanded.

"No one below, sir," the corpsman said. "Topside, I don't know yet."

The chief of the boat stuck his head out of the forward hatch. He was the highest-ranking noncommissioned officer aboard, and overseeing the day-to-day well-being of the ship and her crew were significant parts of his job. "Negligible damage below, Einzvo. Engineer reports he's inspecting the outside stern right now, but so far just a few nicks in the anechoic coatings."

Beck breathed a sigh of relief.

"Sir!" called the senior chief whom Beck had talked to before, the leader of the refueling party. The man walked up the aluminum gangway from the pier. "You better come and see this." The chief's jumpsuit was covered in soot; his eyes were red and his nose dripped black snot. He sounded hoarse, and Beck could see the marks from a firefighting respirator mask against his face. But at least the chief was all right, which seemed to suggest the other crewmen at the back of the hull might be safe.

Beck eyed Haffner. "Sonar, go below and get some rest."

"But, sir—"

"A direct order, Sonar." Beck pointed at the open hatch; Haffner climbed down. Beck envied Haffner his energy, the resilience of youth, but he knew that with Haffner's wiry, birdlike build delayed shock could set in soon.

Beck followed the senior chief wearily, and warily. The chief's whole manner told Beck it would be bad news. They walked toward the dockyard's refueling station.

The station equipment was charred, though the main liquid-hydrogen containment hadn't been breached—Beck knew they'd all be dead now if it had. The ceiling every-where was blackened, and twisted aluminum ducting and broken wiring conduits hung down. These swayed weirdly in the artificial and icy wind from the forced-ventilation ducts.

Overhead lightbulbs were shattered, and Beck felt bits of broken glass as they crunched beneath his boots. Emergency floodlights bathed the scene. Paint was burned and peeled from structural beams; the naked steel was oxidized to rust. The concrete floor was slippery from firefighting foam. Mounds of debris from once-neat stacks of spare parts and supplies and food still smoldered or dripped; firefighters me-thodically hosed down stubborn sources of smoke. Two forklifts and an overhead traveling crane were total losses.

Despite the ventilators going all out, the smell was terri-ble. Beck saw men using digital cameras to record every-thing they could. He saw other men fill body bags, or lay white rubber sheets over smaller pieces of flesh.

"Here, sir," the senior chief said. He had to raise his voice above the continuing roar of the ventilators. The chief led Beck to a body bag. Rescue workers stepped respectfully aside. The chief unzipped the bag.

The thing inside looked barely human. Blood oozed where there once had been skin. The clothing was either dark ash or was soaked with the bright red blood. The stench close up, to Beck, was much too familiar.

The body was burned beyond recognition. The chief reached down and lifted the corpse's identity tags, on a chain around what was left of the neck. Ernst Beck knelt and read the metal tags; someone else had already scraped off the ashes and clotted blood. This was the corpse of Beck's cap-tain, caught on his way from the base admiral's office, in the wrong place at the wrong time.

Before the dismay and grief had a chance to sink in, the base admiral himself strode up.

"Sabotage," the admiral snapped. Almost two meters tall, he towered over Beck. His eyes were hard and his lips were mean and his whole manner said he was not used to being questioned by subordinates.

Even so, Beck asked how he knew.

"The valves for the foam were all chained in the off position. They were chained *on,* like they should be, when inspected half an hour before the refueling started. . . . And the water deluge system, it's fed by gravity alone, it's supposed to be foolproof. But something, someone, put obstructions in the holding tanks. Waterlogged wooden plugs dragged into the distribution pipes the moment the teams yanked the emergency downpour."

"But somebody still had to start a fire, Admiral," Beck said. "Didn't all the equipment get checked?" For incendiaries, or time bombs, he meant.

"A suicide arsonist. That was the easiest part for them to arrange. . . . We were infiltrated. Norwegian freedom fighters." The admiral surveyed the scene, which Beck now realized was being treated like a crime scene. "One or two of these bodies . . . The saboteurs were probably the first to die. If my firemen had been one jot less aggressive attacking the flames with what little they had until we could fix the main problems . . . We averted a total disaster by seconds."

Beck felt stunned and violated that this secure base had been so brazenly, easily penetrated. But he also had to admire the skill and self-sacrifice of the partisans.

"Did they know the *von Scheer* was here?"

"We have to assume so. It can't be just chance, that all this happens right as you're fueling your missiles."

Beck nodded grimly. "That means the resistance knows all about us." The *von Scheer*'s location in northernmost Norway was one of Germany's most closely guarded secrets.

The admiral's face hardened even more. "Yes. Which means the Allies might know already, or they'll find out very soon. You must get under way at once."

"But what about the captain?"

"You assume command. Get the *von Scheer* out of here. She'll be much safer at sea."

"Are those my formal orders, sir?"

"Yes. Verbal, but formal. You're by far the best qualified. I'll send you a messenger with spare keys and the combinations for the commanding officer's safe. Meantime finish inspecting your ship for damage, then begin reactor start-up. You can study your deceased captain's mission orders once you're under way." He nodded to an aide, who handed Beck a thick sealed packet marked in red MOST SECRET.

Beck took it. "Er, yes, Admiral."

"Manage as best you can. This is not your first patrol."

No. Just my first patrol as a captain.

"Yes, Admiral. Of course."

The admiral shook Beck's hand gruffly, then glanced around again at the death and the wreckage. "Such a waste of good men. I'll never hear the end of this from Berlin." Members of the admiral's staff, and shore-support logistics officers, were already gathering, seeking the admiral's attention on urgent details. Standing around, they gaped at the gore and destruction. But Beck had seen more than enough.

He turned to walk back to his ship.

"Wait," the admiral called. "One other thing. You wouldn't have known."

"Sir?"

"Berlin has a passenger for you. That's him now." The admiral pointed to a figure walking down the ramp from the upper, administration level, now that the automatic fire-containment doors had all been raised. Beck saw a civilian, carrying a small suitcase.

The civilian came closer. He wore an expensive business suit and a fine silk tie. He glanced at the blood and burned flesh all around with a look more of disgust than of horror.

"Are you the *von Scheer*'s captain?" the man asked Beck. His voice was very refined. There was a certain aristocratic hauteur to his expression. His posture, his movements, were polished and smooth. And also subtly condescending.

"No. The captain is dead. I'm first officer."

The admiral overheard. *Admirals always do have eyes and ears in the back of their heads.*

"I said you're commanding officer now," the admiral snapped. His tone conveyed, *So act the part and get on with it.*

"Indeed," the civilian commented, taking this interplay in. He held out his hand and Beck shook it as firmly as he could. "Rudiger von Loringhoven," the civilian said, by way of introducing himself.

Von Loringhoven began to walk toward the *von Scheer*'s gangway, forcing Beck to follow him.

"Who are you, exactly?" Beck asked.

"Diplomatic Corps. Are the kampfschwimmer aboard yet?" Kampfschwimmer, battle swimmers, were the German Navy equivalent of U.S. Navy SEALs or the Royal Navy's Special Boat Squadron.

"Yes," Beck said. "Before the fire, with all their equipment . . . If you don't mind my asking, why are you here?" Beck realized that von Loringhoven spoke with a hint of a Spanish accent. There were much easier ways to get from Norway to Spain than by submarine.

Von Loringhoven handed his leather suitcase to a crewman and started down the ladder inside the forward hatch. He didn't request permission to come aboard, or show any other courtesy. Halfway down, von Loringhoven glanced back up at Beck.

"It's all in your secret orders, *Captain*. I should know, I helped write them."

CHAPTER 1

The Omni Shoreham Hotel, Washington, D.C.

Commander Jeffrey Fuller let the hubbub of the cocktail reception swirl around him in the huge grand ballroom of the posh and historic hotel. The crowd moved to its own indecipherable Washington rhythms. The strong conversational currents and nasty undercurrents of glittering socialites and power brokers seemed to be running way above his head, his feet hurt from standing for hours, and he was hoarse from too much talking. The weight of the bronze medallion of his brand-new Medal of Honor felt heavier and heavier on its ribbon around his neck. He tried to remind himself that the whole reception was in his honor, but Jeffrey could see by now that almost everyone had really shown up for selfish reasons. If anything, he told himself ruefully, the nation's capital during this grimmest of wartimes was more unforgivingly competitive, and more politically manic, than ever before.

Still, part of Jeffrey felt very fulfilled. He was surrounded by so much sheer *energy* from all these people, and this moment was the ultimate achievement of his naval career. He was also grateful that, at least for the moment, he was being ignored, lost in the crowd of civilians and of men and women in uniform. He tried to rest his eyes, which hurt from the glare of so many TV camera lights. The reporters must have gotten the footage they wanted of him, because the different clumps of extra glare from those lights were far away in the gigantic room. Jeffrey welcomed his temporary sense of solitude within the mob—this came easily to a submariner, who lived in a cramped and crowded world and needed to make his own privacy, internally, wherever he was.

One of Jeffrey's former shipmates, stationed now at the Pentagon, came by. "Hey, Captain. Way to *go!*" The two of them talked for a couple of minutes, then the other man moved on.

Again, Jeffrey savored a fleeting sense of joy, a tingling in his chest, and a lightness in his gut. *The Medal of Honor . . .* He tried not to remember that winning a medal in battle usually meant that other good people hadn't made it back.

All around Jeffrey wineglasses and cocktail glasses and soft-drink glasses clinked. Tuxedoed waiters circulated smoothly through the hundreds of guests, offering tidbits of snacks on silver trays. The offerings were meager, compared to all the events the hotel had hosted over the years, because of wartime austerity. It wasn't lost on Jeffrey that all the wines were inexpensive labels, and every one of them was American made.

Jeffrey had had little appetite at lunch. Now his stomach rumbled, not that anyone else would notice in this din. As a waiter passed, he grabbed a bite to eat—a cracker with cheese spread.

Jeffrey realized that none of the hors d'oeuvres he'd seen all afternoon included seafood. This wasn't surprising, considering the amount of nuclear waste and fallout built up by now in the Atlantic. Some scientists said the ecological damage wasn't really that severe, that the ocean was very vast and so the toxins were hugely diluted. The relatively small tactical atomic warheads now—used by both sides hundreds of miles from land—weren't much compared to the many megatons the U.S. and USSR and other nuclear powers had

tested in the atmosphere or in the oceans in the early Cold
War. But it was very different, at least psychologically, in an
actual shooting war. No one was taking chances, which was
too bad. Jeffrey loved seafood.

He quickly went from feeling fulfilled to feeling glum.
Some of the atomic weapons detonated in the oceans had
been set off by his ship, on his orders. Jeffrey wondered for
the umpteenth time how many whales and dolphins he'd
killed, collateral damage to the environment as he went after high-value enemy targets. He rationalized that the Germans and Boers had started it all, this limited tactical
nuclear war at sea. Allied forces needed to use nukes in
self-defense. High-explosive weapons just weren't effective
enough when the enemy was firing at you with fission
bombs. And precision-guided high-explosive weapons
weren't the cure-all some pundits had thought they'd be before the war. The Axis had figured out how to distort the
Global Positioning Satellite signals, and how to detect and
jam or kill a ground or airborne laser-target-homing desig-
nator. Some defense analysts had warned about such things,
before the war. Maybe they hadn't been able to get the right
people to listen.

Jeffrey was self-aware enough to witness his own mood
swings. *So here I am, in glamorous wartime Washington,
D.C., wearing my country's highest medal for valor, and I
feel like crap.* He grabbed for another hors d'oeuvre as a
pretty young waitress went by. *I need to raise my blood
sugar. That should help.* The waitress paused politely and
Jeffrey took a dumpling filled with some sort of meat. Then
he watched what he already called "the process" start again.

The waitress saw his star-shaped bronze medallion out of
the corner of her eye. She turned to look at his face, to make
sure it was really *him.* Of course it was him: Commander
Jeffrey Fuller, United States Navy, captain of USS *Challenger.* War hero. The man of the hour. On national TV, and
on the cover of every newsmagazine—the Internet was so
plagued by Axis hackers and misguided hoaxes that most

people used hard-copy newspapers to follow the war and the troubled economy.

"Um, sir, I . . ." the young lady stammered.

Jeffrey met her eyes and waited. Submariners were very good at waiting.

She smiled, and hesitated. Then she positively beamed, and leaned a few inches too close. "Congratulations, Captain." There was a hunger, a wanting, in her eyes. A Medal of Honor groupie? Was there such a thing?

"Thanks," Jeffrey said, friendly enough but distant and noncommittal. He had his mask of command to maintain, his professional demeanor—and he'd never felt comfortable flirting, whatever the context.

She controlled herself and switched to more of a daughter-father mode. "Thank *you,* Captain. For everything you've done, to help protect us."

The woman hurried away, blushing. Maybe she wasn't supposed to talk to the guests. Maybe she'd just felt nervous, suddenly talking to a battle-hardened nuclear submarine captain in his full dress blues. Flirting was natural when people felt nervous.

Jeffrey doubted if that young lady, if most of the civilians here, really knew what the medals on his jacket even meant, which one was which. He knew very few of them had any idea what a person had to suffer through to earn these medals. Today, on the theory that less was more, Jeffrey used only his major decorations: the Navy Cross, with gold star in lieu of a second award, for his first two combat missions in the recent conflict. The Presidential Unit Citation, awarded to *Challenger*'s whole crew by the Department of Defense, for what they did under Jeffrey's leadership on their latest mission, their third, the mission for which he'd just received the Medal . . . And his Silver Star and Purple Heart, won years ago, in the mid-nineties. He'd been a freshly minted junior officer in the Navy SEALs in those days, on a black operation in Iraq, and the SEALs' extraction went bad. Eventually recovered, but unfit for further commando duty, Jeffrey had chosen to transfer to submarines; wanting a career in the navy ever since he was a kid, he'd done Navy ROTC at Purdue, with a major in electrical engineering—good background for his move to the Silent Service.

I was about that waitress's age when I got wounded, Jeffrey reflected. The thought made him feel very old. He was thirty-seven, and this coming summer would turn thirty-eight, if he survived the war that long. He wondered what the navy would order him to do next. He wondered if he really would survive the war.

Out of the corner of his eye, Jeffrey caught a glimpse of Ilse Reebeck. She was a Boer freedom fighter and had served as combat oceanographer on Jeffrey's submarine during all of USS *Challenger*'s war patrols. Originally a civilian consultant, Ilse was now a lieutenant in the Free South African Navy. Jeffrey saw her talking to several African dignitaries, diplomats and generals who'd been invited to the party. Jeffrey was heartened to see that an ethnic Boer could talk with a group of black Africans without them all coming to blows. This boded well for the future. Jeffrey knew there were plenty of "good" Boers. Ilse's family had all been good, and paid the ultimate price for resisting the reactionary takeover last year: They'd been hanged with so many others, on national TV, in Johannesburg, South Africa's capital.

Jeffrey, standing in a corner of the ballroom now—to get breathing space from the increasing press of the crowd—looked steadily at Ilse, trying to make eye contact. He could tell that she could see him. But she ignored him and continued to talk to her fellow Africans. Some of them wore traditional tribal robes, and Jeffrey thought these men looked very powerful. Finally Ilse blinked and subtly shook her head, and still didn't look at Jeffrey. He gave up and looked away.

Ilse was like that. He and she had been intimate, off and

on. Ilse was very emotionally complex. Sometimes Jeffrey felt he was being used, since it was always Ilse who decided when it was time to be close or time to be detached. Today, she'd been altogether standoffish. She wore a new medal herself, the Free South African Legion of Merit, a gaudy embroidered sunburst over her heart, on a wide red sash. Jeffrey thought the whole thing looked overdone. But he'd hoped he and Ilse could share in the sense of celebration today. That wasn't happening, and Jeffrey felt disappointed.

Jeffrey reminded himself that Ilse had personal needs he could barely fathom. What was it like to lose your whole family and your country in one blow? What was it like to be torn from teaching at the University of Cape Town and thrown into a bloody coup and then a bloodier war? If Ilse hadn't been attending a marine biology conference in the U.S. when the trouble started, she might well be dead now too, strung up with her relatives. On top of everything else, she'd played a key role in several recent nuclear demolitions, and must still be reeling mentally from hand-to-hand combat with kampfschwimmer at least as much as Jeffrey was. Kampfschwimmer terrified Jeffrey, and *he* was a former SEAL.

A senator wormed his way over, someone Jeffrey recognized from the newspapers. He chaired an important congressional subcommittee. The senator brought a staff photographer in his wake and quickly struck a dramatic pose, shaking the Medal of Honor winner's hand in both of his own. Jeffrey tried not to blink when the flash went off. The senator disappeared in the crowd as quickly as he'd materialized.

"Son!"

Jeffrey recognized his father's voice. He turned. His father came over from out of the crowd, accompanied by Jeffrey's mother. Both were very well dressed, for the special occasion. Jeffrey's dad, Michael Fuller, wore a gray pinstripe suit that fit him perfectly, even though, like many people, he'd lost a lot of weight since the start of the war. His red-, white-, and blue-striped tie's Windsor knot was also perfect. *Quite a switch from when I was a kid back in St. Louis, when my dad wore polyester clip-on ties and off-the-shelf sport jackets.*

"How are you feeling now, Mom?" Jeffrey was naturally concerned. Her color was healthy, but Jeffrey knew this was mostly due to makeup.

"Good, Jeffrey. Today I'm feeling very good." His mother grinned. When he'd first learned she'd been diagnosed with breast cancer, he worried he might not even have a chance to say good-bye.

Jeffrey's mom hugged him, and he hugged her back very hard.

"I won't kiss you on the cheek this time," she said puckishly. "I got enough lipstick on your face already, posing for all those cameramen." Jeffrey's mother had had emergency surgery less than two months before, and then a new chemotherapy protocol that specifically targeted cancer cells. The treatments were very effective, and were over so fast you hardly lost much of your hair. Her latest medical imagery scans showed her body free of all tumors.

"I managed to escape my various sycophants and camp followers," Jeffrey's father said. Michael Fuller chuckled; he had a biting sense of humor. He and Jeffrey's mother had been right up front at the formal ceremony this morning, when the president of the United States presented the Medal of Honor to Jeffrey in the Rose Garden. Now, with the president off on other pressing duties, Michael Fuller was holding court himself. Since the war began he'd had a meteoric rise in the Department of Energy. Instead of being a local utility regulator, that middle-management bureaucrat Jeffrey remembered from his teen years, his dad had become a savvy political appointee in the nation's capital, one of the dozen most senior people in the DOE.

"You look unhappy," Michael said.

Jeffrey shrugged. "It all gets pretty wearing." He gestured

with his eyes toward the crowd, which kept churning and babbling nonstop. "How do you stand it?"

"It's an important part of my job, the mingling," Michael Fuller said. "*You*, in contrast, look rather uncomfortable."

"This isn't exactly my idea of a good time, Dad. I've lost count of how often I've had a microphone jammed in my face since lunchtime."

"Most of the people in this town would kill to get the exposure you're getting today."

Jeffrey made a sour face. "They don't *need* to kill. They can have it. Right now. Take it."

"Jeffrey," his mother tried to soothe. She touched him on the shoulder. "Your father and I both learned to enjoy meeting so many new people all the time. It's a big game. Don't take everything so seriously."

"I don't have entirely good memories from when I was stationed in Washington," Jeffrey said. At the Pentagon, a few years before the war.

"Huh?" Michael said. He'd been distracted, giving an obviously phony smile as someone important-looking went by. The woman, whoever she was, gave him a pleasant but equally phony smile, then nodded at Jeffrey before she disappeared on the way to the bar, trailed by a retinue of followers of her own.

Jeffrey wanted to change the subject, but his father wouldn't let him.

The man grew stern. "I think, in all honesty, you've taken enough of a break. Lord knows when you'll have a chance to be with so many important people again. I want to see you out there, making contacts, not hiding in a corner like a scared little kid when the grown-ups have company."

That made Jeffrey angry.

Michael Fuller chuckled. "See, son? I know how to push all your buttons. I sit in my office and push people's buttons all day. You need to master the trade yourself if you expect your career to move up much further." He pointed at Jeffrey's Medal. "That thing might get you as far as full captain by pure momentum, but that could be as far as you ever go. If this war ends and we win it, and you don't get killed or maimed, you'll never make admiral once you get tagged as a wallflower."

"Ouch," Jeffrey said. Of course, his father was spot on. Jeffrey could see telling signs of why Michael had been chosen for Washington—and promoted again once he got here—amid major personnel shake-ups since the outbreak of the war.

"Listen to your father," Jeffrey's mother coaxed, but there was a hint of steel in her voice too, and this surprised Jeffrey.

"Speaking of which," Michael said, "I need to get back to the fray myself. There are people I want to talk to, and people who want to see me. . . . There's the deputy secretary of defense." He pointed. "You only get the Medal of Honor once, presumably. *Use* it. I want to see you go up to the DepSec and make conversation."

"What am I supposed to say?"

"Anything. Nothing. Two or three minutes is plenty. He knows who you are, believe me, but Washington people have very short memories. Make sure he *remembers* who you are."

"Good-bye, dear." Jeffrey's mother gave Jeffrey an encouraging pat on the cheek, then walked away holding her husband's arm—gliding across the ballroom floor, the perfect undersecretary's spouse.

Jeffrey felt pretty small. He tried to build up the nerve to go talk to someone important.

It's weird, how I'd rather be commanding my ship, outthinking an enemy submarine captain in mortal combat, than attending a party.

Jeffrey was standing near a row of floor-to-ceiling windows, covered by plush maroon-and-white curtains drawn closed. Idly, he pulled back the edge of a curtain and peeked outside.

The panes of glass were crisscrossed with strips of tape to

keep them from shattering in a blast. Right outside the windows, Jeffrey was confronted by a solid wall of sandbags.

Somebody isn't taking any chances.

Jeffrey put his face closer to the window and peered as far as he could to the left. There was a sliver of a view, looking down into the wide ravine of scenic Rock Creek Park. He could barely make out part of the big stone archway bridge that carried Connecticut Avenue across the ravine. The sky was clear, not yet growing dark. Looking directly up, Jeffrey saw the high, fast-moving contrails of a pair of fighter jets, on combat air patrol over the capital.

Jeffrey pulled himself away from the window and pulled himself together. He stood up straighter and took a deep breath. He saw someone he'd been introduced to briefly before, the four-star admiral who was commander, U.S. Atlantic Fleet. Jeffrey decided to follow his father's advice now. He'd go chat the admiral up.

Before he got there, a murmur of surprise and interest rippled through the crowd. Heads all turned in unison to the entry doors to the ballroom. Even the TV floodlights focused that way.

Over the loudspeakers, someone announced, "Ladies and gentlemen, the president of the United States."

CHAPTER 2

Northeastern Brazil,
on the Edge of the Amazon Rain Forest

In absolute and enveloping darkness, Felix Estabo quietly went through the final stages of forming the nighttime defensive position. He lay flat in the stinking mud, embracing it, concealed under a fern bush festooned with big and very sharp leaves. His floppy-brimmed jungle hat and the insect net draped over his face and neck kept the hungry mosquitoes at bay. Arranged in a circle with him—each man facing outward so that their feet all met in the center—were the others in the eight-man team.

Silent hand-touch signals went around the group from man to man, status reports. All was well. Felix allowed himself a sense of proprietary satisfaction—times like this he felt like a mother hen, though he'd never in a million years say so out loud. Felix's boots picked up a few of his teammates shifting an inch or two to get a little more comfortable. The four men who weren't on watch tried to sleep.

Another bead of sweat formed on the tip of Felix's nose as he lay there. It itched, but to move and scratch would violate noise and motion security; even if they were lucky and the slightest movement didn't get everyone killed, Felix needed to set an example. Although the one thing they knew for sure was that no tribal Indians came near here, other humans might be hunting Felix and his men right now.

More sweat dripped and itched. The temperature was over ninety Fahrenheit—even at night—and the humidity topped 95 percent. The air was almost smotheringly thick.

Felix tried not to fight the relentless weight of his rucksack pressing down on his back. In this tactical situation, you always slept in full gear. He cradled his weapon in his arms, a specially modified Heckler & Koch MP-5 submachine gun. The weapon fired nine millimeter bullets, semi- or full automatic, from detachable magazines that each held thirty rounds. Felix had a dozen magazines with him. But if he was forced to fire just one round, even with his weapon's silencer, the entire mission would almost certainly fail. If it did fail, those dozen magazines would run out fast.

Felix was one of the men off watch, so it was his turn to sleep. He tried to cradle his head in his arms on the uneven ground, with his face cushioned next to the reassuring heft of his weapon. In the Amazon rain forest, roots from towering trees grew right along or over the uneven ground, forming bumps and ridges and tangles everywhere. The team wasn't far above the mighty Amazon River's maximum annual floodplain level. Usable natural cushioning was scarce—very few trees shed leaves or nettles in the tropics. The ground cover consisted mostly of huge fallen branches, or fungus and rotting organic goo, so Felix couldn't fashion a bed as he'd have done on a camping trip. It was hard to find much comfort at all. The men didn't carry ground cloths or sleeping bags or similar luxuries—they were overloaded with other, much more vital equipment.

But Felix was used to it. He was actually enjoying himself, despite the tension and danger and tingling of fear. The heat and humidity and mosquitoes didn't bother him—he'd grown up in Miami. Felix always thought of himself as the archetypal happy warrior. Tonight, he couldn't have been happier. He'd led a clean life. He had a supportive wife and two wonderful infant girls to go home to. Felix's mind was at peace, which was good. He needed every neuron focused on doing his job right now.

Felix was a master chief in the U.S. Navy SEALs, in the field in hostile territory, on a clandestine operation during war. His lieutenant, a promising kid but young and inexperienced as SEALs go, was in nominal charge of the group—but it was Felix, with his maturity and strong grasp of tradecraft, who worked hard to keep the team undetected, safe and alive and on schedule. Every man among them was Latino, handpicked for their language skills and knowledge of local cultures.

Felix was of Brazilian descent. His parents were born in São Paulo, the country's biggest city and main business center. They'd been sponsored to the U.S., given green cards that allowed them to take menial factory jobs in southern Florida. When baby Felix arrived, at a Miami hospital, he was automatically a U.S. citizen. Eventually his parents were naturalized too. Felix was pretty good in Spanish, which he spoke with a Cuban-American accent, and he was fluent in the idiomatic Portuguese that was Brazil's national language.

So his mission was like coming home, visiting the old country. He could blend in well.

Felix wasn't tall, five-foot-six, but he had a blocky, muscular build. When not on an operation, he liked to comb his jet-black hair straight up, forming half-inch spiked bristles with styling gel. His head was very big—his hat size was a whopping seven and seven-eighths—and his neck was broad and strong. In moments of vanity mixed with self-mockery he liked to think he resembled a bullet atop a tree stump— except with a higher IQ. In bars he'd joke with his buddies that either his brain was large or his skull was too thick, he wasn't sure which. And when people saw the old, old scar of a knife wound down his cheek, a jagged line from below his left eye socket to his jaw . . . He smiled to himself at the thought. Nobody in a bar ever messed with Felix.

Again Felix tried to sleep. He listened to the unending sounds of the Amazon rain forest at night. Nocturnal monkeys chattered, high up in the triple canopy formed by the spreading limbs of different species of tropical trees. Some of these trees, Felix knew, were fifteen stories tall or more; their lower trunks could reach a thickness of six or even ten feet. The mosquitoes continued to whine near his ears, but he ignored them. His team had come prepared for such pests. Too overtired to be able to give in to drowsiness and doze off, Felix double-checked by feel that the elastic ends of his sleeves were fastened snug around his flame-retardant jungle warfare gloves. He and the other men swallowed special tablets daily so that the pores of their skin secreted an odorless insect repellent. His one-piece camouflage fatigues were made of layered synthetics to draw away moisture and let it evaporate, to help keep the multitudes of biting or stinging insects at bay, and to double as a diving wet suit when the men had to go in the water. The bottom of the wet suit's legs were tucked tightly into his boots to keep out scorpions and fire ants, which were also nocturnal; ticks and lice and chiggers stayed active all day. Every morning before breaking camp, Felix made sure each man took medications with the team's one daily meal to prevent malaria and intestinal worms and suppress any symptoms of dysentery. Before deploying for the mission, they'd had booster vaccinations for a dozen other diseases, from cholera to yellow fever to smallpox, not to mention anthrax and some bad coronaviruses.

In the inky dark, Felix sensed more than heard bats swooping between the trees and through the brush, feeding on the copious insect life. There were many sorts of bats in the Amazon rain forest. There were also poisonous snakes and big ugly spiders . . . not to mention pumas and jaguars and ocelots, South America's big cats. The countless river tributaries harbored schools of sharp-toothed piranhas, plus several varieties of mean and hungry alligators and crocodiles.

But the most dangerous life form here in the forest was

man. This was why Felix's team avoided moving by the rivers—which were lines of travel and commerce for the native population—and they avoided moving altogether at night. Horizontal sight lines were short, from all the foliage and tree trunks. A surprise encounter after dark could happen much too suddenly, literally at arm's length, spelling disaster. Visibility under the all-concealing triple canopy of leaves and vines was bad enough in the perpetual gloom during daytime. It was because of the short sight lines, tactically, that sounds and smells were so important. That was why, for two weeks before their present mission began, Felix and his team had eaten a special diet to make their body odor blend in with their surroundings. That was also why, during the approach to the coast on the nuclear sub USS *Ohio,* Felix and his men never showered with soap. And that was why, right now, they had to be so quiet. A clicking of metal, the smack of a hand on a wasp or hornet sting, a muffled human cough carried a surprising distance in the rain forest, even above the forest's natural din.

Finally, that was why the team didn't bother bringing thermal or night-vision gear. The devices and their batteries added weight, and they tended not to hold up well under rugged use in such wet and dirty climatic conditions. Instead, at night, the men hid and watched for trouble with the naked eye.

Felix suddenly heard parrots squawking somewhere in the distance. He immediately grew more alert. He was supposed to be off watch now, but as the team's master chief, he was never truly off watch. He'd be lucky to get by on brief catnaps throughout this whole covert reconnaissance patrol. A split second after Felix zoned in on the noise of the parrots, he felt it through his feet as other members of his team grew tense. Two of them, the most experienced enlisted men, continued to sleep. Their unconscious combat minds knew their on-watch teammates would wake them in case of real danger; in the meantime, they were fully determined to get all the shut-eye they could.

The parrot squawking continued, and now howler monkeys hooted and screeched. Felix heard the pounding of hooves as other creatures hurried along through the forest floor's thick red muck. Sheep-sized rodents, the capybara? Miniature deer? Local types of wild boar? Felix couldn't be sure in the dark. He noticed other, quieter stirrings high above him, probably three-toed sloths, moving grudgingly in their lazy way.

The man to his right tapped Felix on the wrist, in code. He was relaying a message from the lieutenant, who was lying in the circle facing directly away from Felix, in the opposite direction from the forest disturbance. The LT wanted an assessment from Felix immediately. Someone might be approaching, and no one the team might meet here was friendly.

Felix tapped the man in a signal meaning "Wait." The men would relay this around the circle one by one, back to the lieutenant—a silent jungle telegraph.

Felix shifted his body slowly and smoothly, like a sniper. Actually, Felix had begun life in the navy as a hospital corpsman on a cruiser, before being seasoned enough to put in for the SEALs. But he had become a very good shot during firearms training, and he'd thoroughly learned what it took to be a skilled sniper or spotter observer.

Felix was careful not to brush against the leaves of the bushes right overhead. He was cautious as he moved slightly, so his arms or legs wouldn't give off a sucking sound from the mud. Gingerly, he shifted his weapon and then brought his hands toward his head, trying to avoid getting snagged on the thorns and needlelike leaf ends abounding in this underbrush. Because it would leave lasting signs that they'd been here, the team dared not do any pruning with the one machete they shared.

Felix cupped his hands to his ears, a standard jungle warfare method to hear better. He rotated his head to pinpoint the source of the zoolike din. He tuned out the endless mosquito hum. He tried to make out luminescent fungi amid the clutter on the forest floor or on the bark of trees—he might notice something or someone walk between him and a fungus. But he could see no subtle, dim blue-green glows from where he lay.

Felix heard more birdcalls—he recognized species of ant-follower birds. He tried to assess the distance to the center of the noises and judged the speed and direction in which the disturbance appeared to move. He heard more monkeys calling, in a way he knew was monkey talk for "no big deal." Felix had been trained in many such things by naturalists who consulted to the navy—it paid dividends for SEALs to be one with the biosphere they worked in.

Now Felix got it. A column of army ants was on the march, devouring everything in its path. The ant birds were specialized feeders. They followed the army ants and snapped up insects fleeing the oncoming ants. . . . The ants weren't coming toward the SEAL team's position. This was a very good thing, because if they had been, the team would need to move, and quickly. No one in his right mind would lie on the ground to let army ants get close. They'd crawl all over you by the hundreds and thousands, and force their way into every opening in your clothes and under your headgear, and then get into your eyes and up your nostrils. Their bites were horribly painful, and even a brave man would scream. Though they weren't likely to kill a healthy large animal, swarms of them could pick a decomposing carcass clean, leaving absolutely nothing but hair and white bones.

Felix tapped a message for the lieutenant, to be passed around the circle. "Army ants. No danger." No danger, at least for now. His teammates tried to relax. The half of them on watch remained alert. Felix was much too keyed up now to sleep.

The pitch blackness of the nighttime rain forest began to lift subtly. Felix's well-adapted eyes could make out shapes in the silvery patches of weak light from the rising moon. The team knew the exact time of moonrise and moonset for each night of their patrol—another reason they hadn't brought night-vision gear. The moon's schedule and also its phase—approaching full—were important parts of the mission profile. So was the weather. Though the sun rose close to six A.M. in northeastern Brazil, almost precisely on the equator, and set near six P.M. all year, the rain forest did have its seasons. The rainy season—given that it was late March—would end within a few weeks. But it was very much still the rainy season now.

Americans often thought of Brazil as being to the south of them, but it was actually southeast. The easternmost tip of Brazil, not far from where Felix lay motionless in all this goo and muck, was two or three time zones ahead of the United States's East Coast. So it would still be daylight in Miami and at Norfolk's amphibious warfare base—where Felix was stationed and where his wife and children lived. This made Felix think of his family, but he forced them from his mind. He knew the wives helped one another constantly, and the base's health care and recreational facilities were outstanding. He did worry that at some point the base might be nuked, but if that happened it was probably the beginning of the end for everybody.

Felix glanced around again, in the subtle moonlight that managed to make its way in dapples down through all the branches and leaves. He'd oriented himself as the team made camp during the very short tropical dusk. But things looked different at night. He watched carefully for the slightest telltale change. No one, *no one* must know the team was here.

He reminded himself that antigovernment leftist guerrillas were active in the area, cut off from the main landmass of Brazil by the miles-wide Amazon River. Felix's present position was a few days' forced march in from the Atlantic, not far north of the Amazon's mouth, with its gigantic water-logged delta and its busy heavy-shipping channels.

There was a railroad line a few days' march from their present location, farther into the rain forest. The railroad was an isolated short line. It ran from a group of manganese mines southward to Porto Santana on a navigable branch of the Amazon. Brazil exported this manganese ore. America needed to buy it. The Axis didn't want America to have it.

The rail line ran through a rain-forest wilderness. It was an obvious target for guerrilla troops. The recently installed prewar electronic Amazon Surveillance System, designed to guard against drug smugglers and animal poachers and illegal lumbering, could tell that guerrillas were training, staging, somewhere vaguely in the area—between the railroad and the coast. But the dense greenery of the canopy cover, and the frequent overcast skies and violent thunderstorms of the rainy season, tended to make surveillance by human beings on foot much better than airborne surveillance. Visual, infrared, radar—all were blocked or distorted, and hopelessly spoofed by false alarms. Ground-based remote-controlled sensors—like seismometers to feel people walking, or urea sniffers to pick up their sweat or body waste—were equally stymied by environmental noise and signal clutter—from the constant wandering of man-sized animals under all the trees. Besides, as Felix well appreciated, the whole Amazon River basin was much too large to cover effectively from the ground by any affordable sensor grid: it was more than half the size of the entire continental United States.

It was really the presence of the railroad that tagged the area as a probable guerrilla target. And therein lay America's problem, and the reason why Felix was here.

There were only two practical ways to reach the area, unless you were lowered by helicopter or inserted from the sea, because the railroad itself—freight trains only, no passengers—was patrolled by Brazilian security troops. One route, from the scattered urban parts of Brazil far south across the Amazon, was by boat and then on foot through the swamps and the jungle. The other way was on foot down from the north, through the French Guyana highlands. Since France was occupied by Germany, French Guyana—a French possession—had seceded and made itself neutral. Like much of neutral soil during war since time immemorial, French Guyana was now a hotbed of intrigue containing all sides. The Pentagon's intelligence assessment was that Germans were helping the leftist guerrillas by coming south through French Guyana. That was a long and difficult trek, since there were no roads whatsoever—this part of the Amazon basin was truly the middle of nowhere.

Felix heard a quick pattering from above and then a loud plop. The quality of the noise told him it was an overripe fruit, falling through the intervening branches to the ground. He watched something the size of his fist scurry along the ground in his field of view. It reared up at him on hind legs for a moment, then scurried away. *A spider.* Tarantula, probably. Their bites were painful but not deadly. Felix wondered if a tarantula's fangs could penetrate his gloves.

In the shadows between the protruding tree roots and creeping vines, he saw something else move. It moved deliberately, with practiced stealth. Slowly, silently, it came for him, closer and closer.

Felix cursed to himself. It was a vampire bat, doing what vampire bats do—stalking a sleeping large mammal. The bat's fangs were razor sharp, so sharp they could slit the hide of a cow or tapir without the victim even waking. Then the bats drank the sweet fresh blood till their stomachs were so bloated they could barely move. The vampire bat would stumble away like a drunken sailor, to digest its tasty meal.

This particular vampire bat had its eyes on Felix's hand. He flicked it in the nose with his thumb and index finger. It jumped back, then tried for him again. He bopped it in the nose, harder. The ugly bat gave up, and went into the underbrush.

Felix sighed. He felt drained from his exertions of the past few days but knew he'd be lucky to get much rest tonight. The constant stress and need for alertness were wearing. By the end of the mission, in another ten days or so if he was lucky, he'd be ready for a nice long break back aboard the *Ohio*. The *Ohio* was an old boomer sub, and the ample space of her missile compartment had been specially converted for SEALs. Compared to the claustrophobic confines of a typical fast-attack sub, where SEALs squeezed into improvised sleeping racks in the torpedo room, the *Ohio* was like an undersea resort hotel.

Felix heard distant thunder. *Another rainstorm coming.* This would cool things off for a little while, though trying to sleep outdoors in a tropical downpour was a losing proposition.

No. Not thunder. Grenades. Now there were pops and stutters and tearing sounds, like rifles and machine guns. They were coming from northeast, farther up the Brazilian coast. Everybody was wide awake now. There was a larger boom, like a Claymore mine, from the same direction, far away and muffled but distinct. Felix was alarmed. He no longer noticed his sweating and itching. He forced himself to stop breathing so hard.

The shooting in the distance died off quickly.

The left hand of the man clockwise of Felix reached for Felix's right hand. Felix felt a rapid series of taps and strokes and squeezes on different parts of his fingers and palm. The lieutenant was signaling Felix again: "Assessment?"

Felix responded, "Somebody triggered an ambush."

"Who versus whom?" the lieutenant asked, still passing hand signals. Felix was glad the LT wasn't breaking silence discipline, even surprised as he must have been by the out-of-nowhere eruption of that violently one-sided firefight. The ambush proved how precarious the SEALs' position truly was.

Felix thought through the LT's question very hard. The noise had been too far away for him to identify it as specific types of weapons. It might have been a Brazilian Army patrol taking out a guerrilla band. Or it could have been guerrillas getting the jump on a poorly trained army squad. . . .

Or it could involve the other team of Navy SEALs—who'd deployed from the *Ohio* at the same time Felix did—sent to cover a different area nearer the Guyana Shield highlands. This worried Felix, because the SEALs would never have started an ambush themselves. None of them were even supposed to be here.

Brazil was formally neutral. American armed forces operating on Brazilian soil was an outright violation of international law. It could be taken as an act of war.

Which is why we didn't just drop in by helicopter, and why the other team can't call for helo extraction or air support.

Yet U.S. national command authorities had deemed the mission important enough to risk it anyway. The SEALs' vital role was to provide military indications and warnings. The U.S. simply *had* to know how far the Axis was willing to go to stir up trouble in South America. If the Axis in fact was active in this part of Brazil, then Felix and the others were tasked to bring back concrete proof—all without being detected. Exactly how this physical proof was supposed to be obtained, Felix and his lieutenant were told they'd best improvise on the spot.

So who hit whom in that ambush? Tensions were already riding too high, with Brazil and Argentina mobilizing along the stretch of border they shared in the middle of the continent. The two countries were on the brink of war, over imagined slights or real provocations. It reminded Felix of India and Pakistan—both of whom were neutral and keeping their heads well down right now—except that the CIA didn't know if Brazil or Argentina had atom bombs. Felix reminded himself that following deadly attacks and near atrocities by the Boers in the South Pacific, Tokyo had announced just weeks ago that Japan was a nuclear power. Japan, neutral up till then, declined to say if she intended to choose sides. After that, the whole world seemed to go crazy—the parts that hadn't already gone mad.

With paranoia and warmongering running rampant everywhere, an illegal U.S. incursion into a neutral Latin American nation, if found out, unmasked, could prove disastrous. There was surely much more to the story, or Felix's team would never have been sent. Felix, a master chief, wasn't fed the big strategic picture by the higher-ups. But he could use his head, and he guessed that the German presence here—if any—was intended to create an annoying diversion, to draw Brazilian troops away from the far-off Argentine front. That, Felix figured, seemed to imply the Germans intended to back the Argentines in any outright fighting. *And* that, *my man, means one way-serious problemo.*

Felix still had to answer his lieutenant. "Ambush adversaries unknown. Possible other SEAL team involved."

"Should we help them?"

Felix was torn. SEALs trusted one another with their lives and never left a man behind. If the other team was in trouble, Felix and the lieutenant should do everything to assist. But there was nothing they could possibly do. The scene of the ambush was much too far away. Felix judged it would take till noontime tomorrow to get there, at the earliest.

Felix was pissed off. *It wasn't supposed to happen like this.* But he refused to just give up. He signaled his lieutenant: "Fire into the air? Create a diversion to relieve the pressure."

It seemed to take forever for the lieutenant to respond. "Negative. Would disclose own position against standing orders. Doubtful slightest real assistance to compromised team would result."

Felix agreed reluctantly.

All at once he heard more shooting from the same area. His heart began to pound with anxiety and excitement.

That particular rhythm of the firing, the bursts all on full auto and the brief but purposeful pauses, told a definite story to Felix's trained ear. It wasn't a bumbling army squad or a rabble of leftist guerrillas. The vicious noises of well-controlled shooting, the perfectly timed crack of grenades, could only be a SEAL team using Special Warfare tactics to break contact with an enemy.

On pins and needles, Felix and his men heard this new act of the drama unfold. Wordlessly they cheered on their friends, praying they'd make their escape. They'd practiced this break-contact drill countless times themselves, with live ammo. For Felix it was like listening to the seventh game of a World Series, from right outside the ballpark, and trying to guess what was happening just from the noise.

Abruptly, the sound of combat halted again. A prolonged and eerie silence took its place. The silence gradually lifted, as if the jungle itself had been holding its breath, and the frightened birds and animals cautiously went back to normal.

"I think they made it," the lieutenant signaled.

Felix concurred. He was almost overcome with waves of relief. He beseeched his God that none of the men were killed or badly wounded. *It would be just like our guys to play dead, then launch a brutal counterambush and make their fighting getaway.*

Felix had a sobering thought. He sent to the lieutenant, "All hostiles in area alerted. Danger to own team high."

"Abort the mission?"

"Negative," Felix responded without hesitation. He reminded himself the LT was young and untried. "Continue, regain surprise."

There was a pause, and the lieutenant answered. "Concur. Maintain fifty percent on-watch status. Break camp at first light and continue recon as planned."

Felix tried to get some sleep, but he wondered. Was his team walking into an elaborate, clever trap? Had German advisers sent a ragtag guerrilla platoon after the other SEAL team to serve as patsies? Was a devious German gambit in play, intended to goad Felix and his team on, and lull them right into another ambush . . . one laid by kampfschwimmer, from whom the SEALs would *not* escape?

CHAPTER 3

J effrey was still at the reception at the hotel. As he approached the commander, U.S. Atlantic Fleet, for a chat, the four-star admiral was standing in a circle with other admirals and members of Congress. The admiral was himself a submariner, and yet Jeffrey got barely a nod from the man before his senior aide, a full captain, cut Jeffrey off. The admiral and his staff needed to rush back to their headquarters in Norfolk, Virginia. The admiral's helicopter was waiting for him and his group in an empty parking lot at nearby Georgetown University. Jeffrey got the impression some sort of crisis had just come up. This impression was reinforced when he saw commander, submarines, Atlantic, and several captains and admirals who worked in undersea warfare at the Pentagon also leave the party very hurriedly, but as discreetly as they could. Jeffrey buttonholed a friend on one of the admirals' staff, but he wouldn't reveal a thing.

Jeffrey was intercepted by two Secret Service agents. "Come with us, please, sir."

Jeffrey couldn't exactly refuse. He wondered if his travel arrangements back to New London were changing at the last minute, for security or because of whatever else was going on. He couldn't spot his parents to make a quick good-bye.

The Secret Service agents led Jeffrey out of the ballroom. Along the way, seeing that he was leaving, some cabinet members and congresspeople moved in. A staff assistant dragged Jeffrey's parents over from out of the crowd, almost physically. Other assistants or interns—or whoever the pushy young people were—insisted that the remaining TV crews come closer. Jeffrey and his mom and dad posed for handshakes and hugs and pats on the shoulder from people who spent more time beaming their glued-on smiles into the cameras than they did really looking at Jeffrey or his folks. This final feeding frenzy ended quickly.

Then the Secret Service agents whisked Jeffrey away, after telling his parents that their son would be back soon. They led him down a heavily guarded side corridor.

Passing through two separate steel doors, with an anteroom between them, Jeffrey was all at once in a temporary communications post. The president of the United States was there, speaking in hushed but urgent tones with some U.S. Army and Marine Corps generals.

The steel door shut behind Jeffrey, with the Secret Service agents stationed right outside. Also stationed in the anteroom, Jeffrey realized now, was an officer with the go codes, in case the president needed to launch a global thermonuclear strike; the thought of it sent shivers up his spine.

"Give us a minute alone," the president said. The generals grabbed their laptops and hats and went out.

Jeffrey was left in a windowless room, standing on the scuffed linoleum, face-to-face with his commander in chief. Jeffrey came to attention.

"Take a seat," the president said. He pointed to one of the beat-up metal convention-hall chairs. The president sat behind a drab desk covered with telephone banks and computer displays. He eyed one display for several seconds, then turned his full attention back to Jeffrey.

Jeffrey took a chair, but sat in it very erectly.

"Feels good to sit down, doesn't it?" the president said.

Jeffrey nodded, cautiously; something was very irregular. Getting a medal and a handshake from the president in public was one thing—talking to him one-on-one with no set agenda was something else entirely.

"Relax, son," the president said in a no-nonsense way. He set the tone by leaning back in his swivel chair, letting his posture loosen up. He gave Jeffrey a smile. Jeffrey perceived in that smile the same depth of character, compassion, humanity, and iron will that millions of voters had seen in the last election campaign. He tried to relax.

"That's the problem with being a retired four-star general," the president said. "All you military guys and gals go into your snap-to-attention mode and stop talking and start obeying. Leave the formalities outside the door for now. . . . Your commodore and my defense secretary were made aware I wanted this chitchat and pep talk in private. Executive privilege, if you will. You'll get a formal briefing soon from your seniors."

"Yes, sir."

The president studied Jeffrey up and down. "You look wilted around the edges."

"It's been a long day, Mr. President."

"Tell me about it. I can't remember when the last time was I didn't have a long day."

Jeffrey decided to say something safe. "I guess it's not just a cliché, sir, when people keep telling each other, 'There's a war on.'"

The president chuckled. "I want to show you something." He reached into his jacket pocket and took out a thin billfold.

Jeffrey assumed he was looking for notes, or maybe would show Jeffrey pictures of his family. Instead the president pulled out a set of dog-eared little photographs and reproductions of paintings. He spread them on the desk as if he were showing Jeffrey his hand in a game of poker.

There were pictures of Dwight D. Eisenhower, Ulysses S. Grant, Andrew Jackson, George Washington.

"Who's this other guy?" Jeffrey was feeling somewhat more comfortable; the president had skillfully broken the ice.

"Zachary Taylor. Know what all these men have in common?"

Jeffrey thought for a second. "They were all elected president after being successful generals in wars."

"Yup. I like to look at them. Role models. Helps keep me going in these difficult times . . . Compared to them I'm the odd man out."

"Sir?"

"They won their biggest shooting wars before they became head of state. I'm the ex-general who got stuck with the Worst World War *after* I got elected."

Jeffrey nodded. That phrase, *Worst World War,* came from a editorial in the *Washington Post* last summer. It was apt.

The president seemed to read Jeffrey's mind.

"We got so fixated on the pillar or the post, conventional weapons or fusion warheads, we missed the awful middle ground of tossing around small atom bombs. The Russians *never* missed it. It was a big part of all their war plans, if they ever went up against NATO. . . . Making them an associate member didn't change a thing. 'Constructive engagement,' my ass. Russian paranoia and jealous resentment of the West go back to the czars, for God's sake. It's burned into their national psyche, and it's obvious now that's one thing that won't ever change."

"I understand, sir." Jeffrey wasn't sure if the president was trying to express regret, or angry hindsight, or what?

"We were so focused on other crises and wars that had to be won. Terrorism, the Middle East, Asia . . . We treated Europe like nonplayers, looked down our noses at Latin America, and forgot about Africa altogether."

Jeffrey nodded politely. *Where is he going with this?*

"The Berlin-Boer Axis bootstrapped themselves into existence very cleverly and we never saw it coming. They used their own twisted brand of voodoo economics to finance a hostile takeover of half the world. Prewar loans from all the big German and Swiss banks and rich insurance companies, to arms makers in Germany and South Africa, with off-the-books covenants saying repayment would come at some future date from war plunder yet to be specified . . . Building a hundred high-tech diesel subs on spec, supposedly for export, then suddenly turning that inventory into a modern U-boat fleet. Group simulator training in modern attack and defense, in secret, using teaching methods and software pioneered by our own Submarine School, to give 'em a cadre of German crews skilled and seasoned even though they'd rarely been to sea." The president got more aggravated, and bitter, with every word.

There was a pregnant pause as Jeffrey waited for him to say more. Jeffrey was caught off guard when he changed the subject completely.

"How'd you like to go on a national war-bond drive?"

Jeffrey was crestfallen, and knew it showed: "Sir, I'd rather get back to my ship."

"Haven't had enough of nuclear torpedoes and SEAL raids for now? Don't want some nice long stateside R and R, meet movie stars and famous talk-show hosts?"

"Very respectfully, sir, my answer is negative on both counts. I need to get back to my ship."

The president smiled. "Good. I wanted to hear you say it. . . . Although the offer was genuine. You've more than earned a break."

"Sir, is there anything else you need from me?"

The president chuckled. "That's just like you, Jeffrey Fuller. Usually people connive to get as much of my time as they can. *You* dare to try to be the first to *end* the conversation."

"Sir?"

"Look, son. Nobody gets the Medal of Honor without coming under a lot of scrutiny. Congress won't approve the award for just anybody. I read your file. You're considered highly talented, and driven, but with some important rough edges."

Jeffrey sat back defensively.

"Don't bristle. If you can't look at your own strengths and weaknesses with cold-blooded accuracy, you'll never go as far as you might in life."

Jeffrey hesitated. "I think that's good advice, sir."

"I wanted the chance to talk to you candidly, Captain. Last month, far away in your ship, you saved me here from having to push the button. . . . I honestly think that for every one of those harrowing twenty-four hours, me in a flying command post waiting in dread for each tick of the clock, and you down in your submarine at the sharp tip of the spear, we have to have been the two most lonely people on the planet. . . . And besides, I've given too many Medals of Honor in this war posthumously. I've seen too many widows and orphans and grieving parents look at a velvet box with a chunk of bronze in it and ask me why their son or daughter had to die. Frankly, it's very refreshing to get to speak to one of the Medal's recipients while he's still alive."

"I never thought of it like that," Jeffrey said.

"I'm not surprised you didn't. Seeing things from the other person's point of view is not one of your strong points."

"Sir?" Jeffrey bristled again.

The president waved a reassuring hand. "Unless that other person is an enemy submarine captain. Then you seem to be able to get inside his head remarkably well."

"You make it sound like I've got some form of 'tunnel intelligence.'"

"You said it, not me. . . . Just a bit of implied friendly advice. Take it to heart. Remember, as a four-star general I had three-stars, and even other four-stars, reporting to me. *You* still have a long way to go to be playing in *that* league."

"Sir, I didn't request this interview."

"No, I did. For a reason. Would you like to know what it is?"

"Respectfully, Mr. President, yes, I would."

"This year, 2012, is a presidential election year. This November, the people will go to the polls to decide who they want to have running the country. Since it's highly unlikely the war will be over by then, and assuming the world has not yet turned into a radioactive wasteland altogether, basically the people will be voting on what they think of the job I've done as the country's commander in chief."

Jeffrey squirmed. "I'm not really into politics, sir."

"I know. You've got a reputation for that in navy circles. Which is good . . . up to a point. But you have to realize that every general or admiral is in part a politician . . . or at least they need to be able to understand and work with politicians well. The interplay between Pentagon and Congress and White House is always a delicate one. It's a rather energy-intensive process. Personal energy and doggedness, keeping things running smoothly, without *too* much animosity or strife."

"Yes."

The president hunched forward. "I need your support in the next election."

Jeffrey was flabbergasted. He shook his head, "Sir, I don't think I can continue this discussion. I think, I mean . . . I think it might even be unconstitutional, for an officer on active duty to endorse a particular candidate."

The president stared at Jeffrey, raised his eyebrows again, and then laughed. "That's not exactly what I had in mind."

Jeffrey felt himself blushing.

"No. Don't feel bad. I'm glad to see you're not an opportunist. You don't have an inflated view of your place in the world."

"I *try* not to, anyway," Jeffrey said.

"The best way you can help me is to help your country. . . . Do you feel ready for another war patrol, immediately?"

"Yes, Mr. President."

"I mean *really* immediately. Like getting under way tonight."

So a major crisis is definitely on. That's why all those submarine admirals were acting all stirred up.

Jeffrey ran a quick mental tally of the status of his ship.

"If we can load what we need and get out of dry dock on such short notice. Yes."

"You did it once before. I mean do *you,* personally, with whatever scars you bear inside from what you've been through in combat lately, feel ready this very instant for more?"

Jeffrey nodded. His adrenaline was pumping now. *This* type of challenge he liked.

The president stood and walked to an easel, picking up a marker pen and pulling off its cap. "Remember easels?" he said.

"They're a bit old-fashioned, sir."

"Sometimes I like to be an old-fashioned guy. . . . I gave many a briefing using marker pen and paper, back when I was in your pay grade, an ambitious young officer myself. . . . Are *you* an ambitious person, Captain?"

Jeffrey was taken aback again by the president's change of subject. "Yes. I have to say I am."

"Good. Because your next mission task is very ambitious. I wouldn't want to think you weren't up to it."

Jeffrey decided to hold his tongue.

"The better you understand what's involved, the better you'll do your job and be able to motivate your people." The president began drawing squiggly curves along both sides of the blank page on the big pad on the easel. He tapped points on the curve on the left.

"The U.S., Canada, Mexico," he said. "All Allies . . . Central America, mostly neutral so far, except for our friend Costa Rica, which is too bad because Panama won't let our warships use the canal. South America, also mostly neutral, except for Venezuela and Chile, at opposite ends of the continent from each other."

Jeffrey nodded. The U.S. received a lot of oil and natural gas from Venezuela, shipped through the Caribbean and Gulf of Mexico.

The president pointed to the right side of the easel chart and worked his way down the page. "The UK, Occupied Europe. The Afrika Corps' big holdings, our Central African pocket, and the Boers down here."

"Yes." Jeffrey nodded. Libya was a nuclear no-man's-land since the Germans had nuked Tripoli—without real provocation—at the war's outbreak. Egypt and Jordan were protected from Axis incursions by Israel's small but potent nuclear umbrella. Most other Middle Eastern nations were neutral, as was every country in Asia.

The president stepped back and looked at the map he'd drawn. He added a series of little *X*s. "The U.S. East Coast ports and navy bases." He drew a line from the U.S. diagonally across the map to the middle of the African west coast. "Our main line of supply, for the moment, to our forces holding out in Africa . . . At least until we can pick up the pieces in the Indian Ocean and get supplies to them that way. The loss of Diego Garcia was a very hard blow."

"I understand."

"The Congo basin and surrounding highlands are some of the best defensive terrain in the world. Steep mountain escarpments, massive river barriers to cross, pestilential jungles . . . That's the main reason the pocket has survived this long."

"The Sahara and Kalahari Deserts are owned by the Axis," Jeffrey stated.

"Germans here." The president pointed to the Sahara, in the northern part of Africa. "Boers here." He pointed to the Kalahari, in the south. "Us in the middle, but most of our tanks in that theater ended up on the bottom of the sea."

"I remember." In the initial ambush that had started the war, three American aircraft carriers were also sunk or damaged beyond practical repair.

"Here's the deal, Captain. The Axis is making a big buildup in both their parts of Africa. It's evident they intend to launch a new offensive soon, out of the good tank country in the deserts and into the Congo basin. They intend to envelop the Allied pocket, cut it off from both coasts. . . . We've known for months we don't have anything *near* the massive airlift capacity needed to keep the pocket open in the face of a major enemy offensive. It's just too far to fly, planes spend too much time in the air compared to on the ground unloading. And it's simply too vast an area, with huge numbers of soldiers and civilians needing sustenance, for the cargo tonnage to make it through by air."

"It sounds pretty serious, sir." Jeffrey knew Germany possessed a culture of war fighting on the Dark Continent that went well beyond General Rommel's famous exploits: in World War I, they'd had a big troop contingent in southern Africa, jockeying with the British over colonies both countries held there. That German Army—including loyal native formations—performed brilliantly in the awful jungle. They had been undefeated in the field when German resistance in Europe collapsed in 1918. . . . And South Africa under old apartheid owned a strong and self-reliant defense force, well blooded repulsing incursions by then Communist-dominated neighboring states. The Boers thus could draw on a whole generation of white males, now in their late thirties and up, every one of whom had two years of hardening military service—before democracy was forced on them from the outside in '94. These men and their sons now formed the core of the Boer Army; the many South Africans of English ancestry—and blacks faced with the choice between obedience and starving—further bulked up combat units or worked in logistics and admin support. Pro-apartheid South Africans also had a long track record of secret collaborations with foreign powers on nuclear arms—in the seventies and eighties it was Israel. . . . Later it was the schemers behind the new Imperial Germany.

"We intend to punch through the Atlantic with a major resupply convoy, to get food and medical supplies and weapons and ammo to the pocket. A really *huge* resupply convoy, Captain, escorted by the most powerful naval fleet ever assembled. I won't say how many carrier battle groups, it's classified and you don't need to know. Their air wings and the weapons load-outs on all the cruisers and destroyers and frigates will be optimized for a balance of antisubmarine warfare and cruise-missile defense. Not to mention protection by a lot of our fast-attack subs . . . I won't say the number, you *do* need to know, but this room might not be secure enough."

"Yes, sir." Gears began to turn in Jeffrey's head.

"We expect the Axis is as aware of this resupply effort as we are of their upcoming offensive. So both sides are locked in a deadly race, our convoy versus their land attack. Who can get the jump on whom, which of us achieves our big goal first . . . We expect the bad guys to throw everything they have at sea at the convoy and escorts. And they're rushing right now to get their land offensive ready and moving. . . . It's very touch and go how much of the convoy will make it, and whether the remnants will even get there before the Axis land push opens and our pocket gets pinched off. The time pressure here is appalling."

Jeffrey digested all this soberly. He knew from old wargames of the USSR assaulting NATO in Europe that the Pentagon expected 50 percent losses in Atlantic reinforcement convoys hounded by Soviet attack submarines. Now Germany had nuclear subs, including fast and quiet ones she'd grabbed from France. "The situation sounds very critical, Mr. President."

"It is. *Believe me,* it is."

"Just where does *Challenger* come in?"

The president drew a big question mark over Northern Europe on the briefing map. "You know the Germans with help from Russia have built a new ceramic-hulled nuclear submarine similar in basic concept to our steel-hulled SSGNs."

Jeffrey nodded. SSGN was the designation for a handful of *Ohio*-class strategic-missile boomer subs whose missile tubes and related weapons-targeting equipment were modified. Each of the two dozen vertical tubes in the "Sherwood Forest" aft of the sail—"conning tower" in old-style parlance—was fitted with a sleeve. Within that sleeve the tube held seven Tactical Tomahawks or other cruise missiles instead of a single submarine-launched ICBM tipped with multiple hydrogen bombs. A single SSGN could carry about 150 Tomahawks, a very strong force for projecting power onto land.

"Until today we had no idea where the new German SSGN was being hidden, Captain. Now we're pretty sure we do. Infrared and visual satellite surveillance data seem to jibe with a garbled report the Brits say they got from a Norwegian resistance group. A short-lived but odd heat signature out of ventilator shafts from under a mountain in northernmost Norway. Sabotage attempted but failed. Then suddenly increased signal traffic between Russian surface warships in the Norwegian Sea. All of this just within the last hour or two . . . The different pieces of the puzzle strongly suggest the German SSGN is putting to sea, if she hasn't already."

"Armed with a hundred fifty nuclear-tipped supersonic antiship cruise missiles." Jeffrey made it a statement not a question. He was truly stimulated, and very worried, now.

"Yes. And we don't know if they've got any of those scary Mach eight missiles left. . . . The Axis is under huge time pressure too, getting their SSGN into combat. One of the few things we do know about this monster is its name, by the way. The *Admiral von Scheer*."

"Cute," Jeffrey said sarcastically.

"Yes, the ironic historical reference has not been lost on our naval intelligence people."

"The *von Scheer* is going after the convoy. Our convoy's sailing is forcing their hand."

"Roger that." The president drew a dotted line on the map, from the question mark in Northern Europe diagonally down toward the mid-Atlantic. "And you, Captain Fuller, and your crew and your ship, are going to go after the *von Scheer*."

"Sink the *von Scheer*, protect the convoy, relieve the African pocket."

"Precisely. We're playing a very high-stakes game of dominoes here. If the *von Scheer* sinks *you,* or gets past you and destroys the convoy, all the dominoes fall. If we lose our toehold in Africa, I don't want to think how we'll ever dislodge the Axis from there or continental Europe."

"Understood." A big buildup in Britain and then a D-day-like invasion across the English Channel were out of the question in the face of atomic weapons. Jeffrey realized his new orders demanded the utmost from him tactically, with serious strategic consequences depending on whether he won or lost against the German SSGN. Part of him groaned inside, knowing how relentlessly taxed his body and mind would be in the impending confrontation. His skills at thinking on his feet, and at keeping his crew focused and level-headed amid deafening chaos and grinding uncertainty, would be tested to the ultimate limit.

"Good," the president said. "I'm glad to see you're taking this so seriously. It's a very serious business."

The president took the pen and drew a question mark on South America. "Another danger area. Instability and risk." He drew a dotted line from Brazil and Argentina up toward the mid-Atlantic. "Notice where all the lines intersect."

"Right in the Atlantic Narrows," Jeffrey said.

"Yup. The narrowest part of the whole Atlantic Ocean, where the northeast tip of Brazil juts out toward the western-most tip of North Africa. A nautical choke point, one that's going to become a tactical nuclear maelstrom soon."

"If the Axis can gain control of that part of Brazil," Jeffrey said, "and given what they hold in western Africa, they'd be able to cut the Atlantic Ocean in half around that choke point. Subsonic cruise missiles launched from the opposing coasts could overlap their reach, hit any surface ships or planes that try to move north or south." Cruise-missile design always traded off range against speed, Jeffrey knew. Tactical Tomahawks, which went about as fast as a Boeing 747, had a range of nearly 1,500 miles; the North Atlantic was more than twice that wide. The *von Scheer*'s Mach 2.5 Modified Shipwrecks, in contrast, ran out of fuel after 500 miles; the South Atlantic was up to ten times that far across.

"I'm sure that's exactly the Axis objective, Captain. . . . There are many levels to what's going on here, wheels within wheels. We still don't know quite what the Germans are up to in Latin America, but we strongly suspect their agents and moles and sympathizers are behind Brazil and Argentina being on the verge of open hostilities. It is definitely in the interest of the Axis Powers for fighting to break out in South America. It costs the Berlin-Boer nasties little, and costs the Allied cause a great deal."

"Everything's happening at once."

"The masterminds of the Axis are too good at moving countries around like chess pieces. They're also very good at seizing the initiative and forcing us to react defensively. One thing I learned as a West Point plebe is that if you keep losing the initiative and can't regain it, you lose the war."

Jeffrey studied the map, with all its *X*s and question marks and intersecting lines, for a very long time.

The president cleared his throat. "You'll be filled in more on your specific role by your direct superiors shortly. I wanted to give you the overall picture myself. So I could see your face, know who you are as a person. I'll feel a lot better, understanding what sort of man is captain of USS *Challenger*. I'm a big believer in personal relationships. A politician has to be. As a former military man, I'm a believer in knowing my key subordinates well. Your place in all this will be very key, and your ship is no ordinary submarine."

The president looked at the map, and for a moment his face was haggard and drawn. His eyes looked pained and sad, as if he was thinking of all the death and destruction to come in the next few days and weeks. The body count in this war was terrible already.

Then the president set his jaw and his eyes cleared and

grew harder. Jeffrey sensed the meeting was wrapping up. The president came closer. Jeffrey stood.

"I see now why you're such an effective commanding officer, Captain. You're a very direct guy. You zero in on your mission, period. You don't look over your shoulder when it's your job to lead the charge. . . . When we win this war, our country is going to need good men and women to pick up the pieces and help the world rebuild. *If* I'm reelected this November, and can steward the country into a thriving new peacetime somehow, there are going to be all sorts of important jobs to be filled here in Washington, inside and outside the military."

Jeffrey thought of that map again, the intersecting lines in the Atlantic Narrows. The impending clash of forces might determine the whole outcome of the war. Things might get so hot that atomic weapons would start to be used without restraint on land. The war, up to this point such a volatile trade-off between immensity of hitting power and compulsion for survival, could escalate in the days to come into a fearsome doomsday scenario.

"I have to ask you again, Mr. President. Exactly what is it you want from me?"

"Nothing you don't want to give me."

"Please don't be so cryptic, sir."

The president pointed at the easel map. "Just get out there, and win another resounding victory, and come home alive."

CHAPTER 4

When Jeffrey left the president, the crowd at the reception was just thinning out. *Boy, if they only knew what I know now.* Every nerve in his body felt electrified.

Jeffrey tried to act as calmly as he could, to maintain the air of decorum befitting a Medal of Honor winner, and to protect the secrecy of what he'd just learned. There were nosy reporters everywhere, and the country was entering a heightened state of national emergency—triggered by the sailing of the *von Scheer* and the relief convoy. Jeffrey expected to be rushed back to New London, Connecticut, any moment, to rejoin *Challenger* in her home port and then get under way. He decided to stop in a men's room while he could.

As he unzipped his fly he heard a loudspeaker announcement: "NBC drill. This is a drill. Lockdown is in effect until further notice."

NBC stood for nuclear-biological-chemical. The drill meant the staff and building engineers were rushing through standardized measures to make the hotel airtight. The ventilation system was stopped and the rooftop intake and outlet vents were shuttered automatically. All public and service entrances and exits were also sealed.

Such drills were a common aspect of life on the U.S. East Coast these days, in major structures from office towers to hospitals to schools. The threat-detection hardware and communications gear, and the procedures and the practice drills, went back several years, to the wave of increased homeland protection forced upon the country by the War on Terror. All this was coming in very handy now: Jeffrey knew radioactive dust, from the battles that raged out at sea, sometimes reached the coast in local hot spots that could be dangerous. Civil defense was no joke. There were stiff fines for people leaving home without their gas-mask satchels. National Guard units were on call 24/7 in all jurisdictions, outfitted with mobile decontamination equipment; the National Weather Service tracked the movement of winds from the Atlantic carefully, with a network of sampling stations to check for radioactivity every minute. And government price controls went well beyond enforcing prewar levels on many staple goods, to defend against panic inflation. Now controversial laws set mandatory *minimums* on house and apartment sales—based on prewar market appraisal data—to prevent any mass exodus from vulnerable areas. Some people argued these severe executive orders were unconstitutional, but the president stood firm and told the people to stand firm too. If you can't find a willing buyer at prewar prices, the president addressed the nation on live TV, then wait to sell after the war. Jeffrey figured that by the time dissenting lawsuits reached the U.S. Supreme Court, the war would be over in any case, one way or another.

Jeffrey finished washing his hands. As he walked to the ballroom, the crowd continued its murmur and hubbub, largely undisturbed by the NBC drill. Swallowing iodide tablets was part of most people's daily health routine; *nobody* used unfiltered tap water. Survivalist books, and emergency supply stores, did a land-office business—Geiger counters and gas-mask filters were two top-selling items. The populace adapted as best they could.

Jeffrey suspected the actual purpose of this particular drill was to establish zone security as the president was escorted from the hotel. He guessed these Washington old-timers knew it too.

Sure enough, in moments the drill was lifted. Jeffrey's trained submariner ear sensed the air circulation fans start up again, even as the reception's din increased.

Jeffrey noticed Commodore Wilson standing in one conversation group. A full captain, Wilson was the commanding officer of *Challenger*'s parent squadron in New London/Groton. He was Jeffrey's boss. Half a year ago, Jeffrey joined the ship as executive officer, while Wilson was *Challenger*'s captain. The two men, so far, were being promoted upward in lockstep. Though a loving husband and father to his wife and their three daughters, Wilson was a very tough and demanding guy to subordinates.

The commodore saw Jeffrey. "Where have you been?" he snapped. He didn't wait for an answer. "We need to be going. Where's Lieutenant Reebeck?"

———

Jeffrey, Wilson, and Ilse were standing with some Federal Protective Service bodyguards in the vestibule to a side entrance of the hotel.

Ilse came up close to Jeffrey. "I'll be much too tired to have dinner with you later," she said in a meaningful undertone.

"I'm occupied myself," Jeffrey said evenly. He knew he'd be swamped getting *Challenger* and her crew ready for sea and for combat. Jeffrey ached for more combat, for a chance to tangle decisively with the *von Scheer*.

As they waited for their transportation to arrive, Jeffrey was troubled by his discussion with the commander in chief. The president, as a man, had distinct charisma, an infectious eagerness to get on with the job, no matter how trying and grim. Jeffrey could detect, even in that close-range private interaction, no trace of the self-aggrandizing narcissism that could turn a national leader into a demagogue. Yet all the open references to politics as a profession, and the unveiled hints of backdoor support in the corridors of power, left Jeffrey wondering what it might be like to work in Washington after the war. *Helping direct a new reconstruction abroad. Occupation of the aggressors once subdued, and war crime trials. Foreign aid. New global alignments. Hoped-for return to a time of plenty at home.* The possibilities were almost too big to contemplate. In comparison, commanding a warship in battle was a simple and straightforward task.

Blue water in my service record is what I want. . . . Besides, so much has to happen first. The war has to be won before anyone can realistically plan for the peace.

But Jeffrey knew he couldn't have *Challenger* forever, even assuming the ship and he survived. The navy didn't work that way. It was up or out, for officers. Commanding a fast-attack submarine—or any other vessel—was supposed to be just one rung on the ladder. Selection boards for rear admiral required solid performance in land assignments too. Someone bucking for his or her first star had to look well rounded indeed—fewer than one in a hundred full captains ever made the cut for flag rank. After all, Jeffrey's own inner voice nagged, the Pentagon itself, with its spiderweb of connections with Congress and command links to the executive branch, sat on solid dry land, not out in blue water.

Jeffrey's father and mother hurried over.

"On your way out?" Michael Fuller said, annoyed.

Jeffrey nodded sheepishly. He'd been too cowed by the insistent Wilson to ask for time to look for his folks. Jeffrey was glad his father found him before the transportation showed up.

"Let me stay here and chat with Jeffrey," Michael said to his wife. "Use the car, dear. My driver can take you home so you can lie down."

Jeffrey's mother kissed her husband on the cheek. Then

she turned to Jeffrey. "Good luck. Keep safe. Call us when you can." Jeffrey hugged his mom good-bye. She walked away, accompanied by Michael Fuller's government chauffeur: undersecretaries rated official automobiles. Jeffrey wondered when he would ever see his mother again. He might be killed on his next mission. His mother's breast cancer might recur, in the chest wall this time, where there was nothing the doctors could do.

"Finally," Commodore Wilson said. Two town cars pulled up.

"Let me go with you to the airport," Michael Fuller said to Jeffrey. "We can spend a few more minutes talking. I'll take the Metro home." The Metro, the Washington subway, was very overcrowded because of wartime gasoline rationing coupled with a surge in local employment.

The bodyguards didn't argue. Jeffrey's father had pull.

Wilson and Ilse got into one of the town cars, Jeffrey and his father into the other. They sat in back, with Michael on Jeffrey's left—it was navy etiquette for the senior person to enter first so he or she could exit last. In the front passenger seat, his eyes very alert and an Uzi submachine gun in his lap, sat a bodyguard. District of Columbia police cars, one in front and one behind, started their flashers. The motorcade moved out.

———

The group of autos weaved through side streets rather than heading directly to the airport. Jeffrey figured this was for extra security. Seeing all the precautions needed just to *get to* the airport made him glad he'd be taking navy transport to New London; commercial airline check-in was a nightmare.

Jeffrey's father lowered the armrest between them, to relax. "So how did you make out? I lost track of you there for a while."

Jeffrey turned to his father. As deadpan as he could, he said, "I spent half an hour alone with the president."

"Of the Naval War College?"

"No. Of the United States."

"You're kidding." Michael Fuller seemed impressed, even envious.

"I wish I was."

"What did you talk about?"

"It's secret."

"Good," Jeffrey's father said at once. "Loose lips sink ships. . . . Like I already told you, this town's gossip circuit is too leaky as it is."

In the front seats, the driver and bodyguard ignored Jeffrey and his dad, intent on possible threats from outside the town car.

Jeffrey looked around. It was late afternoon, still light, with a gentle breeze and clear blue sky. A handful of people, mostly young or very old, strolled the spotless sidewalks. Some men and women between twenty and seventy walked more purposefully, with heavy and bulging briefcases, the beginning of evening rush hour for those who worked the early shift and then brought more work home. Some of them, Jeffrey thought, were probably heading *to* their jobs, if their assignments—civil service or private sector—helped the city and the national government keep running around the clock.

"A bit of advice?" Jeffrey's father said.

Jeffrey hesitated. "I'm all ears, Pop."

"You've got to maintain a rather difficult balance here, son. I know I just told you to mingle more, but part of you has to forget all this fancy publicity. *Just do your job.* Keep your head down with other officers."

"Huh?"

"Campus politics get ugly. You're in a very competitive business. You're already attracting jealousy. Self-appointed enemies, at your level, and up."

Jeffrey felt a shiver along his spine. This was something he hadn't even thought about.

"Not everybody loves a winner, son. That bauble around

your neck could turn into a lightning rod for resentment by the people who come in second or third."

"Are you saying this for a reason, Dad?"

"Obviously you need better antennae. Didn't you see those sidelong glances back at the hotel?"

"Frankly, no."

"I'll do what I can from where I sit," Michael Fuller said. "I know what you aren't good at, son."

"That's a rather odd way to offer a relative help."

"You'll get pigeonholed behind your back, if you aren't careful. As a war fighter who's reached his peak of competence, topped out at the single-unit operations level . . . Washington isn't a family business, Jeffrey. But every connection helps. You're my kin, my own flesh, even if we didn't talk for so long . . . Maybe *especially* because we didn't talk. I'd hate to lose you now, sunk in the ocean. But I'd hate almost as much to see you break your heart dead-ended on the beach, after going out there again and then coming home safe."

Jeffrey hesitated. There'd been deep worry, poorly disguised, in his father's tone of voice. "Dad, do you know something you're not supposed to know?"

Michael Fuller shook his head. "Remember, I've got a security clearance too, and 'up there' contacts in the Pentagon. My work at homefront conservation, fuel allocations and lubricants and all that, depends a lot on knowing supply and demand, the total picture. I therefore cannot do my job without access to the needs and plans of the fleet. The very *near-term* plans." He gave Jeffrey a meaningful look.

"I really can't comment, Dad."

"Then don't. Just remember, son, for later, God willing, the games they play in this town, they play very rough."

Jeffrey's procession halted at a red light. Cross-traffic moved, using the opposing green. One big truck rolled into the middle of the intersection. It reminded Jeffrey of a traveling carnival ride, painted in moving, gaudy red and yellow triangles. Then he realized it was a cement mixer. Jeffrey's traffic light turned green, but the cement mixer still sat there.

Spill-back. Washington rush-hour traffic jams are infamous. Still, you'd think that with carpooling, and gas rationing, in a residential neighborhood . . .

Jeffrey glanced behind him. He saw the town car with Wilson and Ilse, and the other police car, and craned his neck to see behind him more. Past the rear of their little motorcade, in the far intersection, was a fire engine—a long and heavy ladder truck. No sirens, but its flashers rotated as if it was returning from a run.

In front of Jeffrey's car, the cement mixer hadn't moved. The big hopper holding the wet cement continued to revolve. The red and yellow of the hopper, the bright red of the fire truck, and the flashing lights of the fire truck and the police cars gave the scene a strangely festive look. Jeffrey turned and watched as six firemen dismounted and opened equipment bays in the side of their truck.

Jeffrey's heart leaped into his throat as his bodyguard shouted into a walkie-talkie. The firemen now held assault rifles and rocket launchers. Three more armed men left the cement mixer's cab. They took up firing positions under the massive vehicle. *Things* hit the front of Jeffrey's car with terrible force. Jeffrey and his father flinched and ducked.

Despite himself, Jeffrey looked up. The glass was pockmarked but the bullets hadn't penetrated the armored windshield—yet. Now Jeffrey recognized the unmistakable rapid-fire *boom-boom-boom* of AK-47s. He saw glass in the police cars shatter, the cars jumping and sagging as their tires were ripped to shreds. The policemen tried to shoot back, using their riot shotguns and pistols. The noise of the firefight grew. It was a very uneven contest. Bullet-riddled men in blue collapsed to the asphalt, writhing in expanding pools of blood.

CHAPTER 5

"S it tight," Jeffrey's driver shouted. "We're armored all around!" A voice crackled over the bodyguard's walkie-talkie, something unintelligible to Jeffrey.

"Christ," Jeffrey's father said as he stared back at the fire engine. "He's aiming a rocket launcher."

Jeffrey saw a fireman crouch on the ladder truck. He held a long tube over one shoulder. At the front of the tube was the bulge of an ugly warhead. It looked like an RPG-7, Russian made—aged, like the attackers' rifles, but flooding the world's arms markets and impossible to trace.

There was a flash and a blast of smoke and dust. The warhead tore at Jeffrey's car, skimming over the intervening vehicles.

Jeffrey heard a ripping sound overhead. The incoming rocket missed the top of his car by an inch and kept going. As Jeffrey watched, it hit the cement mixer in the side.

There was a deafening concussion and a flash of searing flame. Shrapnel flew, pelting other vehicles, breaking windows in nearby buildings, chipping bricks on their facades.

The hopper of the cement mixer continued to revolve.

There was a four-inch hole in its side, and wet gray concrete poured from the hole as the hopper turned around and around.

Bullets continued to crack through the air. Jeffrey's car jumped with every impact. He saw the fire truck taking hits, and silvery dents appeared in the red of its sheet-steel side. Pedestrians on the sidewalk cowered, pinned down; some were trying to use their phones, but hysterical fumbling and frustrated rage seemed to show that the cell phones were jammed. Both sides of the street were littered with now-abandoned civilian cars.

One of the attackers climbed higher on the fire truck with another rocket launcher, trying to get a better shot at Jeffrey's vehicle.

Jeffrey's bodyguard saw it too. He hefted his Uzi and did a calculation. Enemy bullets were grazing the auto from both front and behind—to crack the door invited instant death.

Just one of those rocket-propelled shaped-charge warheads will turn this car into an inferno.

A wounded cop emptied his revolver at the enemy with the rocket launcher. The launcher fired at the same time the man who held it fell straight back off the truck. The warhead came in at an angle, barely missing the left side of Jeffrey's car.

The warhead detonated against the pavement. The blast lifted Jeffrey's town car violently. It bounced down on its reinforced suspension. Jeffrey's arms and legs felt numb from the punishment. His ears ached from the noise. The side windows of his car on the left were pitted by sharp steel fragments, and the glass was partly obscured by soot. Other autos—private cars and taxis—were starting to burn.

"We can't take any more of this," Jeffrey's father said.

Again the bodyguard's walkie-talkie crackled.

"Sit *tight*," the driver yelled. "Help is coming!"

Jeffrey watched in horror as a spray of bullets ricocheted off Ilse's and Wilson's car. He saw the headlights shatter,

chrome molding twist and break, sheet metal tear, and fiber-
glass fracture. The whole vehicle shivered on its springs.

The sound of firing suddenly intensified.

The three men under the cement mixer turned and aimed
the other way, away from Jeffrey. The ground around them
was slippery as concrete continued to pour from the hopper—it still rotated mindlessly, coated more and more by the
clinging goo.

Those three attackers opened fire again, shooting at something or someone on the far side of the cement mixer, where
Jeffrey couldn't see. There was another hard concussion.
The three attackers disintegrated. Fresh concrete quickly
covered the gore. The hopper finally stopped; the cement
mixer's powerful diesel engine was burning now, and soon
the entire front of the truck was engulfed in roaring red
flames. The flames reached threateningly for the fuel tank
down behind the cab; the tank was leaking from shrapnel
punctures. Jeffrey felt the radiant heat through the windows
of his car.

More AK-47 slugs came at the back of Jeffrey's car. The
attackers were smashing their way through the rear windshield, concentrating their fire in a single spot. Bullets
chewed and chipped at the armored glass.

A handful of men in black uniforms ran from around the
far side of the cement mixer. They took up positions and began to engage the attackers on the ladder truck.

Friendly troops. Who are they? Their only insignia were
small American flag patches on their sleeves.

The smoke of burning rubber and diesel was thick. The
stench of it got into Jeffrey's car.

The men in black combat fatigues advanced steadily.
Some fired their weapons on full automatic while others
dumped empty magazines and reloaded their assault rifles.
The weapons didn't look at all like M-16s. They had boxy
optical sights, with a little video imagining screen and mirrors to see around corners. The men worked their way up the

street. They shot and moved with skill, darting from cover to cover, advancing relentlessly.

A rapid-reaction force. Are there enough of them?

AK-47 rounds from the fire truck poured in Jeffrey's direction. Bullets hit the back bumper and pounded into the trunk. The vehicle jolted with each heavy impact.

"Jesus," Jeffrey's father said under his breath. Streaks and puffs of dark smoke drifted everywhere outside.

The friendly troops worked their way past Jeffrey's car, closer to Ilse's. Now Jeffrey saw they wore thick flak vests and ballistic-ceramic battle helmets, and talked to one another by tactical radio with microphones next to their lips.

Jeffrey looked around. He saw a young woman lying on the sidewalk, curled up and clutching at her abdomen. There was a lot of blood, and she looked pregnant.

One of the friendly troops shouted something. Jeffrey read his lips. "Grenade!"

The man aimed a grenade launcher at the ladder truck. The launcher was clipped beneath the barrel of his rifle. The launcher and rifle kicked. There was another tremendous concussion—against the side of the fire truck.

Jeffrey saw his chance. He unlocked the door and dashed from the car.

"What the—" the bodyguard shouted. Jeffrey couldn't hear the rest. Ricochets screamed; rifle reports were much louder outside the car; the smell of burning things was awful. There was more blood on the woman's dress already, and Jeffrey needed to drag her behind good cover and stop the bleeding fast. The bodyguard opened his door enough to take aim across the top of the town car. He emptied his Uzi at the ladder truck. Hot spent brass flew everywhere.

A man in black ran up to Jeffrey with his rifle held at port arms. In that fleeting instant Jeffrey saw that a wire ran from the rifle to a computer pack on the soldier's thigh; he also wore a keypad strapped to his forearm; there were tiny disk and rod antennas on his shoulders over his flak vest.

With his left hand the soldier grabbed Jeffrey by the front of his uniform, throwing him backward into the car and slamming the door.

The soldier screamed to Jeffrey's driver. "Go! Go! *Clear out of here!*"

Jeffrey landed with his head in his father's lap. His father looked down at Jeffrey and his expression seemed to say he wasn't sure if his son was very brave or incredibly stupid. Jeffrey sat up and refastened his seat belt.

Bullets continued to snap in all directions. The attackers were putting up a stiff resistance. The friendly counterattack began to slow down—the closer the engaging troops got to the fire truck, the more lethal was the return fire from the assassins dressed as firemen.

"How the *fuck* are we supposed to clear out of *this?*" The bodyguard cradled his smoking Uzi, and now the stink of burning inside the town car was very strong.

Jeffrey saw what he meant. On the near side of the street was a row of apartment buildings, beyond a line of parked cars. On the opposite side of the town car sat all the abandoned and shot-up cars in the other lane of traffic on the two-way street. Beyond those were more parked cars by the other sidewalk—that most had near-empty tanks because of the fuel shortages was the only thing that kept the whole street from becoming one huge gasoline-fed conflagration.

Beyond that far sidewalk, Jeffrey saw a wrought-iron fence. Beyond the fence the ground dropped off too steeply.

"Hold on," the driver said. He did something with the gearshift.

He began to make a broken U-turn, forcing other autos out of the way. The transmission protested, but gradually the town car worked itself sideways. The car backed up, smacking into cars parked on the same side of the street, in front of the buildings.

The driver floored the accelerator, in very low gear. He aimed at the narrow space between two cars left in the street. The town car elbowed them aside, but then the engine stalled from the effort. More smoke from everything burning stained the windows with oily yellowish soot. More bullets smacked and pitted the window glass. It was becoming harder and harder to see outside. Jeffrey caught glimpses of another wave of men in black, except these sported white armbands with big red crosses, and their helmets bore red crosses in circles of white. They carried not weapons but heavy satchels of combat first-aid supplies. These men crouched near the wounded, opened their satchels, and went to work fearlessly under fire.

Jeffrey's driver restarted the engine and backed up, very hard. Jeffrey and his father were thrown around against their seat belts. The driver changed gears and pressed down on the gas. The town car lurched forward, smashing into two parked cars on the opposite side of the street. There was a screech of smoking rubber, and for an endless moment the armored town car didn't move.

Then the two parked cars were shoved up onto the sidewalk and out of the way.

The town car flattened a stretch of the wrought-iron fence. The car began to run downhill, accelerating. Jeffrey looked back. The tires—designed to be bullet resistant—were throwing up divots of grass and clods of earth. Jeffrey saw the car with Wilson and Ilse following him, looking banged up but intact.

The cars rumbled down the slope at a frighteningly steep angle. Bushes were dragged under the car and spat out behind. The noises of shooting receded, but the fight they'd left behind seemed barely diminished. Jeffrey spotted people in the park, hiding behind pathetic cover, benches or sapling trees. Some of the people had children with them, or dogs.

The cars leveled off and made a tight turn and accelerated; the going was very rough. They were on a path in Rock Creek Park—here the park comprised the sides and bottom of a wide and deep ravine. Both town cars continued along the pavement of the walking path as fast as they possibly could. Rock Creek was close beside.

Jeffrey heard sirens now. On the opposite side of the ravine, a parkway paralleled the creek. A parade of police čars, fire engines, ambulances was trying to catch up with Jeffrey. But they were out of reach. To Jeffrey's immediate left was the twenty-foot-wide creek, water churning in its rugged course. The creek was lined with stands of trees too old, too sturdy, to smash through.

Jeffrey's driver pressed on hard. Outside the battle-scarred windows, tree trunks and overhead branches went by in a blur. The cars zoomed under the high archways of road bridges carrying cross streets above the park. They reached a place where the ravine's bottom narrowed, and the sidewalk they'd been using came to an end.

"Shit!" the driver shouted. He slammed on the brakes and the car slewed sideways. Jeffrey's bodyguard yelled into his radio; the voice that answered from somewhere safe was maddeningly calm.

The way ahead was blocked by thick felled trees. Behind the trees were men in green Park Service uniforms. The men were unpacking rocket launchers.

They expected this to be our escape route all along. . . .
The first wave didn't get us, but this one will. We're sitting ducks.

To the right was the rising embankment, hopelessly steep. To the left, still, were trees and creek, an insurmountable barrier. Just behind Jeffrey's car, the one with Wilson and Ilse, with their own driver and bodyguard, also fishtailed to a halt.

If the armored town cars tried to turn around they'd just give better broadside targets. If they tried to flee in reverse the rocket launchers couldn't miss.

"Make a stand right here!" Jeffrey's bodyguard said. He reloaded his Uzi with a long and heavy ammo clip. The driver pulled another Uzi from its mount under the dash.

Both men pulled out pistols. The driver turned to Jeffrey and his father. "You know how to use these?"

"I think so," Michael Fuller said. "Which thing is the safety?"

Great, Jeffrey told himself. *My dad's a bunch of help.*

Jeffrey took one of the weapons. He recognized a nine-millimeter Beretta, a standard military-issue weapon.

But the bad guys have assault rifles and rocket launchers.

"When I yell 'Go,'" the bodyguard said, "everybody pop their doors and roll out and start shooting. Some of us might make it."

Jeffrey knew it was useless, even before the new wave of attackers opened fire.

AK-47 bullets came at the town cars in short but terrifying bursts. These attackers were firing green tracer rounds so their victims could *see* the rounds in flight as they passed. They peppered the side doors of Jeffrey's car. Four grown men were pinned in Jeffrey's auto. The bodyguard's plan to shoot their way out would be suicide.

Whoever they are, these attackers know exactly what they're doing. They're just too good.

Behind this deadly incoming suppressive fire, Jeffrey saw an attacker kneel and take aim with a rocket launcher. The man seemed to point it right at Jeffrey, right through the dirty, punched-up armored windshield of the car. The warhead's antitank shaped charge would fill the car with a supersonic jet of white-hot gas and metal vapor, cooking everyone alive.

Somebody important really wants me dead.

Policemen on the parkway stopped their cars. They were trying to shoot at the attackers with whatever light weapons they had. Some of the attackers shifted their fire in that direction.

Jeffrey's father made eye contact and took a deep breath, and let it out. "Whoever thought we'd buy it, both, like this?"

Jeffrey felt deeply violated, and angry. Not because he would die. He'd always known that someday—in combat or in old age—he would die. He felt enraged at this latest defamation of the nation's capital, at the heartless sacrifice of civilians so a gang of paid assassins could get at *him*. Jeffrey also felt guilty. *People are dying here because of me.*

The attacker with the rocket launcher exploded. A solid wall of bright red tracers poured at him out of the sky. There were brilliant flashes from the automatic-cannon rounds. The rocket launcher's warhead and propellant fuel burst in half-blinding secondary detonations.

Above the pounding of his heart and the roaring in his ears, Jeffrey heard the noise of powerful turbines and the steady beat of military-helicopter rotor blades. He looked up in time to see two army Apache Longbow gunships racing by. More bursts from their chin-mounted Gatling guns pulverized the attackers' position, mutilating the barricade of fallen trees.

"That's it," the bodyguard said. "We got air support! *Let's move it!"*

Jeffrey's father looked doubtful. "Can't we just get out and ford the stream?"

"Negative! There could be snipers *anywhere!"*

The town cars started up again. The ride was terribly rough. Both cars wobbled and bounced on their torn-up tires. Smoke was coming from under the hood of Jeffrey's car.

How many more attack waves has the enemy prepared? How much more can this vehicle take?

Still both autos pressed on hard, forward along the ravine beside the creek. The Apache helicopters flew top cover, and the crowd of emergency vehicles kept pace along the parkway. Now there was no clearance between the creek and the embankment. The town cars tilted sideways, their damaged suspensions complaining. They threatened to lose all traction and smash against the heavy trees still lining the creek.

The parkway crossed overhead, and now the road was on Jeffrey's right. Both town cars veered onto the road, swerving through panicky oncoming traffic. They got into the right lane and Jeffrey's driver stepped on the gas. Suddenly the right rear tire of his car disintegrated altogether, from too much shrapnel damage, and the car sagged down on the wheel rim.

The driver just kept going. A steady shower of sparks and smoke was left in the wake of Jeffrey's vehicle; the grinding noise of steel on the roadway was nearly unbearable. The smoke from under the front hood was getting heavier and heavier. The front windshield was gathering an ever-thicker coat of soot and oil and dirt. There were countless bullet pockmarks. The bodyguard had to open a window and stick out his head to help guide the driver as he steered. The car was hard to control and kept weaving onto the grassy shoulder.

"Watch for land mines!" the driver shouted.

"I'm trying to!" the bodyguard yelled.

"Terrific," Jeffrey's father mumbled.

Jeffrey looked behind again.

The other car still followed, but had had to drop back so the driver wouldn't be blinded by the smoke from Jeffrey's car. Jeffrey and his father began to choke on all the fumes.

"We're almost there!" the driver said.

The ravine grew broader and both side slopes became less steep. The town cars emerged from the park and jumped the curb and skidded to a halt. In front of them, barring further progress, was the wide Potomac itself. In an open area beside the river sat a huge Marine Corps transport helicopter. Both army Apache gunships orbited vigilantly overhead.

Heavily armed marines had already formed a perimeter. They motioned for everyone to get out of the cars.

The noise of the Marine Corps helo was painfully loud, even with its engines just on idle. The stink of the turbine exhaust added to all the other burning smells. There was grit in the air, blown by the spinning main rotor blades; the small tail rotor spun much faster, in a blur. The entire helo was painted in camouflage, a blotchy pattern of matte dark green and black and brown.

"Those men, the attackers," Michael Fuller shouted in Jeffrey's ear. "They looked liked Russians!"

Jeffrey nodded. "Former Spetznaz probably! Special forces, in the pay of the Axis now!"

Michael Fuller hesitated. "Is it always like this?"

"Is what like what?"

"The combat!"

Jeffrey looked his father right in the eyes. "Welcome to my world!" Jeffrey reached out a sweaty, smoke-stained hand. Jeffrey's father shook it; Michael Fuller's hand felt like an ice cube.

"I'll see you, Dad!"

Marines hustled Jeffrey and Wilson and Ilse to the helo. The crew chief handed them cranials and floatation vests. The cranials were collapsible flight helmets. They opened like a clamshell, had built-in hearing protection, and came with big padded eye goggles. Jeffrey and Wilson and Ilse quickly got ready for the flight.

So close to the aircraft, conversation was impossible. The crew chief used sign language to show each of them where to sit. They climbed inside the helo. The seat frames were made of stark aluminum tubing, and the seat backs and bottoms were simple thick black vinyl sheets. Shoulder straps came over each shoulder. They clipped into the buckle of a belt that covered both thighs. Jeffrey pulled all the fittings very tight.

The helo was an SH-60 Seahawk. The transport compartment had seating for ten. On board were Jeffrey and Ilse, sitting side by side facing forward at the rear of the compartment. Wilson sat up front, facing Jeffrey. The only other passengers were the crew chief and his assistant, who slammed the door.

The engine noise grew stronger, even through the sound-proof ear cups of Jeffrey's helmet and the insulated padding of the fuselage walls. The vibrations through the seat and through the floor rose to a heavy rapid shaking. The Seahawk took to the air.

The helo rose quickly and headed out over the Potomac. The Pentagon was a huge gray squatting presence up ahead, the oblique perspective from the helo making the five-sided building seem oddly elongated and flat.

Jeffrey saw a thinning pillar of black smoke, rising from where the first ambush broke out.

They flew past Theodore Roosevelt Island and over bridges; the interior of the aircraft had a metallic, oily, hot-plastic smell. Then the helo was rushing along the Potomac, closer to and then right past the Pentagon and the airport, at 150 knots, at barely a hundred feet above the river.

The Apache helos flew armed escort. Jeffrey could see their Gatling guns pivoting in their chin mounts, scanning both banks of the river, cued to sights mounted on each gunner's special helmet. Each Apache's pilot sat above and behind the gunner in the long and narrow two-man combat helicopters.

Jeffrey tried to slow his pulse and just enjoy the ride and savor life. He'd hated the feeling before of just being a passenger, of having to huddle passively while others fought and died protecting *him*. He wasn't used to this, and it galled him. He much preferred to be in charge, both of himself and of the ones who did the fighting and killing and dying.

The engine sounds swelled louder, and the rotor vibrations got more rough, each time the helo banked steeply right or left to follow the river. But the steady vibrations were reassuring. There was no incoming fire from either side of the Potomac. The direction of the golden sun, low on the horizon now to the right, confirmed for Jeffrey that the helos were heading south.

Then Commodore Wilson caught Jeffrey's eye. The muscular black man gave Jeffrey a sidelong glance and pointed at Jeffrey's chest, then shook a finger. Jeffrey looked down and saw why. His Medal of Honor was gone. It must have been torn off when he tried to get out of the town car to help that wounded pregnant woman lying in the street.

CHAPTER 6

A half-hour flying time south of Washington, Jeffrey's helicopter banked again, hard left and then hard right, along a wide curve in the Potomac near Fredericksburg, Virginia. Now that he was coming down from the emotional highs of combat and survival, he felt drowsy and thirsty and couldn't really concentrate on organized work. That would come later—all too soon, when he rejoined his ship.

For now, buddy, just enjoy the ride.

The helos still followed the river, the Seahawk with its passengers and the Apaches with their Gatling guns. The Potomac began to open out and formed a broad tidal estuary, lined by scenic inlets and coves. Beyond the houses and occasional towns on both sides of the water, rolling southern pine forests stretched to the visible horizons. The forested terrain was sometimes sliced by roads, or railroads, or rights-of-way for high-voltage power lines. Once Jeffrey saw a freight train, with eight diesel locomotives and an endless stream of cars. The diesels were painted olive drab for

camouflage—it was their straining exhaust plumes that gave
them away.

Jeffrey's Seahawk turned right and again headed south.
Out of both sides of the aircraft, suddenly, he saw Chesapeake Bay. The water reflected the blue of the sky, shading
to green in shallower places. Yellow-white sand beaches,
grassy salt marshes, and tree-studded swamps rolled past as
the helo kept up its high-speed dash. The two army Apaches
continued flying escort, one close to each shore of the huge
and elongated bay.

Civilian marinas were closed for the war's duration, and
Jeffrey saw no pleasure craft at all. The lowering sun cast a
pink and melancholy glow on the deserted beaches, the sandbars, the marshes and abandoned cottages, and the many
cargo ships moored in the sheltered bay; Jeffrey was sure
these ships were waiting to sail in the convoy to Africa. Now
and then he could see the three helos' shadows cast on the water. The shadows appeared to pursue him, each one dark and
insubstantial, sometimes far off and sometimes close. Jeffrey
felt as if he were being chased by the ghosts of the dead.

The Seahawk's crew chief listened on his flight helmet's
headphones for a moment, then said something into his lip
mike. He caught Commodore Wilson's eye and held up both
hands balled into fists. He opened and closed all ten fingers
three times. Wilson nodded.

Thirty minutes until we land, Jeffrey knew the hand signals
meant. *Land where?* More massed cargo vessels stretched
below.

Jeffrey saw a U.S. Coast Guard cutter, one of the new
class that were really major warships, steaming toward the
mouth of the bay, to the battle-torn Atlantic. The cutter's
bow wave creamed high, foaming white as she made flank
speed, nearly thirty-five knots. Her wake spread out behind
her, faithfully following the ship like a V-shaped tail. Two
helicopters flew ahead of the cutter, towing paravanes
through the water to sweep for mines.

Jeffrey saw various aircraft at different altitudes, near and far. An air-force AWACS plane, its powerful radar enclosed in a saucer disk above the fuselage, coordinated military air traffic and monitored civilian airliners too. The AWACS also stood guard against enemy airborne incursions.

Four-engine long-endurance maritime patrol aircraft came and went; these planes carried airdropped antisubmarine torpedoes. Jeffrey saw a navy blimp. The blimps could stay aloft for days between refuelings and bore many sensors to keep a sharp eye on the sea. Jeffrey suspected that well concealed on the ground were other types of radars, antiaircraft guns, and anti-cruise-missile missile launchers—and hidden tanks and machine-gun nests.

Jeffrey seriously doubted that the land defenses all along the East Coast would ever face a full-blown invasion. That wasn't a part of the Axis master plan. Berlin had openly said so. They were far more clever and calculating than to waste resources on such an impossible, preposterous task as a military occupation of the United States. Far better to unleash their unspeakable violence on the high seas, in international waters, to sever America's lines of communication and trade abroad. Far more effective, for Axis aims, to *isolate* the U.S. than to invade it: let fear and deprivation gnaw away at American voters, until they chose en masse to allow Europe and Africa to fester on the far side of a gigantic ocean. Let Americans be frightened into accepting a new status quo, whittled down into making peace with a new Axis empire—at the price of America's diminishing to a second-rate, also-ran power.

The real war being fought in and for the U.S. homeland was a psychological war. The targets weren't factories or rail yards but people's feelings, their confidence in their leaders and in themselves, and their willingness to risk eventual mass destruction *here* to benefit occupied foreign countries *over there*. Axis submarines had already launched harassment raids against several coastal American cities and bases, using supersonic cruise missiles with conventional warheads. The risk of nuclear escalation, intentional or inadvertent, was ever present and constantly rising—and the Axis made very sure the American public knew it.

Ahead of the Seahawk, Jeffrey saw land instead of water. The bridge-and-tunnel road link across the mouth of Chesapeake Bay loomed ahead of him, at an angle on the Seahawk's left. The Seahawk banked to the right, into the now-setting sun. The Apaches peeled off and headed back toward Washington. The cargo ships moored on the water gave way to navy ships tied up at piers. The Seahawk's engine noise changed pitch again, and the aircraft leaned back on its tail. The ground came up quickly, and the helo settled down on a concrete pad. It took a moment for Jeffrey's senses to reorient from the heady exhilaration of flying to the mundane, narrowed perspective of a creature tied to solid land.

Fun's over. Now back to work.

The crew chief squeezed past Jeffrey and Ilse and opened the passenger-compartment door. Jeffrey unbuckled, then followed Ilse and Wilson out of the aircraft. At first his legs wobbled a bit as he readjusted to walking on the ground. A safe distance from the helo, he and Ilse and Wilson took off their goggles and folding helmets and floatation vests, handing them to the crew chief. The pilot and copilot, still in the cockpit, shut down the engines and systems; maintenance and refueling teams already were setting up; heat rippled off the now-silent turbine engines atop the fuselage.

Jeffrey glanced around. He and Wilson and Ilse were in the middle of the sprawling, bustling, heavily defended Norfolk Navy Base. Nearby, Jeffrey knew well from his younger days as a SEAL, was the separate and equally sprawling Norfolk Amphibious Warfare Base. In *that* direction, at the far end of Pamlico Sound, sat the U.S. Marine Corps' Camp Lejeune, with its barracks and obstacle courses, its shooting ranges and beaches for practice assaults. Closer lay the runways and hardened hangars of Oceana Naval Air Station. And in *that* direction, just across the nearby waters of historic Hampton Roads, were the Newport News Shipbuilding yards, where they made nuclear subs and nuclear-powered supercarriers. It had been right there in Hampton Roads that the world's first ironclads, the USS *Monitor* and the CSS *Virginia*—formerly the *Merrimack*—fought each other to a standstill in the Civil War.

Next to the helicopter pad, an aide stood by an unmarked but very navy-looking white van. He waved for Wilson's party to come over.

Jeffrey yelled into Wilson's ear, above the noise of other helos taking off or landing. "Sir, I thought we were supposed to go back to New London."

Wilson gave him a disapproving look, but then smiled. He cupped a hand to Jeffrey's ear; with the decibels roaring all around them, the exchange would be totally private. "Captain Fuller, view today as practice for tomorrow, and *learn* from it. Sometimes you don't think enough. Other times, like right now, you assume too much. They're both bad habits. Fix them pronto."

Wilson walked on, and Jeffrey followed. Wilson leaned to Jeffrey's ear again.

"The Medal you lost on that street back there in Washington can be replaced. You, as my most hot-running ship commander, I'd rather not lose. I want you to live long enough to win another Medal, not come back in a box yourself, or end up as radioactive fish food."

Jeffrey and Wilson and Ilse were seated in a conference room deep underground, in Norfolk's hardened communications and planning facilities belonging to commander, U.S. Atlantic Fleet. There were more than two dozen people crammed in the room—most of them generals or commodores or admirals, or high-level members of their staffs. One side of the conference room was made of soundproof glass, and the curtains were drawn open. Through the glass,

Jeffrey could see the main war room itself. Large maps and situation plots covered the walls on big flat-screen displays. Men and women in uniform sat at consoles. Officers, with the gold cords around one shoulder denoting an admiral's aide, hurried back and forth purposefully. Enlisted messengers dashed hither and yon.

The preliminaries in the conference room were long over, and the four-star admiral himself, Admiral Hodgkiss—commander, U.S. Atlantic Fleet—had the floor. The atmosphere was very tense. The feeling of urgency in the big war room, right outside, was infectious and mounting. Hodgkiss himself was a stiff and formal man at the best of times, and Jeffrey could see that this evening he was feeling the pressure like everyone else: the pressure of the relief convoy's impending confrontation with the modern U-boat packs, of the Axis land offensive soon to open in Central Africa, and of the sailing of the *von Scheer*. The admiral finished laying out the many knowns and unknowns and uncertainties—the uncertainties seemed to predominate.

The admiral looked around the room. "All of you. My staff, the submarine squadron commanders, carrier battle-group commanders, everybody. We need a total effort now. I expect each of you to use your head, and stay sharp and put your forces in harm's way aggressively. Show me real initiative every minute when the shooting starts, or I won't hesitate to relieve you. Take a deep breath and savor the smell of gun smoke clinging to Captain Fuller's clothes. Get addicted to it! Don't defend yourselves against the U-boats. *Attack* the U-boats! We're gambling everything on this throw of the dice. We *have* to get our convoy through, and we *have* to keep the pocket open. If we don't, the war is probably as good as lost."

Just then a messenger knocked. Hodgkiss's aide, a full captain, let the man in. He handed Hodgkiss a communiqué. Hodgkiss read it and frowned. He turned to the room at large.

"This is as good a time as any to take a short break. . . .

Everybody be back here in ten minutes. We need to discuss fleet dispositions to protect the convoy en route and sink or scatter the wolf packs. We need to go over the plans for landing and off-loading on the Central African coast, depending on whether we still have control of the beaches and surrounding waterspace and airspace, or not, when the convoy and escorts get there. . . . And Captain Fuller, I want to see you in private."

Jeffrey followed Hodgkiss nervously down the hall, to a smaller meeting room that was unoccupied. The admiral sat, gesturing for Jeffrey to sit facing him across the table.

Hodgkiss stared at Jeffrey very hard, without saying anything, as if to take Jeffrey's measure, to weigh him in Hodgkiss's unforgivingly objective hand.

Hodgkiss was short and skinny, and incredibly intelligent. As a former submariner who now bore immensely broad responsibilities, he tended at times to distance himself from the submariner community. He controlled huge numbers of naval assets, going far beyond fast-attack subs. His empire included such surface combatants as Aegis cruisers, and naval aviation—both the planes and their carriers—plus powerful marine amphibious warfare groups. Hodgkiss could be rough on his subordinates and had the reputation of being a man you did *not* want to displease. In both his wiry build and his overbearing manner, he reminded Jeffrey a lot of the late Hyman Rickover, self-proclaimed father of America's nuclear navy, the maker and destroyer of careers.

Hodgkiss had been the admiral Jeffrey could barely get himself to talk with in the reception back at the Omni Shoreham Hotel.

Hodgkiss put the message slip on the table, looked Jeffrey right in the eyes, and without preliminaries, began to speak. "The Russians just made a formal announcement to us through their ambassador. I quote, Any first use of thermonuclear weapons by the United States anywhere in the eastern hemisphere will be taken as a first use against the Russian Federation itself. Retaliation in kind will be massive and swift. Unquote." He waited inscrutably for Jeffrey to react to this bombshell.

"Does the statement say Allies, sir, like the UK or the Free French, or just the United States specifically?"

"Smart question, son. The United States, specifically and only . . . They're telling us we better not be first to escalate past tactical fission bombs. And *this*"—the admiral tapped the message slip—"puts the Axis Powers explicitly under Russia's hydrogen-bomb umbrella." Neither Germany nor South Africa possessed any H-bombs. France's had either been evacuated before her capitulation or destroyed by French Special Forces.

"Why now?" Jeffrey asked.

"You tell me. Answer the question yourself."

"They know about the *von Scheer*. They know about the relief convoy and the African land offensive. They're protecting themselves in case things get out of hand and we're tempted to escalate. They're also throwing more weight behind the Axis."

"Concur. I'm sure they're also reacting to something else."

"Admiral?"

"Their certain knowledge that last month you almost started World War Three."

Jeffrey wasn't sure how to respond.

I acted under orders that originated with the commander in chief, delivered to me through the proper chain of command.

And I didn't *start World War III.*

Hodgkiss shot Jeffrey an amused look, as if he'd read his mind; part of the admiral's scary reputation was that he was very good at reading minds.

The admiral chuckled. "If you can't take the heat in here, how are you going to manage out in the deep blue sea? No one's blaming you for anything, at least no one in the Allied

High Command, including me. You just got a big fancy medal for what you achieved last month. I wanted this little chat, one-on-one, because your role in what's coming next will also be very important."

Jeffrey hesitated. "Yes, sir." *Everybody keeps telling me that today.*

"Commodore Wilson is quite aware of this tête-à-tête outside his formal chain of command. He approved, naturally enough. I didn't ask him about it, I *told* him." Hodgkiss chuckled again. "I promised you'd fill him in on the highlights as soon as you two get the chance."

"Yes, sir, Admiral. Of course." Jeffrey felt less uncomfortable.

Hodgkiss became more intense. "HMS *Dreadnought* is already on station on barrier patrol in the Greenland-Iceland-UK Gap. Now that we know the *von Scheer* is leaving from Norway, *Dreadnought* is our first line of defense. Her and our best steel-hulled submarines like *Seawolf* are also deployed in the gap." The *Seawolf* class was very deep diving and fast, optimized for open ocean sub-on-sub combat in a late Cold War scenario. *Dreadnought* was the UK's ceramic-hulled equivalent to *Challenger*. "Since the *von Scheer* can pick her place to infiltrate the gap, and *Dreadnought* and *Seawolf* can't be everywhere, it is my informed view that *von Scheer* will break into the Atlantic. That's where you and your ship become indispensable to me."

Jeffrey thought it best to hold his tongue.

Hodgkiss picked up the message slip. "This Russian ultimatum should trigger another question."

Jeffrey began to sweat mentally, thinking hard.

This guy knows how to put me through my paces without wasting time.

"Admiral, does the announcement make any specific reference to them retaliating against first use of tactical nuclear weapons in open land warfare well outside Russia?"

"Good, you got it in one. To answer you: No; it does not.

The attached assessment by our analysts says the Russians wish to sidestep that rather loaded topic."

"To keep both us and the Germans and Boers guessing."

"And to keep the Germans and Boers feeling dependent on Russian help . . . It also indirectly raises the wild card of atomic fighting spreading ashore in Central Africa, which would be our worst nightmare."

Jeffrey found the thought appalling—but this was exactly the sort of stress that always made him feel emboldened. "The best way to discourage that, sir, is for our landing to be fast and powerful and well dispersed. Get our tanks and vehicles and helos well in past the beaches quickly. Then stay mobile, don't bunch up. Don't tempt the Axis with concentrated targets for fission weapons."

"You're up on your theory. . . . Your job is to help turn theory into fact. This is your prime motivation, Captain. Stop the *von Scheer*. Make sure the convoy gets there with minimal losses so our marines and army troops can do all the things you just said they should do. Helos and eighty-knot air-cushioned landing craft and fast amphibious armor are useless if their parent ships can't get in range intact."

"I understand."

Hodgkiss changed subjects abruptly again—another of his trademarks. "*Challenger* has gotten under way, using a twofold subterfuge. Step one is that the Axis has almost certainly been tracking her captain since his helo flight from Washington, and her captain is here in Norfolk, not in New London. That's *you,* Commander Fuller, CO of our navy's most capable undersea warship." The admiral smiled disarmingly. "Step two is that *Challenger* has gotten under way using a new form of concealment for which special codename project clearance is required."

Jeffrey was confused. "I'm supposed to stay put, as a deception, so the Germans and Boers think my ship is still in dry dock?"

"Negative," Hodgkiss snapped. "You join your ship

covertly, by mini-sub, when she reaches the Norfolk area. *Challenger* has your executive officer in temporary command." He raised his bushy eyebrows at Jeffrey. "I presume, Captain, that your XO has your confidence to safely make the transit here through friendly waters?"

"Of course, sir."

"Lieutenant Reebeck is not coming with you this time." Now Hodgkiss gave Jeffrey a quizzical look. Jeffrey realized someone, somewhere, had decided Jeffrey and Ilse had better be separated. Then he remembered he himself considered asking that Ilse be transferred off *Challenger* after his previous mission.

"Lieutenant Reebeck will remain here at my headquarters, with Commodore Wilson, to assist me in divining your probable tactics and intent, since we will frequently lose communications contact with your vessel. Lieutenant Reebeck will also apply her skills as combat oceanographer to help the larger effort."

Jeffrey digested this. It made good sense from the wider context of the admiral's tasks and areas of control.

He waited for Hodgkiss to go on.

"No, Lieutenant Clayton and his SEALs are not on *Challenger*. They will not be joining you either."

"Then—"

"You will be taking on a different team of SEALs, by rendezvous with another submarine's minisub, as you reach your principal operating area."

Hodgkiss leaned back and folded his hands behind his head. Jeffrey let down his guard—and instantly regretted it.

"Why aren't you wearing your Medal?"

Jeffrey hesitated. This was embarrassing. "It was lost, sir."

"Yes, I know. I know exactly where, and when, and how. The question was purely rhetorical."

"Sir?"

"Before we resume the other meeting and move on to general business, I wanted to personally make a point to you, Captain."

"Admiral?"

"This time, once you join *Challenger,* you are *not* to go gallivanting off with the SEALs and expose yourself to enemy fire on land. . . . If necessary to destroy the *von Scheer,* your ship and crew are expendable. *You,* as an individual, separated from your ship, are not."

CHAPTER 7

In the western Barents Sea, east of Norway, Ernst Beck sat alone in his cabin—the captain's cabin of the *Admiral von Scheer*. Beck brooded, about what had happened already, and about what his own next actions would be.

The ship's real captain was dead. And Beck needed to take the *von Scheer* into the sharpest teeth of Allied antisubmarine defenses very soon. By an accident of geography, the only fast way from Norway into the North Atlantic Ocean was through the Greenland–Iceland–United Kingdom Gap. This nautical choke point—the G-I-UK Gap—had been a major focus for both NATO and the Soviets during the Cold War. Right now, running this formidable gauntlet was the price Ernst Beck had to pay for the *von Scheer*'s hidden construction up by the bleakest Arctic wastes, so near Russian aid and Russian protection.

Help wipe out a massive Allied convoy to the Central African front. Sink USS Challenger *once and for all. Which happens first doesn't matter—just don't come back to port until they've both been done.*

Beck knew that even though German submarines had

nuked the gap's SOSUS hydrophone lines at the start of the war, the U.S. and Britain by now would have planted more. They were even using small and stealthy mobile, autonomous, roving multisensor platforms to detect and localize undersea intruders. A large number of the Allies' very best fast-attack submarines would be deployed in and around the gap. Perhaps a dozen of them at once, each in its own preassigned barrier patrol box . . . in reinforcing lines on both the near and far sides of the gap. Not to mention airborne and space-based and surface warship surveillance systems—and antisubmarine torpedoes and mines.

Beck rubbed eyes that still burned from the effects of smoke and seawater. He sighed to himself.

My first deployment as captain, the von Scheer*'s first combat sortie, could end quickly, stillborn. And right now, as per my basic orders, I'm sneaking the ship in the wrong direction—east into the Barents Sea, not west toward the gap—and I don't even know why.*

Beck looked around the cabin. He'd had so little time to adjust to being the man in charge, and even less time to grasp the immensity of the tasks before him. A photo of his wife and sons was attached to the wall, in the same place where so recently another man's wife and children seemed to stare at Beck accusingly.

The deceased captain's personal effects had all been left behind at the U-boat base under the mountain up a fjord in occupied Norway. The base admiral's staff would sort through everything and return the dead man's possessions to his family with a letter of condolence. Beck was sure the letter would say only that he'd been killed in action defending the Fatherland. Given the victim's rank, the condolences would probably be signed by someone senior in Berlin—and routed from Berlin too, to reveal nothing about the location, let alone the cause, of this latest tragic loss. *This latest of many, many a tragic loss.*

Beck listened as *von Scheer*'s air circulation fans issued their reassuring hushing noise from the ventilator grilles in the overhead. The air had that familiar smell of a nuclear submarine submerged: pungent ozone, oil-based lubricants, enamel paint on hot metal, nontoxic cleansers, warm electronics, and stale human sweat. The ship was running as deep as the local bottom terrain would permit: three hundred meters, about one thousand feet. A strong blizzard raged on the ocean's surface. Beneath thick overcast, the waves topside were high. But the *von Scheer's* deck was rock steady as she moved at an ultra-quiet fifteen knots.

Weather here in the Barents Sea is almost always dreadful this time of year—off the Kola Peninsula, Russian turf, their chunk of the Scandinavian landmass, near Polyarny and Murmansk . . . and the major installations of Russia's Northern Fleet.

Beck looked up from reading his orders when a messenger knocked. He stood and cracked the door so the messenger couldn't see the classified documents stacked on his cabin's little fold-down desk.

The messenger was very young, perhaps eighteen. He snapped to attention and handed Beck some standard reports from the ship's engineer. Beck eyed the forms on the old-fashioned clipboard. All was in order with the *von Scheer's* twin nuclear reactors. The big pump-jet propulsor at her stern was working perfectly. So was everything between, from the steam generators to the main turbines and condensers, to the massive dynamos the turbines spun, to the solid-state power-control circuits, to the permanent-magnet DC motors that made the propulsor shaft turn. Beck initialed the forms in all the proper places—a captain's paperwork burden never ceased.

Beck gazed at the messenger's face. He saw someone youthful but hard, obedient and proud—yet somehow shallow in spirit, not given to introspection or philosophy or moral doubt.

A well-honed fighting machine, like the von Scheer *herself, except made of human flesh. A component of a weapon system, really, more than a person. Trained, to the finest standards of classic German craftsmanship and discipline, but with little development of underlying* self . . . *A member of my crew.*

Outside, in the passageway, personnel traffic quickly became more hectic. The watch was changing, as it did every six hours. The midnight watch was coming off duty; the morning watch was coming on. One of Beck's more experienced officers would be passing the deck and the conn to one of the others, according to a preestablished schedule. That officer would decide on all aspects of internal ship's machinery status, and direct the *von Scheer*'s movements as well—but formal accountability, and ultimate blame, always lay on Beck's head as commanding officer.

The cooks would be in the middle of serving breakfast now. Beck took a deep breath and savored delicious odors wafting from the galley: fresh-baked bread, ham, scrambled eggs. It made his stomach rumble, but he had work to do. He'd grab a light snack later, or maybe just wait until lunch.

Beck opened his cabin door another few centimeters while the messenger stood there stiffly. He wanted to see his men as they went by, toward the control room and the torpedo room forward, or aft to the wardroom or enlisted mess and the berthing spaces. Farther aft was the big missile compartment with its vertical cruise-missile launch tubes, and then came the shielded reactors, with the engineering spaces toward the stern.

Some chiefs nodded politely to Beck; the enlisted men mostly avoided meeting his eyes; the few officers he saw mouthed a polite *guten morgen*. Good morning.

Overall, Beck liked what he saw. Although this was the *von Scheer*'s maiden combat patrol, covert shakedown cruises and training exercises had melded these men into a sharp team. Now, by their facial expressions, their postures, their crisp appearances, they showed they were eager and ready for battle. There was a collective excitement to put more Allied ships where they belonged: at the bottom of the sea, in fragments.

Beck nodded to himself. You could tell a lot from body language, when over one hundred men lived in such close quarters inside a submarine's pressure hull, with no windows and no mental or physical privacy at all. He'd known most of these men for about eight weeks, the intense time since he joined the *von Scheer* from recuperation and leave, after his previous mission. There was much yet to be done, to test the men and test himself, but they seemed prepared to begin the ultimate testing. They'd accepted his role as new captain seamlessly. Beck's reputation as a strong tactician preceded him, spread by those few among the crew who'd been with him before and survived. The Knight's Cross around his neck—which he wore even with his workaday black at-sea submarine coveralls—empowered him with much credibility. Its sparkling inlaid diamonds were a visible reminder to each man aboard that Beck had gone places, done things, made decisions, scored kills that most of them could only dream about.

This aura and mystique is something that, as their commanding officer now, I fully intend to maintain and exploit.

Satisfied with the engineer's report and everything else, Beck dismissed the messenger. Then, on second thought, he told the youth to have someone bring him a fresh cup of hot tea.

———·———

The empty tea mug sat on the deck off to one side of Ernst Beck's desk. On his desk now was the large envelope with the secret-mission orders given him by the rear admiral, the orders that Rudiger von Loringhoven had helped to write. The envelope was open.

Beck was not at all pleased. The envelope contained a brief letter of instructions, and another thick envelope within it. The letter stated that von Loringhoven was to serve as a special adviser to the *von Scheer*'s captain, on matters pertaining to the ship's broad patrol routing and target priorities. Von Loringhoven, though a civilian diplomat, was seasoned at working with naval attachés of Germany and several foreign powers. He'd been thoroughly briefed on the overall war situation by the Foreign Ministry. He'd conducted background discussions with the grand admiral, commanding, Imperial German U-boat Fleet, to prepare him for this cruise. He was well versed on the latest Axis stratagems and war aims.

Fine. But none of this says why von Loringhoven is here.

The letter told *von Scheer*'s captain to open the second envelope, the one under the cover letter, only in von Loringhoven's presence. While exercising final discretion as commanding officer—to assure the ship's successful completion of her mission and to preserve her safety as much as the rigors of war would allow—*von Scheer*'s captain was nevertheless to render von Loringhoven every assistance that tactical circumstance permitted.

Wheels began to turn in Ernst Beck's head.

This letter is addressed to a dead man, who outranked me, and who knew things I don't know. It would have been irksome enough for a full commander to have a civilian breathing down his neck. My deceased former superior owned the jovial personality, and the proven leadership skills, to make such an arrangement work. I'm less senior, and not feeling nearly so jovial.

Beck decided to begin by standing on ceremony. Von Loringhoven, as a diplomat, should appreciate this. He picked up the intercom headset for the Zentrale—the control room.

A response came immediately. "Acting first watch officer speaking, Captain." This was the weapons officer, Lieutenant Karl Stissinger. Beck had given him the job as acting executive officer and moved the assistant weapons officer, a junior-grade lieutenant, into the weapons officer's position. Then a senior chief became acting assistant weapons officer, and everyone else in that department moved up a slot. Though the men were saddened to lose their captain, and some still seemed a bit stunned or disturbed by the death and its cause, overall they were pleased. Everyone had in essence been promoted, and if this patrol was successful these promotions were sure to be made permanent.

"Einzvo," Beck said, "please send a messenger to my cabin."

"*Jawohl.*"

"And you don't need to call yourself 'acting.' You're the einzvo, period. It's better that way both for you and the crew."

"*Jawohl.*" Stissinger sounded confident, and pleased.

It felt strange for Beck to be calling someone else einzvo. *I'll just have to get used to that, myself.*

The messenger arrived. This one also was young, fit and trim, intelligent but obviously not a deep thinker.

Is he old enough, in years and life experience, to understand the true meaning of mortality? Is he wise enough to grasp how absolutely final his own death would be? . . . Does he think at all of the Hereafter, or is he preoccupied as I am with the constant living purgatory of this godforsaken war?

"Ask our official passenger to join me here."

In a few moments Beck heard a knock, not at his cabin door but at the door to the small shower and toilet he shared with the executive officer's cabin.

Von Loringhoven was using the executive officer's cabin. He'd been quite insistent on this. For mission security, he said. If the acting einzvo was a mere lieutenant, used to sharing a cabin with two junior officers aboard the crowded *von Scheer,* let him continue doing so.

Now von Loringhoven seemed to want to sneak around, and not even walk the two meters through the corridor and mingle with the crew.

"Come." Beck projected his voice toward the stainless-steel door to the head and tried to hide his annoyance. He felt the deck nose down a few degrees as the *von Scheer*—with Stissinger's new weapons officer at the conn—followed a dip in the seafloor, still hugging the bottom for stealth. With a quick dart of practiced eyes, Beck checked the readouts on his cabin console: latitude 71 degrees 58.37 minutes north, longitude 31 degrees 24.08 minutes east. Course 041 true, depth 324 meters, speed 15.0 knots. Course 041 was roughly northeast, farther into the Barents Sea, into Russian home waters.

Only ship's course and speed on the console were steady. The little red digital figures showing the *von Scheer*'s position and depth changed rapidly.

All this ran through Beck's head with no effort, in a fraction of a second. He realized he was avoiding the main issue: his first private discussion with Rudiger von Loringhoven.

Von Loringhoven came into Beck's cabin. He showed none of the respect or awe one would anticipate from a nonmilitary guest in a nuclear submarine commander's inner sanctum. In fact, von Loringhoven was too blasé about the whole experience of being on the *von Scheer,* as far as Beck was concerned. He thought there was something quietly amoral about the set of the man's eyes.

"Ach," von Loringhoven said. "I see you've begun to open your orders."

Beck tried to be pleasant. "Are you ready for me to unseal the inner envelope?"

"Yes."

"Please sit. Is there anything you need in your cabin, to be more comfortable? Can I have something brought from the wardroom for you?" Beck hoped the diplomat would say yes to the last point so he could get some solid food himself.

Von Loringhoven used the guest chair. "No. The relief convoy from America to Central Africa will be moving very soon. Our land offensive in Africa, to crush the enemy pocket and link with the Boers, should begin any day. Other things must be carefully coordinated. Time is of the essence. Let's proceed."

Beck opened the envelope. Inside were several typed pages, a high-density data disk, and another sealed envelope. The typed pages began by instructing Beck not to open this new sealed envelope until he had completed the mission task detailed on the latest pages, as supported by the intelligence and oceanographic information on the disk.

Beck furrowed his eyebrows. He looked at von Loringhoven. "How many more envelopes-within-envelopes are there here?"

"Several."

"Why is it being done like this?"

"Security."

This guy is playing it too tight-lipped for my taste. Is he baiting me? Rubbing in from the start the difference in social class between us? The restoration of the Hohenzollern crown had driven a resurgence of acute elitism among Germans of noble blood. The *von* before someone's last name marked his family as aristocrats. Some people enjoyed this side effect of having a kaiser on the throne again—whether the kaiser was a figurehead, pressured into taking the job, or not. The glitter of court life had great appeal to those who could now openly call themselves a baroness or count and have it mean something. . . . It was also a great incentive for outstanding achievement and valor, since hereditary titles could be newly awarded to deserving individuals whatever their prior background.

"You ought to appreciate the reason as much as anyone," von Loringhoven said.

"What?" Beck caught his mind wandering. *Or was I daydreaming?*

"For the step-by-step security. It's possible as captain, if something went wrong, that you might not go down with the ship. Last time, as first officer, you didn't. You could be captured and interrogated. What you don't know you can't reveal under sweet talk or torture."

"But what about you?"

"I'm sorry?"

"You have full knowledge of *all* the orders?"

"I do."

"What if something goes wrong and *you* don't go down with the ship?"

Von Loringhoven withdrew a palm-sized pistol from his pocket. "To avoid capture, I am to shoot myself in the head."

———

Von Scheer's control room was cramped, with more than twenty men sitting at consoles or standing in the aisles. The overhead was low, covered with a maze of pipes and cables and wires. The lighting was dim red, to make the screens easier on watchstanders' eyes, and also to emphasize that the ship was at battle stations—just in case. Other colors, blues and greens and yellows, danced on different console screens.

Beck sat down at the two-man desk-high command console in the middle of the control room. He studied his screens. The gravimeter display showed the shape of the seafloor in detail, derived from a real-time analysis of gravity fields in different directions, as measured in widely spaced spots on the ship. This instrument was very valuable, because it emitted no signals at all, was not impaired by loud noises and atomic bubble clouds in the sea, and—just like gravity—it could see through solid rock. The gravimeter's one disadvantage was that it couldn't detect a moving object, such as an enemy submarine's dense reactor shielding and core.

Beck took the conn—decisions on ship's depth and course and speed, from minute to minute, were now his to make. He noticed von Loringhoven standing nearby but outside the main flow of crew traffic through the Zentrale, watching with measured curiosity; Beck put him out of his mind.

Beck studied the other data on his screens, to establish full situational awareness. The seafloor here was a gently rolling plain. Bottom sediments varied almost randomly, with patches of sand, or gravel, or mud in different places. Because the atmosphere above the sea was so near freezing, and the water was mixed by continual storms, the water temperature was nearly constant from the surface to the bottom. It was impossible for convergence zones to occur in the south Barents Sea. The water was much too shallow for a deep sound channel to form. The currents were confusing at all depths, as the last tendrils of the Gulf Stream ran north along the coast of Norway, in conflict with the Arctic's wind-driven counterclockwise gyre.

Sound propagation here was very poor. The subtle signs of *von Scheer*'s passage would go undetected except at point-blank range.

Beck was satisfied. This was a good place for his ship to hide while on the move.

He glanced to his right. There sat the einzvo, Karl Stissinger. Beck knew he'd grown up in East Germany, under long and dreary domination by the Soviets. Stissinger's father had been a sergeant in the East German Army, a member of a motorized rifle regiment, and would surely have been killed quickly if the Warsaw Pact and NATO had gone to war. To Stissinger's father's generation, and to Stissinger's as well, the Soviet collapse must have seemed like some kind of miracle. But freedom in the east at first brought a new type of poverty, and high unemployment, and when Stissinger came of age he joined the navy.

Beck looked at Stissinger in profile. He would be very important to the captain—as any einzvo is. And if something should happen to Beck—serious injury, illness, or death—he would need to assume command, the same way Beck had done.

Could Stissinger handle it, if I'm put out of action, vaulted that *far beyond all his training and experience?*

Stissinger's face was lit by the red of the overhead fluorescent lights and by the different displays on his console. He was handsome, tall, blond, with a flat abdomen and narrow hips—everything Ernst Beck was not. Stissinger was unmarried, and quite a ladies' man ashore, from what Beck heard. Stissinger had served in diesel subs in the Bundesmarine, the peacetime German Navy, after East and West Germany were reunited in 1991. In more recent years, he'd been assigned to help, from the beginning, on the secret construction of the *Admiral von Scheer*. He received training on nuclear submarine technology and tactics from experienced Russian instructors. Some of those instructors were ex-submariners, veterans of the Cold War against America and Great Britain, who welcomed the chance to pass on their knowledge to an appreciative new audience—they also liked the generous steady paychecks for their services. Their government enjoyed getting German payment in diamonds and gold while having someone else take on America and cut her down to size.

Beck knew America only ever had five SSGN guided-missile nuclear-powered submarines; the purpose-built one was long gone to the scrap yard, and the four modern ones· had been modified from *Ohio*-class ballistic-missile subs, so-called boomers. But Russia had been building SSGNs in quantity for decades—the *Kursk,* one of eleven sister ships in the *Oscar II* class, was an SSGN. In any armed conflict with the United States, these SSGNs were intended to trail American carrier battle groups and then take out the carriers and their escorts using salvos of supersonic antiship cruise missiles.

The *von Scheer* could serve a similar purpose, or direct some or all of her missiles at targets on land. The Russians were very good teachers of SSGN tactics against the U.S. Navy—and against the convoys that navy would try to protect. Beck had learned much from them recently too. But one key aspect of SSGN operations had deeply troubled him and still did.

Once an SSGN begins to launch her missiles, even submerged, she tosses aside any vestige of stealth and gives her position away completely. A murderous counterstrike would be quick in coming from a ferocious First World opponent, especially during tactical atomic war. Beck seriously questioned how he could keep the *von Scheer*'s very first salvo from being her last, once the engagement with the enemy began.

Beck turned his mind back to Stissinger. In battle, Sonar and Weapons reported to the einzvo. Stissinger would play a crucial role in attacking hostile targets and evading inbound fire. His fire-control technicians and weapons-system specialists worked consoles along the Zentrale's port side; other men were stationed in the *von Scheer*'s large torpedo room below.

Stissinger was a stickler for detail with his men. They seemed to like to work for him because they always knew exactly where they stood. He trusted his chiefs and gave them the independence they needed to do their supervisory jobs properly. He inspired his junior officers by keen example, and made sure they constantly got better and steadily matured at *their* jobs. The ship's other two full lieutenants, the engineer and the navigator, had readily accepted Stissinger's new seniority above them—they were professionals too.

Perhaps most important of all to Beck, Stissinger was loyal. In the last two months he'd always taken orders well from Beck when Beck was first watch officer. Stissinger displayed an ideal blend of obedience and initiative; his initiative showed in the shrewd and efficient ways he got things done. He never transgressed the boundaries of what Beck told him to do or not do. As einzvo, Beck thought, Stissinger ought to be excellent at helping him run a tight ship.

I'll soon know how well Stissinger and the officers and chiefs and men stand up to the rigors of nuclear combat. . . . And I'll see how well this von Loringhoven holds up under pressure too.

Beck waited to begin the first task in his mission orders. If there had been some misunderstanding between nameless, faceless persons on shore, this impending meeting could lapse into a sudden, vicious exchange of nuclear fire. It was bad enough that he still hadn't had the chance to put the *von Scheer*'s latest dockyard work through proper testing under way.

"Einzvo!" Werner Haffner called out. He sat at the forward end of a line of eight sonar consoles that lined the starboard bulkhead of the control room.

"Yes, Sonar?" Stissinger asked.

Beck caught himself. He'd almost answered Haffner himself, from old habit. *Get a grip. Von Loringhoven still watches, calm and catlike. And the crewmen observe my every move, reacting to each inflection in my voice, taking cues from me on what to think and feel and do.*

"New passive sonar contact on the starboard wide-aperture array," Haffner reported. "Bearing is one-three-five." Southeast. "Range is ten thousand meters." Five sea miles. "Contact is submerged."

"Contact identification?" Stissinger asked, doing his job.

"Nuclear submarine," Haffner said. "Possibly two nuclear submarines."

"Why was first detection made so close?" Beck broke in. Sound-propagation conditions had improved in the last few tens of sea miles. The *von Scheer*'s passive listening sonars were very powerful. Beck was testing Haffner and Stissinger as their first real wartime mission began.

"Contacts have just rounded Tiddly Bank, Captain," Haffner said. "Previously were obscured by intervening terrain rise."

"Very well, Sonar." The correct answer—Beck had been watching the shallow water of the bank on the gravimeter. The two new contacts' positions popped onto his main situation plot.

Von Loringhoven, standing patiently in the aisle, nodded complacently.

This civilian doesn't appreciate how precarious things are. Are these new contacts simply sticking to the plan, or were they lying there in ambush to outnumber me two to one? Has Russia even changed sides and I've been too out of touch to know it?

"Einzvo," Beck said. "Give me new own-ship course leg to determine contact course and speed. I want target motion analysis, to validate the instant ranging data from our wide-aperture array." It was always best to cross-check the systems and algorithms—especially at the start of a cruise.

Stissinger conferred with Haffner, studied his screens, and ran software. He passed the recommended course change directly to Beck's console through the ship's fiber-optic local area network.

"Pilot," Beck ordered, "steer zero-one-zero." Almost due north. The chief of the boat, during battle stations, was the ship's pilot. He sat at a two-man computer-assisted ship-control position at the front of the compartment. He and a junior officer—aided by the autopilot routines—managed all the ballast and trim tanks, and handled *von Scheer*'s rudder and bow planes and stern planes as well.

The chief of the boat acknowledged. Hearing his voice, Beck had another flashback, to a different chief piloting a different submarine. To squash the poignant memories quickly, he peered past Stissinger's head at the waterfall displays and sound-ray traces dancing on the sonarmen's screens.

Soon Haffner and Stissinger had the data Beck wanted. Arrows attached themselves to the contact icons on Beck's main plot; their direction and length indicated each contact's course and speed.

"Pilot," Beck ordered, "slow to three knots." Bare steerageway, to maximize hydrophone signal-to-noise sensitivity.

More information began to come in to the sonarmen.

"Good tonals now," Haffner stated.

Stissinger turned to Beck. "Submerged contacts are two Russian Project 945A submarines, Captain. Course is directly toward our rendezvous point. Speed fifteen knots."

"Very well, Einzvo. Navigator, plot a course for the rendezvous point." The rendezvous was halfway between the Tiddly Bank and the Thor Iversen Bank to its north.

Von Loringhoven pursed thin lips. "Sierra Twos, to use

the NATO nomenclature. Twenty years old, but upgraded,
quiet. Eight torpedo tubes, with plenty of tube-launched antiship missiles, and mines, and those nasty Shkval rocket
torpedoes, and regular eels."

Eel was German Navy slang for torpedo.

"Well able to protect themselves," Beck said as casually
as he could. "Stealthy." Shkvals scared Beck. He'd had
enough of such things when the fuel for his own Mach 8
missiles exploded; both missiles, unfueled, still sat in their
launching-tube canister aft.

"Yes," von Loringhoven said. "Sierra Twos are stealthy.
With the latest refits and upgrades, they're very, very
good. . . . A lot of that, you know, is thanks to long-term dividends from Russia's American spies. The Walker gang,
Ames, and so on. Plus the *other* traitors, the ones the Americans *haven't* caught." The diplomat chuckled.

———

Beck brought the *von Scheer* directly under the two Russian
submarines. They'd reached the rendezvous before he did,
so they sat halted while *von Scheer* still needed to move.
Even so, with them holding the sonar advantage, they didn't
react to his presence at first.

Recognition codes, from the data disk in Beck's orders,
were exchanged between the *von Scheer* and the two Russian
fast attacks. All three submarines used covert acoustic communications. Messages—either data or voice—were digitized and transmitted as a series of pulses in the
one-thousand-kilohertz band, forty or fifty times above the
range of human hearing. The frequency of the pulses
changed thousands of times each second to prevent interception by enemy hydrophones.

A message came back from the more senior of the two
Russian captains. He had the courtesy to send the message
in German. "Greetings. You are very quiet. We did not even
hear you until you signaled."

"Good," Beck said. "Einzvo, return the greeting. Say something complimentary, like thanks for helping Germany build such an excellent submarine. Then tell them to proceed due west and follow the deception plan."

Stissinger acknowledged and smiled. Beck gave the helm orders to keep *von Scheer* under and between the two Sierra IIs. The titanium-hulled Sierras maintained a steady depth of two hundred meters, shallow for them. The *von Scheer* hugged the bottom terrain, for stealth, at a depth that varied from three hundred to four hundred meters in this part of the Barents Sea.

"Those captains would kill to get their hands on our blueprints," von Loringhoven said.

"Are you worried?" Beck said.

"No. Just making conversation . . . They'd love to see what good German engineering did beyond what the Russian experts could give us."

"And what our own American spies could steal for us, that Russia doesn't know about?"

"That too, *mein kapitan*."

Beck and von Loringhoven stood at the horizontal digital plotting table at the rear of the control room. The navigator and his assistants maintained a constant track of the ship's position, based on inertial navigation systems checked against dead reckoning.

All three submarines, still moving in formation, had increased their speed to twenty-five knots to make better time as they neared deeper water.

"Any minute now they'll start," von Loringhoven said. "We're coming up on the North Cape–Bear Island barrier."

Beck nodded. The North Cape was the northernmost tip of Norway. Directly ahead, west, lay the Norwegian Sea, leading to the G-I-UK Gap. The North Cape–Bear Island–Svalbard Gap came first, stretching from mainland

Norway to tiny Bear Island about two hundred nautical miles due north. Bear Island sat on the sprawling Spitsbergen Bank, shallows leading farther north to the gigantic, desolate islands of mountainous Spitsbergen; Svalbard was one of those islands. As usual, in March, most of Spitsbergen was frozen hard into the polar ice cap; the edge of the solid ice in late winter extended close to Bear Island this year.

Bear Island and Spitsbergen were Norwegian possessions—which meant that they were occupied by Germany.

"I bet those Russian captains are grateful these are friendly waters now," von Loringhoven said.

"I'm sure they are," Beck said.

Norway had been an active part of NATO. The North Cape–Bear Island–Svalbard Gap was once the West's forward line of defense against the Soviet Northern Fleet's subs and ships. Looked at from the other direction, it also formed the gateway into the Barents Sea, where American carrier battle groups would be in easy striking range of Russian naval bases, and air-defense radars, and Russian airfields. Now, instead, the barrier gap and the airfields of Norway were German.

Even so, the Russians needed to keep up appearances in order for the subterfuge to work. And once again, the feeling of risk and danger for Beck was heightened.

A failure to communicate, by a bureaucratic dunderhead at one of our shore-command centers, could mean I'm about to be blown to bits by friendly—German—forces.

Beck reminded himself that, running submerged in wartime, a submarine had no friends.

"Contact on acoustic intercept!" Werner Haffner shouted.

"Keep your voice down," Beck snapped. "Put it on speakers, and identify." Young Haffner was the excitable type.

The control-room speakers came alive with the sounds of the nearby ocean: crashing waves and wind-driven sleet squalls, whale songs of different species, swishing schools of polar cod, and the occasional tumbling iceberg.

"Both 945A contacts have gone active," Haffner stated. His reedy voice was level.

Everyone in the Zentrale waited nervously for something more to happen. *Are things going according to plan, or has it all got muddled by the fog of war and both Germans and Russians are about to start shooting?*

After an interval on tenterhooks, a deep-toned ping filled the air in stereo. The rumbling made coffee cups shake in their holders. A few crewmen jumped in surprise or fear; Beck gestured for them to be steady. After a pause, there was a different series, three high-toned pings that pierced Beck's skull.

Stissinger shook his head as if his ears hurt. "The 945A to starboard is using the single deep tone, Captain. The 945A to port is using the three-part high-pitched tone."

"Very well, Einzvo. Any signs of weapon-launch transients?" Beck wasn't taking chances.

"Negative, sir."

"Very good. Sonar, engage acoustic-masking signal-processor feedback routines. . . . And turn down the speaker volume."

In sixty seconds, the deep-toned ping and then the three higher-pitched ones repeated.

"Actively suppressing echoes with out-of-phase emissions," Haffner said. "Wide-array transducer complexes and electromalleable rubber tiles all functioning nominally."

Stissinger turned to Beck and translated Haffner's technobabble into practical terms. "Nobody should be able to steal an echo off our hull, Captain."

"In theory. That's why we're doing this in German waters first."

The two Russian submarines were pinging at full power, not to search for contacts, but to announce their presence to anyone in earshot, like a foghorn. According to recent international notices to mariners, this was how neutral submarines were supposed to safely transit choke points in declared war zones, if they chose not to run on the surface for identification instead. To make sure the submerged submarines were genuine neutrals exercising their rights of innocent passage— and not enemies pulling a bluff—the belligerent side in control of the constricted waters would send small probes to study the intruder's acoustic signature and visual appearance from very short range. Or they might use airdropped sonobuoys, augmented by blue-green laser line-scan cameras. The laws of war did not allow combatants to board and inspect warships of neutral countries—only merchant ships could be subjected to such blockades or quarantines.

Stissinger reported that the two Sierras were slowing. Beck ordered the pilot to reduce speed so as not to draw ahead and increase his own vulnerability. Beck used his light pen on the gravimeter display to show the pilot a fold in the bottom terrain in which to nestle the *von Scheer*.

"Captain," Stissinger said a few minutes later. "Our on-hull sensors are detecting scattered blue-green laser light. Assess that friendly surveillance probes are examining the two Sierras."

"Very well, Einzvo . . . Everyone stay focused. This is a dress rehearsal. Next time, across the Norwegian Sea, we'll all be using live weapons. Get used to the tension *now*. We'll be informed soon enough if our signature down here is too blatant."

Stissinger acknowledged crisply.

Beck waited to learn if the *von Scheer* was stealthy enough. If things went wrong, in this mock infiltration of a German-owned barrier, and the problems couldn't be corrected easily, he would have to get his ship through the G-I-UK Gap somehow, some other way—or die trying.

Beck had a wild thought that the *von Scheer* had already been found out and localized, and the Allies were truly desperate, and a massive enemy air-launched strike would tear in at the *von Scheer* any second—and collateral damage to meddling Russian fast-attacks be damned.

But no enemy air strike materialized.

"New message received, sir," Stissinger said. "All clear to proceed. The two 945A ships are accelerating."

"Very well. Pilot, have engineering make propulsor RPMs to keep pace."

"*Jawohl* . . . Engineering acknowledges."

"Use extra care to keep proper station as we follow the bottom down off of the continental shelf."

"Understood." They would soon reach water more than three thousand meters—ten thousand feet—deep; these Russians couldn't go below six or seven hundred meters.

All three ships sped up, maintaining formation.

"The 945As now steady at twenty-five knots."

"Very well, Einzvo."

"Sir," Haffner said, "at this speed the Russian vessels are giving off machinery noise again." He passed a diagram of the decibel levels to Beck's console. Beck, a former sonar officer himself, read the frequency power spectrum quickly.

"Own-ship status?"

"Own ship is ultraquiet, Captain. No sound shorts. Assess our flow noise is masked well by the moving pair of 945As."

"Very well, Sonar."

Beck hoped this trick worked next time, crossing the G-I-UK Gap, when the stakes were so high and the play was for keeps.

It would take two days to go from Bear Island to the G-I-UK Gap. The more time passed—running drills, making plans, waking, sleeping, eating—the more Beck had to wonder.

The Allies know that Russia is helping Germany. What if they pay extra *attention when Russian fast-attacks go by? Intell says that so far they haven't, so as not to antagonize Moscow . . . but that was before the fire in the underground U-boat pens, with heat and smoke up the chimney . . . and Norwegian partisans, who must know the* von Scheer *has sailed.*

CHAPTER 8

Before dawn, Felix and his lieutenant roused the sleeping members of the team. Everybody stayed on guard, lying or crouching in their defensive circle from the night before. Dim streaks of moonlight stippled the ground. The moonlight pierced between the tree trunks and leafy branches and hanging vines, dappling the ferns and roots and fungi in an otherworldly silver-gray glow. It was extremely humid and hot. Mosquitoes, biting flies, and other insects continued their background hum and chirp. The air was thick with the musty, musky stench of jungle rot and fermentation.

Felix listened on high alert as the earliest risers among the daytime birds and animals began to stir. To his eyes, the eerie patches of moonlight carried an air of expectancy: of approaching sunrise, and of unknown dangers to come.

This was the time each day that Felix hated, because for a few unavoidable minutes now the team would be most vulnerable. An armed enemy might blunder into them before the SEALs were ready. The team might have been noticed many hours ago, and attackers might have spent all night creeping close for a dawn assault.

One by one each SEAL rushed through a silent, meticulous, well-practiced routine of cleaning himself and burying body waste. One at a time, each man quickly ate his single high-calorie meal of the day and drank one entire full two-quart canteen; each had one more full canteen for later. They replaced their floppy jungle hats with battle helmets—the folded hats went into their rucksacks, along with all the breakfast trash. The helmets were covered with raggedy patches of cloth and plastic to break up their outlines in the bush. Mosquito nets draping from the helmets protected their faces and necks. They raised the nets just long enough to touch up their camouflage makeup using small compacts from their rucks. There was no incoming fire.

Amid the all-cloaking underbrush, beneath the towering trees, the team did buddy checks of one another's equipment, clothing, and weapons status.

Like the other men, Felix had a K-bar fighting knife in a waterproof sheath strapped to one thigh and a survival knife strapped to the other. His backup pistol was safed in its shoulder holster, beneath his left armpit. His Draeger rebreather scuba gear, and big combat swim fins and dive mask, rode under his rucksack in a special harness—their considerable weight was borne by his hips and lower back; a dirtproof cover protected and hid the diving equipment.

There was a round in the chamber of Felix's German-made MP-5 submachine gun. He gently eased the quiet selector lever off safe to sustained fire. He nodded to his lieutenant. The lieutenant signaled the team to move out.

───────

The silvery moonlight had faded away and was replaced by the pink diffuse glow of a short equatorial dawn. Traces of sharper yellow sunlight filtered down through the trees obliquely, backlighting a morning mist that burned off almost at once. Now the sun was higher in the sky; the few shafts of light that hit the ground were more vertical. The heat and the humidity intensified. The rancid odors wafting everywhere grew stronger. Sometimes toucans or parrots flew by, but were barely seen, their gaudy colors muted in the deep rain-forest gloom.

Felix's team patrolled closer to the railroad for the Brazilian manganese mine—the railroad that would probably be the objective of more insurgent guerrilla sabotage raids— the guerrillas who might or might not be getting aid from Axis advisers.

The eight SEALs had split into two teams of four; each team formed half a circle. The lieutenant led the first team, which served as point and covered their left flank as they moved. Felix led the other team, covering their right flank and also covering and sanitizing their rear. The tension was unrelenting. Each man's every motion was a risky compromise between the need for speed and the need for silent invisibility. Crouching, crawling, duckwalking, they maintained course by compass—GPS was useless because of Axis signal hacking, and there were no distant landmarks to guide on in the bowels of the Amazon rain forest.

The SEALs worked forward steadily. They cautiously peered around trees, and over bushes or fallen logs. They watched for any signs of human presence or human activity. They listened intently for clues to what was happening around them. The continual animal traffic discouraged booby traps or mines, but everyone was careful for trip wires or suspicious fist-sized bumps or dips in the ground, or freshly dug earth.

Felix made very sure they left no traces. Thorny vines, snagged on equipment or clothes and tugged in the direction of the SEALs' travel, were rearranged at random. Leaves that were disturbed and twisted in passing, with their undersides showing a different color or texture than their tops, were righted so they wouldn't stand out. Boot prints in the puddles and mud, and scuff marks on roots and trunks, were altered artfully. This part of the work was especially tiring. Felix needed intense concentration and acute manual dexterity every minute, every hour. The weight of all his gear seemed to increase constantly. After each rest break, it was that much harder mentally to get up and resume.

His Draeger and combat fins weighed three dozen pounds. A full canteen weighed five pounds. Each prepackaged, dehydrated daily meal in his rucksack weighed more than a pound. Each concussion grenade he carried weighed one pound; each white phosphorus smoke-incendiary grenade weighed two pounds. His helmet and flak vest and weapons and ammo and first-aid supplies were also heavy.

Soon the team of eight SEALs would divide up into pairs, each pair patrolling one arc of a four-leaf-clover pattern. After going full circle, the four pairs would reunite. The team would then advance several more miles, still navigating by compass. Then they would do another cloverleaf, and on and on. This way they could scan a broader area, on their covert reconnaissance for Axis presence in the rain forest.

Felix remembered the firefight he and his team had listened to the previous night. He wondered what shape that other SEAL team was in, and who had ambushed them.

Felix heard a sharp crack, and a deep rolling rumble, very close. Everyone froze and waited for incoming fire. But this time it was thunder, not a grenade.

Soon there was a steady drumming sound overhead. The daytime gloom of the rain forest grew much darker. Driblets of rain began to fall. Felix saw an electric-blue flash of lightning through the trees. There was another blast of thunder. The driblets of rain became a crushing downpour.

The lieutenant signaled a pause in order to refill their empty canteens. The men used their upturned floppy hats to help catch the rain and funnel it into canteen mouths, through fine mesh filters. The water was very dirty. Over their heads, in each level of the multiple-canopy tree branches, dwelled entire ecosystems. Plants lived on other plants, which lived on branches of the larger trees, and died and rotted. Bugs and bacteria thrived in puddles caught on leaves or in forks in the trees, a hundred feet in the air. Different birds, rodents, and mammals populated different zones of altitude, eating and mating and defecating. Frogs, snails, ants, spiders, termites—all led their daily existences high above.

The rainwater that reached the ground was truly filthy. Felix and his team added water purification tablets to their newly filled canteens. The tablets made the water stink of chlorine and taste even worse. They used powdered tea mix, fortified with extra tannin, to cover the taste; the tannin also helped fight tropical diarrhea.

The rain continued to drum and pour. With their canteens replenished, the lieutenant signaled for the SEALs to move out. The rain was so heavy it pelted their faces with mud splashed back up from the ground. The runoff gushed in streaming rivulets and formed ever-widening pools. A wind began to rise, slashing the treetops. The team closed up amid the almost solid, streaking vertical torrent to keep in better touch now that sight lines were so reduced and the noise of the rain was deafening. They moved faster, since the rain would obliterate much of their spoor. Moving faster also gave them better forward momentum—in case they crashed into an enemy patrol that crashed into them.

Now, with two full canteens instead of one, and water-logged from head to toe by the all-surrounding thunderstorm, Felix carried a much greater weight load. The rain was cold, so cold it made him shiver.

The rain had stopped, and the rain forest was steamy, stinking, baking hot. Felix's team halted for a brief rest. The two compass men compared notes to cross-check their navigation. Felix and the lieutenant surveyed the ground ahead. It was time for the team to turn due west. Ahead in that direction, on the near side of the railroad, lay the Pedreira River, which the men would have to cross to continue their recon. The Pedreira ran south, paralleling the railroad, until the river fed the Amazon itself. Crossing the river would be a time of maximum peril, but it was necessary.

Quietly, the team reviewed their plan and rechecked one another's equipment. Again the lieutenant led the point element and Felix oversaw securing and sanitizing their rear. Tomorrow they would trade places, with Felix in front and the lieutenant protecting their backs, and Felix was already looking forward to it. Tonight, maybe, once across the Pedreira, he might get some sleep for a change. And tomorrow, the mental and physical strain of taking point, as wearing and dangerous as it was, would be a welcome change from the constant peering and smoothing and rearranging, the endless stooping and kneeling and patting and brushing, that it took to maintain secrecy as the SEALs covered more and more distance.

Felix was jarred by another crack. He knew at once it wasn't more thunder. He ducked as his whole body tightened instinctively; his heart was in his throat. Razor-sharp steel from a fragmentation grenade whizzed overhead. Felix heard crackling bursts from AK-47s. *None of my guys are carrying Russian weapons.* Then Felix heard the *puff-puff-puff* of silenced MP-5s responding. He lay flat just in time. There was a tremendous blast, and hundreds of metal pellets tore through the air. Pieces of bark and shredded greenery flew and fell. Tree branches rocked and swayed from the mighty concussion.

That was a Claymore mine. And not one of ours.

Every sight and sound and smell became ten times more vivid; every trace of fatigue in Felix vanished.

Felix's lieutenant shouted in Portuguese. The team had been ambushed by antigovernment militants—the Brazilian Army didn't use AK-47s either. Felix crawled forward. He and the lieutenant pulled white phosphorus grenades from their rucksacks and armed them. As bullets zipped overhead or slammed into trees or kicked up muck, they lobbed the grenades well to their front and yelled for their men to withdraw. They took disciplined care with their throwing so the grenades didn't hit a tree and bounce back.

The grenades exploded. Burning white phosphorus spewed

in all directions. Thick, choking smoke covered the ground and spread through the trees. Fires began, from the heat of the incendiary grenades, even with everything soaked. The grenades would form a good antipersonnel barrier. White phosphorus burned human flesh down to the bone; it was unquenchable.

The SEAL team crawled to the rear, quickly taking turns firing their weapons back through the smoke. Felix let loose a three-round burst and heard an enemy scream.

"Let's go," Felix shouted.

The SEALs stood and regrouped on the run. On and on they ran, away from the ambush site.

The lieutenant cursed. "We're compromised," he said in Portuguese, "and we haven't found out a single useful thing."

Felix concurred, did a head count, and turned and fired another burst through the drifting white phosphorus smoke. "I don't think we're being pursued," he said between ragged breaths. "Irregulars . . . Must have thought we were Brazilian Army, tired and bored after lunch." He vaulted a protruding root as the other SEALs kept pace. One of the enlisted men fired a burst toward the ambushers, then another.

"Didn't expect us to be so alert," Felix panted. "Surprised we reacted so fast and violently." He ran on, breathing heavily, reviewing the action in his mind. "They set off that Claymore a moment too late." *Pant, pant.* "Most of their bullets went high."

The lieutenant nodded. He was shaking now from the surge of adrenaline and gasping too fast to speak.

Felix signaled the team to halt and take up a defensive position. The men quickly checked one another for wounds or equipment damage. They were okay. Felix listened; he let a few minutes go by. The bird and animal noises told him his team wasn't being followed.

"Which way now?" he whispered to the lieutenant.

"Let me think."

Felix didn't like this. To accomplish their mission, they needed hard proof that Axis agents were operating in this area, if indeed they were. To come back empty-handed meant failure.

We have to at least probe farther in. If Axis agents aren't involved, we need to see much more to know it for sure.

"Head north," Felix whispered, still speaking in Portuguese. "Outflank these guerrillas, then turn west. Get behind them."

"Concur," the lieutenant whispered. "Move through their rear. See what we learn that way . . . But why not outflank them south?"

"We came from south. North, we cover new territory."

The lieutenant nodded. He began to catch his breath.

"We change our route formation. Column, single file. I want more weapons covering west in case the hostiles come at us again."

"I don't know, LT. We still need good all-around defense." Felix gestured out at the jungle. "We don't know who else is hiding where."

"Negative."

"But—"

"Do it my way."

Felix had to agree—the lieutenant was the man in charge.

An old saying ran through Felix's mind, seeing the LT's hardened attitude: *It's better to be sure than right.*

The only thing is, in Special Warfare clandestine ops, being sure but wrong gets people killed.

The team re-formed into a column, well spread out. On the lieutenant's order, the compass men—stationed near both ends of the column—began to guide everyone north. The lieutenant remained near the front of the column. Felix stayed near the rear and picked his way between the tree trunks and the roots.

The underbrush was thin, because so little sunlight reached the ground. Clumps of dense growth—the kind he had chosen for the place where the team had sheltered last night—formed only when old trees died and toppled, or when standing trees were broken or felled by lightning strikes or hurricanes. Such gaps in the trees made openings through all the canopy layers, under which more dense brush could spring up. But away from these overgrown patches caused by major deadfalls, the dangling vines and protruding roots were more annoying than anything green that grew out of the ground. Progress on foot took care, but there was no need to hack a trail with swinging machetes.

Felix was worried. His team appeared to be in the middle of a hotbed of trigger-happy bad guys. Sooner or later the Brazilian Army would send units to investigate all the shooting. This would make the SEALs' job even harder. The rules of engagement for this mission allowed them to fire only in self-defense and required them to keep that fire to a bare minimum. Their goal was information, not body counts. *Any* body counts, while they were violating neutral territory, could have extremely negative repercussions. Guerrilla murderers and terrorists were one thing. Killing a Brazilian Army recruit or officer by mistake was something Felix didn't even want to think about.

The terrain was gradually rising as the team worked north, and Felix noticed that the species all around them were subtly changing. He reached out to hold a particularly thick and thorny vine away from his face and body. The SEALs were penetrating a clump of closely spaced trees, whose trunks bulged with the round mud nests of ants and termites. No one wanted to bump into one of these nests and the SEALs' rate of movement was slowed. Felix had a sense of foreboding. He walked practically on tiptoe now, his eyes darting everywhere. He scrutinized the terrain as he quietly placed each foot—away from any twigs that might snap. He watched the rain forest constantly for signs of some stranger watching him. His ears worked so hard he felt as if they were stretching out from his head.

The next men in his team in front and behind were barely visible. They were forced to group closer together. Otherwise, they wouldn't be able to communicate by hand signals and might even become separated and lost—with disastrous results. By now, Felix was dripping with sweat instead of rainwater.

The team eventually cleared the stand of trees. Among thicker trunks with different bark, spread wider apart, they were able to increase the distance from man to man in their column. They probed on.

To their front an enemy weapon opened fire. Then everything seemed to happen at once. Felix heard shouts and screams. More fire began to pour in from the flank—from the *right* flank, from *east*.

Felix had never heard the sound of these weapons before. *We've been suckered. The ambush, this time, is perfect.*

"At them!" Felix screamed. The best tactic was to charge the flanking enemy. To take cover in this situation amounted to suicide—that weapon to their front, firing straight down along the SEALs' column, would pick off every man fast.

Felix led his men to the right. Everyone fired on full auto. The enemy fire increased. The men began to be driven back.

"The LT's hit!" someone screamed. Felix recognized the voice—his point man. Still, strange weapons poured in fire. Again, clumps of bark flew everywhere as bullets pounded into trees. Vines danced and fell as they were riddled. The mud insect nests that bulged from trees exploded.

Felix belly-crawled toward the front of the column. As he passed each enlisted man, he steadied him and urged him to return the enemy fire and charge the enemy ambush again. They tried, but the fire was just too heavy. It came at them knee-high or lower, well aimed and effective. The men were forced to huddle in folds in the ground or hide behind trees. They fired their weapons half-blindly into the distance. Their muzzles flashed and spent brass bounced and clinked. Moving parts in the silenced weapons clattered. The men changed magazines steadily. Burned bullet propellant went up Felix's nose.

Felix reached the lieutenant. The man was dead, his skull shattered. His brain sat in the mud on the trail, in almost perfect condition, as if it had been removed by a surgeon. That strange weapon to the front fired yet again, a slow but steady explosive *bloop-bloop-bloop*. It sounded like a cross between a heavy machine gun and a grenade launcher. The noise of it hurt Felix's already-ringing ears.

Felix pulled out a pair of white phosphorus grenades. He fell back, then threw one toward the strange heavy weapon, and the other to his right, toward the flanking enemy riflemen. He ducked behind a tree.

Both grenades exploded. Felix charged forward, relying on the choking smoke screen for protection. He hefted the lieutenant's body across his shoulders. The heavy enemy weapon fired another three-round burst. More shrapnel filled the air. Felix took out another smoke-incendiary grenade, his last. Over his shoulder, he tossed it at the dead man's brain—this was as good a point of aim as any. Felix ran to the rear with his lifeless, dripping burden. The third white phosphorus grenade burst behind him. Again Felix felt the radiant heat and coughed on the fumes of searing phosphorus. Bits of it landed near him and made the puddles steam and hiss.

"Withdraw," he shouted, still speaking Portuguese for disguise. "Follow me! Break contact!"

Felix had realized what that strange enemy weapon was. He'd heard that the U.S. Army was developing something like it.

An objective crew-served weapon. A highly portable two-man miniature cannon that fired one-inch-caliber explosive rounds on full automatic. These weapons had laser range finders, and electronically fused each round before it was fired. The fuses could be set precisely by timer so the weapon made lethal air bursts at any specific range its crew wanted to target.

Explosive rounds from such a weapon were pounding at the SEALs. One round had taken off the lieutenant's head.

At least the smoke grenades are blocking their range finder. With that, and the trees in the way, it'll be harder for them to zero in on us.

Felix ordered his team to retreat to the south, regrouping on the run into an all-around circle formation. The enemy, whoever they were, followed in close pursuit. More incoming explosive shells detonated, near the ground and high in the air; the eardrum-splitting concussions were fast, and bright, and hot. Birds and monkeys screamed. Dislodged seeds and heavy ripe fruit rained from far above. Entire branches crashed to the earth. Enemy bullets tore by like angry, burning bees.

The SEALs took turns firing back the way they'd just come while others ran ahead and reloaded. Then the SEALs who'd fired would rush for safety while their teammates unleashed vicious fire at the enemy. The men did this over and over again, taking turns, covering more and more distance each time. The enemy continued coming after them, returning the fire. But the noise of reports, the incoming rounds, were the only signs of the enemy—Felix couldn't catch one glimpse of who was shooting at him.

Felix heard more *bloop-bloop-bloop* sounds, overlaid on more sharp concussions each time a grenade round exploded in the air or against a tree. The jungle was thick with flying shrapnel and bullets now, and kicked-up debris. There was painful pressure in Felix's ears from the punishing noise.

A big rotting fruit bashed down on Felix's helmet; pungent juice from it dripped into his eyes. A wounded sloth slammed into the earth and Felix almost stumbled. He shot it once in the head to end its agony.

The dead lieutenant's body, with all its equipment, was an almost unbearable weight across Felix's back. *SEALs* never *leave a man behind, dead or alive.* From somewhere deep inside himself, Felix found the strength to carry on. He spun and fired a long burst from his submachine gun. He turned and ran. Grenade rounds probed toward him, but the enemy gunners were guessing the range.

Then bullets pounded into the lieutenant's body from behind. Felix staggered, more from fright than from the force of the impacts. He hurried on.

Felix did a head count on the run. The rest of the team was

following, but one man had been hit in the arm. The bullet struck the side of his shoulder, next to the edge of his flak vest. He seemed okay, at least for now. The wounded man was keeping up with the others, and there didn't seem to be much blood, but he was having trouble reloading with his injured arm. Other men had lacerations from wood splinters or steel shrapnel—they kept running.

Felix's heart pounded hard as he splashed through the puddles and mud. His back ached terribly from the deadweight of his lieutenant, and his breath came in overrapid painful gasps. He turned and fired his weapon again.

Bullets punched hard and squarely at his chest. Only his flak vest saved his life. Felix turned again to cover more distance and lead the withdrawal. He yelled for two of his men to throw more smoke incendiaries behind them.

Felix glanced at his chest. Sticking from his flak vest were what looked like long thin nails. They had little fins at their protruding ends. Each was bent, from its own momentum after it struck the ceramic plate of his vest. Each was smoking hot.

Fléchette rounds.

Felix yelled for his men to pick up the pace.

They'd been ambushed by a very sophisticated enemy. The weapons were state-of-the-art. The air-burst shrapnel rounds were ideal to take out men in helmets and flak vests—the shrapnel would hit faces and arms and legs. Fléchettes were perfect for use against the extremities of men in body armor too. The United States had decided not to use them in combat because the wounds they caused were so cruel. Each fléchette had such kinetic energy, and yet was so thin, that hitting anywhere unprotected in a human body it would fishhook—twisting and caroming inside to mutilate organs and rip blood vessels and sever nerves. A fléchette in the knee could ricochet and lodge inside your liver. One in the elbow could end up in your spine.

I think we found what we came here for.

Physical proof of German interference. This last ambush hadn't been led by any insurgent band, using sloppy tactics and weapons designed fifty years ago. These were German Special Forces, maybe even kampfschwimmer.

Their goal is to do whatever it takes to kill or capture U.S. Navy SEALs on Brazilian soil. Then after they do their own interrogation, they'll have local Axis sympathizers turn us in to the government. Those earlier half-botched ambushes were a setup after all. They were waiting for us.

Another grenade round flew past Felix's head and embedded itself in a tree. He flinched, but it failed to detonate.

Felix was taking a terrible risk, but he had his orders. He stopped and used his survival knife to dig the intact round out of the trunk of the hardwood tree. He prayed its fuse was defective, a dud, or that it was programmed to burst after covering more distance and hadn't flown its minimum arming range.

Just in case, Felix put it in his rucksack—outside the back panel of his flak vest, and covered by the dead lieutenant's corpse.

Now we just have to break contact and get far away from here.

Felix shouted for his men to throw every white phosphorus grenade they had. A solid wall of heat and smoke flew up.

The enemy continued pursuing. Felix was impressed by their tenacity and stamina, as much as he was by their weaponry and tactics. He began to worry they were forcing him into another ambush, with more German Special Forces blocking the SEAL team's rear.

Felix and his team reentered the stand of closely clumped trees. He handed the dead lieutenant to one of his men. They'd brought a body bag, just in case, and they placed the corpse in it quickly. This would avoid leaving more of a blood trail for the enemy to track. There was still enough blood and gore on Felix for what he planned to do next.

He ordered his team to split up. Most of the men would head east, at right angles to the pursuing Germans. Felix and one other SEAL would continue south, and make as much noise as they could to draw on the enemy.

Felix picked the most experienced unwounded man to assist him. They took two weapons, from the wounded and dead, to supplement their own. They began firing back down their escape path, toward the Germans, with one submachine gun in each hand.

Without the terrible weight of the lieutenant's body, Felix felt a renewed surge of energy and strength. He and the other SEAL, impelled by a desperate cunning, charged ahead to lay a false trail. They emptied the magazines from all their weapons in the direction of the Germans. Then they shouldered the weapons and doubled back, literally walking backward, dashing toward the Germans as quickly but as quietly as they could.

"Here!" Felix ordered in a hoarse whisper. He used a canteen to wash the lieutenant's blood from his gear. He and the other SEAL pulled special plastic sticks from their rucksacks. They ran west for several yards. They bent double and used the sticks and walked backward again, hurrying east, and picked up and followed the footprints of the other men in their team.

The sticks ended in fake boar hooves. Still bent over, glancing between their legs so they wouldn't trip and ruin everything, the two men disguised their trail by pressing the stick ends into the mud and earth. Right and left hooves, front and rear hooves, over and over and over. They did this until the pain in their lower backs and knees made them feel as if they'd never walk again. Then they stood and flew east as fast as they could.

———

Felix's team had reunited one hour later and was hurrying north on the run. Their shrapnel injuries wore field-expedient bandages. The men took turns carrying the dead lieutenant's body. The man with the shoulder bullet wound had been given a transfusion of blood expander to delay shock and help him keep moving. But Felix knew he had internal bleeding—the high-velocity fléchette that entered his shoulder had lodged somewhere in his chest cavity.

Felix chose to head north because this was the direction the enemy would least expect him to take. North meant away from the Amazon, and farther away from the coast. It brought the team closer and closer to the Araguari River, a populated area and major obstacle, the last place a team of SEALs would want to be. The Araguari ran east, not toward the Amazon but to the coast and the South Atlantic Ocean.

"From now on," Felix told his men between labored breaths, "I do the talking."

Felix maintained a grueling pace. There was real danger the Germans had figured out his plan and were coming after him. There was danger the Germans were in contact with other hostile units near the Araguari, or in the big town ahead on the river, Ferreira Gomes. The team had many miles still to go. They splashed through puddles and dashed between trees with all their equipment.

From here, Felix could count on nothing but his and his men's nerve and their will to survive. The sun was getting lower in the sky. Once it set, their progress would be badly slowed by poor visibility. The wounded man would die. German or Brazilian forces would close in. Time was vital. The enemy already knew the team was present; caution was thrown to the wind in a high-stakes gamble for life.

"Faster," Felix urged as they ran. Each breath was sheer agony. The strain in his legs and back muscles was painful beyond description. His eyes teared from the effort, but his tears were masked by sweat. His insect head net was lost somewhere, torn off as he ran, but his speed through the rain forest kept most bugs from homing in.

Felix eyed his men. They were all grouped together now to boost one another's morale through simple companionship. On and on they hurried. Arms and legs pumped endlessly; chests heaved. Heads in helmets bobbed. Fourteen different feet rose and fell, pounding the earth relentlessly, jaggedly out of rhythm for mile after mile. The combined

huffing and puffing sounded like an overtaxed steam loco-
motive struggling up a hill. Rucksacks and dive-gear sacks
bounced heavily with each stride.

Each face was a mask of utter exhaustion. Felix forced
himself to smile. He looked at his men with pride. To talk he
drew a breath so deep his stomach pushed out at his flak
vest. "And you thought Hell Week was bad."

The man who was carrying the dead lieutenant looked at
Felix blankly. There was grief in his eyes, for the loss.

"Don't think of death until later. Just *put out* for me, for
the team." Felix threw his head back to pull in more air.

The wounded man tripped. Felix reached and caught him.
The man lost consciousness and wouldn't revive. Even with
other guys lugging his gear, Felix was amazed he'd managed
this far. He quickly inserted another transfusion of blood expander and lifted the SEAL in a fireman's carry; SEALs
took turns running beside him, to hold the plasma bag high.

With this new burden over his shoulders, Felix gave his
men another forced smile. They still had so far to go.
"Faster. Quit slacking off. *The only easy day was yesterday.*"

At dusk, Felix hid in the stinking trash dump, making obser-
vations. His team rested in the jungle growth behind him.

The small village beyond the outskirts of Ferreira Gomes
was crawling with Brazilian Army troops. From things they
said to one another, Felix knew the troops were preparing to
make a sweep to the south. He wasn't surprised—he'd heard
the noise of helicopters during the late afternoon.

The wounded SEAL was in very poor condition now. Felix was sure that if he didn't get into surgery before dawn, he
would die.

Felix didn't like the options. He couldn't afford to wait for
the Brazilian troops to leave. They might take hours yet, as-
sembling for a night reconnaissance—he saw some men
with night-vision goggles. Even if they did depart soon, to

scour the country Felix and his team just covered, they'd
surely leave behind a rear element for communications and
logistic support.

We'll just have to brazen it out.

Felix crawled backward out of sight of the village. Dogs
barked, chickens cackled, pigs oinked, but they'd been doing
that already because of the army troops. Felix pulled rotting
fruit rinds and maggot-ridden animal bones, and even more
unspeakable waste, off his clothing and equipment. But the
garbage pile had been high ground of a sort—and he was unlikely to be disturbed by playing children, or villagers
dumping trash, without enough warning to slip away.

Felix rejoined his worn-out men. He led them forward,
along a well-beaten trail running from some cultivated fields
into the village. Felix already knew that most of the villagers
had gone indoors because it was getting dark—and also to
avoid interfering with the well-disciplined, orderly troops. He
saw and smelled wood smoke coming from village shacks on
stilts grouped around a main clearing. He also smelled delicious cooking smells, even above his own stench.

"Hey!" Felix yelled. "*Hey!* Patrol coming in!"

"Password!" a young and scared private shouted from behind a straw-thatched storage shed.

*If he thinks that shed is good cover, I'd hate to see what
his marksmanship's like. . . . Still, I'd rather not find out.*

"Password?" Felix shouted. "How should I know? Special
Forces! We've been wild-westing it for two weeks!"

The private came forward, shrugged, and let Felix and his
men go by. The private stared wide-eyed at the wounded
man—carried now on a stretcher improvised from saplings
and uniform shirts—and at the dead man in the body bag—
carried now by two men using the handles on the bag's sides.

"Be careful out there," Felix said to the private. "You could
be next!" As expected, he saw that the soldier held an M-16.

In the village, a Brazilian Army sergeant spotted Felix
and walked over. He sniffed when he got closer, then tried
not to breathe too deeply. "Do you need an evacuation? We

can call back a helicopter." The sergeant looked up at the sky. It was growing dark very quickly. "But I'm not sure they land at night."

"No," Felix bluffed. "Thank you, but we have our own arrangements."

"I think your man needs a hospital."

"Yes. Leave that to us."

"I think I should tell my lieutenant."

Felix hesitated. "Please be quick. We have a schedule."

"Yes, yes. Quick."

This is where it gets dicey.

The lieutenant approached. He seemed capable and battle-hardened, not someone easily fooled. He wrinkled his nose at his first whiff of Felix.

Good. The more I stink, the less he'll really look at me, and the less he'll think to ask me awkward questions.

Felix knew the best way to lie was to use as much of the truth as he could.

"Special Forces, sir. We met some opposition. Our officer was killed. We have our own plan of egress. Classified mission orders."

The lieutenant called the sergeant over. "Give me the map."

As they wasted precious minutes and the sky became increasingly dark, Felix showed the lieutenant the vague area of where he'd made contact with the enemy—it had poured rain again that afternoon, and the brushfires from the fighting had surely been snuffed. Felix was certain the Germans would be hiding or gone long before the Brazilians could get anywhere near them on foot.

A villager lit straw torches. They gave off dancing yellow light.

The lieutenant went to brief his squad leaders by red flashlight. Felix led his men in the other direction, toward the river. The Araguari was high and running fast, and Felix could hear it even before the torchlight outlined the near edge of the riverbank against the wet blackness beyond. To his great relief, there were a handful of boats tied up at a rickety pier, at an indentation in the bank sheltered from the main flood current.

To steal a boat at this point, they'd have to wait some time for all the villagers to be asleep, and even then they might be caught—some shacks with light in their windows were close to the pier. Time was one thing the team's wounded man did not have. Getting caught would surely start a noisy, attention-getting argument with the natives, or an even more compromising waterborne chase. *No, outright theft, discovered quickly* or *at first light, is definitely not advisable with genuine Brazilian forces right here.*

Felix found an old man who owned one of the boats and said he needed to requisition it. He told the man to speak to the authorities in Ferreira Gomes, and he'd be reimbursed. That ought to create enough bureaucratic confusion to cover the SEAL team's tracks. Felix wasn't happy about needing to tell this sort of lie to an innocent villager.

The man wasn't going for it. He threw up his hands. "How am I supposed to get upriver to Ferreira Gomes without my motorboat?"

Felix forced himself to hide his real annoyance. "How much?"

"Huh?"

"How much for the boat?"

"It's not just a boat. It's my livelihood." The boat smelled of dead fish, and the inside looked greasy and slimy.

"How much?"

Felix and the man began to bargain. They settled on a price in local currency.

"How far are you going?"

Felix refused to say.

"You'll need petrol."

Felix sighed. "How much?"

Again they haggled.

"You'll need lanterns. It's dark."

"All right. Lanterns. What kind?"

"Kerosene."

"Full?"

"Yes, I'll fill them."

"How much?"

The man named a figure.

Felix sighed again, as if he regretted having to part with hard cash. The total price agreed to was high but not unreasonable.

Felix nodded to one of his men, who'd been leaning exhausted against the wall of the fisherman's shack—the walls were made of old plywood, with no glass in the windows, and the roof was rusty corrugated tin. The SEAL pulled a roll of worn Brazilian bills from a pocket of his rucksack. Felix counted out the proper payment and handed it to the fisherman.

Felix gestured for his men to get in the motorboat. With all their equipment and the lieutenant's body, it almost sank right there.

Felix turned to the fisherman. "Order and progress!" The Brazilian national motto.

"Huh?"

"I said, 'Order and progress!' "

"Whatever. Hurry up. If you're going east you'll hit the *pororoca*." The old man turned and went into his shack. The *pororoca* was a huge wave—a tidal bore—that rushed in at the mouth of the Araguari every twelve hours.

Another time bomb ticking on our heads.

Felix started the motorboat's engine and left the pier. It ran surprisingly well. As skilled as he was in small-boat handling, the current was just too strong for the overloaded boat. The men had to bail for their lives and balance carefully, and even so they were in danger of capsizing any second.

When they were out of sight of the village, Felix turned down the kerosene lamps. He told the men to jettison their unneeded equipment in a deep part of the channel. This improved the freeboard just enough to keep the boat from swamping. They kept their weapons and ammo—they didn't have much ammo left. They also kept their diving gear. Felix relit the lanterns, and put one at the bow and one at the stern.

This way no one will think we're trying to hide.

By lantern light the racing water was silt-laden mocha brown. Felix revved the engine to maximum power. Dirty smoke poured out of the exhaust, and the motorboat went faster. The vibrations were so strong he was half afraid the boat would shake apart. But there was no compromising now. If an enemy was setting up to shoot at him from the bank, speed was everything. If they were too slow getting downstream and out to sea, they'd nose under the boiling forward face of the next inbound *pororoca*—and they'd never come up. Water around the fast-moving boat splashed higher; the men continued bailing for their lives.

The moon began to rise. First Felix saw its silver aura from below the horizon, and then the moon itself emerged. It reflected off the river sometimes, between the galleries of trees that lined both banks. The stars Felix could see overhead were very sharp and steady. He prayed it didn't start to rain—without the moon and stars he couldn't see far enough ahead to steer, and a downpour like the last one would drown them all. One of his team, an expert in first aid, was doing what he could for their injured man.

The injured man, his equipment and flak vest removed now, lay motionless. He didn't moan or writhe. He just breathed slowly, and his respiration was more and more labored.

"There's too much fluid in his chest," Felix said. "It's occluding his lungs." As a former hospital corpsman, he knew about such things.

"I can try to rig a tube," the first-aid man said. He meant insert a drain so the built-up fluid wouldn't press against the lungs and heart.

Conditions here were hardly ideal, but Felix nodded.

"I'll start," the aid man said. One of the other SEALs brought a lantern closer. Bugs swarmed around the lantern light. Flies were drawn to the blood. Other flies and mosquitoes bothered Felix. He tried to ignore them.

Felix followed the twists and turns of the rushing river down to the sea. The noise of the outboard motor was very loud, a higher tone than the roar of the rain-swollen Araguari. The stench of gasoline and kerosene and fumes helped cover the smell of rotting garbage that even Felix splashing himself with river water couldn't remove. The engine and lamp smoke also helped repel the insects, which would only get thicker as they neared the coastal swamps.

Felix looked at the moon and gave thanks to God for being alive. He gingerly felt for the unexploded grenade round in his rucksack. He fingered the bent fléchettes embedded hard into his flak vest; he was sure the surgeon on the *Ohio* would find another fléchette in the wounded man's chest somewhere, plus who knew what sorts of bullets and shrapnel in the lieutenant's corpse.

Felix glanced into the boat. Some of the men continued bailing, using their helmets. Others helped steer with oars they'd found in the bottom of the boat—if the boat veered broadside to the current they were doomed instantly. The aid man cared for his patient. The boat rocked in the current, and shipped a lot of water, and Felix and his team were barely holding their own.

One man killed in action. One wounded in action, condition critical. Mission accomplished, but at a high price.

Felix estimated their rate of speed along the bank.

Maybe we'll beat the tidal bore, and maybe we won't. If we do we kill the lights and sneak out past the reefs and sandbars. . . . We aim for a spot where the surf isn't running too high. We lower our sonar distress transponder and hope a minisub from the Ohio *hears it and picks us up before broad daylight.*

CHAPTER 9

To leave the Norfolk Navy Base covertly and rejoin USS *Challenger,* Jeffrey sneaked in disguise aboard a *Virginia*-class fast-attack submarine, and hitched a ride out to sea. The *Virginia* boat submerged as soon as she could—to begin her own deployment protecting the African relief convoy. Jeffrey was forced to watch inside the control room, a mere passenger. He felt cheated of having the captain's important privilege: that last view of the outside world and that last breath of fresh air, up in the tiny bridge cockpit atop the sail, before the sail trunk hatches were dogged and all main ballast tanks were vented. His only glimpse of the early-morning twilight was via the photonics mast, as another captain had the conn. The view on a video display screen just wasn't the same.

Jeffrey grabbed some sleep in the executive officer's stateroom fold-down guest rack. He had been up all night in briefings and planning sessions in Norfolk. A messenger woke him when the *Virginia* boat was beyond the continental shelf, saying that the minisub from *Challenger* was ready to pick him up. The entire rendezvous and docking took place submerged, for stealth. *Challenger* herself lurked more than thirty nautical miles away, for even more stealth.

Jeffrey greeted the two-man crew of his minisub—a junior officer and a senior chief—then went into the mini's transport compartment and took a catnap. He woke when he felt the minisub maneuvering for the docking inside *Challenger*'s pressure-proof in-hull hangar, behind her sail.

The mini's crew went through final mating and lockdown procedures. The big doors of the hangar swung closed. Ambient sea pressure around the mini was relieved. The crew undogged the bottom hatch and opened the top hatch of *Challenger*'s mating-trunk air lock. Jeffrey quickly climbed down the steep steel ladder. Minisub maintenance technicians were ready with tool bags to climb up.

Jeffrey came out of the air lock into a narrow corridor inside his ship. His executive officer, Lieutenant Commander Jackson Jefferson Bell, was waiting for him.

"Welcome back, Captain," Bell said.

"Good to see you again, XO." The two men shook hands firmly and warmly.

"How's the baby?" Bell's wife had given birth to their first child, a son, a couple of months before.

"Great, sir." Bell grinned. To Jeffrey he was a changed man since becoming a father, somehow more mature and mellow, and more involved with life. Jeffrey felt a bit jealous.

"Lieutenant Willey has the deck and conn," Bell said. Willey was the ship's engineer.

"The crew has a basic idea of our mission parameters?"

"Yes, sir. I was briefed by Commodore Wilson's deputy and also had a private talk with commander, Sub Group Two." He referred to the rear admiral commanding the three New London fast-attack squadrons—Wilson's boss. "I've told the men about the convoy sailing for the Central African pocket, sir, and our role to seek and destroy the *Admiral von Scheer*."

"Good. Let's make the CACC our first stop." CACC,

command and control center, was the modern name for a submarine's control room.

Jeffrey followed Bell down the corridor. The lieutenant commander was a couple of inches taller than Jeffrey was, fit but not as muscular, and a couple of years younger. Bell's walk was confident. His posture projected pent-up positive energy. He was clearly pumped from having been in command of the ship in Jeffrey's absence. Jeffrey smiled to himself. *I'm gonna need Bell's skills and support more than ever, on* this *mission.*

Crewmen Jeffrey went by perked up when they saw their captain. He smiled and gave them quick hellos.

It's good to be back. Jeffrey took in the familiar sights, sounds, and smells of his command. The flameproof linoleum tiles on the deck. The imitation-wood wainscoting that covered the bulkheads. The bright red fire extinguishers and axes. The gentle breeze of coolness through the ventilator ducts. The triangular Velcro-like pads on the deck that marked valves for the emergency air-breathing masks. The long and narrow pipes along the overheads, with clusters of fittings for those valves—and all the other exposed bundles of pipes and wires and cables flowing like purposeful rivers everywhere.

Bell had put the ship at battle stations for the rendezvous, just in case. Jeffrey squeezed past damage-control parties stationed in the corridors. Again he greeted his crew. Some wore thick and heavy firefighting gear. Most of the men were barely out of their teens.

The control room was rigged for white—normal daytime fluorescent lighting. Jeffrey stood in the aisle. Lieutenant Willey sat at the two-man desk-high command workstation in the center of the compartment. Bell sat down in the other seat, as fire-control coordinator. The overall atmosphere was one of concentration and great care: although *Challenger* was still in heavily patrolled home waters, an enemy threat could appear at any time—an Axis submarine, a mine, anything. Jeffrey let Willey retain the conn. He told him to go deep and head due south at the ship's top quiet speed: twenty-six knots.

Jeffrey liked the lanky and straight-talking Willey. He had been an engineer himself, on his own department-head tour, between his stint at the Pentagon and his more recent planning assignment at the Naval War College. Like many nuclear submarine engineers, Willey had an air of intensity and overwork. Besides his turns on watch as officer of the deck and conn in the CACC, he was responsible for a million details of keeping *Challenger*'s entire propulsion system in good shape. Willey's turf was the whole back half of the boat, from the reactor compartment to the hot and cramped engine room and turbogenerator spaces to the pump jet behind the stern. He had broken a leg in combat on *Challenger*'s first war patrol in December, but that hadn't stopped him—leg in a cast and all—from going right back out with Jeffrey on their next emergency assignment. By now, Willey's leg was well healed.

Jeffrey went back and forth between checking the status of the ship's important systems with Bell on Bell's display screens, and greeting—and sizing up—the other main members of his battle-stations team.

Challenger's chief of the boat, whom everyone called COB—pronounced "cob"—sat in the left seat of the ship control station at the front of the control room. COB was a salty master chief of Latino background, built like a bulldog, with a leadership style to match. COB came from a clan of Jersey City truckers, but he liked to brag that as the black sheep of the family, he instead had gone to sea. COB was—among many other things—effectively head foreman and shop steward for all of *Challenger*'s enlisted people. He was in charge of their training, morale, and discipline. The oldest man aboard, in his early forties, COB's many years of navy service gave him potent credibility. Now, at the ship-control station, he managed the ship's ballast and trim tanks, compressed air banks, pumps of all types including the powerful bilge pumps, and the hydraulic systems. COB constantly scanned his dials and readings and indicator lights. Flow diagrams and schematics danced on his screens. He worked switches to fine-tune things, as slight differences in temperature and salinity in the surrounding water altered the water's density, and with it *Challenger*'s buoyancy—her tendency to rise or sink.

Next to COB sat the battle-stations helmsman, Lieutenant (j.g.) David Meltzer. Meltzer was a tough kid from the Bronx who always walked with his chest puffed out, as if he were asking the world to give him something even more interesting and hard to do. Meltzer spoke with a heavy Bronx accent he made no effort to disguise and wore a class ring as a Naval Academy graduate. Jeffrey thought very highly of him. Meltzer sometimes acted as the pilot of *Challenger*'s minisub; in the past few months, he had driven Jeffrey, Ilse Reebeck, and a team of Navy SEALs to and from land combat more than once. Meltzer was cool under fire. As helmsman, he controlled *Challenger*'s depth, course, and speed, based on helm orders from whoever had the conn—the job was not an easy one, when combat called for fast and tight maneuvers of the nine-thousand-ton vessel in close proximity to bottom terrain.

On the control room's port side was a row of seven sonar consoles, each with two large screens, one above the other, a computer keyboard, track marbles, and sets of special headphones. At the front of the row sat Royal Navy Lieutenant Kathy Milgrom, an exchange officer, and also part of a controversial experiment. Before the war broke out, the Royal Navy began placing women in fast-attack sub crews. This was partly an outgrowth of European Union court rulings about equal rights in all military combat units. It was, to some, a natural extension of the Royal Australian Navy's success with coed crews on their *Collins*-class diesel subs, going back more than a decade. And maybe most important, to its proponents, and especially now with this war, using women on the UK's nuclear submarines doubled the available supply of talented people.

Kathy Milgrom was especially valuable to *Challenger* because she'd served as HMS *Dreadnought*'s sonar officer. The ceramic-hulled *Dreadnought* had been operational months before *Challenger* completed post-shakedown maintenance and workup training. Milgrom was in the thick of the fighting in the North Atlantic, starting in the summer of the previous year, whereas Captain Wilson took *Challenger* into battle—with Jeffrey as his XO—for the first time last December. With the brain trust Lieutenant Milgrom represented, from her working directly with Ilse Reebeck on sound propagation and oceanographic nap-of-seafloor tactics in very deep water, she'd be a vital resource to *Challenger* in their hunt and showdown with the *von Scheer*. Jeffrey gave silent thanks to the British commodore who'd recommended her temporary transfer, and to the U.S. Navy brass who, with some note of caution, had approved it.

The sonar chiefs and enlisted technicians had no trouble accepting Milgrom's leadership as sonar officer and did everything possible to meet her very high standards of job performance. Right now every sonar console was manned. Keyboards clicked, and sonarmen listened intently on their headphones, as waterfall displays cascaded slowly down different screens. Other screens showed jagged graphs that squiggled constantly, or confettilike charts of scalloped arcs and sine curves. All this told Jeffrey that *Challenger*'s hydrophone arrays were working hard to pull in even the subtlest noises from outside. Advanced signal processing software gave meaning to the incoming jumbles of multitudinous sound waves that wafted past the ship from everywhere.

Occasionally something would streak diagonally across a waterfall display like a shooting star or comet. Jeffrey knew these were nearby overflying aircraft. Murmuring came from the sonarmen, and Milgrom and her senior-chief sonar supervisor spoke as new contacts were reported and then classified.

The last main player in Jeffrey's control-room team was *Challenger*'s navigator, Lieutenant Richard Sessions. Jeffrey walked to the rear of the control room, where Sessions worked at the digital navigation plotting table. Sessions came from a small town in Nebraska. His hair and clothing always tended to look a little sloppy no matter what he did, but there was nothing sloppy about his work. He and his assistants precisely monitored *Challenger*'s position on a large-scale nautical chart. This chart, on the big horizontal main navigation computer screen, also showed the day's top-secret Allied submarine safe corridors. From time to time, Sessions recommended course corrections to Lieutenant Willey to make sure the ship stayed well inside these corridors and thus avoided friendly fire—unstable deep-sea currents and underwater storm fronts could make the ship's position drift. Willey would relay conning orders to Meltzer at the helm. Meltzer acknowledged and worked his split-yoke control wheel.

On the navigation display, Jeffrey eyed the trace of *Challenger*'s course since departing New London. He had some questions for Bell about that. Bell was busy talking to the fire-control men and weapons technicians, who manned consoles along the control room's starboard side. Some of these consoles tracked all the different sonar contacts held by Kathy Milgrom's people, and projected their future positions compared to *Challenger*'s while simultaneously feeding data to the main situation plot on Bell's and Willey's screens.

In actual combat Jeffrey would sit where Willey was sitting. The master plot showed estimated range and bearing to each contact, the contact's likely course and speed, whether it was airborne or on the surface or submerged, and also marked the time and place of its closest approach to *Challenger*—the latter was vital to avoid any risk of collision. The plot was busy with icons for merchant ships, warships, and planes.

Bell's weapons officer, Lieutenant Bud Torelli—called Weps for short—worked at a special console on a lower deck near the torpedo room. This separation from Bell was intended to enhance the safety and surety both of handling the atomic warheads at all times, and of launching their torpe-does properly in battle. Torelli kept in constant touch with Bell by intercom and sound-powered phone and fiber-optic LAN as needed.

Jeffrey saw Bell was drilling his weapons-systems spe-cialists, having them practice on the friendly surface con-tacts by pretending to aim mock weapons at each one. *This is where everything comes together,* Jeffrey told himself. *In the days to come, getting in the first shots and not missing will decide if I succeed or fail.* The real-time linkage—be-tween raw data from sonar and accurate knowledge of a tar-get's range, course, and speed—depended on powerful target-motion analysis algorithms, some of which used math so advanced it was classified. *The validity of this informa-tion hinges on the skill of almost every person in the CACC.* Reliable data was essential to placing warheads on a moving target quickly and unerringly—a good firing solution was the only way to score a kill.

The dependability of my ship, her stealth, her power to take damage and stay in the fight depend on every person in the crew.

Jeffrey looked around the control room one more time. He pictured the bustling activity elsewhere aboard. Junior offi-cers, chiefs, and enlisted personnel supported the three de-partment heads—Willey, Sessions, and Torelli—and filled places in the watch, quarter, and station bill throughout the vessel. There were 120 people in *Challenger*'s crew.

Speaking of my crew, and of getting under way from New London . . .

Jeffrey asked Bell to come with him to the captain's stateroom.

First, Bell spoke to the CACC phone talker and modified the drill. "XO is a casualty. Continue targeting exercise."

The phone talker spoke into his bulky sound-powered mike without missing a beat. "Fire-control coordinator is down." The youngster listened on his headphones as a phone talker on a lower deck responded.

The CACC phone talker repeated what he'd heard. "Weapons officer reporting to CACC smartly. Assistant weapons officer is manning special-weapons console."

"Not bad," Bell said half to himself. He followed Jeffrey aft, the few paces to the only stateroom on the ship that only had one rack.

———

Jeffrey and Bell sat in Jeffrey's stateroom. The door was closed.

"You hid under a *garbage barge?*"

"Well," Bell said, "more like half under it, half inside it. It was very big."

Jeffrey laughed. "That's great. I'd love to meet whoever comes up with these things."

Bell smiled. "So would I." He took a pad and pen from Jeffrey's desk and sketched out the shape of the special barge. "I guess, Skipper, from the thing's layout, the way there was good headroom for us to hide tied up and surfaced, it was sort of like a catamaran more than a barge."

"So you snuck in through the stern under a smoke screen, hid under this arcade running down the middle of the hull, and the tugs pushed you and this big trash scow merrily down the river and through Long Island Sound."

"Pretty much. They lay infrared-proof smoke screens all the time, you know, when ships go in or out and just to keep the Axis guessing. The tricky parts were squeezing in to begin with, without breaking something, and then getting through Hell Gate in one piece so we could use the East River." Hell Gate was the portal from the west end of Long Island Sound, near La Guardia Airport and the Triborough Bridge, into the East River, which ran down one side of Manhattan—tidal currents in the narrow Hell Gate were infamously treacherous.

Jeffrey looked at Bell's drawing of the special barge again and shook his head in amazement. He knew that a major dredging operation in the early 2000s had greatly improved the depth and clearances of shipping channels in the Inland Waterway around New York Harbor and Long Island Sound. This work, which took years and cost a fortune, was proving invaluable now.

"So where did they toss out the garbage?"

"Way beyond Sandy Hook, past the edge of the continental shelf. I'm told it was all nontoxic stuff not suitable for landfill. We untied first, and dived, and steamed away real quick. But I gotta tell you, Captain, the noise of all that refuse pouring overboard and falling through the water, and then smashing into the bottom mud, was really something over the sonar speakers."

"And you've been using the Gulf Stream for concealment as you came south?"

"That was Lieutenant Milgrom's idea, based on things she and Reebeck worked on in the past." Sonar conditions in the Gulf Stream were very confusing because of chaotic temperature mixing and unpredictable side eddies.

"Okay. Great. Chalk one up to SubGru Two for supporting us as effectively as ever. . . . A garbage barge. The Axis probably don't even know we've sailed."

Bell looked a little worried. "Let's hope so, anyway. They must suspect *something,* sir."

"Yeah. The Germans probably know we know the *von Scheer* is on the way. They know we won't just sit on our backsides. If anything, their failed attempt to have me and Ilse killed in Washington will put them even more on their toes."

Bell sat there thoughtfully.

Jeffrey leaned forward to dispel the beginnings of a negative mood about what the future might bring. "So how's my ship?" *Challenger* had received some hasty repairs and upgrades since returning from her previous deployment.

"The new fiber-optic acoustic towed array is just terrific, Captain. Milgrom and her people are very turned on about what it can do."

"Good. We'll need it."

"And we finally have all eight torpedo tubes in working order again."

"This I'm *real* glad to hear. What kind of weapons load-out could they give us? Was that inventory page I saw on your status display for the exercise, or a wish list, or was it real?"

"It was real. High-explosive Tactical Tomahawks in all twelve vertical launching-system tubes. A mix of warheads, like ground penetrator and cluster minelet. And a well-balanced, full load in the torpedo room. High-explosive AD-CAP fish, a few more Tomahawks, and improved versions of our newer toys."

"Improved how?"

"The unmanned undersea vehicles are mission reconfigurable now. We have a decent supply of the plug-in black boxes so the vehicles can probe for us in different sortie profiles."

"And we really got the Mark Eighty-eight Mod Twos they promised?" Mark 88s were *Challenger*'s custom-made deep-diving nuclear torpedoes. They were vital to take on a ceramic-hulled opponent, since conventional Mark 48 Improved ADCAPs had a crush depth of about three thousand feet—and ceramic fast-attacks subs could dive maybe five times deeper.

"We sure did, Skipper. A bit faster, a bit longer range, and the variable-yield warhead is booped up to a maximum of one kiloton."

Jeffrey nodded. "Finally we have parity with the Axis torpedo-warhead punch."

"I've already started reviewing how that can alter our tactics," Bell said. In the past, the Mark 88 warheads went up only to a tenth of a kiloton. But the higher yield could be a mixed blessing, Jeffrey knew. Extremely quiet submarines tended to detect one another at very short range. The whole point of using tactical nukes was they had a kill radius vastly larger than any conventional warhead—large enough to defeat most noisemakers and evasive maneuvers. But there was real danger, in a close-quarters melee, that a submarine would be damaged or even sunk by its own atomic warhead going off near its enemy's hull.

"Okay," Jeffrey said. "Ship's material condition is otherwise in good shape?"

"Affirmative." Bell gave him a rundown of items out of commission or on reduced status; the list was short. "Though of course we won't know for sure until we shock-test everything, Captain."

Jeffrey knew what his XO really meant. The shock test would come when they engaged the *Admiral von Scheer*.

"How's the crew?"

Bell sighed, his face clouding enough for Jeffrey to be instantly concerned. "Going out again with so little rest is hard on people."

"What else is new? We're at war. . . . What are you bobbing and weaving about, XO?"

Bell shifted in his chair uncomfortably. "A few of the guys came back from leave, well . . . Let's say, they were visibly three sheets to the wind."

Jeffrey was shocked, and angry. "*Drunk? Some of my people reported back drunk?*"

Bell looked down at the floor.

"Who are they?"

Bell reluctantly told him.

"Crap," Jeffrey said. "Older men. Married. This isn't good, XO. You putting them on report?"

"Well, the corpsman had them diagnosed with nonspecific flulike symptomology and confined them to their racks till they sobered up. COB and I decided their hangovers would be sufficient penance. We can dodge any formal paperwork till after this patrol. . . . The option to push it further's really your decision, sir."

Jeffrey looked at his hands. "*Why*, XO?"

"You mean why did it happen?"

Jeffrey nodded.

Bell took a deep breath. "I think it's obvious. They're scared."

"We're fighting for national survival. Who isn't scared?"

"It's just that, well . . . Even if the ship has nine lives, each time we head out into the blue we use up a handful more. Ditto for your narrow escape in Washington yesterday, sir. The men know all about it, and in their eyes you *are* the ship. The guys pretty much feel like we're playing Russian roulette. Sooner or later, Captain, the bullet with *Challenger*'s name on it has to come up. It's just a matter of statistics."

"But they all got the Presidential Unit Citation last time!"

"I know."

"That ought to have been *good* for morale."

"That's the problem, I think. It created this artificial emotional high."

"You mean, a false sense of closure, and escape."

"Yup. Then having to turn around so fast for another deployment, it just meant more of a group mental crash."

Jeffrey sat there, pondering. "I'll have to go around and talk to the men."

"I think that would help a lot," Bell said. "You might not realize quite how much they worship you."

"Without us both getting sacrilegious, XO, I hope their *faith* in me isn't misplaced."

Bell hesitated. "There's something else. Well, two things."

"What?"

"The guys were all kind of attached to having Lieutenant Reebeck around. They knew she had rather special talents, and they thought she brought the ship good luck."

"You mean they thought she was some sort of *mascot?*"

"I don't know if anybody would put it that way, Skipper. But they think this leaving her behind, now, suddenly, is *bad* luck."

Jeffrey grunted. This was one subject he did *not* want to push any further. "What was the other thing?"

Again Bell shifted uncomfortably. "When we were in the hardened underground dry dock." Cut into the rock bluffs opposite the New London base, on Connecticut's Thames River.

"Yes?"

"*Jimmy Carter* limped home." The USS *Jimmy Carter* was the third and final *Seawolf*-class boat. She'd been specially modified during construction to have a stretched hull, with extra space for carrying SEALs, their equipment, and commando warfare planning and communication facilities. The *Carter* had been commissioned in 2004; the first of the four modified *Ohio* ex-boomers wasn't fully ready until 2007.

"Damaged?"

"Damaged. Her XO wouldn't tell me much at first. Secrecy, the usual. But I saw several body bags come off."

"I don't like where this is going."

"I gather they'd tried to raid the German underground U-boat pens at Trondheim." Trondheim was on the coast of central Norway. "Somebody senior thought that's where the *von Scheer* must've been hiding. But apparently all the activity there was fake, a big deception, to draw us off from where *von Scheer* really was, far up in the nether reaches by North Cape, hard on the border with Russia."

"So what happened?"

"The Germans were waiting for the SEALs. They took heavy losses and failed to penetrate the base. The *Carter* was badly banged up getting away."

"Any word on Clayton and Montgomery?" They were two SEALs, a lieutenant and a senior chief, who'd been with *Challenger* on recent missions. Jeffrey and Bell—and a lot of *Challenger*'s crew—had gotten to like Clayton and Montgomery a lot, living so tightly together and sharing the dangers of war. Clayton was very even-tempered and easy to talk to. Montgomery had a dry sense of humor and an extremely sharp tongue, but people tended to trust him and he exuded strong natural charisma.

Bell looked at Jeffrey. "It seems likely from their previous experience that they both would have been on that raid. Now we don't know if they're alive or dead, and nobody in New London would tell us."

Jeffrey frowned. "It doesn't bode well that we're picking up a different team this time."

"I know, Captain. That's what the whole crew's thinking. New SEALs are not a good sign. The idea Clayton and Montgomery might be dead is getting our people down. Uncertainty is even worse than knowing for sure. It gnaws at you."

"All right. Once you and I go over one more thing, I'll make the rounds and get everybody cheered up. We can't have them thinking dark thoughts based on hearsay and guesswork. And this business about us playing Russian roulette is bullcrap. This ship's crew are all professionals. They're not supposed to mope and feel sorry for themselves when we're fighting for our country's whole way of life. Their job is to make the *enemy* be the one to get the willies and have self-doubt."

"It'll make a difference, sir, them hearing that from you."

"I'll fill them in on the big picture, this relief convoy to Africa and everything. I know you already did that. But getting it again, from me, should boost their sense of purpose."

"Yes, Captain."

"We have the consoles for this Orpheus gizmo?"

"Affirmative. Installed and tested. My understanding is the off-hull equipment will come when we rendezvous with *Ohio*."

"So Admiral Hodgkiss told me . . . And so I will tell each member of my crew. Next stop, the Caribbean Sea. Then we head for the one place where the Orpheus setup will work, and do the most good. . . . Orpheus. Is that a code name, or an acronym for something tongue-twisting, do you think?"

"I believe it's a code name, Captain. I doubt they'd use an acronym, sir, on the off chance an Axis agent or mole could figure out what the letters stood for."

Jeffrey rose to signal he was ending the meeting. "It's good to know, XO, given what we'll be facing against the *von Scheer,* that just for once it's the Allies who've come up with a secret weapon that could turn the tide."

CHAPTER 10

Two days later, nearing the Greenland-Iceland-UK
Gap, Ernst Beck sat alone at his desk in his tiny, austere cabin. To one side of his laptop lay the heavy
packet of remaining unopened envelopes within envelopes
that Rudiger von Loringhoven had given him. Since the *von
Scheer* left Norway, the packet had already been stripped of
its two outermost layers: the rendezvous with the pair of
Russian submarines in the Barents Sea and then details for
piercing the G-I-UK Gap. Some of those latter details were
displayed right now on Beck's laptop screen.

Beck reached over and palmed his intercom mike. In the
control room, the junior officer of the deck responded.

"Have the einzvo report to my cabin."

Beck stared for a moment at the unopened packet. Its contents, he knew, would guide his actions stage by stage in the
cataclysm to come. *The Allied relief convoy, and USS* Challenger. The SMS *von Scheer* was the threat to draw *Challenger* out, and the convoy was the flypaper to make sure that
threat stuck.

Beck's latest phase orders, like those before, were couched

in the dry, precise terms he'd long since learned to expect from Berlin. Well-composed naval orders gave wide discretion to commanders at sea to exercise initiative while adapting to real-world conditions as they unfolded on the spot. But formal naval orders routinely ignored the human emotions their dictates would surely evoke in those whose duty it was to carry them out in a life-or-death global struggle.

Beck sighed.

The crisply worded orders always sidestep the tension of waiting, the chaos and confusion of actual battle, the crew's grinding fear or terrified panic, the agony of wounds. The orders never touch upon the constant dread of escalation of the wider war. And they never address the crushing load they put on a captain's shoulders: the near-inhuman demands for brutal, decisive ruthlessness and always-mounting tactical innovation—to deceive or slaughter the enemy in clever and subtle new ways.

Someone knocked on Beck's door.

"Come."

Karl Stissinger entered. "Good morning, Captain."

"It's time," Beck said. He gestured at his laptop screen.

Stissinger nodded. "Shall we fetch our mysterious guest, sir?"

"He asked to be called Baron von Loringhoven in public, by the way."

Stissinger raised his eyebrows. "Oh, a *baron,* is he?" Stissinger chuckled. "The way he's been hiding and having messengers bring all his meals, there's wide speculation he might even be a count. You know, Captain, as in Count Dracula?"

"Not so loud," Beck said. "He's right next door."

"In what should be *my* cabin, with him sharing it as our guest."

"He said privacy was needed, for security."

"I believe it. The messengers say he's always huddled over papers and maps and documents, and keeps scribbling on a thick notepad. Each time they bring a new meal tray, he turns everything upside down before asking them in. The previous meal, the leftovers, sit shoved in a corner. Besides his computer, he just has the reading light on, day and night. Never uses the overhead fluorescents, and the men swear his bed looks completely unslept in."

Beck nodded. "He seems to take what's going on very seriously." He pointed at the door into the head, the bathroom he shared with von Loringhoven. "I've heard him take a shower a couple of times. And I know he pisses and shits like any mortal." Beck grinned lopsidedly. "You can tell the men I seriously doubt he's a vampire."

"Yes, sir."

"Anyway, let's see if our baron wants to join us in the Zentrale for the latest excitement."

The *von Scheer* was at battle stations, running deep. Beck and Stissinger sat at the command console. Von Loringhoven stood, wedged in behind them, so he could look between their shoulders at their status plots. Way over their heads, the surface Gulf Stream current ran northeast, back the way they'd come. The air and water temperatures were well above freezing here; there was rain and wind and heavy seas, but no ice.

"Sonar," Beck ordered, "put passive broadband on speakers, volume low."

Werner Haffner acknowledged from his console, past Stissinger's seat on Beck's right. Now Beck heard the sounds of biologics—lobster and herring that had so far survived the heavy oil spills of war—and the gentle murmur of bottom currents flowing along rough terrain. He also heard a steady eerie mechanical pulsating throb: the two submerged Russian submarines that concealed *von Scheer* from above.

Beck kept one eye on the tactical plot and the other on the gravimeter. His orders told him exactly which route to take. Ordinarily Beck would not have liked such restriction. But now, with the need to move in formation with the pair of Russian Sierra IIs—yet remain undetected himself—he understood the requirement for things to be organized in advance.

"This is good," Beck told Stissinger. He knew von Loringhoven would be in the conversation too, simply by his physical proximity. "This is exactly what I would have done."

"*Jawohl*," Stissinger said respectfully.

"Explain," von Loringhoven said.

Beck glanced at the diplomat for a moment, then pointed at the gravimeter display. "Our two friendly Ivans are taking the deepest part of the gap, right between the northern tip of Scotland and the Faroe Islands. The water here goes down a thousand meters plus, in most places. This valley between the European continental shelf, here, and the Faroes Rise, here, is ideal for us to hide in by hugging the bottom."

"I see that," von Loringhoven said. He gave Beck a look as if to say, *Don't you think I can read a nautical chart?*

Beck decided to ignore his irritating attitude. Otherwise, this could be an extremely long cruise. "It's all a very neat bluff. This route is shortest for the Russians to get from their home port to the Atlantic, so it's natural they'd come this way, just as if they've nothing to hide. Plus, after we pass Scotland we go right down the west coast of Ireland, which is the last thing the Allies would expect the *von Scheer* to do. They're much more likely to be looking for us way up near Greenland or Iceland."

The two Russian submarines pinged on their sonars again. They were continuing to signal their presence as neutrals—to invite inspection by Allied antisubmarine forces and avoid accidental attack.

"We're about to see how well this works," von Loringhoven stated. "We don't know how thoroughly the Brits will

probe beneath the two 945A boats." His tone was distant, almost sarcastic.

Is he really such an arrogant bastard, Beck asked himself,
*or is he just scared and won't admit it? Either way, doesn't
he have the common sense to behave better in my control
room, in front of* my *crew?*

The Russians slowed to seven knots. Beck ordered the pilot to slow the *von Scheer,* to keep station. Then he ordered
that one of his ship's two nuclear reactors be shut down to
reduce the *von Scheer*'s noise signature. In an emergency, it
would take several minutes to bring the reactor fully back
on-line. This would sacrifice a lot of the ship's propulsion
power when it might be needed most. But the *von Scheer* was
truly boxed in—by dry land to north and south, and by
minefields and enemy forces in other directions. *Absolute
stealth, not escape speed, counts the most.* Beck ordered that
the air-circulation fans, and other nonvital equipment, also
be turned off. To further save amperage demand—and remind everyone to make as little noise as possible—lighting
shipwide was cut to dim red.

The air in the control room quickly grew stale and humid
and warm—from the people and from electronic gear. The
repeated bass and high-pitched sonar tones from the Russians filled the control-room speakers every minute or so. It
made Beck feel as if he were one of several vessels on the
surface in thick fog, feeling their way half-blind in the days
before radar.

Beck ordered Stissinger to launch two remote-controlled
undersea probes through two of the *von Scheer*'s eight over-
sized torpedo tubes. These battery-powered, reusable probes
would check out the bottom rocks and muck ahead for antisubmarine detectors that could be problems for the *von
Scheer.*

Stissinger whispered with his weapons technicians and relayed orders to the torpedo room. Rapidly, the unmanned
undersea vehicle probes were launched, attached to fiber-

optic tethers; Beck windowed their sensor readouts on his console.

"Isn't that risky?" von Loringhoven said.

"To not use the probes and trust to blind luck is riskier," Beck mumbled. "And please keep your voice down."

The ship's copilot took control of one probe to gain cues to help the pilot steer Beck's vessel. One of Stissinger's senior-chief weapon technicians controlled the other probe. The darkened Zentrale grew hushed.

"Einzvo," Haffner called out in a forced whisper. "New passive sonar contacts. Airborne contacts, approaching from east, assess as Royal Navy helicopters possibly based in the Orkneys or Shetland Islands."

"Captain," Stissinger murmured, "the Brits have sent their inspection team to take a good look at the Russians."

Beck nodded. In a few minutes, he could barely hear the beating of rotor blades and the whine of engines coming straight down through the sonar layer, playing over the speakers.

"Aircraft are hovering near the Russians," Stissinger said.

"Sounds of dipping sonars," Haffner reported softly. The Royal Navy was using high-frequency pings, above the range of human hearing—for better image resolution of returns off the Russian hulls. "New surface contacts, weak, closing. Warship tonals."

"Traces of blue-green laser light also now," Stissinger said. "Assess helicopters making close inspection with line-scan cameras . . . And Royal Navy frigates, distant, approaching."

"Fine," von Loringhoven said. "They'll see two Russian submarines." The Zentrale crew became even more hushed.

"Our own acoustic masking routines continue to function nominally," Stissinger said. "Line-scan cameras are too shallow to pick us up down here in the bottom terrain."

"Very well, Einzvo." Beck tried to sound calm, but he couldn't allow himself to relax. He saw several crewmen hunch closer over their consoles, as if they were literally ducking to hide from the enemy undersea cameras way overhead.

Beck understood better than any of them how savagely fast this delicate ballet of deception could all come unglued.

"Captain," the copilot said.

The urgent call hit Beck like an electrical shock. "What is it?" he snapped in an undertone. "Give me a proper report."

"New contact on off-board probe."

"Concur," Haffner said. "New passive sonar contact by one of our unmanned undersea vehicles." The vehicles had hydrophones and other mission sensors. "Strong contact. Range is short."

"Classify it," Stissinger ordered.

"Nuclear submarine. On the bottom. Same depth as us!"

"Quiet," Beck snapped. He looked at Stissinger. "A nuclear sub at a thousand-plus meters? Identify it. *Seawolf* class? *Dreadnought*? Either way we've got big trouble."

"New contact signal strength increasing," Haffner said through clenched teeth. "Contact is approaching our location."

"Copilot," Stissinger ordered, "pass control of the probe to me."

"Jawohl." The copilot was a junior officer. His voice now sounded very tight.

Stissinger gripped the joystick on his console. Through the fiber-optic guidance wire, he directed the probe in a wide arc around to the side of the hostile deep-running nuclear sub. Beck saw Stissinger's hand was white knuckled on the control stick. He knew his XO was aiming for a better acoustic profile of the hostile contact.

Using folds in the terrain and rubble from ancient undersea earthquakes, Stissinger snuck the probe nearer and nearer the inbound submarine. Then his senior chief reported that the other probe's cameras had spotted a line of acoustic- and magnetic-anomaly sensors freshly emplaced on the bottom just ahead.

The tension in the control room rose sharply.

Beck told himself there was no reason to think the *von Scheer* had been spotted, yet. Maybe this was just routine Allied procedure to guard the gap and also keep an eye on Russian submarine movements.

Don't kid yourself. They know the von Scheer *is on the prowl, somewhere.*

"Good tonals now," Haffner said in an almost yell. "Inbound contact is definitely nuclear-powered, definitely American."

Stissinger turned to Beck. "Probe's magnetic-anomaly sensors confirm unidentified vessel is steel-hulled, not ceramic, sir."

"A *Seawolf*," von Loringhoven said. "But she's practically at her crush depth. Or below it. Something doesn't make sense."

Beck shot him a disapproving look. "Quiet in the Zentrale." Baron or not, this guest had to learn to keep his mouth shut.

"Better tonals now," Haffner hissed.

"It's *NR-One*," Stissinger said disbelievingly. The one-of-a-kind *NR-1* had been a pet project of Admiral Hyman Rickover years ago.

"What's *NR-One* doing *here?*" von Loringhoven said.

"I said be quiet," Beck snapped. "We've got difficulties, Einzvo. That little sub out there may be unarmed, but she's optimized for deep-sea surveillance and recon."

"Concur, Captain." Stissinger sounded extremely worried. The aged *NR-1,* with her eight-man crew and powerful sensors, could find the *von Scheer* and unmask her . . . and then, by acoustic comms or radio buoy, call in overwhelming firepower.

In a pinch, those two Russians will flee for their lives, and we'll be naked down here, and damned to destruction.

"Do something," von Loringhoven said. He'd read Beck's mind, and now was almost pleading. *A coward, under the facade?*

Beck stared hard at the gravimeter and a nautical chart. This bluff of hiding under Russian subs was about to unravel completely. *NR-1* moved closer and closer. The stale air in the Zentrale grew stifling, suffocating. Crewmen squirmed in their seats; sweat-soaked backsides squeaked on vinyl.

"Arm nuclear torpedoes?" Stissinger prompted.

Beck thought fast. *This is my first real test as captain. And an awful test indeed.* "Negative. Make no mechanical transients. . . . Pilot, bring the boat up to one hundred meters." The two Russians were moving slowly, above the layer, at fifty meters. "Rise on autohover, get us up there quickly. Cut the wires, jettison both probes."

Beck watched as *von Scheer*'s depth decreased. On the gravimeter display, the local terrain receded beneath the ship.

"What are you doing?" von Loringhoven demanded.

"Upping the ante," Beck said. "I told you to be quiet."

The diplomat bit down whatever he was going to say next.

"Einzvo. Sonar. We're about the same size and shape as a U.S. Navy strategic-missile sub, correct?"

"An American boomer?" Stissinger asked. "Er, yes, Captain."

"Use our active wide-aperture arrays and the bow sphere. Take the sound profiles we have of Allied submarines. On our way up, as we pass through two hundred fifty meters, start making us sound like a barely audible newer *Ohio*-class vessel."

"Understood," Haffner said. "Working on it, sir." He and his sonarmen got very busy.

"Captain?" Stissinger said.

"We know they'll know we're here. There's only one way we stand a chance to get through now unmolested. . . . We aren't that far from Holy Loch."

"The reactivated Allied submarine base?"

Beck nodded. "The strategic-missile subs are controlled by different authorities from their tactical antisubmarine forces. That's what I'm counting on, delay and confusion while they sort things out. If the Royal Navy and *NR-1* think we're a U.S. boomer, turning the tables and trailing a pair of Russian fast-attacks to grab some intell, they'll leave us alone. They'll be extra careful to not draw attention to us, *especially* if they think we're exploiting Ivan to hide from the Germans."

Stissinger exhaled unsteadily. "Remind me to never play poker with you, Captain."

Crewmen were clearly aghast at the sleight of hand Beck was proposing to pull off. If it worked, they'd soon be free in the North Atlantic and could insert into the superbly concealing bottom terrain of the vast Mid-Atlantic Ridge. *But still, if those jettisoned Axis probes are found here by* NR-1 . . .

"What if your ploy doesn't work?" von Loringhoven said.

"If the einzvo reports enemy weapons in the water, we return fire and take as many of them with us as we can."

"You didn't arm nuclear warheads."

"That's correct." As von Loringhoven turned livid, Beck held up a forceful hand. "There is *no way,* Baron, that I'm going to use atomic bombs so close to civilian population centers, enemy or not."

CHAPTER 11

Felix Estabo woke that morning in his coffin-sized sleeping rack aboard the USS *Ohio*. Felix had an uncannily accurate internal body clock—he didn't have to glance at his watch to tell that it was 0450 local time. Every night, worldwide, no matter the jet lag and season, he decided exactly when to get up—and next morning he would, within a minute or so.

For a few seconds, without stirring, Felix listened to the sounds of the ship, the gentle ventilation and subdued electrical hum. He knew the *Ohio* was running deep, heading northwest, away from South America and into the Caribbean Sea. As always on rising, even before pulling off his blanket and yanking open the privacy curtain of his rack, Felix said a brief prayer.

Today, barely forty-eight hours after rejoining *Ohio*, Felix was especially grateful to be alive. He was sad that his lieutenant had been killed back there in the rain forest of Brazil. He was glad his man with the chest wound had come through surgery okay. The trickiest part had been moving the injured SEAL from the fisherman's motorboat—as it be-

gan to sink once and for all off the mouth of the Araguari—
down into the minisub, submerged at thirty feet for stealth.
But a one-man pressure-proof transfer capsule was carried
in the mini for just that purpose. Held safely inside at a
steady one atmosphere, warm and dry, already wounded
men were spared the added physiological strains of diver
compression and decompression, and of immersion in the
sea that might be icy cold or might contain sharks. A navy
corpsman was part of the minisub's crew on combat missions, and the *Ohio*—unlike American nuclear subs in
peacetime—carried a medical doctor who specialized in
trauma surgery.

The rest of Felix's team weren't seriously injured, though
shrapnel had to be pulled out of their bodies under general
anesthesia, and many, many stitches were required. Ironically, Felix himself was the only man to escape with nothing
but minor abrasions from bushes and vines.

Then Felix asked God to protect the *Ohio* and everyone on
her. No expert in submarine combat, he did know that the surrounding waters might hold naval mines—planted by infiltrat-
ing Axis U-boats or dropped from disguised, pseudoneutral
merchant ships. The *Ohio* might even be ambushed by a U-
boat at any time. Felix pictured the nightmarish blast and influx of crushing water if the ship hit a mine or was hit by an
inbound torpedo. The absolute worst would be getting sunk by
friendly fire, in the tragic and wasteful confusion inevitable
during a shooting war.

Felix pushed these morbid thoughts from his mind. He
knew that the *Ohio,* as a former strategic-missile sub, was
slow by modern standards but was also exceedingly quiet,
and her refitted sonars were state-of-the-art. Her officers and
men—it was the Blue Crew for this rotation—inspired total
confidence.

The ending of his prayer was for the safety and well-being
of his family.

Felix got out of bed and stood up straight; because of his
seniority, he had the middle rack in a tier of three—the easi-

est to enter and exit. He was careful to not make noise, since people around him still slept. But the advantage of the *Ohio,* as an ex-boomer, was her roominess. She carried a powerful complement of SEALs: sixty-six men, including command and planning staff, plus communications and logistics personnel. Each SEAL had his own rack in a dedicated bunk area, with separate climate control from the rest of the ship. The air at the moment was kept warm and humid; Felix was lucky not to have to risk a chest cold or worse coming back from the jungle to the dry and freezing air of a typical fast-attack sub.

He was still very stiff and sore from his physical exertions on the bloody but successful mission, and his whole body ached, as if he'd run a competitive ultramarathon—which, indeed, he had. His chest was black-and-blue from the impact of enemy bullets against his flak vest. Even after almost ten hours of uninterrupted sleep, he felt weary and drained. But he knew from experience that strong hot coffee and a nice big breakfast were just the thing to restore his vigor and spirit.

Felix answered the call of nature, then shaved and showered, in the well-equipped multiple-person head belonging to SEAL country on the *Ohio.* His shower was very short, to save water, and he had to be careful not to bang his elbows as he scrubbed himself: each stainless-steel shower cubicle was barely the size of an old-fashioned phone booth. He also had to be careful when flossing his teeth, or he'd poke the guys at the sinks next to him in the face; the other SEALs, all early risers, were also awake. The head got crowded and busy fast—the air was filled with drifting steam from the showers, and with profane locker-room humor from SEALs wearing towels. Felix admired his neighbors' tattoos, and sometimes saw scars from old wounds; he himself wore no tattoos, just a necklace crucifix.

After dressing, Felix made the rounds of his team, to cheer up the wounded who were confined to their racks and speak with the ambulatory wounded, to buck up everyone's morale. Even on the spacious *Ohio,* there was no separate sick bay, just a cramped cubicle used by the ship's corpsman to dispense medicine for routine complaints. The *Ohio*'s wardroom table, where ship's officers ate their meals and did briefings and paperwork, doubled as an operating theater; the tables in the enlisted dining compartment became the triage center; seriously hurt personnel, including the SEALs, used their own narrow sleeping racks as the closest thing to a hospital bed available. While clandestinely violating neutral territory, the ship could not afford to betray her presence by evacuating badly wounded men to any surface ship or shore facility—everyone involved knew it and understood. A walled-off part of the ship's food freezer had been turned into a morgue.

Felix's men appreciated the visit from their master chief. They were visibly more chipper as he teased and joked with them all. They'd held a brief memorial for their lieutenant the day before—and life simply had to go on. Felix left each man feeling much better, with smiles on their gaunt, pain-drawn faces and their depression dispelled. Mourning was a luxury Felix had scant time for. He knew his men's biggest problem of the moment would be boredom, with all the tricks it could play on one's mind. Because of their wounds they couldn't really exercise to burn off energy, and for now they weren't on active mission status—so they had no immediate combat tasks to get ready for. Instead, they could watch movies, or play video games or checkers or cards, or talk or sleep or read or listen to music. Felix resolved to make sure his men's needs were attended to so they wouldn't go batty. It was hard enough for most SEALs to deal with the claustrophobic confines running submerged in a nuclear sub at the best of times.

Here I go again, Felix the mother hen caring for my brood.

Felix himself enjoyed the coziness and intense companionship aboard a submarine, but other SEALs thought he was strange.

To stretch his legs and get some kinks out of his body, Felix took a quick trip around the multidecked missile compartment. It filled the whole middle portion of the submarine's hull, and he was impressed by its dimensions.

The modified *Ohio* was a hybrid warship, and even with her massive size, space was at a premium. Many of her huge missile tubes, which once held sub-launched ballistic missiles tipped with thermonuclear warheads, now carried seven Tactical Tomahawk cruise missiles apiece. Ten of those two dozen tubes were dedicated to Special Warfare operations: two for air locks that SEALs could use to board minisubs or directly enter the sea in diving gear, two for explosives and ammunition storage for their missions, and up to six for other SEAL equipment stowage. The missile compartment also now had decontamination showers, and areas for postmission rig and weapon wash-down and cleaning— and an extremely good physical-training exercise and weight room. Virtual-reality practice aids helped keep the SEALs' marksmanship and battle reflexes sharp while they traveled impatiently from place to place—squeezed inside a giant sardine can that had no windows.

The *Ohio* did have four tubes in her torpedo room, with a supply of war-shot fish that was small—only about a dozen—but deadly nevertheless.

Felix made his way forward. The corridors were narrow, functional, and stark. During the morning change of watch, the passageways and ladders were very crowded. Often men had to stand sideways in order to jostle past one another. If two submariners had potbellies, this clearance was awkwardly tight. Including the SEALs, there were two hundred people aboard the *Ohio*. The watch was changed every six hours, round the clock.

Even before he reached the enlisted dining space, Felix noticed the delicious smells of breakfast. He heard the subdued noise of clattering plastic plates and the enthusiastic babble as crewmen chatted over their meals. He waited in line, cafeteria-style. The mess-management specialists already knew him well—even without the old facial scar, Felix's compact muscular build and his upbeat personality would cause him to stand out in any crowd. The cooks piled plates high with the foods they knew he liked most, now that he'd been released from the bland pre-packaged jungle warfare odor-control diet regimen.

Felix took his tray and sat at the six-man booth that was unofficially reserved for chiefs. Now, at 0545 ship's time, oncoming watchstanders had already eaten, and it was the offcoming watchstanders' turn to dine. The atmosphere was a little more relaxed. Felix talked with a friendly mix of his own SEAL peers and some of the *Ohio*'s submariners. They traded the standard joshing, each saying he thought the other was utterly crazy for his career choice. Felix's answer, as usual, was that both SEALs and submariners were undersea warriors, so to the rest of the naval community—and to the outside world at large—both types of men must seem mad. Beyond that, the chiefs avoided shoptalk, as was the custom at meals. They mostly spoke of their families: how their kids were doing in school, wives and cars and pets and housing and overdue bills and such. By long-practiced tacit agreement, they left their worries unvoiced—of death, or escalation, or a spouse who might ask to divorce.

As Felix finished his breakfast, a messenger came and asked him to report to the Special Warfare command and planning center. Felix gulped the last of his coffee, bussed his dirty dishes, and headed aft.

He took a steep steel ladder down one level. The Special Warfare command center was a compartment that once held electronics needed to fix the *Ohio*'s exact position and then coordinate launching her two dozen Armageddon rockets. The very thought gave Felix the creeps. With all that equipment removed, the SEALs now had different consoles and workstations to support the various missions U.S. Navy frogmen trained for. Many of the consoles in the blue-lighted compartment were manned. Message traffic was monitored through *Ohio*'s low-observable floating-wire antenna. Upcoming SEAL sorties from the sub were mapped out and then rehearsed, using simulators and planning software. Felix made a point not to look, in order to maintain mission security.

Running into the master chief of the ten-man SEAL command and communications staff, he was told, "Commander McCollough wants to see you." The chief pointed to a small meeting room. The door was closed.

Felix knocked and entered. McCollough sat at a worktable, going over status reports and briefing documents; the commander wore neatly starched and precisely creased khakis, with his rank insignia on the collar tabs. When he saw Felix, he stood. As a chief, Felix also wore khakis—the main difference was the anchor on each collar tab, instead of bars or oak leaves.

"Morning, Master Chief," McCollough said.

"Morning, sir." In the SEALs, relations between officers and enlisted men were informal—the navy didn't salute indoors anyway. The room they were in was drab, linoleum floor tiles and painted metal bulkheads—a study in gray on gray.

McCollough shook Felix's hand. This was the first sign Felix got that they'd have a serious discussion.

"Sit. Please." The commander pointed to a chair beside his own. The two men were about the same age, but McCollough was a good foot taller. McCollough spoke with a heavy Boston Irish accent that Felix liked. He also enjoyed the commander's lively sense of humor and his tolerance of the practical jokes of which most SEALs were so fond. As was the way in the SEAL teams, McCollough—as a commissioned officer—had spent much less time on field operations than Felix. The fact was, the SEALs worked their chiefs quite hard, but moved their officers up and away from the day-to-day grit rather quickly.

"Feeling rested?" McCollough asked.

"I wouldn't mind a month on leave." Felix meant it, but he smiled. His smile was short-lived. He knew at once McCollough's question wasn't small talk. Right now the commander was stone-faced, even dour.

"I need someone to lead another team, on a different sort of op."

Felix thought fast. "You want my advice on picking the best lieutenant still fit for duty, sir? What sort of op?" The *Ohio* had seven separate eight-man teams under McCollough's command. The team that had deployed from *Ohio* to the Brazilian coast—the one Felix and his men heard fighting off an ambush the night before they themselves were hit—had come back with several wounded, including their LT and their chief. With the death of the lieutenant of Felix's team, there remained five lieutenants or lieutenants junior grade to choose from.

"What sort of op?" McCollough repeated Felix's question. "The sort of op I want you to lead."

"Sir?"

"You did a real good job back there. I need somebody mature and hard, not another kid with daydreams of glory, with his head stuffed full of all the generalist nonsense naval officers are supposed to know to enhance their 'upward mobility.'"

"I'm not sure I like where this is going, sir."

McCollough suddenly smiled, a disarmingly puckish grin. Felix knew that look. The commander used it to win people over to something he knew they wouldn't welcome—something procedural, bureaucratic, dealing with navy regulations and hierarchy.

"Master Chief, I put you in a few weeks ago for what I prefer to view as a well-deserved battlefield promotion. I can think of no better time than now to inform you that the Senate's rubber stamp came through. You've been formally approved as a limited duty officer with the rank of full lieutenant."

"Thanks but no thanks, Skipper," Felix said immediately. A limited duty officer was a chief or other enlisted person who'd won a commission through merit. The *limited* meant that, lacking the generalized training McCollough just mentioned, the officer's future assignments would be confined to their existing specialty—in this case, SEAL operations.

McCollough sighed. "Look, do me a favor and take it for now. Once we're through with this deployment, if you haven't changed your mind . . ."

Felix shook his head vehemently. "Master chief is what I am, and what I want to be till I retire. It's the best social club in the world. None of this officer politics crap, none of these jump-through-hoops promotion selection boards and mumbo-jumbo fitness reports. Let me just do what I love to do."

"You see, my man Felix, that last part is exactly the idea. This next op, I need someone who can *command*. You'll be off on your own with a team, exposed, beyond any means of support, and you may go head-to-head with kampfschwimmer in a knock-down-drag-out with no retreating allowed this time."

Felix thought for a minute. "Sir, does this have something to do with repercussions from my team's last action? The hard proof of Axis involvement in northern Brazil?"

"The answer is yes, and no, and I don't know. We sent your report up the ladder, with my full and unconditional endorsement. But questions like yours, the answers don't filter back down."

"I understand."

McCollough cleared his throat pointedly. "So quit evading the issue. To command, by navy regs and age-old custom, you have to be a commissioned officer. . . . You do get a raise, you know."

"Effective immediately?" Felix's wife and kids could always use the extra money.

McCollough nodded.

"But what about your exec?" McCollough's deputy was a lieutenant commander, seasoned and mature himself.

"One, he doesn't have the language skills. Two, I need him here. We have too much to do, getting ready for other near-term ops. And three, he just isn't as good in the field as you are. I don't think anyone in my complement is as good in the field as you."

"First you bribe. Now you're trying to flatter me, sir."

McCollough smacked the table. His face turned red. "I never flatter anybody and you know it! Take the promotion! I don't have all day to waste coddling you. And *you* don't have any time to waste getting ready for this assignment."

"Uh, okay, Commander. Okay. But it still stands, if I don't like it, later, you send in the forms and I go back to master chief forever?"

"If you and I are still alive in a month, that's a promise. Meantime, get ready to leave the ship. You're taking men from my third platoon and transferring to *Challenger* once we rendezvous."

"Jeffrey Fuller's boat?"

"That ought to make up somewhat for your inconvenient change in rank."

"Yeah, if I don't mind being squashed to the size of a peanut, down at fifteen thousand feet."

"*Challenger*'s crush depth is classified. Keep your educated guesses to yourself. You should know better."

Felix was taken aback. "Sir, what's really the matter?"

McCollough sighed, and rubbed his bloodshot, overworked eyes. "After we drop you off, we're heading across the Atlantic. My men are tasked for antimine warfare and sabotage around the extreme north flank of the pocket to help prepare waterspace access for the convoy landings. Plus joint suppression of enemy air defenses in coastal Saharan Africa." JSEAD. "Clandestine intelligence, surveillance, reconnaissance, and targeting for *Ohio*'s Tomahawks and other Allied warships and planes." ISRT. "Sexy-sounding catchphrases from the Pentagon, but it's going to be a bloodbath. . . . You ought to be glad you're getting off now."

"You know I don't see it that way, sir. Don't send me on some sideshow." *Not now, when my friends and teammates are going to be put in harm's way.*

"I'm not—and it won't be a sideshow. You lead a team

that is also preparing the waterspace in a big way. Something new, when you and your men deploy from *Challenger*. Something real important, a breakthrough if it works. You're going to be a force multiplier, in a very big way." A small group whose efforts greatly leverage the power of main-line fleet units. "My exec will give you briefing materials. Study them hard. The operators from third platoon are already trained. You'll have to use both of *Ohio*'s minisubs to shuttle your men and the special equipment across to *Challenger* quickly."

"Yes, sir." *This is getting interesting.*

McCollough reached in a pants pocket. "You'll need these." He passed across to Felix a pair of not new collar tabs. Each had the two silver bars of a full lieutenant.

Felix had a sinking feeling. "Where did you get these, sir?"

"From someone who should have listened to you better than he did, and paid the price." Felix's dead lieutenant.

"Mother of God."

"Wear them in his memory."

Felix hesitated.

"If you think they're cursed, *I* think you're the man to break the curse." McCollough stood. Again he shook Felix's hand. "The rendezvous with *Challenger* is eighteen hundred tomorrow evening. That gives you less than thirty-six hours. . . . And congratulations, *Lieutenant* Estabo. I might not see you before you go. . . . Ask my exec for the Orpheus package."

CHAPTER 12

Thirty-six hours later, in the Caribbean Sea aboard *Challenger*, Jeffrey sat alone in his cabin rereading his orders for the umpteenth time. The USS *Ohio* was nearby: *Challenger's* minisub, and the pair of minis from the other sub, were busy completing the transfer of SEALs and their gear.

Since reboarding *Challenger* off Norfolk, Jeffrey had decided to set the proper tone from the start. As much as possible, he intended to delegate. In this, his second deployment as *Challenger's* captain, with no *acting* in front of *captain* to limit or excuse his role, his hands-on style of leadership needed to change. He simply had to let go of the day-to-day nitty-gritty, as familiar and reassuring as it might be, or he'd be overwhelmed. There was just too much else for him to think about, on a higher level. He had to roll his sleeves back down, button the shirt cuffs nice and tight—and let his officers be the ones to plunge into details.

So far, this new tone of leadership was working well. People seemed to appreciate the increased trust he was placing in them. At the moment, Lieutenant Sessions, the navigator, was officer of the deck in the control room, and had the conn. Lieutenant Commander Bell, the executive officer, was overseeing *Challenger*'s end of the underwater rendezvous.

Jeffrey took a deep breath to relax. He smiled to himself. This little corner of the eastern Caribbean Sea—hard by the Lesser Antilles just west of Guadeloupe—was crowded. *One ceramic-hulled fast-attack sub. One big boomer-turned-SSGN. Three Advanced SEAL Deliver System minisubs at once . . . This has to be some kind of record.*

All the islands of the Caribbean, Jeffrey knew, from Cuba and Jamaica down to Trinidad and Tobago, were the exposed tops of huge mountains that jutted steeply out of water more than fifteen thousand feet deep. For the rendezvous, *Challenger* needed to hover shallow, to respect the diving limits of the steel-hulled *Ohio* and minis. Jeffrey was eager to be on his way, but wasn't terribly nervous about an enemy attack: with Puerto Rico to his north, and ally Venezuela to his south, with Cuba officially neutral but rabidly anti-Axis, these were friendly waters. The Lesser and Greater Antilles helped bar entry by hostile submarines. The local area was regularly swept for mines.

Jeffrey was far more concerned about the bigger picture of his orders. Alone in his stateroom, he envied his officers and men. They could focus on specific tasks in the here and now, difficult as they might be. This would give them a sense of purpose and shared camaraderie, and occupy their thoughts in a positive way. On Jeffrey's shoulders, and Jeffrey's alone, rested the far larger burden: that his superiors had guessed right, that the engineers and scientists were more than just starry-eyed tinkerers—and that *Challenger* would get where she needed to be to set up Orpheus, and do what she needed to do while using the secret device's help, before it was too late. For all the plans and preparation, for all everyone's efforts and well-meaning aid back on shore, Jeffrey could still be caught fantastically out of position, and out of range.

Captain Fuller knew that all through history, naval battles and even entire wars sometimes hinged on which ships or squadrons were in the right or wrong place at a single, un-forgiving moment in time.

———————

The SEAL team leader, newly arrived on *Challenger,* came to Jeffrey's cabin to report aboard and introduce himself. The two men hit it off in a big way on sight. Something about the dark-skinned Brazilian American, with his lively eyes, ready smile, and confident, bone-crushing handshake, made Jeffrey feel less worried about the future.

"I'll show you yours if you show me mine," Felix Estabo joked.

Jeffrey laughed. In private, they were comparing war stories from their time in the SEALs, and talking about their wounds.

"Forget it," Jeffrey said, and started to crack up completely; Felix had exactly the sick sense of humor that he himself enjoyed. "An AK-forty-seven round through the bone of my left thigh. You'll just have to take my word for it." Jeffrey gestured at the door into the head he shared with the XO's stateroom. "Privilege of rank, Lieutenant, so you won't be catching glimpses in my shower, either . . . Even if you *were* a master chief this morning, and even if master chiefs *do* secretly outrank captains."

And this was another reason Jeffrey liked Felix a lot: the SEAL was a very down-to-earth and practical man, who knew how to work the system and get things done. He was career navy, just like Jeffrey. At different times, they'd been through the same SEAL training and testing: they shared a lot of common ground. Plus, Felix was outside the strict chain of command of Jeffrey's vessel, so they both could afford to be a bit informal while alone.

Felix stroked the scar down his own face. "You're just jealous, Skipper. *This* thing"—he pointed to the scar—"was one heck of a chick magnet back in high school."

Jeffrey was surprised. "That one's not from a German bayonet?"

"Nope. Miami gang thugs jumped me when I was fifteen. I wandered into the wrong neighborhood after dark."

"You're lucky you lived to talk about it."

"Well, let's say they were drunk or stoned or both, and I was neither, and they kept falling over each other to draw first blood. Besides, I was very motivated. They just thought it was cool to mug or cut up a Latino kid. I was fighting to survive."

"How many of them were there?"

"Five. Fortunately they only had knives."

"So what did you do? Run?"

"Nope. Before I really saw them they got me cornered in this alley."

"Then what?"

"Backed up to cover my rear, grabbed a garbage can lid as a shield, picked up a whiskey bottle and broke it, and let them come at me."

"And you were what, fifteen? Weren't you scared?"

"Captain, frankly I just did what I had to do. I'm sure you've been there."

"To myself I call that the warrior gene."

"Anyway, somebody in one of the buildings called the cops, and by the time they got there I'd taken one bad cut to my face, and I put three of my 'assailants'—that's what the policemen called them—in the hospital."

"With?"

"Lemme see. One badly broken kneecap. One sucking puncture wound to the chest. And one, shall we say, very severe impact to the groinal area."

"You sound like you *enjoyed* the whole business."

"Looking back, sort of, yeah. I guess you could say I found my calling that night. The cops, you know, they tried to convince me to do the Police Academy after high school. I think they liked my moves. They were great guys, don't get me wrong, Captain. But I was on the swim team, I really liked being around the water. So it was a no-brainer, to join the navy when the time came, then put in for the SEALs. And lo and behold, here I am, Lieutenant Felix Estabo, former master chief, suddenly an officer and a gentleman."

Someone knocked.

"Come in."

A young messenger entered. Like many of the crew, he wore a blue, flame-retardant cotton jumpsuit with a zipper up the front and his name embroidered on a patch on one side of his chest. Although the other side lacked the silver dolphins qualified enlisted men wore—he was still fairly new to the ship, and to submarines—his jumpsuit did have the ribbon for the Presidential Unit Citation. That had been Bell's idea, for everyone to wear theirs, to strengthen group cohesion and morale.

"The XO said you ought to have this immediately, sir." He gave Jeffrey an envelope. "The *Ohio* grabbed it for us off the broadcast, the last time they raised their satellite mast."

"Okay," Jeffrey said. "Thanks." The messenger left and shut the door; Jeffrey appreciated help from *Ohio*—to receive high-baud-rate signals, a sub had to raise a satellite dish on a mast above the surface, breaking stealth.

"What is it?" Felix said.

Jeffrey opened the envelope. He read. Attached to the message text was a download of a photograph.

Jeffrey made eye contact with Felix. "It's confirmed the *von Scheer* is loose in the Atlantic."

"How do you know?"

"The message doesn't say. They wouldn't, for security, in case of signals intercept by the enemy. But from this"—he held up the message papers—"it's quite definite the *von Scheer* broke through past the UK more than two days ago."

Felix frowned. "That means they could be almost anywhere."

"There's a postscript for me personally with this," Jeffrey said. "From commander, U.S. Atlantic Fleet."

"*Really?* A four-star, huh? What's the postscript say?"

"Literally, 'Good luck, and don't screw it up.'"

"Four-stars talk that way?"

"It's sort of a private reference, to when he and I spoke one-on-one in Norfolk. And basically yes, Admiral Hodgkiss can talk that way."

"What's that picture with it?"

Jeffrey took the hard-copy photograph, and taped it to the wall of his cabin, next to the picture of his folks. "*That* is the commanding officer of the *Admiral von Scheer*."

The picture was obviously cropped and enlarged, from a group portrait probably taken before the war. It showed a man in German naval uniform, of average height, a bit overweight, with the beginnings of a receding hairline. He looked modest, even-tempered, intelligent. His features were undistinguished, not especially handsome or dashing; he even seemed a little shy.

Felix got up and studied the photo. "How do they know he's the one?"

"Again, it doesn't say. You and I can guess. Reports from moles, message traffic decrypts, collated with file photos or old news clippings, things like that."

"In other words, use my imagination."

"Yeah. But this message says the information is good. Rated A-one, completely reliable and confirmed by multiple sources."

Jeffrey pursed his lips as he finished the message.

"What's the matter?" Felix said.

"I know this guy."

"Well? A NATO combined assignment or something?"

Jeffrey turned and stared at the picture. "No, not like that. I mean I've met him in battle before."

Felix hesitated. "Is he good?"

"He's still alive. That says a lot."

"You don't seem happy, Captain."

"I'm not. If I know him, that means he knows *me*. My tactical style, my strengths, weaknesses, how I like to fight."

"I guess that's not good news. . . . You think the Germans know you're in command of *Challenger*?"

"After all the publicity over my Medal?" Jeffrey snapped bitterly. "How *couldn't* they?"

"Sorry, sir. Just asking."

"*I'm* sorry, Felix."

Jeffrey stared at the picture again, long and hard. He tried to read the eyes that seemed to be peering back at him. "His name is supposed to be Ernst Beck. He was the first watch officer, last time. Naval intell knows hardly anything about him."

"The exec?"

Jeffrey nodded. "Just that he's married, with two kids . . . Plus whatever I can piece together from when I clashed with his ship before Christmas."

Jeffrey tapped the face of the *von Scheer*'s captain and took a very deep breath. "Simply put, Felix-the-ex-master-chief, our job is to kill Ernst Beck before he kills me."

CHAPTER 13

fter sneaking through the teeth of Allied defenses in the G-I-UK Gap, Beck's ship and the two Russians steamed southwest, submerged, past Ireland. The Republic of Ireland, neutral in World War II, was a staunch friend of the U.S. and UK in the present crisis. Ireland's flotilla of coastal patrol craft were a constant thorn in Ernst Beck's side, until he left them behind. The noise signatures of other enemy ships and planes and sonobuoys the *von Scheer* crept past echoed within his head. The transit beyond the British Isles had been a test of resolve and fortitude for everyone in Beck's crew.

Then, while running shallow under the Russian fast-attacks, Beck had received an intelligence download, through *von Scheer*'s on-hull very-low-frequency underwater antenna: HMS *Dreadnought* was somewhere north of Iceland, and USS *Challenger* was stuck in dry dock in her Connecticut home port.

The same download told him that the relief convoy from the U.S. to Central Africa had set sail, at about the same time *von Scheer* and the Russians rounded North Cape. *Sooner than I'd hoped. Now every hour counts. I'll have to hurry.*

At a prearranged point, over the very deep Porcupine Plain—between Europe and the Mid-Atlantic Ridge—*von Scheer* and the Sierra IIs parted company. The Russians turned toward Halifax and New England on some mission of their own. Spying? Trying to trail real U.S. boomers? Maintaining a forward presence just in case, or for show? Beck had no idea.

He did hope that if—make that *when*—the Allies saw through the deception, they'd go chasing after the Russians, on the theory that the *von Scheer* would still be close.

Beck knew the *von Scheer* was by no means safe from attack, even then. Allied forces hunted for her everywhere. He kept his ship at battle stations, rigged for ultraquiet. The men were released to eat or use the head a few at a time. Far enough from land to have a clear conscience, Beck ordered deep-capable Sea Lion nuclear torpedo warheads armed, ready for anything.

It was time to substitute one source of mind-twisting stress for another. But within her design envelope, going deep meant greater sanctuary for any sub that craved the defensive, wanting to hide. In measured stages, Beck carefully took his ship into the concealing bottom terrain, almost five thousand meters down, close to the *von Scheer's* crush depth. All present in the Zentrale gritted their teeth, hoping and praying grimly that nothing in the hull or internal sea pipes would give way.

Once he was sure his command had suffered no engineering problems or flaws on the nerve-racking dive—building to a pressure of five thousand metric tons per square meter of hull—Beck passed the deck and conn to one of his officers. Stissinger could get some rest, but for the sub's captain it was time to deal with yet another form of stress.

———

Beck asked von Loringhoven to meet with him in his cabin. Behind closed doors, he and the diplomat had the confrontation Beck now knew had been inevitable. Von Loringhoven tried to evade the real issues and insisted that Beck open the next layer of his sealed orders.

Beck shook his head slowly and firmly. "Herr Baron, my instructions are to provide you with every assistance, but only as appropriate to the safety and combat readiness of my vessel. I can only continue to tolerate your presence on my ship under certain conditions." He drew on his own anger, and on the prestige of the Knight's Cross that hung around his neck, to stand up to the aristocrat passenger.

He almost tripped into thin air when von Loringhoven answered with modest submission.

"Forgive my impertinence in your control room, Captain. I think that lack of sleep has caused me to become a rather poor listener."

Beck recovered quickly, saving face. He suspected the diplomat had just pulled some verbal jujitsu: letting Beck's own annoyance—meeting no resistance—throw himself off balance.

Now Beck was *really* annoyed: von Loringhoven showed he had known exactly what misbehavior the captain was going to unload on him about.

"Baron, we are not at some embassy or diplomatic ball. We are at sea on a naval warship, and we are at war! Do not play your word games with *me*. When I give you instructions, whether to be quiet in the Zentrale or to stand on your head and sing Christmas carols, you will from now on show me instant, unquestioning obedience!"

Von Loringhoven rubbed his eyes. Beck saw his jaw lock subtly, not with aggression, but to stifle a yawn of fatigue. "I apologize, Captain."

"*Do* you? I am serving you formal notice right now, Baron, that any further attempts at conversational rugby with me will undermine your credibility completely! I do not have the time or the patience to coddle your ego any further. And I will *not* permit you to continue to treat this ship as some sort of plaything at your personal disposal. *Is that clear?*"

"Yes, Captain. Yes. Your message is clear."

"And I order you to get some proper sleep at once."

"Soon, yes."

"Anyone who stays awake for days at a time becomes dysfunctional. *Anyone.* You are turning into a safety hazard, a liability, and this cannot be permitted to go on."

Von Loringhoven nodded. "I promise to sleep at least six hours each day. I had so much work to catch up on, so much to digest and visualize and rehearse. You will understand better, I think, Captain, as we proceed with our mission."

"Why do I feel like I'm talking to a recalcitrant child? Don't tease or mock me, Baron. I may seem a simple sailor to you, but for a landsman to underestimate an undersea battleship's commander can be a fatal error in judgment. *Fatal.* I'm warning you for the only time."

Von Loringhoven looked down at the floor. He seemed contrite and cowed. Beck wondered how sincere any of this was, and how long it would last. Beck was a man of honor, and never gave his word lightly; he would keep a solemn promise made or oath taken, unto death. He wondered if any diplomat or *any* civilian could understand what such commitment meant.

"Now, it is time to open the next phase of my orders. And I know what you're thinking, that you already know what they say. Your knowledge does not impress me. To flaunt it is nothing but small-minded disrespect. *Understood?*"

"Perfectly so, Captain."

"Very well. Are you ready?"

Von Loringhoven nodded.

Beck went to his safe and removed the envelope. He returned to his desk and sat facing von Loringhoven.

Opening the outer seal of the remaining package of nested envelopes, he began to read. The instructions told him to have the kampfschwimmer team leader present, the battle-swimmer commando who'd embarked with his men and equipment back in Norway before the sabotage fire.

Beck palmed his intercom mike and sent a messenger to get the kampfschwimmer lieutenant from his sleeping-and-working area aft in the missile compartment.

Then he read further, and his jaw dropped.

He looked up at von Loringhoven in amazement, feeling a mix of awe and revulsion. All he could think to say was, *"Mein Gott."* My God.

Von Loringhoven smiled. The smile, for once, conveyed no trace of a sneer or smirk.

"But this will delay our attack on the convoy," Beck said.

"Not by long, Captain. All in good time."

Someone knocked.

Beck projected his voice. *"Come."*

The kampfschwimmer lieutenant entered. He was tall, alert, and very fit. He braced respectfully to attention.

Beck held up the diagram printed in the latest orders. "I don't believe this. Show me."

The kampfschwimmer turned around and pulled up his shirt and undershirt.

In the small of the man's back, implanted into the skin on each side of his spine, were two small white plastic surgical fittings with plugs. Intravenous ports. *Gills.*

CHAPTER 14

Jeffrey sat in the captain's place, at the head of the ward-room table. The dinner dishes were cleared, though coffee service remained on the table. Several people, himself included, were enjoying another cup. Felix, as a guest, sat on his right. Bell was on his left. Sessions was in the control room, as officer of the deck.

Lieutenant Milgrom started the formal briefing. She seemed intense, but not overtired as Jeffrey felt: since Ilse Reebeck wasn't on the ship to share a stateroom with Milgrom, Bell had decided that she should use the VIP rack in the XO's cabin. Milgrom and Bell arranged their schedules to sleep at different times; no one would look askance, and freeing up the three-man officers' stateroom that Ilse and Kathy had been using allowed three male officers to get their regular quarters back. Bell's next administrative nightmare would be finding places for sixteen SEALs to sleep, with the torpedo room already completely crammed with weapons and part of *Challenger*'s junior enlisted crew hot-racking—sharing bunks—as it was.

Milgrom's laptop was wired to the big flat-screen TV on

the wall of the wardroom, on the opposite bulkhead from Jeffrey's chair. She touched her keyboard, and a briefing slide came up on the screen.

"Lord," Jeffrey said, "it looks like all the veins on someone's retina." *A retina the size of the Atlantic Ocean.*

"In a sense," Milgrom said, "that's precisely the point. Orpheus lets us *see* out to vast distances, like a gigantic eye."

"And in the middle, where all the veins come together like where the optic nerve would be, that's *us?*"

"Precisely, Captain. The Orpheus connections and consoles, set up with help from the SEALs."

"Okay. Go on." Jeffrey was being intentionally standoffish today, not to Milgrom in particular but to all his officers. By playing devil's advocate, making them work to sell him on the idea of Orpheus, he'd make sure they got a better handle on it and did a better job with it in combat.

"That seeming 'retinal scan' was the map of the relevant portion of the network of transoceanic undersea telephone cables, the old electrical ones. Mostly abandoned, most of them cut near one shore or the other." Milgrom brought another slide on the screen. "This diagram shows the basic concepts behind how Orpheus picks up signals."

Jeffrey looked at the picture. The physics were familiar enough from all his technical training.

"Point one," Milgrom said, "the earth's magnetic field isn't shielded by seawater. It penetrates the ocean's deepest depths."

Jeffrey nodded.

"Point two, an electrically conductive material, moving through the lines of force of any magnetic field, produces an electric current."

"Which is exactly how a generator works," Jeffrey threw in.

"Point three, seawater is highly conductive."

"Yup." *That's one more thing that makes being on a ship or sub so dangerous. The hazard of lethal electric shock, when you mix salt water and steel with heavy voltages, is high.*

"Next," Milgrom said, "a submarine's hull form, moving through the sea, creates an internal wave in the water. The fluid around the bow of the hull is forced up and down in a characteristic, predictable manner."

"I'm with you so far," Jeffrey said, mostly to be polite and keep the briefing moving.

"These principles, brought together, are the basis of Orpheus. When a submerged submarine advances through the ocean, the seawater that the bow dome pushes out of the way moves up and down in the earth's magnetic field. This creates electrical currents. There is no way to prevent or mask these telltale currents. The submarine's quieting does it no good. Attempts at using sonar layers or terrain masking to hide from the SOSUS hydrophones do it no good."

"That part isn't new," Jeffrey said rhetorically. "The idea was looked at during the Cold War as a way to localize and track enemy subs non-acoustically. The result, unless I missed something, was zilch."

Milgrom went on, unfazed. "The Cold War era did not have ceramic-hulled nuclear submarines, Captain. The problem with this detection method in the first thousand feet or so of the water column is confusion by environmental noise—signal clutter, in other words—from waves, passing whales, and thermal downwashes and such. That, plus the problem of how to have a platform, to cast a net as it were, with a large and steady search area that an enemy submarine cannot intentionally maneuver to avoid."

"Granted." A platform meant a ship or plane or sub.

"A ceramic-hulled submarine, however, running at ten or fifteen thousand feet, is far enough away from surface waves and large biologics to avoid that problematic signal-to-noise ratio. At the same time, said deep-diving submarine is close to the fixed, preexisting network of undersea electrical cables stretching from continent to continent all along the ocean's bed. When the submarine passes over such a cable, the electrical current caused by the hull pushing its way through the water will, by induction, generate a small and subtle sympathetic current in the cable. That sympathetic current, induced point-blank by the passing submarine, will flow along the entire length of the cable, at the speed of light. . . . The key to Orpheus is to harness this phenomenon."

"By patching into the cables," Jeffrey stated, "where a bunch of them crisscross."

"That's where my men and their equipment come in," Felix said. "We create the crucial node, the observation post the enemy can't sneak past or avoid."

Milgrom brought up another slide. "Lieutenant Estabo?"

Felix stood. "This nice little artist's conception gives you the layout. Because parts of the cable hookups involve some very fine manual work, our hardwired anchor station needs to be in shallow water, *here*." He pointed at a place beside a craggy island on the slide. "Shallow because of limitations on humans making repeated dives with the scuba equipment we've got . . . The satellite dish needs to be high and dry and stable, to get a good continuous lock on the geosynchronous commo bird." He pointed to the schematic picture again, where a big dish sat on the island, aimed at a satellite in space. "The minisub, *here*, brings the divers and equipment to the cable anchor point and to the islet, and strings the transducer line out to deep water. That line lets the ground station, and *Challenger*, and the mini all talk by covert acoustics." Transducers were a type of underwater microphone.

Jeffrey nodded.

Felix continued. "Then the mini sits over the cable-hookup anchor station, which is now connected to all the old phone cables, all underwater. More new wires of our own run from the anchor station sitting on the bottom to the Orpheus consoles inside the mini. Other wires run from the mini up to the beach on the islet and the satellite dish that talks to Norfolk. And then there's the transducer line, also from the mini."

"So the minisub is like a spider in its web," Jeffrey said.

"Or like a fly caught in the web. Depends on your point of view, sir." Felix shrugged. "Anyway, all this gets us what we want, without *Challenger or* the mini needing to raise an antenna mast for hours on end and give themselves away. My team will be exposed on land, sure, but we earn our daily bread by taking such risks. If we could do everything from a rubber boat or raft instead, we would. But small boats are just too unstable. We need solid ground to emplace that satellite dish and supporting equipment. . . . Notice that *Challenger* herself is not tied down by any physical linkages, so she remains fully mobile and stealthy and tactically flexible." Felix sat.

"How long will you and your men need?" Jeffrey asked. "To make the cable hookups and establish the ground relay station and everything?"

"Working in shifts around the clock," Felix said, "once we get there, about twenty-four hours."

"And the place we're heading to is neutral territory."

"Also correct," Felix said. "Won't be the first time, for me. If anyone asks, we're Brazilian. Not that there'd be a soul there who would ask."

"Okay, thanks," Jeffrey said.

Milgrom cleared her throat and resumed. "Of course, powerful software is needed to sort out and interpret these subtle electrical clues to the enemy submarine's passage. The Orpheus consoles have microchips optimally designed for the particular type of maths and signal-processing required. In theory, it will be possible to tell the *von Scheer*'s exact location along the cable, as well as her depth and course and speed, from the shape and the decay rate of the internal electrical waves induced, even if she's many hundred miles away from the Orpheus station. This data would let us calculate an intercept course and sneak up on *von Scheer* with surprise."

"In theory," Jeffrey said.

"As Lieutenant Estabo already anticipated in his discussion of the hardware layout, sir, this is why we need the land-based portion of the equipment. A voice-and-data satellite relay to Norfolk, whose supercomputers may catch whiffs of signal our portable consoles miss, to feed such information back to us. And for Atlantic Fleet to pass us any other detections made on *von Scheer,* from elsewhere, to redirect *Challenger* if need be."

"*If* we can get there in time," Jeffrey said a bit sourly.

"If not," Milgrom said, "it is my understanding that other escort platforms will be tasked to prosecute the contact, just as they would be sent after any Orpheus contacts we detect too far beyond our own effective interception range. Again, that's why we need the satellite communications dish."

"What other escort platforms? We absolutely require a ceramic-hulled sub if we're to stand an adequate chance of killing *von Scheer. Dreadnought* is way up by Greenland last I heard." HMS *Dreadnought* was the only Allied ceramic-hulled sub besides *Challenger.* "I doubt she can get between *von Scheer* and the convoy at this point, given the geography and distances involved. *Von Scheer* could leap out of the Mid-Atlantic Ridge terrain anywhere from east of Maine to east of Miami for all we know."

"Understood, Captain. The convoy routing plan accounts for that."

"*How?*" Jeffrey already knew the supposed, official answer; he worried that that answer was too pat.

"Sir"—the assistant navigator broke in—"the convoy is avoiding steaming over the Mid-Atlantic Ridge until they reach the Atlantic Narrows, where the ridge can't be avoided. . . . Lieutenant?"

Milgrom brought up a slide that plotted the convoy's path versus sea-bottom topography. The assistant navigator used it to elaborate his point.

"Berlin can read the same terrain maps we can," Jeffrey responded. "Who says they'll do what we expect them to do? Maybe the *von Scheer* won't hide in the ridge. Maybe she'll sneak out over one of the North Atlantic abyssal plains and savage the convoy from there."

"That's where our other platforms come in," Milgrom repeated.

"*What* other platforms?" Jeffrey pressed. *The idea of a formal briefing is to cover every conceivable base and not hold back from tough questions.*

"Antisubmarine aircraft, surface ships, and steel-hulled fast-attack submarines."

"All of which might not be decisive enough against a ceramic-hulled SSGN hiding three miles down. We're in a situation where 'might not' could spell disaster."

"Yes, sir," Milgrom said reluctantly.

Jeffrey relented. The U.S. and UK had fewer than sixty nuclear-powered fast-attack subs left in commission between them, because of budget cuts and then war losses—and after nine months of constant hard fighting, many of these were in dry dock for repairs, or at sea but barely battleworthy. With heavy worldwide commitments, the submarine forces were spread too thin. Each country could afford to build only one ceramic-hulled submarine, because of the huge costs. But all this certainly wasn't Milgrom's fault.

"What other kinds of detections would Norfolk relay us?"

"Acoustic, or magnetic anomaly, or . . . or *von Scheer*'s missile launches."

There was a long and uncomfortable silence.

Jeffrey looked around the room, to take the pressure off Milgrom and pass it equally among his people. "We better all hope the higher-ups guessed right, about where we and the SEALs are supposed to set up our ambush location."

"That's the point, sir," Bell said. "You just need to look at a chart. Because of the layout of shorelines versus ocean, and the layout of all the old phone cables, we're being sent to the one spot in the whole hemisphere that really *is* the optic nerve, the point of maximum searching-and-tactical focus."

Jeffrey grunted. He wished he could share Bell's upbeat take. *But what's the alternative? Putter around half blind and half deaf in the Mid-Atlantic Ridge, six thousand miles between Central Africa and Greenland, and hope I get lucky? Hope I meet the* von Scheer *soon enough in that gi-*

gantic undersea mountain range, and I get off the first, deci-
sive shots . . . before the convoy meets the von Scheer? *. . .*
At least Orpheus gives us a fighting chance.

Milgrom and the assistant navigator presented their plan
for getting from the Caribbean to the Orpheus point with an
optimum balance of speed versus stealth. Jeffrey approved.
Bell outlined the enemy threats that *Challenger* might meet
en route. Jeffrey nodded cautiously.

"Meeting's adjourned," Jeffrey said. Everyone waited for
him to stand up.

Jeffrey stood, and walked to the screen on the bulkhead,
still showing the assistant navigator's final slide. He contem-
plated *Challenger*'s next destination, that lonely, tiny dot of
land almost lost in the Atlantic Narrows. He reread the label
next to the dot, on the nautical chart on the screen:

THE ST. PETER AND ST. PAUL ROCKS.

CHAPTER 15

Beck sat at his command workstation in the Zentrale. Stissinger sat to his right. Von Loringhoven stood between them again, watching over their shoulders. The control room was crowded and hushed. Dim red lighting emphasized that the ship was still at battle stations and ultraquiet. Depth gauges around the control room, and windowed on Beck's console screen, read 4,800 meters.

The *von Scheer* was so deep that the deck of the Zentrale was actually warped from the pressure squashing against the outer hull. Extra damage-control parties were stationed around the ship. Beck hoped they wouldn't be needed. At this depth, five thousand meters—three miles—down, the slightest flooding would be catastrophic. If a single weld or valve joint failed anywhere that was exposed to full sea pressure, the ocean would blast in with a force beyond comprehension. The noise would be painfully loud, like artillery fire. The solid jet of water could instantly cut a man in half. It would ricochet everywhere, making the source of flooding impossible to find. Above the quickly rising water in the bilges and then on the decks, the air would become an atomized mist of stinging, blinding seawater. The flooding would drive the internal atmospheric pressure up very fast, making the air turn hot—burning hot—and the steaming salty mist would short out critical electric equipment. Men would die in horrible ways as the *von Scheer* herself was drowned and crushed from within.

Those thoughts were bad enough. The reality of what Ernst Beck was seeing was, in some ways, worse.

The ship was at the exact location specified in his orders, verified by the inertial navigation plot. The sonarmen and weapons technicians were all on high alert. Two remote-controlled off-board probes, designed to work at such depths, had already scouted the general area for any lurking threats.

At the moment, a kampfschwimmer chief and enlisted man were working at a console at the rear of the Zentrale, intensely focused on their task.

Video imagery was shown on the control room's main display screens. Some of the images came from active laser line-scan cameras outside the ship. The images were crisp and sharp, at least within the effective range of the laser beams. Other pictures came from passive image-intensification cameras. Those views were murky, diffuse, even where floodlights pierced the darkness; backscatter glowed off floating silt. The live feeds all came in through fiber-optic tethers.

Ernst Beck saw the seafloor, a short distance beneath the *von Scheer*. The ship was holding perfectly steady as the pilot and copilot busily used the small auxiliary thrusters fore and aft to counteract the sluggish bottom current. The bottom at this location was a mix of clay ooze, washed down off dry land in Europe, and scattered basalt boulders. The boulders were jagged and rough, because at this depth there'd been no polishing by Ice Age glaciers, no weathering by wind or waves, no cycle of freezing and thawing. The water temperature was constant at four degrees Celsius—just above freezing. The terrain rose gradually toward the west. In the far distance soared the central peaks of the endless

Mid-Atlantic Ridge, magma hardened as it emerged from the earth over eons.

On the imagery projected from outside, Beck saw bioluminescent glows and flashes from clouds of microbes and hideous fish. Over the sonar speakers, he heard the clickety-clack and popping of deep-sea shrimp.

This water was transgressed, defiled, by man. Near the *von Scheer,* settled on the bottom, sat the wreck of a U.S. Navy destroyer. Between the *von Scheer* and the wreck, divers walked—impossibly—on the bottom. Two of them turned to the cameras that other men carried. Through their faceplates, Beck recognized one as the kampfschwimmer lieutenant in command.

As Beck watched, they gave a quick thumbs-up, then continued toward the sunken destroyer, walking freely on the seafloor five kilometers down.

———

The six kampfschwimmer divers wore backpacks, hooked up to their intravenous ports—those implants Beck had thought of as gills. Inside their full-body diving clothes and helmets that looked like spacesuits, Beck's briefing papers had told him, they breathed a saline solution suffused with oxygen. They breathed the liquid as if they were breathing air.

"I'm informed that once you get used to it," von Loring-hoven said, "breathing the fluid seems natural."

"It must be strange at first," Beck said.

"These kampfschwimmer are well trained. The reason their suits are soft is so the fluid, and their whole bodies, can equalize to ambient sea pressure. Even the best mixed-gas rigs would kill a man past the first thousand meters."

"I know."

"Breathing the fluid isn't new. Lab mice, and men, did it fifty years ago. You just can't do it for long, because there's no way to get the carbon dioxide out of the lungs. It's not the lack of oxygen that's the problem. It's the buildup of carbon dioxide in the body that would be fatal in minutes—in seconds, at this great depth."

"Someone obviously solved that problem."

Von Loringhoven nodded. "The new part is the backpacks. They include a form of dialysis apparatus. The carbon dioxide is removed directly from the blood, much as other wastes would be deleted for a hospital patient suffering from kidney failure."

"It sounds rather dangerous," Beck said.

"The descent under pressure can be done surprisingly quickly, as you saw. The decompression period is long, as you'd imagine, several days. That's why the kampfschwimmer brought those individual pressure capsules. Once they return they'll stay inside the capsules, breathing saline and having body wastes dialyzed for quite some time. . . . And that's the other advantage of the backpacks. With the intravenous hookups they like to call gills, the men can be fed nutrients continually while they work. This gives them tremendous endurance."

"I suppose it's hard to eat underwater when you're breathing through a scuba mouthpiece."

"The thin plutonium lining of their suits keeps them nice and warm, no matter how lengthy their toils. It's quite safe, as long as a suit doesn't tear and someone actually ingests plutonium. That's one reason the suits are lined with multiple layers of Kevlar."

"I have to insist on a thorough radiological survey before the men come back into my ship."

"Of course. It's standard procedure."

"How often has this been done before?"

"You mean operationally, in a war zone?"

"Yes."

"I'm not sure. It's all top secret, need-to-know. The Allies haven't the slightest idea we possess this capability."

———

"Oh, Jesus," someone said.

"Easy," Stissinger cautioned the man.

Beck felt repugnance too. The "dialysis divers," trailing tethers for their cameras and other equipment, had reached the sunk destroyer. The wreck was recent. One of the line-scan cameras showed the corpse of an American sailor, his lower body trapped in mangled wreckage. *Things* like giant worms crawled on the corpse, feeding. Bone on the skull was already exposed.

"Do we have to see this?" Beck asked. "Can't they just get on with it?"

"Feeling guilty?" von Loringhoven said. "The records show you sank this ship on your last patrol."

"I suspected as much." Beck saw more of the destroyer as the divers worked their way around and over the wreckage.

"You can understand now why this can't be done by a robotic sub, using grapnels. We need human judgment, in real time, and practiced manual skills on the spot."

The destroyer lay on her starboard side. Beck watched as the divers avoided the ragged stump of her mast. She was an *Arleigh Burke*–class vessel, and huge—as long as the *von Scheer*—and had a wide beam for a destroyer; the top of the hulk, her port side, rose almost twenty meters off the ocean floor amidships. The twisted remnants of her four exhaust stacks, in two pairs surrounded by big air intakes for the gas-turbine propulsion plant, were aimed at the divers' cameras. They seemed to be aimed at Beck, as if they were saying, *You did this to us. You.*

There was a large debris field in the foreground. Fragments of the ship's superstructure littered the bottom. Unnamable objects spilled from fractures in her hull and cracks in her decks. As the dialysis divers searched and inspected, and their cameras panned around in the freezing blackness, Beck saw more corpses. They were much too fresh to be fully decomposed, for their bones to have dissolved from the pressure. The sight of seamen burned, mutilated, crushed, with tatters of clothing and pieces of half-eaten flesh waving at him in the bottom current, was profoundly disturbing to the captain. As loose and dangling equipment jangled in the half-knot current, noises came over the sonar speakers, like the sound of ghosts dragging chains.

Not one man in the control room said a word, except for the two kampfschwimmer at their console behind Beck. They spoke to the diver team, who responded by typing on keypads worn on their chests. Some of the men in Beck's crew seemed grateful that their job required them to stare at their sonar screens or threat-tracking plots, forcing them to avert their eyes from the tomb, the hallowed ground, that the divers were going to plunder. Sailors were sailors, whatever their nation. Every man in the control room—and Beck assumed this included von Loringhoven—knew how easily the corpses might have been *them*.

From the way her mast stump and stacks were bent, and the destruction of the bridge superstructure, Beck judged that the destroyer had taken a near miss from an airburst off her port bow, caused by an atomic cruise missile. She seemed to have burned while sinking, but must have sunk quickly, because the fires were snuffed before her main magazines could explode. The fires topside had been fierce while they lasted: Beck saw aluminum melted and fused. Paint was blistered or totally charred. She probably tumbled underwater before striking the bottom—the hard impact had made a crater in the seafloor muck. It strewed debris in a wide area, splitting her seams along many frames.

This was fortunate, because the antisubmarine torpedo launchers on her external decks were all smashed. To find what they were looking for, the divers had to go inside the hulk. The pictures on the Zentrale screens seemed to jiggle and jump around; the imagery would spin, then focus on something, then spin or bounce to focus on something else.

Beck watched in morbid fascination as the divers began to search the ordnance-handling areas, ammunition hoists, and magazines. Much was twisted beyond recognition, and space to work in was tight. Shapeless tangles of multicol-

ored pipes and wires and ladders, and sheet steel crumpled
like cardboard, formed jagged obstructions. Some voids
were filled with viscous pockets of buoyant, sticky engine
fuel, caught there after the hull tanks ruptured apart. Some
watertight doors were jammed hopelessly shut; others stood
gaping, burst wide open, with dogging bars sheared from
their bracket mounts by brutally destructive forces. Everywhere mud and silt drifted, along with flecks of insulation
and plastic, and the divers' helmet lights cast haunting shadows. To enter this terrible place, Beck thought, took great
courage.

Clearly the divers had reviewed the plans of this destroyer
class very thoroughly. They showed an impressive ability to
make sense of the mess that seemed to Beck incomprehensi-
ble. He wondered if the divers had practiced by studying
video of the damage to the USS *Cole,* a sister ship of this destroyer. Maybe their training had also included a briefing by
the Russians on how to work around and inside the carcass
of the *Kursk*—and her severed torpedo room.

At last the divers found what they were looking for: intact,
or mostly intact, American-made atomic torpedo warheads.
The cameras showed the team of divers working far inside
the hull, within what was left of one of the magazines. Two
divers stayed outside the wreck with one camera, as safety
monitors, and to make sure the cable feeds running into the
hulk weren't snagged. Using special tools, working slowly
and carefully, the four inside divers dismantled the American torpedoes, removing the warheads and placing them in
special, shielded carrying cases.

"They're looking for the ones in the best condition," von
Loringhoven said. "They're taking three, just in case."

"Just in case what?" Beck knew the wrecked ship's magazine was full of self-oxidizing weapon propellants, and
damaged high explosives too. The divers could potentially
set something off, causing a massive detonation that would
damage the *von Scheer.*

"We need samples, for intelligence purposes."

"Why aren't the divers going after crypto gear?"

"It's doubtful any survived in usable form."

"Our side hasn't salvaged Allied atomic warheads before?"

"We have, but I'm not privy to details. And I assume the Allies have salvaged some of ours."

Beck grunted. He hadn't thought of that. "So why are we grabbing more, with a relief convoy to Africa on the move? We seem to be taking considerable, and unnecessary, risks, at a most inappropriate moment. And we're wasting precious time by doing so."

"We need at least one warhead, of specifically American manufacture. It has to come from an antisubmarine torpedo so it's pressure-proof enough."

"Enough for what?"

"Enough to use the physics package . . . Ah, I see the divers are finished. They're starting back to the *von Scheer*'s air lock." One special air lock opened downward, through the bottom of the SSGN's hull, and had a winch for lifting personnel and cargo.

Beck didn't like the way von Loringhoven had just changed the subject. "To use the physics package for *what?*"

"Like I said, intelligence. Research. Berlin doesn't tell me everything."

Beck decided to play along, for now. The one thing he did know was that von Loringhoven was lying.

The kampfschwimmer dialysis divers were back inside the *von Scheer,* safely ensconced in their decompression capsules. Their plutonium-lined diving suits hadn't sprung any leaks. The three atomic torpedo warheads were now in the radiological containment area, within the kampfschwimmer working space in the missile compartment.

Beck sat in his cabin, feeling utterly exhausted. Von Loringhoven knocked from inside the bathroom they shared.

Beck rolled his eyes. "Come."

Von Loringhoven entered.

"I really wish you'd stop doing that," Beck said.

"I apologize again, Captain. I'm just beginning to grasp how many unwritten rules there are to proper etiquette aboard a submarine. You were right, of course, to tell me that I am not now in an embassy or at a diplomatic reception."

"Speaking of which, Baron, I am formally inviting you to dine with me and my officers in the wardroom tonight. . . . I'm sure security won't be compromised. If anything, by hiding from everyone and eating alone, you're only drawing the wrong sort of attention to yourself."

"Thank you, Captain. I would be honored to join you and your officers for dinner."

"Good. Now. I've been told by the kampfschwimmer chief that one of the warheads retrieved is in usable-enough condition that we can continue on our way."

"Excellent."

"It is thus time to open the next envelope with my orders."

Von Loringhoven nodded. "At your convenience, Captain."

Hmm. The guy does seem to be showing a little respect and humility now. Maybe there's hope for him after all.

Beck opened his safe and retrieved the latest envelope. Each time, the package grew thinner and lighter, but he could tell there were several more layers of sealed orders within orders.

Ernst Beck read. "Ach." He had to grin. "This is all nicely thought out. There's some risk, especially for the kampfschwimmer, but less than I expected for *von Scheer*."

"You see now why the Russians turned toward Nova Scotia. We want the Americans to think you're aiming to catch the convoy from behind, from the north."

Beck nodded. "And the strongest convoy defenses will be protecting their eastern flank, standing between the cargo ships and the hostile Euro-African coast as they head for the Congo pocket."

"Precisely. And to throw ourselves against the Americans' strongest defenses is foolish."

"And thus we cut ahead and attack from where they least expect and they're least prepared. From their *front,* from south of the convoy, and with accurate firing solutions from very long range . . . I want to check a nautical chart." Beck switched on his laptop, connected to the *von Scheer's* onboard fiber-optic local area network. "Look with me, Baron."

Von Loringhoven came around to Beck's side of the little fold-down desk.

"Right here is the place." Beck tapped a spot on the map with his light pen. "Of course, we still have details to work out, but we have several days to get there. . . . I suggest, Baron, that you and I both make up for our sleep deficit. I'll have a messenger fetch us a good meal now, then wake us both in time for dinner."

"Delightful."

Beck used his intercom to dial the wardroom pantry chief. They spoke briefly. Beck hung up.

"Fresh ham, hot carrots, also fresh, and freshly baked bread, for two, is on the way. Eat with me here, Baron."

"With pleasure."

"Excuse me for a moment while I speak to the einzvo." Beck stepped out of his cabin and walked the few paces to the Zentrale. The acting weapons officer had the deck, while Stissinger kept an eye on things. Beck approached Stissinger.

"Our guest has accepted the invitation to dine in the wardroom tonight." He touched the side of his nose, knowingly, and saw an answering sparkle in Stissinger's eyes.

"We'll make a good shipmate out of him yet, Captain."

Beck gave the weapons officer and navigator orders to get the *von Scheer* under way, toward the craggy, broken bottom terrain of the Mid-Atlantic Ridge: "Nap of seafloor cruising mode. Mean speed of advance twenty-five knots. Base course southwest until we reach the east side of the main ridge flank, then base course south. Maintain rig for ultraquiet."

Both men acknowledged; Stissinger calmly monitored their performance. Beck returned to his cabin. Von Loringhoven sat there patiently.

Beck started to clear the papers and computer from his desk. But first, he took one more look at the nautical chart on the laptop screen. "A clever stratagem," he said expansively, "and a good choice. A useless menace to navigation, hundreds of miles from land. A perfect place to set up a land-based satellite downlink station, and an undersea acoustic link to talk to us while we can hide. . . . My only trouble is the real estate belongs to a neutral country."

"Don't concern yourself," von Loringhoven said. "Efforts are under way that ought to remove that worry from your mind."

"Specifics?"

"Not yet."

"Funny, I somehow knew you'd say that." Both men chuckled, sharing a good laugh for the first time since they'd met.

Beck looked at the map a final time, examining their destination. "Desolate, unoccupied, a radioactive wasteland now. It's the last place I'd ever think to choose . . . which is probably exactly why Berlin chose it. And it *is* so centrally located." He turned off his computer just as two messmen arrived with the meal trays.

On both trays were two shot glasses filled with schnapps.

Beck raised the first glass. "To a successful voyage, and now to a nice long well-earned nap."

Von Loringhoven raised his glass. "To a successful voyage, and to more good work by our kampfschwimmer." He downed his schnapps in one gulp.

For a moment, Beck thought there was a soulless predatory look in the other man's eyes. It sent a chill up his spine, enough to ruin the feeling of warmth brought on by the schnapps.

Von Loringhoven raised his second glass. "To our destination, our ear to Berlin's sea-surveillance satellites, the St. Peter and St. Paul Rocks."

CHAPTER 16

Four days later, near the St. Peter and St. Paul Rocks, Jeffrey stood in the aisle in *Challenger*'s control room. A main display screen on the forward bulkhead, above COB's and Meltzer's ship-control stations, showed him and everyone else the big picture. *Challenger* lurked deep in the western foothills of the Mid-Atlantic Ridge, eleven thousand feet down. Farther west was the flat and open Ceara Plain, four thousand feet even deeper than that, off the northeast coast of Brazil. *Challenger*'s minisub lingered shallow, near the St. Peter and St. Paul Rocks. The mini was careful to keep a direct acoustic line of sight to Jeffrey's ship, southwest of the Rocks.

The two vessels communicated by covert undersea acoustic link, which transmitted voice or data by a series of digitized pulses. The pulses were incredibly short, at frequencies extremely high and changing thousands of times each second—so the likelihood of intercept by an enemy was very low. The range of the link was up to thirty nautical miles, depending on local oceanographic conditions.

Most of the Orpheus setup work was complete. Robotic undersea vehicles, launched from *Challenger* and controlled by the ship's technicians or by specialist SEALs in the mini-sub, had tapped into the undersea telephone cables. Thin wires from those taps were strung to a place by the Rocks, in sheltered water one hundred feet deep. SEAL divers had rigged those wires into an anchor and relay station, ready for use by men at Orpheus consoles in the minisub, and ready for linkage by fiber-optic to a satellite transceiver site that the SEALs would create on the Rocks.

"Captain," Lieutenant Milgrom reported, "Lieutenant Estabo is calling from the minisub. He indicates he's ready to transfer to the Rocks."

"Ask him how Orpheus is performing so far."

"Wait one, sir." She spoke into her microphone and listened on her headset. Classified signal-processing software encoded and decoded the two-way conversation and generated the sonar pulses *Challenger* sent to the minisub; the mini had identical software, though her sonar arrays were simpler and less powerful.

"Sir, his men are just now calibrating the consoles. Lieutenant Estabo prefers to establish the satellite link with Norfolk first, to double-check each other using raw incoming Orpheus data."

"Very well. Tell him to proceed."

Milgrom spoke into her mike, then signed off. To deliver Felix to the Rocks, the mini would have to move in closer, and the line of sight, the acoustic link, to *Challenger* would be blocked.

Jeffrey looked at the main display once more. Bell had the conn, and Jeffrey glanced over the man's shoulder at the tactical situation plot. Something just didn't add up.

"XO, Sonar, I want you both in my stateroom."

Officers traded places as Bell passed the conn to Lieutenant Sessions. One senior chief, the assistant navigator, took over for Sessions. Another senior chief, the sonar supervisor, sat in for Milgrom. Bell and Milgrom followed Jeffrey to his stateroom.

"What's the matter, Skipper?" Bell asked. He stood, because Jeffrey was standing. Milgrom stood too, and frowned, because Jeffrey was frowning.

"Sonar, when was the last time you heard a nuclear detonation in the North Atlantic?"

"Days, sir. We've heard hardly any since departing New London."

"And how long has the relief convoy been under way?"

"About a week," Bell said. "Pretty much the same as us."

"And where is the convoy right now?"

"Right now? Streaming down toward the Atlantic Narrows."

"We're just picking up traces of their signature, sir, on our wide-aperture arrays," Milgrom said.

"A week. Why haven't the U-boats attacked?"

Milgrom and Bell looked at each other. Bell spoke for both of them. "I guess we've all been wondering, Captain."

"And our latest intelligence download from Norfolk confirmed what our sonars have heard. Or haven't heard."

Milgrom and Bell nodded; when *Challenger* went shallow to launch the minisub with Felix and his men, Jeffrey had used his floating wire antenna to grab short text messages from headquarters. Jeffrey summarized what he'd been told then.

"The convoy escorts picked up a few false contacts, dropped high-explosive torpedoes or depth charges, and then nothing. No confirmed contacts, no confirmed kills . . . They blew up biologics by mistake, or bleary-eyed observers were just seeing things, or nervous sonar techs heard sounds that weren't there."

Milgrom and Bell nodded again, reluctantly.

"Don't you see what's happening?"

"Sir?"

"Atlantic Fleet's whole take on the shape of the battle has been all wrong. *The defensive tactics, the carrier and escort dispositions, everything, they've been all wrong.*"

Bell nodded.

Milgrom glanced at the XO. Her face turned grim. "The Axis have been one step ahead of us the entire time, haven't they, sir?"

Jeffrey looked into space and worked his jaw. "For a solid week the carrier battle groups and escorting ships and fast-attacks have been at general quarters almost nonstop. Their antisubmarine helos and aircraft have been flying patrols on high alert around the clock. Men and women will be exhausted, close to dropping on their feet, from lack of sleep and interrupted meals. Equipment will be worn down more and more, to the point where critical failures are almost imminent, from the aggressive operational tempo. Crews on the merchant ships will be going crazy from the endless waiting game. . . . And nobody's sunk one single U-boat. And I think I know exactly why."

"Yes, sir," Milgrom said; she obviously realized why too.

"The *real* battle, the battle the Axis intend to fight exclusively on their own terms, hasn't even started yet. Their submarines are massed much farther south that we expected."

Bell looked. "You mean—"

"Yup. In a day or so, the convoy starts to go through the Atlantic Narrows. The Axis knows we're coming, and they know our ships can't hide. Then, for another entire week, the convoy and escorts try to run the South Atlantic. The carrier battle groups and our available fast-attacks are mostly deployed for a fight in the *North* Atlantic, that was supposed to have come from the *east,* from Europe, already. Now they're out of position to give good mutual support against a massed threat to the south. If they come steaming through the Narrows one at a time, they'll get torn to pieces. Think about it."

"Oh, God," Bell said.

"To the west, thousands of miles away, will be the neutral, unhelpful shores of South America. To their east and then their north will loom the bulge of occupied North Africa, menacing the convoy's left flank the whole way. To the south, against their *other* flank, are Boer home waters."

"I see what you're leading to, Captain," Milgrom said.

"*That's* where they'll strike. *That's* what they've been waiting for all along, sitting fat and happy and stealthy and rested and fresh. The convoy-versus-U-boat fight won't be in the North Atlantic at all. It'll be in the one place where the enemy holds every card, geographically, logistically, strategically. . . . They'll have mobile antiship and antiaircraft cruise-missile launchers moving along the coast, shooting and scooting, working in concert with the wolf packs. The whole fight will be on the last leg of the convoy's journey, in the *South* Atlantic, with the tail of support for U.S. forces stretching back six or seven thousand miles, stretched to the breaking point."

Bell hesitated. "What should we do? Reposition the ship? Is all of this work by the Rocks just a waste?"

Jeffrey stood there in his stateroom with the door closed. "XO, I wish I knew."

CHAPTER 17

E rnst Beck sat alone and lonely at the head of the wardroom table. Two great men looked down at him, one
alive and one dead.

To his left, on the bulkhead in an expensive gilt-edged
frame, hung an oil painting of the new kaiser, Wilhelm IV.
To Beck's right, on the opposite bulkhead, hung a portrait of
his ship's namesake, Admiral Reinhard von Scheer—commander in chief of the High Seas Fleet at the height of World
War I.

Reinhard von Scheer wore a thin black mustache; the hair
at his temples had started to gray; his eyes were dark and
piercing. The artist of the portrait had captured von Scheer's
expression skillfully, and brought the man forever to life.
Von Scheer's intelligent face was poised somewhere between a dissatisfied frown and a benevolent smile. The smile
looked like it was just on the verge of winning out over the
frown. From history, Beck knew the admiral had been daring
but prudent, inventive but cautious, a brilliant tactician under
fire . . . and an iron-willed opportunist who at Jutland—
Skagerrak to the Germans—damaged a vastly superior

British force and then escaped against all odds with his own squadrons mostly intact.

Beck looked Admiral von Scheer in the eyes very thoughtfully. He remembered that he himself sat in a different dead man's place—the *von Scheer*'s original captain, his former commanding officer, had until recently used this sacrosanct chair at the head of the wardroom table. *Did he feel Reinhard von Scheer gazing down at him, testing him, challenging him, as I do?*

Beck had lost track of the time when the einzvo, Karl Stissinger, walked into the wardroom, right on schedule. Always empathetic and perceptive, Stissinger saw his captain locked in a staring match with the long-deceased admiral.

"That's one contest you can't win, sir," he joked. "I tell myself it's just dabs of oil paint on canvas; *he* isn't really here, but those eyes, those *eyes* . . . Even a century later you don't want to let that man down."

Beck turned to Stissinger and smiled wanly. "I know. It's like he's our conscience, watching us from that wall. . . . I try to imagine the weight on his shoulders, that fateful day and night, with fifteen-inch enemy battleship shells pounding at him incessantly. Armor-piercing shells the weight of small autos, smashing at him and his ships and his men. The noise, the smoke, the fear, and the tension. The drenching bursts of near misses, the bone-breaking shudder of hits, and the fires."

Stissinger shivered and glanced at the other painting, as if to change the subject. "Our new kaiser, on the other hand, is what one might call an enigma."

Beck let out a deep sigh. "Before the war, I used to think the people who wanted a kaiser again were all hobbyists or hotheads. Sure, Wilhelm the Second abdicated and fled to royal relatives in Holland in 1918, but he always assumed he'd come back once Versailles died down. In the thirties, General von Hindenberg wanted to restore him to power, you know, but Hitler had other ideas. Wilhelm must have died a bitter man."

"As I recall, Captain, he spent the last twenty years of his life in exile in the Netherlands, chopping down trees for exercise. He chopped down something like fifty thousand trees. He must have gone mad, if he wasn't half mad to begin with."

"Some people said, and *still* say, the Versailles Treaty itself was a major war crime. Enslaving and plundering our nation just to satisfy French and British vindictiveness and greed . . . And Wilhelm had good reason to go mad. He abdicates voluntarily, for the good of the nation, right? Then he watches from refuge in Holland as Edward the Eighth abdicates in the thirties over that scandal with Mrs. Simpson. *That* didn't end the *British* monarchy at all. The next in line stepped in. . . . It must have all seemed so *unfair*. . . ."

Beck looked at the picture of the new kaiser. Wilhelm III, crown prince in World War I, had never gotten to assume the throne. After the coup last year in Berlin, when the ultranationalists restored the crown to have a figurehead, the sudden-kaiser chose the name Wilhelm IV, for tradition and continuity—or because he was *told* to.

Stissinger looked at the picture. "I frankly wonder, sir, how happy he was to get the title."

"No one knows. He puts on a good-enough face in public. Maybe they threatened his family. 'Take the job, or else.'"

"Wouldn't surprise me, sir."

"He's an ornament, pure and simple," Beck said. "Willing or unwilling, he has no real power at all. . . . Sometimes I feel bad for him."

"It's a weird contrast, the two paintings. Don't you agree, Captain? Two men, one a proven combat leader, maybe even a genius, in a major war Germany lost, and the other a ceremonial hostage in a war that it looks like we'll win."

"Yes," Beck said. "A very strange contrast."

"Anyway, Captain, Haffner reports we're just beginning to pick up traces of the convoy and escort ships on sonar."

"Already? They're still very far."

"Screw cavitation, propulsion-plant noises, hulls as they pitch through the swells. It's a really *huge* contact, sir. Noise leaks into the deep sound channel," he said, referring to a layer in the open ocean that acts as an acoustic superconductor, in which sounds can travel for hundreds of miles with little signal loss.

"They're still a day or two away from running right over us, I should expect."

"That's the navigator's estimate also, Captain, based on his best guess of the cargo ships' speed. Twenty knots sustained, if they're lucky. A slower actual rate of advance, from course doglegs and zigzagging to try to confuse our forces."

Beck glanced at a clock. "Our guests are late." He reached for the intercom near the captain's place, but the wardroom door opened. In walked the lieutenant in command of the kampfschwimmer group, Johan Shedler. Since the salvage of the American warheads from that sunken destroyer, Beck had begun to look at Shedler with respect, even awe—the man appeared refreshed, returned to normal by now, after his long decompression from his deep dialysis dive.

"Sorry I'm late, Captain. I needed to oversee a few things. My men are almost ready."

"Good, good," Beck said. "Sit. Please." Shedler's full team was sixteen men—only half of whom had been fitted out with and trained to use the dialysis packs.

Shedler glanced with curiosity at the thick envelope of sealed orders by Beck's place on the table, then stood up again almost immediately, at attention, as Rudiger von Loringhoven entered the wardroom.

"Ach," von Loringhoven said with evident self-satisfaction. "I see we're all here." He held a sheaf of notes and papers under one arm.

"Let's begin the briefing," Beck said. "We're running out of time."

Stissinger and Shedler paid careful attention. Portions of what they were about to hear were unfamiliar to them, Beck knew, and they both had important parts to play in the details. The purpose of this briefing was to lay out all the pieces for ample study, minimize the chance of ambiguity or miscommunications, even belabor the obvious in order to assure foolproof implementing of the whole complex attack plan.

Beck started. "The entire arrangement is designed to provide us with supremely accurate, real-time targeting data on the Allied convoy and escorts while *von Scheer* herself stays stealthy and at a safe distance. Stealthy, that is, at least until we salvo-launch our missiles from near the Rocks, at the limit of their fuel supplies, five hundred sea miles south of their targets."

"Perfect firing solutions," von Loringhoven emphasized, "against the most high-value enemy targets, from far beyond the range of *von Scheer's* sonars. Perfect firing solutions, from well beyond the outer screens of the carrier battle groups' submarine and surface escorts and airborne protection. We'll even be outside the longest over-the-horizon detection range of their AWACS radar planes, with your cruise missiles hugging the wave tops."

Stissinger nodded.

"Berlin has sea-surveillance satellites in geosynchronous orbit," Beck said. "The hardware was disguised in German-built vehicles belonging to Third World neutrals lofted by the ArianeSpace consortium before the war. So the Allies have no idea of our actual space-based targeting capabilities."

Stissinger smiled. Beck addressed his next remarks to Shedler. "Your team's role is so important because the data we need has to come in via radio, and radio at such frequencies can't penetrate the sea."

"Understood," Shedler replied.

"The land installation you erect amounts to an interface between the open air and the deep ocean. The two mediums admit two different methods of communicating, radio waves versus sound. Your portable satellite dish is one-half of the link. The transducer line you'll lay underwater forms the other half. The black boxes you brought in your equipment from Norway contain electronics for the interface, and they in turn feed proper signals into the transducers. Digitized acoustic-message bursts will then be picked up by *von Scheer*'s passive sonar arrays. In short, those bursts will take the information that comes down from space via radio, and send it on to us to use while we remain concealed and tactically mobile. You'll be stuck in the open, Lieutenant, working on the Rocks, but you buy us important time and a vital safety margin. The only alternative to a land-based interface relay of this type would be for us to raise an antenna mast above the surface ourselves, and revealing *von Scheer* too soon that way is simply out of the question."

"I understand, Captain."

"You and your men will have to work very quickly to get set up. Remember, the Allies have sea-surveillance assets too. Once you're spotted, the danger for all of us mounts."

"The Allies may assume," Stissinger offered, "that the kampfschwimmer presence, their data uplink even if it's seen, doesn't relate to *us,* Captain. There are many other Axis submarines. Besides, it's natural our side would want control of the Rocks. They're the only land in the whole Atlantic Narrows. They represent a military high ground of sorts. There are *lots* of things the Axis might use them for. Signals intelligence, visual surveillance, even occupy them briefly just to deny them to the Allies at a crucial moment in the battle." He shrugged.

"Timing is everything," Beck said. "The faster we all move, obtaining the targeting data and then getting rid of our missiles, the better our chance to keep the Allies guessing until it's too late. Then we all make our escape while they're still reeling, reacting, confused. That's where your role comes in, Einzvo. You'll be supporting me in an engagement like none you've ever seen. Discipline and teamwork among the crew must be precise in order to program each missile and then execute each step of every launch in such rapid succession. There is no margin for error. None."

"I'll see that all goes well, Captain."

"And as soon as our first missiles broach the surface," Beck said, "we give *von Scheer*'s exact position away. Once our last missile is launched, prompt recovery of the kampf-schwimmer and evasive maneuvers by *von Scheer* against incoming retaliatory fire become a matter of life and death. Sonar, Ship Control, Engineering, every department and every station must put out a maximum effort for me."

"Understood, sir. The men will perform."

"The whole point," von Loringhoven said, "is that setting up this ground station, getting the data from such long range by satellite, maximizes that *other* crucial factor, the distance from us to the escorts and thus the duration until such return fire via missile or aircraft can even reach us. And besides, jamming and spoofing the Allied surveillance and communication circuits is an essential part of the plan. Information warfare experts elsewhere will trigger prearranged virus attacks, just as you ripple your missile salvos, Captain."

"Well . . ." Beck was perhaps the only man at the briefing who fully understood the uncertainties and risks of what was proposed.

"It certainly gives us the best way to lay down accurate fire and live to tell about it," Stissinger said. He was warming more and more to the overall plan. "Since the Allies use random formations for their carrier groups, and they shift the formation shapes constantly, we won't know which ship in a clump of warships is which. They'll use heavy passive and active electronic countermeasures too. If Berlin tells us exactly where the high-value targets are, sir, and their course and speed and zigzag habits, we shoot fan spreads of missiles with a very high kill probability."

Beck frowned. "Launching our missiles from extreme range maximizes their transit time, and gives the enemy the greatest margin for evasive maneuvers too. That's the one thing that bothers me."

Von Loringhoven shook his head. "Your missiles go Mach two point five. From five hundred sea miles away, they'll reach their target coordinates in less than fifteen minutes. . . . That's why you carry so *many* missiles, Captain. You saturate each target coordinate zone. The Americans will have no escape."

"The Americans call that overkill," Beck said with irony, mostly to himself. "You shoot enough weapons to nuke your opponent several times over."

"And what's wrong," von Loringhoven said, "with destroying our enemy several times over? With the carriers and marine amphibious warfare ships and escorts out of the way, our wolf packs can then close in and savage the cargo ships at will. Even were there no Axis interference, it would take those merchant vessels a solid week to steam from the Atlantic Narrows to the Congo-basin coast. With such a long gauntlet to run, subjected to coordinated and merciless U-boat attacks, and not one friendly nation in sight for thousands and thousands of miles, a worthless trickle at most will ever get through to the Allied pocket."

CHAPTER 18

Jeffrey and Milgrom and Bell were still sequestered in Jeffrey's stateroom. Jeffrey had moved the discussion to a different question. They were once again, hurriedly, going over what little they knew about the *von Scheer*, to try to work out more specific tactics for when the fateful confrontation came—if it ever did. Jeffrey and his key people had been doing this often since leaving Norfolk. It became their daily mantra, a benediction almost, but unlike meditation or prayer, this convocation gave no peace of mind. And as Jeffrey said, pointedly, now could well be their final opportunity to brainstorm before the maelstrom of battle began. Then there'd be no pause button, no calling time-outs, no do-overs.

They knew the *von Scheer* was a very big ship, much bigger than *Challenger*. She was almost certainly slower than *Challenger* if both made flank speed. How much slower, Jeffrey didn't know—and knowing could be the difference between life and death in a stern chase or dogfight. Running at the same speed, Milgrom suspected, knot for knot, *von Scheer* would be even quieter than *Challenger*: bigger meant more room for quieting gear, more room to isolate noisy machines from the hull.

But they had no good noise profile on the *von Scheer*. They didn't know what her hybrid Russian-German propulsion plant sounded like. They didn't even know if she had one reactor or two, one propulsor at her stern or two, or even if each propulsor was a screw propeller or a pump jet.

Milgrom pointed out that *Challenger* did have some sonar advantages. *Von Scheer*'s bigger size made her a bigger target on hole-in-ocean passive sonar—a larger spot in the water that was too quiet because the hull blocked ocean noises from farther off. And since ocean sounds or nuclear blasts bounced off the target and served to give it away in the same way as the echo from an active sonar ping, a larger hull meant a larger ambient-sonar contact too. "We can expect a longer detection range against the *von Scheer* than she against us in those modes, sir," Milgrom said.

"We have another advantage, Skipper," Bell said. "*Von Scheer* has to go shallow to launch her missiles. Otherwise they'd implode in the tubes. Going shallow, she loses the help of concealment by bottom terrain. She leaves herself wide open to easy tracking on active sonar, and a preemptive attack by us from below . . . or by other Allied forces from above."

"And then there's the wild card of Orpheus," Jeffrey said, "our secret eye on *von Scheer* looking up from the bottom of the sea . . . assuming the gadget actually works."

———

Felix stood behind the pilot's seat in the cramped, red-lighted control compartment of *Challenger*'s minisub. There was just enough space for him to squeeze between the back of the seat and the front of the pressure-proof bulkhead to the lock-in/lock-out chamber. The mini was all of eight feet high externally, and inside Felix could barely stand up straight.

The mini was too small to have a gravimeter, but the nautical charts were detailed and the inertial nav position was accurate. At four knots, submerged, it took an hour to go from the edge of the undersea ridge—where Felix lost direct contact with *Challenger*—to the immediate vicinity of the Rocks. Instrument panels bristled with buttons and readouts. Computer screens showed depth and course and speed, ballast and trim, and the condition of the minisub's atmosphere. Other screens showed sonar displays and a tactical situation plot. Right now there were no threats.

The very existence of the St. Peter and St. Paul Rocks was an accident of nature. They just happened to be in a most strategic location, where the Mid-Atlantic Ridge stopped curving south and took a sharp turn east along the Romanche Fracture Zone—a gigantic transform fault in the ocean floor straddling the Atlantic Narrows. At the eastern edge of the Romanche fault, hundreds of miles nearer Africa, the Mid-Atlantic Ridge resumed its southern procession, all the way through the South Atlantic Ocean to Antarctica. The St. P and P Rocks—as Felix and the others called them—were, in fact, a part of the Mid-Atlantic Ridge, right at the elbow of that sharp turn east. The Rocks were the only dry land of any sort, anywhere near the center of the Narrows. *The relief convoy has to steam through the Narrows. The Germans have to know all this too.*

Compared to the seafloor down in the sprawling abyssal plains on opposite sides of the endless and massive ridge, the St. P and P Rocks were the summit of a mountain range three miles high. Compared to local sea level, though, the highest point of the Rocks peaked barely sixty-five feet above mean high water.

"We're at periscope depth," the copilot said. "Want to take a look, sir?" The copilot was a senior chief in the SEALs, qualified to operate the minisub—he'd come with Felix from the *Ohio*. The pilot, also a senior chief, was a submariner from *Challenger*. This was standard doctrine for using the ASDS minisub in combat: teamwork, a marriage of cultures, between two of the navy's different elites, submariners and SEALs.

"Do it," Felix said.

The copilot flipped some switches. The fold-down periscope mast was raised hydraulically, and one of the control compartment's display screens lit up with scenery from outside.

It was first light, just before sunrise. The sky facing east was a beautiful golden yellow.

From this angle, with the top of the periscope just above the sea, the St. Peter and St. Paul Rocks didn't look like much.

A jumble of stones sticking out of the water. Four main chunks, plus a few tiny islets. Barely eight hundred feet from end to end, running north-south. Barely a football field's worth of total dry-land area, and barely two square feet of it flat. More than five hundred miles from mainland Brazil. Just over a thousand from Africa. Not a place someone would ever choose to go.

The minisub rocked gently in the minor swells. Felix could make out white water where the swells broke here and there against the edges of the rocks. The weather forecast was good, and he could already see it would be a nice day. The lightening sky was clear and azure blue, with scattered high fluffy clouds that glowed pink in the sunrise. The sunrise was happening fast, even as Felix watched through the digital periscope display. The Rocks were only thirty miles north of the earth's exact equator.

"I better get suited up," he said. This was the part he wasn't looking forward to at all.

———

Beck stood near the bottom of the lockout trunk that led into the *von Scheer*'s pressure-proof internal hangar for her minisub. The rest of the kampfschwimmer group, and their equipment, were already loaded. Beck was saying good-bye and good luck to Lieutenant Shedler; the two of them were alone by the heavy watertight door that sealed the entrance to the trunk.

"I appreciate what you're doing for us." Beck gripped Shedler's hand in both of his firmly. "Godspeed to you."

"You make it sound like a suicide mission, Captain."

"Whatever our friend the baron said back there in the wardroom, Lieutenant, the moment you and your men break the surface, the clock begins to run out on all our lives."

"If we come under attack by air," Shedler said, "we can pull back underwater and take shelter in the minisub. It's combat-hardened, remember."

"What about nuclear bombs?"

"The Rocks are already a radioactive wasteland. We're prepared to deal with that. We'll just have to work quickly, and get you the targeting data you need before the Allies have time to retaliate. With luck we'll be up and down, out and back, before they ever know what hits them." Shedler, always so sure and optimistic, turned serious. "Just promise me one thing, Captain, if you can."

"Name it."

"If something does go wrong, don't leave us behind."

———

Beck and von Loringhoven were making small talk in the wardroom. Beck drank hot tea, Von Loringhoven black coffee. They used expensive china cups and saucers; the wardroom silverware was exquisite sterling; the embroidered tablecloth was antique, imported from old Persia.

"French coffee is good," von Loringhoven said idly, "but the coffee in Buenos Aires is much better."

"You've been stationed in Argentina?"

"Once, earlier in my career, before the war."

Beck felt the *von Scheer*'s deck tilt as the ship nosed down. He watched the readouts on the captain's console next to his end of the table. The ship's depth mounted steadily.

Stissinger returned from the control room. "Minisub safely away, Captain. In-hull hangar pressure-proof doors are closed and sealed. We're heading back to the bottom. Navigator has the conn."

"Very well, Einzvo," Beck acknowledged formally.

"Thank you for joining us," von Loringhoven said to Stissinger.

"Thanks for inviting me, Baron, but I'm still not sure why I'm here."

"My instructions are that the next portion of your captain's secret orders are to be opened and read in your presence. I thought that three of us in the captain's cabin might be crowded. The wardroom gives us space to spread out. The large flat-screen display lets us look at maps and charts together in comfort."

Beck interrupted. "We need security."

"At your convenience, Captain."

Beck grabbed the intercom handset and called the control room. He asked the chief of the boat to have a senior enlisted man posted outside the main wardroom door, and another outside the door that led from the wardroom into the pantry. "Chief, tell the guards to admit no one without my permission."

In a few minutes, the guards were posted outside.

"Open the next envelope whenever you like," von Loringhoven said.

Beck's curiosity was aroused by the change in procedure. "Why *now,* before we've completed our next mission task, the Rocks and the convoy? And why with my einzvo this time?"

"Once Shedler and his men reach the St. Peter and St. Paul Rocks, things will move very quickly."

Beck nodded. *That's putting it mildly. We'll soon go from daintily sipping coffee and tea under fine oil paintings in gilded frames to dealing out supersonic mass death, and then become absorbed in a fight for our lives.*

"Management of the battle time line, by *our* side, is now more essential than ever," von Loringhoven said.

"Granted," Beck replied.

"In order to destroy the convoy, and achieve our broader war aims, and utterly defeat the Allied Powers, many things must be delicately coordinated and synchronized. Lieutenant Shedler will help us seize the tactical initiative. We three here, Captain, have a broader duty, to seize the larger, *strategic* initiative. Destroying the Allied convoy, alone, will not win us the war. It will just bring the enemy closer to losing. The convoy is not the last of your mission tasks on this vessel's deployment."

Beck glanced at Stissinger, who shrugged.

"Once you read the orders," von Loringhoven said, "you will understand. Contingency plans have been carefully made in Berlin. You both, as the *von Scheer*'s senior officers, must study those plans in detail now. Now, before Shedler's sudden appearance on the Rocks is noticed by the Allies, and that event in turn begins an unforgiving contest, and starts an inexorable race."

"And I'm to take these new directives into account, in shaping my further decisions after the *von Scheer*'s missiles are launched?"

"Precisely. And I assure you, these orders are valid, from the highest levels in Berlin. You can double-check the authenticator codes against your private passwords on your computer if you wish. If you prefer, I'll leave the wardroom while you do so."

Beck ripped open the latest envelope. Hastily, he began to read. Before Stissinger even had a chance to move close to look over his shoulder, the captain felt his heart begin to pound.

As he read further, he could feel himself turning livid. He put down the hard-copy orders. He could see Stissinger reading now, staring at the papers in disbelief. Beck turned to face von Loringhoven accusingly.

"What this says is an outrage! It's a crime against humanity!"

CHAPTER 19

Felix's minisub was nestled in a sheltered area where the four main chunks of the St. P and P Rocks formed a west-facing U-shaped lagoon. The water here was very shallow, less than thirty feet. The minisub, weighing sixty-five tons and all of fifty-five feet long, was trying, for stealth, to pass for a dead whale. This was believable, Felix knew, because there were two dead whales, real ones, washed up and stranded against the rocks, decomposing.

Felix wore his Draeger rebreather and diving mask, swim fins, and knives. He had his firearms—his MP-5 submachine gun and his backup Beretta pistol and ammo—in a waterproof equipment bag. He also wore a full-body rubberized antiradiation protective suit, colored flat black and with shreds of ragged cloth and plastic for camouflage. This suit included thick gloves and boots, thoroughly sealed to the main part of the outfit. Felix's Draeger oxygen rebreather—the latest prewar German model enhanced by an American contractor—had a nominal endurance of twelve hours. It would double as his respirator once he reached the land—a compressed air tank, in comparison, would weigh the same but give him only thirty minutes. A regular gas mask might have been most convenient, but it had two big flaws: The filters needed changing now and then, and changing them required a clean environment, and the Rocks were anything but clean. And a gas mask was useless for scuba diving.

The protective suit was hot and sweaty, and would only get more uncomfortable the longer Felix wore it. But he was used to being hot and sweaty. It was one more reason Commander McCollough had chosen him and his new platoon for this task.

On the outside of Felix's full-body suit was a buoyancy compensator and a weight belt. His knives were worn outside, strapped to his forearm and his thighs so he could reach them. His Draeger was worn underneath so he could breathe through its mouthpiece without risk of toxic contamination. The suit included a soft all-enclosing helmet with a big plastic faceplate. It was under this that Felix wore his dive mask so he could equalize his eyes and nose to the pressure of the sea.

Inside his suit, Felix also wore radiation dosimeters attached to his body.

Felix stuck his head into the mini's control compartment. The pilot and copilot were ready. Felix shut and dogged the hatch into the central hyperbaric sphere. He stuck his head out of the rear hatch, into the aft transport compartment. Some of his men were there, either manning the Orpheus equipment or resting from a work session out on the Rocks or underwater. Felix nodded to them encouragingly, and gave a quick wave, then dogged the rear hatch. He stood in the lockout sphere, with an enlisted SEAL as his dive buddy. They did a final equipment check on each other's gear. Felix awkwardly used the intercom to indicate they were ready.

The air pressure in the sphere began to rise. Felix kept swallowing to clear his sinuses. The pressure held steady, at less than two atmospheres—the mini was shallow. When the copilot announced that the lockout sphere was equalized,

Felix opened the bottom hatch. It dropped down on its dampers. Beneath him was a pool of dark and dirty water.

Felix gripped his mouthpiece firmly in his teeth. He held his dive mask in place with his left hand, through the soft clear plastic of his protective suit faceplate. He sat on the coaming of the bottom hatch, then slipped into the water.

———

"Captain," Werner Haffner reported from the sonar consoles, "the minisub is calling on the acoustic link. Lieutenant Shedler is asking for you."

A very troubled Ernst Beck got up from his command console and grabbed a microphone from the overhead. He asked Haffner to put the conversation on the sonar speakers. Rudiger von Loringhoven stood in the aisle, smug now, almost gloating about his victory in the latest mental game with Beck.

Damn him. He knew about those orders even before we departed from Norway. But Ernst Beck had a job to do, a duty to follow. And he knew he needed a very clear head to do his job and survive.

The *von Scheer* was hovering close to the bottom, northeast of a long and narrow undersea rise that was topped at its farthest end by the jutting St. Peter and St. Paul Rocks. The *von Scheer* hid in the eastern foothills, tucked tight inside a huge L-shaped bend of the Mid-Atlantic Ridge—behind the ship, farther east toward Africa, sprawled the Guinea Plain, five thousand meters deep or more.

"Go ahead," Beck said into the mike, keeping his voice as even as possible, forcing down his moral revulsion.

"Sir . . ." Shedler's voice came over the speakers, scratchy and distorted. "Nearing the Rocks. At periscope depth. I see human activity."

Von Loringhoven tried to grab the mike, but Beck stepped away from him. "Clarify," he said to Shedler.

"People on Rocks."

"Who?" the diplomat demanded. "What are they doing?"

Beck repeated the questions into the mike.

"Not sure," Shedler said. "Topography on Rocks all up and down. Much of view blocked, far side of steep slopes, from my current position. Heavy shadowing with sun so low in east. People seen wear protective suits."

"Military? Enemy?"

"Unknown. Not close enough to see weapons or not, or nationality. Risk of them spotting my periscope head."

"The Rocks do belong to Brazil," von Loringhoven said. "A weather station, perhaps?"

"Weather outpost, Lieutenant?"

"Possible. Do appear establishing some technical installation. Could be study radiation on Rocks, effect on environment. I'm guessing."

"We can't abort the mission," Beck told Shedler. *Duty, always duty. The source of pride has become instead an inescapable prison.*

"Understood, sir," came back over the sonar speakers. Shedler knew Beck required the targeting data.

Von Loringhoven caught Beck's attention. "How long do they actually need to have their land station up and running for us to get what we want from Berlin?"

"Wait one, Shedler," Beck said into the mike, and turned to von Loringhoven. "The download should be quick once they get a good lock on the satellite. . . . It'll take them longer to transmit the numbers to us down here from the minisub."

"Why?"

"The undersea acoustic-link baud rate is much slower than their big SHF antenna's data rate." *SHF* meant "super-high frequency," the band used by naval satellite downlinks.

"I have an idea," the diplomat said. "May I please join in the direct conversation?"

"Sonar, patch the baron in." Beck reached and handed von Loringhoven a mike.

"Lieutenant," von Loringhoven said, "can you hear me?"

"Yes, Baron."

"I suggest a cover story. Granted, Brazil is neutral, but we can use that, assuming the intruders are in fact Brazilian. Some of your men speak Portuguese?"

"Two. Enough to get by."

"If you claim you're submariners in distress when you swim ashore, by international law you're entitled to seventy-two hours' safe harbor to make repairs and transmit messages asking for help from your higher command. Tell the Brazilians that if they give you an argument."

"Repeat, please, more slowly."

Von Loringhoven spoke more slowly, with fewer words.

"Understood, Baron," Shedler said.

So did Beck. "Tell Brazilians a half-truth, Shedler. You swam from the escape trunk of a damaged German diesel U-boat. Ship unable to blow main ballast tanks to surface, and diving planes jammed, so unable to maneuver to shallow depth."

"That's good," von Loringhoven said. "But keep it simple, Lieutenant. The key to a good lie is not to volunteer too much. Tell your men to stay low-key, resist the urge to blurt out things, if they aren't good natural liars. And be careful. Some of the Brazilians might understand German and not let on."

Again the baron, not used to the limitations of the acoustic link, needed to repeat himself.

"Yes, Baron. We'll act shaken up, exhausted, worried, because parent submarine is in distress."

"Say your satellite link is an emergency radio," Beck said.

"Set it up under their noses," von Loringhoven said. "Get the data download. Then say you have to swim back to your submarine."

"Understood," Shedler's voice answered. "What about our weapons?"

"Take them with you," Beck said. "Credible since you're at war with Allied Powers. Also, we don't *know* the people you see are neutral. . . . But for God's sake don't shoot a real Brazilian by mistake!"

———————

Felix smoothly raised his head out of the tepid water and wiped smears of spilled fuel oil off his faceplate. He squinted in the sunlight and peeked around as a quick security check, then more carefully took stock of his position. He felt thankful for his airtight protective suit, and not just because of the lingering radiation. Everything he saw around him looked revolting, and he was sure the smell, should he be exposed to it, would be much worse.

The St. P and P Rocks had once been the home to a teeming colony of seabirds; a century before, sailing ships stopped here to harvest valuable cargoes of guano—built-up bird droppings, rich fertilizer in an age before modern chemicals raised crop yields.

But a convoy-versus-U-boat battle raged near here a few months back. Atomic weapons, detonated close to the Rocks, burned everything black. The guano, the thin scrub brush and moss, the seabirds—everything was charred. Dead fish of all sizes and species, discolored, bloated disgustingly, bobbed in the swell or washed against the base of the Rocks. Then there were the two dead whales, their sides split open from rotting, bones exposed through layers of blubber that had turned green or black in the relentless tropical sun.

Felix headed for the usable patch of more or less flat high ground, following the wires and fiber-optic cables leading out of the water. He paused to raise his dive mask onto his forehead, under his suit. Once out of the water, he felt much heavier, especially wearing a Draeger, but he was used to this, and it was good to be out in the open, after days in a sub or a minisub. Despite the eye exercises he'd done every day to maintain depth perception while cooped up, it took a little time to get used to focusing on objects at a distance.

Felix removed his swim fins and attached them to his external load-bearing harness. He donned his pistol holster, shouldering his submachine gun with its sling. He began to trudge inland—he had to laugh that anywhere here was really inland—and started to climb.

On what the map called Southeast Rock, on a saddle between two jagged volcanic formations, lay a jumble of man-made stones. This was the foundation and other remnants of a long-abandoned and toppled lighthouse. A more modern lighthouse, of less rugged construction, had been built fifteen years ago. That one had been hit by the heat and the shock waves from several atomic airbursts. All that was to be seen of it now were scattered bits of metal and melted glass.

Felix's on-watch land-side team was busy setting up their satellite communications link on the saddle. Looking south, Felix could see the St. P and P Rocks' highest point, a volcanic spire whose sides were almost vertical. In the other direction, in the shallows on the northeast side of the Rocks, lay the hulk of a cargo ship—one victim of the convoy-versus-U-boat fight. The hulk was some sort of old dry-cargo vessel, not a tanker or a modern container ship. It must have drifted here, ablaze, and run aground. Now the hulk was completely burned out, blackened like everything else, except for spots and streaks where sea salt had oxidized its tortured steel a matte red brown.

As Felix walked he heard a sickening crunch. He looked down and saw he'd stepped right onto the skeleton of something large, maybe an albatross. He had to shake his foot to dislodge the brittle rib cage.

Felix spoke with some of his men. This was a difficult chore. They had to use one hand, to grab and hold their Draeger mouthpieces through their protective suits or faceplates, and then shout to one another through the muffling effect of the suits.

Radiation detectors confirmed that contamination of the Rocks was still heavy. The alpha and beta rays wouldn't penetrate a human body's outer layer of dead skin, let alone get through the SEALs' heavy suits. But the radioactive particulates lingering on the Rocks—the isotopes of plutonium and uranium and lighter fission by-products—would cause multiple cancers if inhaled and allowed to lodge in the living tissue of the lungs. If a suit seal were to be broken, and a man's skin torn, carcinogens could also enter the body through even superficial wounds.

The uncomfortable suits contained a layer of Kevlar to prevent such deadly penetration. Even so, all the SEALs worked very carefully. No one wanted to slip on the oily mess that covered the Rocks—charred guano, convoy-ship waste that had condensed from the mushroom clouds and fallen as black rain, and worse. No one wanted to take a spill and go sliding down the rough stones into the water.

And then there were the penetrating neutrons and the gamma rays. The suits would help, but the REM count—a measure of accumulating radiation exposure—said no one would want to stay in the area more than a couple of days, tops.

Felix was therefore happy that things were just about ready to start. The huge, collapsible satellite dish was unfolded and erect. Using portable consoles with keyboards—all battery-powered and hardened against radiation—his men checked the acoustic link into the water to the minisub. *Challenger* had belatedly launched an off-board probe to serve as a communications relay, and the men were trying to verify that it also allowed them to speak and transmit basic data directly to Jeffrey Fuller on his ship.

The minisub positioned itself above the bottom anchor and cable relay point for the Orpheus gear. Divers left the minisub and made a hardwired hookup. Now signals from a spiderweb of distant telephone cables were flowing into the consoles in the mini. Those signals were also coming ashore and being transmitted via satellite to analysts with supercomputers in Norfolk.

Felix sat down to wait. He had eaten, and drunk, and used the tiny head on the minisub before coming ashore. For most of the next twelve hours, he'd be confined in his protective suit, as were his men. His major challenge was to stay alert and support his men's morale and spirit—despite the depression the truly hideous moonscape inspired in him—as the SEALs stood watch on the land-based equipment and suffered inside their saunalike suits. He wished it hadn't been such a warm and sunny day. He envied the men who'd be working the night shift.

Felix glanced up at the dazzling sky. The pure white clouds and very clear air were a stark contrast to the ruin on the Rocks. He peered toward the horizon. Except for the Rocks, microscopic in their isolation, the glistening ocean stretched as far as the eye could see, vast and empty and blue. The prevailing wind, and surface current, both came from the east—the surf was slightly heavier on the eastern side of the Rocks. The unbounded vistas, breathtaking under different circumstances, only added to Felix's melancholy; the total lack of signs of any living wildlife anywhere—no soaring seabirds or dolphins playing—made him feel even worse.

"Sir," one of his men yelled in Felix's ear. "Something seems to be messed up." The SEALs spoke to one another in Portuguese, acting as if they were Brazilian, just in case.

"What do you mean, 'messed up'?"

"The moment we got everything up and running on Orpheus, the minisub consoles and Norfolk both came back with the same indication. It has to be a technical problem, bad data or a faulty hookup somewhere. It's too soon to make any sense."

"Crap," Felix said. "Just what we need, having to recheck miles of wiring now of all times."

"I know, LT. The minisub and Norfolk, they both say there's a deep-running enemy sub right on top of us." The man turned and pointed toward the northeastern horizon. "Just a few miles *that* way."

"Lieutenant!" another SEAL shouted from down the far slope of the saddle. "Divers coming out of the water! One is yelling in bad Portuguese! They say they're from a damaged German U-boat! Requesting official safe-harbor status!"

Felix turned to look through his binoculars.

His heart almost stopped. The Germans were hamming it up, but he wasn't fooled for a minute. Their posture, their body movements in and around the water, and their equipment, including their weapons, all pointed to their true identities.

Waterproofed, silenced Heckler & Koch MP-5s, carried by crewmen from a sinking German submarine? And Draeger rebreathers inside rubberized black full-body suits, instead of escape lungs and orange life vests and open-water exposure suits? . . .

Kampfschwimmer.

As casually as he could, Felix ducked behind a ledge of rock. He gestured for his men to take cover as well—subtly, not abruptly. He grabbed the microphone for the acoustic link to *Challenger* and the minisub in one hand, and the mike for the satellite voice link to Norfolk in the other.

"Enemy contact, contact, contact! Kampfschwimmer on the Rocks! Positive submarine contact on Orpheus, bearing northeast. Repeat, northeast! *At practically point-blank range!*"

Stone chips flew and ricochets whined—the kampfschwimmer weren't fooled either. The battle for the Rocks was joined.

CHAPTER 20

Felix Estabo's shouting came over the sonar speakers on *Challenger*. Everyone in the control room looked as if they'd suddenly been jolted by cattle prods, but Jeffrey never felt more alive in his life.

At last the waiting is over. The combat begins.

"Minisub, minisub," Jeffrey shouted into his mike for the acoustic link. "Maintain your position! Maintain your position! Keep feeding me Orpheus data as long as you can!"

"Minisub, acknowledged," came the reply over the sonar speakers.

"Ground station, ground station, hold your position! Hold the Rocks at all cost!"

Something garbled and breathless came back.

"Chief of the Watch," Jeffrey ordered COB, "sound silent battle stations antisubmarine."

COB acknowledged. Phone talkers spread the word throughout the ship—the general-quarters alarm, and the 1MC loudspeakers, made too much noise when stealth was vital. In seconds, more enlisted men and chiefs dashed into control from aft, some still pulling on clothing or shoes.

They manned and powered up empty consoles or stood in the aisles to help or learn or supervise.

Next to Jeffrey, Bell quickly reconfigured their screen displays. At battle stations, as usual, Bell was fire-control coordinator.

"Sonar, threat status?" Jeffrey snapped.

"No new contacts," Milgrom reported coolly.

She always is a cool one under fire. Milgrom's even tone helped get the others settled and focused.

Jeffrey stared at the gravimeter, at the large-scale nautical chart: the saw-toothed peaks of the local part of the soaring Mid-Atlantic Ridge and the jutting and dwarfish Rocks with the mini nearby. Terrain all around them was jumbled and jagged. . . . South-southeast of the St. P and P Rocks, and just a few hours distant at flank speed, the Romanche Gap plunged twenty-five thousand feet deep—almost as deep as Mount Everest was high.

And the SMS *Admiral von Scheer* could be anywhere.

Except for Orpheus. Beautiful, beautiful Orpheus. I'm sorry I ever doubted you. Admiral Hodgkiss was right all along.

"Helm," Jeffrey rapped out, "ahead two-thirds, make turns for twenty-six knots. Make your course zero four five. Nap-of-seafloor cruising mode."

"Ahead two-thirds, turns for twenty-six knots, aye, sir," Meltzer acknowledged at the helm. "Make my course zero four five, aye. Nap of seafloor, aye." Meltzer turned his engine-order telegraph, a four-inch dial on his console. He worked his control wheel. "Maneuvering answers, ahead two-thirds twenty-six knots! My course is zero four five, sir!" The helmsman's burly Bronx accent sounded tough and determined.

"Northeast, Captain?" Bell asked. His job was to play devil's advocate as Jeffrey led the attack against what seemed the devil himself.

"It's the last thing they'll expect. They're on the other side of the mountain. We know where they are, but they don't know where we are, if they even know we're here at all."

"But going so shallow?"

"This way we'll maintain contact with the mini and the Rocks as long as possible. And it's the shortest route to the *von Scheer*'s position."

"The kampfschwimmer must have reported resistance from the SEALs by now. *Von Scheer* will guess Estabo's men got there by submarine."

"Yes, but they won't know *which* submarine. They're supposed to think we're in dry dock."

"There are a dozen other passes we could take across the ridge, Captain. A straight line is too obvious."

"We need to do the unexpected."

Bell nodded reluctantly. "Understood, sir."

"Cheer up, XO. We can't be in two places at once, but neither can the *von Scheer*. Let Beck be the one to keep guessing."

Challenger's bow nosed up steeply as she began to climb the flank of the ridge by the Rocks. Her depth would go from eleven thousand feet to just a few hundred in less than ten miles.

"Sir," Bell said, sounding worried all over again, "why are kampfschwimmer on the Rocks to begin with?"

"To keep the Rocks from us."

"But they have to have planned this for days. How did they know *our* guys would be there?"

Jeffrey ignored Bell in favor of something more urgent. "Fire Control, arm and load nuclear Mark Eight-eight Mod Twos, torpedo tubes one through eight."

Bell relayed commands to his weapons officer below. Jeffrey and Bell entered the warhead-arming passwords on their consoles.

"Preset all warhead yields to maximum, one kiloton."

"Maximum, one kiloton, aye," Bell repeated for absolute clarity. He typed commands on his keyboard.

The torpedo tubes were loaded one by one. The main work was done by hydraulic assists, but the warhead-arming hookups had to be connected and then passworded by hand.

"Make tubes one through eight ready in all respects including opening outer doors."

Jeffrey would proceed with fish wet, ready to charge on their way to his opponent in an instant. He preferred to make the mechanical transients of loading and flooding the tubes, and opening the outer doors, while the intervening terrain still masked him from his enemy.

This task done, Bell glanced at Jeffrey again insistently. "The kampfschwimmer, the Rocks. We're missing something, Captain. Something important."

In a flash of insight, Jeffrey saw it. He blanched.

A satellite dish to an Axis sea-surveillance bird in space, and an acoustic link into the water, would give von Scheer *all the firing-solution data against the convoy that Ernst Beck could ever want. . . . And from way outside the longest reach of the escorts' radar pickets . . . I came here to look for Beck using phone cables under the ocean. He came here to look for the convoy with sensors outside the atmosphere.*

Jeffrey grabbed for a microphone. "Ground station, ground station, I repeat. Estabo, Estabo, *hold the Rocks at all costs!*"

Felix Estabo's voice came back, reverbed and scratchy over the undersea acoustic link. He sounded muffled too, from speaking through his protective suit helmet. "We're trying! I—" There was a noise on the link like that of men shouting and scrambling. There was a screech like a bullet ricochet. There was a fast *puff-puff-puff* as a silenced weapon close to Estabo's open mike fired on full auto. Then the mike clicked off.

"*Targeting data,* XO," Jeffrey said. "The Germans want the Rocks to set up a link to get long-range targeting data."

"Yes, sir, that has to be it."

Jeffrey's heart raced. "Data for Ernst Beck to launch his missiles at the Allied convoy, unmolested by the escorts . . .

If the Germans seize control of the Rocks for just a few minutes, our first detect on the *von Scheer* will be the sound of dozens of Mach-Two-plus missiles salvoing into the air."

Once her missiles are away, the von Scheer *is spent, an empty shell. . . . To sink her after she launches against the convoy will be no victory.*

Jeffrey knew that every second counted badly now, both underwater and on land.

———

Felix cursed doubly when one of his men was hit by a bullet through his helmet's soft plastic faceplate. The man began to scream, in English, before he bled out inside his suit from a severed main artery. *My first killed-in-action as leader . . . And so much for our Brazilian disguise.*

The kampfschwimmer heard it too. The energy of their assault redoubled.

"Dig in?" one of Felix's chiefs shouted.

Felix looked at the ground on the slope where they were taking cover. Two inches down it was solid basalt. "We'd need jackhammers!"

More bullets whizzed overhead. The protective suits kept Felix and his men from hearing them well, from feeling their passage disrupting the air—and this added to the danger. The chief was trying to control his team using hand signals alone because they hadn't taken radios—whose signals would be blocked whenever basalt outcroppings stood in the way, and whose electronics would be damaged by fallout gamma rays. With the SEALs' fields of vision impaired by the helmets of their radiation suits, near-chaos reigned. Felix heard another SEAL scream in agony. Then one of his people bellowed in triumphant rage—he'd just shot a kampfschwimmer dead.

Felix peeked around a rock for a split second to use his binoculars. He ducked, barely in time, as an incoming three-round burst sent dust and pebbles flying.

"I see no mortars or hand grenades! I think they just have direct-fire weapons like us!" Rifles and pistols.

"They're trying to outflank us!" the chief yelled back.

Felix looked at the lay of the land, the folds in the slopes, the jagged escarpments.

So this is how it feels to be in full command, as an officer. This is what it's like to have chiefs taking orders from me.

It was scary, but Felix found he wanted it.

"We have to hold the high ground!"

"Firing line across this side of the island, or circle in an all-around defense?"

Felix looked about again and thought as fast as he could. Razor-sharp spines led down from Southeast Rock's central saddle in both directions, right into the sea. If his men spread out along the spines and fired down from the top, they might keep the Germans pinned down on the opposite side of the Rock.

But Felix and his men hadn't come prepared for a major firefight. They only had so much ammo.

If each kampfschwimmer brought just one more magazine than each of my SEALs, we've had it. Or if the Germans are only slightly better shots, or have slightly better fire discipline, or use slightly better tactics . . .

The uncertainty stabbed him in the chest like a bayonet.

So this is the burden of command. I've already lost the element of surprise to the enemy. My logistics are inadequate. My commo's barely functioning. I have to make too many choices at once. . . . And my men are bleeding and dying.

"Chief, this isn't Iwo Jima! We have to stop thinking like Marines or infantry!"

Felix grabbed the mike to the minisub. To his relief the line still worked. "We need reinforcements. Every man not needed to run the Orpheus, suit up on the double. Head north underwater, outflank the Germans clockwise, come up on Northwest Rock and support us from there. Take the kampfschwimmer in enfilade."

The chief in the mini acknowledged. Northwest Rock

faced the opposite slope of the central spines of Southeast Rock. From there, fresh SEALs could attack the Germans from behind.

An enlisted SEAL shouted. Kampfschwimmer were charging up the slope in a coordinated rush.

Felix told his chief to get his men spread out along the spines and conserve their ammo but drive the Germans back. The chief made hand signals, and the SEALs began to act. With every weapon silenced, the battle was strangely quiet—but it would be a person's final mistake to think the bullets were any less deadly.

Felix gestured for the chief to follow him. They belly-crawled across the open ground on part of the saddle and huddled in the ruins of the stone lighthouse. The location would serve as his command post, the pivot point in their battle to hold the Rocks. Felix dragged the microphones along with him. He tried to keep their wires concealed, and tried not to break either mike. But the conspicuous satellite dish was already riddled by the kampfschwimmer, and its preamplifier box was totally smashed. Then the whole dish toppled flat: Felix lost contact with Norfolk. The Germans continued their uphill rush.

Some kampfschwimmer were knocked down by American bullets, but they crawled or hobbled away behind boulders and draws—and Felix saw no blood trails. He realized their suits were lined with Kevlar, like the SEALs'. To stop them, he knew his men had to stick to head shots. He told his chief to give the order.

———

Over the sonar speakers in the Zentrale, Ernst Beck listened to his acoustic link. The kampfschwimmer chief in the mini-sub, watching the Rocks through the periscope, was relaying Beck a blow-by-blow description of the battle.

"Their charge has been repulsed, Captain! The Americans still hold the high ground!"

"This will never do," von Loringhoven said.

Lieutenant Shedler was leading from in front, on the St. Peter and St. Paul Rocks. Because he was under fire, his men couldn't set up a communications link to the minisub, or to Beck. The captain knew he had to do something himself.

Beck and Stissinger peered at a detailed topographical map of the Rocks and surrounding waters.

Beck used the acoustic link. "Chief, shift the minisub's position south. Send the rest of your men into the water. Have them come up on Southeast Rock and take the SEALs from behind."

"*Jawohl*. Moving now."

"How did the SEALs ever get there?" von Loringhoven asked.

"That's a very good question," Beck replied. "More to the point, what do they want? What was that satellite dish for?"

There was an awkward silence.

"Targeting data from SOSUS hydrophones?" Stissinger suggested.

"Perhaps." Beck considered everything he knew—why *he* was there by the Rocks, the enemy convoy that was coming, the defense plans U.S. commanders are likely to have made. "If you're right, Einzvo, that would seem to prove the SEALs came via submarine."

Von Loringhoven looked like he'd been slapped. "Find it! Destroy it!"

"Baron, you don't have to tell me how to do my job."

CHAPTER 21

After another fitful, nightmare-ridden attempt at a few hours' sleep, Ilse Reebeck had just come back on duty to the console she'd been assigned at the Atlantic Fleet Command Center in Norfolk. The past several days of waiting for news from *Challenger* had been even more nerve-racking for her than for the others in the big war room because Ilse had served in battles on *Challenger* three times before. She knew most of the chiefs and enlisted men well. She was good friends with Kathy Milgrom, and the two had had fun "pajama parties" in their shared stateroom on the ship. COB had been Ilse's mentor and father confessor as she tried to fit into a military hierarchy. And Jeffrey Fuller, of course, was someone she went back and forth between liking and hating—a roller coaster she hoped would continue, for the way it seemed to meet her deeply conflicted emotional needs. She desperately wanted *Challenger* to win, and Jeffrey Fuller and the others to survive.

But the past few days of draining quiet had meant high stress for everyone. It felt worse than sitting on thumbtacks, to wait for news that the U-boats were finally moving in. Ilse could observe the gradual progress of the convoy ships on the war room's main displays, and she could follow the maneuvers by the escorts. She saw plots of each suspected contact with an enemy submarine, but then not one contact proved real. Instead, she read on tally boards—or overheard conversations—as the terrible wear and tear at sea took a mounting toll on ships and aircraft and people.

Then, out of nowhere, as Ilse finished her second coffee of the morning, pandemonium struck. Communications contact had just been established with the SEALs on those tiny islets amid the Atlantic Narrows, a third of the distance to the other side of the world. Almost at once, news came of a definite Orpheus contact on the *von Scheer,* and then kampfschwimmer attacked, and the satellite link to the Rocks went totally dead.

Admiral Hodgkiss walked over to Ilse. She found the man to be unfriendly and intimidating at best. The last few days, he'd become increasingly short with people—even his own staff approached him with trepidation.

"Good morning, Lieutenant Reebeck."

Ilse began to rise to attention. She'd come far enough along the path from civilian consultant to uniformed personnel to follow military courtesy by instinct—most of the time. She was also smart enough to know that it was rare for any four-star to address someone of her junior status directly.

"Don't get up," Hodgkiss said. He stood next to her and looked at the big status plot on the wall. The last known position of the *von Scheer* had just popped onto the screen. "I guessed half right," he said, as much to himself as to Ilse. "And in this game there's no partial credit."

"Sir?"

"I did get *Challenger* in range of the *von Scheer* after all. I miscalculated badly where the Axis would mass all their U-boats."

Hodgkiss turned to his senior aide, a full captain, on the other side of the room. He barked for the man to come over. Ilse felt like a fly on the wall as they talked. The captain's face was grim.

"To recover we need to take a monumental gamble," Hodgkiss said.

"Admiral?"

"The U-boats are all waiting south," Hodgkiss told the captain. "The sons of bitches let us chase our tails this whole past week. It wasn't a running battle of attrition after all. It's going to be a mass attack where we'll least be able to cope."

"Yes, sir."

"I want the convoy ships to stop and circle right where they are, with just enough speed for steerageway. I want the escort formations to redeploy."

"Sir?"

"The warships go through the Narrows in a solid wall, not piecemeal. When we're ready, the convoy groups start moving again. The escorts sweep ahead while giving full mutual support. I want three carrier battle groups to then peel off and form a new line to cover the North African coast, priority given to Axis mobile antiship cruise-missile launchers. The carrier fighter-bomber squadrons and cruiser Tomahawk batteries find those land-based launchers and pound the living shit out of 'em. Understand me?"

"Yes, sir. But all this will delay the relief convoy."

"I know, maybe by several days."

"The Axis ground assault in Africa might hit before the convoy reaches the coast to unload."

"I know. If we lose the coast we probably lose everything. But unless we wait and do this right, the convoy doesn't reach the coast at all."

"Understood, Admiral. But I need to report that enemy jamming is increasing."

"Then start drafting orders *now!* Get them out while we can! Get on it!"

Hodgkiss's aide hurried off.

"And set up a conference call for me with someone on top in the air force!" the admiral yelled after him.

"Yes, sir!"

"Now, Lieutenant Reebeck."

Ilse almost gulped. She knew the upcoming battle would be one for the history books. *The Battle of the South Atlantic*. And now the man whose name would be forever attached to that battle was talking to *her*.

"Admiral?"

"We need to give *Challenger* as much support as possible."

"Yes, sir."

"And we've just lost the only stealthy way *Challenger* had to talk to us."

"Yes, sir."

"And we dare not ask her to violate radio silence herself with the *von Scheer* so close."

"Understood, Admiral." Ilse knew they could use extremely low frequency radio to send an order to *Challenger* to come up to two-way antenna depth—or they might drop a signal sonobuoy from an aircraft.

"So tell me what to do."

"Admiral?" Ilse was shocked he'd ask such a question. Then she realized he was testing her. "You mean, sir, tell you what Jeffrey Fuller would do."

"Good, you got it in one."

"I think Commodore Wilson would be a better person to ask, sir."

"I already did. I want to hear what *you* have to say."

Hodgkiss stepped closer, invading Ilse's personal space. She knew that if she stood she'd be several inches taller than he, but that didn't make the man any less of a potent authority figure.

Ilse thought hard. She glanced up and down, between the big status plot on the wall and the small-scale nautical chart on her workstation screen, which showed the Rocks and that local part of the Mid-Atlantic Ridge, with an overlay of the surface water temperature and salinity.

"He'll go right for the *von Scheer*. He'll do everything he can to keep her from launching her missiles."

"How?"

"I think he enjoys risking death, sir. He'll push himself right to the edge."

"I told him he was expendable in a one-for-one trade with *von Scheer*."

"He'll definitely use that. He'll act suicidal on purpose, to bend the enemy captain's mind." Ilse felt acid stomach hit as the full implications sank in. *Expendable.*

"How does that apply right now?" Hodgkiss prodded.

"The *von Scheer* needs to go shallow to launch her antiship missiles?"

"Yes. The missiles aren't very pressure-proof. We don't think she can do it from below one hundred fifty feet."

Ilse glanced at her console; satellite radar and microwave sensors told her a surprising amount about the upper part of the ocean. Self-propelled oceanographic probes, programmed to skim the surface periodically and transmit data dumps, told her even more—though reception from them was deteriorating. "One hundred fifty feet's above the sonar layer near the Rocks."

"Are you telling me Captain Fuller would take *Challenger* above the layer now that he's made Orpheus contact?"

"I think he might."

"He wouldn't hide in the bottom terrain?"

"Not if hiding won't help him to sink the *von Scheer*. Captain Fuller is extremely aggressive, sir. He's also very inventive on tactics. Going shallow, he might make the *von Scheer* think he's a steel-hulled sub, and lull the *von Scheer* by disguising his true capabilities. And going shallow gives his sonar arrays a much better field of view. . . . He might even use active sonar and reveal himself if that lets him draw a good bead on his target."

"Invite incoming fire on purpose?"

"That could be part of it, yes."

"Kampfschwimmer on the Rocks. The one thing I didn't plan for. Now we're deaf and blind at the absolutely worst imaginable time." Hodgkiss sounded disgusted. "If *von*

Scheer gets away from *Challenger,* or sinks her, we're back to square one and the entire convoy's at very grave risk. Especially with my altered escort dispositions. They'd make an even better group target for *von Scheer* than before."

"Understood, sir."

"Would he abandon the SEALs on the Rocks, or try to help them?"

"If his priority is the *von Scheer,* he'll know that the SEALs are expendable. . . . I've seen him order people to their deaths before. He won't like it one bit, but he'll do it."

Admiral Hodgkiss looked Ilse right in the eyes. "How sure are you of any of this?" He kept looking right at her without blinking.

Ilse returned the stare as bravely as she could. Admiral Hodgkiss had such a strong persona he could be frightening. "I'm as sure as I can be, sir."

"I read all of Captain Fuller's patrol reports. It may please you to know that I concur with your assessment of him, Lieutenant."

"Yes, sir."

The admiral looked up at the main screen. He seemed to make a decision, then spoke half to himself. "I'm taking one huge gamble. I may as well take two."

Hodgkiss turned and shouted for his aide again.

CHAPTER 22

Felix fired another short burst from his MP-5, then ducked behind the scattered man-made stones of the ruined lighthouse. He was sweating profusely inside his hot protective suit. He'd already used up the built-in drinking bottle, and he knew he was in danger of becoming dehydrated. If that or a German bullet didn't get him, heatstroke soon would.

Then his team of reinforcements from the minisub came out of the water on Northwest Rock. Felix and the headquarters chief hand-signaled to their men along the spines of Southeast Rock; the men increased their rate of fire. The SEALs on Northwest Rock took up positions and started to shoot. The kampfschwimmer were forced to withdraw back toward the water.

Felix ordered his men to charge. While the other team made the kampfschwimmer scatter and keep their heads down, he and the surviving SEALs began to dash down the slope, using fire and movement to protect one another.

Then he and his men took enemy fire from behind. Felix realized the kampfschwimmer had sent reinforcements too.

They were trying to do to him exactly what he was doing to them: catch him in enfilade—kill him using fire from two directions at once.

Felix and his men had no choice but to take cover and shoot back the way they'd just come. The kampfschwimmer who'd been withdrawing saw this and got emboldened. They waded across to Northeast Rock, shooting at the SEALs on Northwest Rock, Felix's reinforcement team. The seesaw struggle of evenly matched Allied and Axis elites grew brutal and vicious.

Hot lead continued to fly, and ricochets continued screeching. Silenced muzzles smoked and spent brass flew. The supply of full magazines steadily dwindled. Felix sweated and panted; his mouth was terribly dry. The stale taste from his Draeger told him he was hyperventilating—breathing faster than the chemicals in the rebreather could absorb his carbon dioxide and give him fresh new air.

Felix fired in one direction and then the other. Clumps of men advanced a handful of yards, then were driven back.

Then Felix had a horrible realization. He hyperventilated harder. *We had the proper tactics but we picked the wrong location.*

"Chief!" he shouted to get the man's attention.

"Sir!"

"The high ground! *This* spot isn't the high ground!"

The chief shook his head, then ducked as a well-aimed bullet almost took him in the face. "I don't follow you, LT."

"*Challenger* and *von Scheer*. They'll use nuclear torpedoes." Felix pointed out at the ocean.

The chief's eyes widened; his face grew pale.

"The waves they kick up will wash right over the Rocks!" Felix had to pause to draw a breath. "When the fireballs break the surface, the heat and shock front and gamma rays, they'll cook us alive!"

"Retreat to the minisub?"

"We can't! Orders! We can't abandon the Rocks!" Felix drew another breath. "If we go in the water at all, the undersea warhead concussion power will force our livers out our assholes and make shit spray from our mouths!"

"What do we do?"

Felix looked north. It had been there the entire time, staring him in the face, and he hadn't been thinking.

That was the whole point. This *wasn't* Iwo Jima. It wasn't anything *like* Iwo Jima.

"The cargo-ship hulk! That's the real high ground, Chief! From there we control the Rocks by fire! It's the only place we stand a chance to survive the nuclear blasts!"

The chief set his jaw with new determination.

Felix clapped him on the shoulder. "We have to occupy the cargo-ship hulk!"

Felix ducked as more bullets poured in. He was forced to shift his position. In their black suits, everyone looked the same, but Felix had too visibly been acting like an officer.

So much for the joys of command.

The incoming fire died off suddenly.

Felix suspected a trap. He peeked from around a rough, charred boulder and caught fleeting glimpses of movement on Northeast Rock, black against the black there. The kampfschwimmer were pulling away from him and heading north.

"The Germans are going for the hulk! *If they get there before us we've had it!"*

———

Jeffrey gripped a microphone as he stared at the gravimeter readouts. *We have our quarry localized. Now we need to track and target Beck.*

Using one mode, the gravimeter gave Jeffrey a perfect picture of the seafloor terrain around the Rocks, like a 3-D bird's-eye view—as if the water weren't there—with *Challenger*'s position plotted as she moved along at top quiet speed. In a different mode, the imagery was like looking out the front windshield of a car—but with eerie clairvoyance, because the gradiometers could sense through solid rock. Right now Jeffrey had both modes on his command workstation screens to help him think and visualize tactics.

"Minisub, minisub," Jeffrey called through the mike, "any more contact with Lieutenant Estabo?"

"Negative, negative," the submariner chief in the mini responded. "Kampfschwimmer came at them from behind. I think the Germans cut the hydrophone wire by the Rocks. We have no commo signal, sir, not even acoustic carrier tone."

"What's the last you heard from Estabo?"

"He asked for reinforcements."

"Who's left in the mini?"

"SEAL chief copilot, two enlisted SEALs aft at Orpheus consoles."

"Do you copy anything at all on radio?" The mini had her own small floating wire antenna.

"Negative, sir. Enemy jamming keeps getting heavier."

"Okay. Okay. Don't raise any masts. Do nothing that might make a datum." Give their position away. "Do you have enough cable to stay hooked into the Orpheus grid but move the mini farther from the Rocks?"

"We can manage a mile from the feed-in anchor. That's all."

"Good. Stay shallow, but get out to deeper water." Jeffrey glanced at his screens. "Head two five zero." West-southwest. "That'll give you six hundred feet of water. I don't want you right by the Rocks when tactical nukes start going off. The tsunami effects, understood?"

"Yes, sir."

"I don't want German combat swimmers finding you. They might be looking for an Allied mini already."

"Understood."

"Keep the bottom hatch dogged. Be careful who you let in. . . . Be careful who you let get near you. They might plant limpet mines, even drop them on you like bombs if you try going deep."

There was a thoughtful, pregnant silence on the line for a minute. "Acknowledged."

"Good luck. Out."

Jeffrey turned and looked at Bell. "Estabo's on his own. At least the mini can hide underwater, watch for threats with her cameras and sonars."

Bell nodded. "Estabo seems like a man who knows how to take care of himself, Captain."

"I hope so. I hate abandoning people."

"Sir, what the chief on the mini told us—that the radio jamming is worse. It seems like more confirmation."

"I think I see where you're going, XO, but say it."

"Electronic countermeasures support from other German forces, all of a sudden? From land, from space, from U-boats, I don't know. But I think it's another sign *von Scheer* is preparing to launch."

"Bring up the map of all the old phone cables Orpheus uses. Put it on your console, XO, my displays are swamped."

Bell typed on his keyboard. "We do have a bit of an information explosion going, don't we, Captain?"

Jeffrey ignored the remark. He did *not* want to think about his ship exploding.

The large-scale map came up on Bell's screen. The two men studied it together, elbow to elbow.

"So this is the cable the *von Scheer* crossed when Orpheus first picked her up." Jeffrey pointed to a jiggly line that ran north, past the east side of the local rise capped by the Rocks.

"She came from east to west." Bell moved his hand from right to left on the map. "Just about here." He pointed to a spot on the map. "She must have been moving in to deploy her minisub with the kampfschwimmer."

"This one other cable is real important to us now," Jeffrey said. It also ran north, but on the west, the left side of the Rocks. "Orpheus hasn't sensed *von Scheer* cross over that cable, yet."

"So she has to be somewhere between the two, Skipper."

"Yup. The question is whether she's still north of this rise here by the Rocks. Or has she been moving southward, sneaking east of the Rocks running deep, while we've been moving north, going shallow and to the west?" Jeffrey moved his hands while he talked, as if the *von Scheer* and *Challenger* were twirling past each other with the Rocks stuck in the middle, screening them both.

"Why would she move south, Captain?"

"To look for us? Beck has to know there's another sub in the area."

"But he's not a fast-attack, Captain. It's not his job to go hunting for an enemy and offer combat."

"You're right, XO. And that's our other trump card, in addition to Orpheus. We *are* a fast-attack. We get paid every day to go looking for trouble and mix it up with our adversary."

"I admit that's an important observation, sir, but very dangerous if we're wrong. Remember, Beck used to be XO on a fast-attack. And he knows you, sir."

Jeffrey frowned. "Our problem is that the Rocks split this whole area between the two phone cables into separate playing fields. North, and south. Which one do we play in?"

Uncertainty piled on uncertainty.

"Go north, sir," Bell said decisively.

Jeffrey smiled. "Why so sure?"

"Our priority is protecting the convoy. The convoy is north. Beck's priority is attacking the convoy. The convoy is north."

"North it is." Jeffrey knew everyone in the control room who wasn't wearing sonar headphones heard snatches of this talk. For clarity, he said, "Helm, steady as you go."

"Aye aye," Meltzer said. "My course is zero one five, sir." A bit east of due north.

"Until Orpheus tells us otherwise, XO, we assume *von Scheer* is north of the Rocks, somewhere between these two cables."

This give-and-take between a submarine's senior officers, in the control room before and during an attack, was an old and valued Silent Service tradition. Brainstorming approaches and tactics, thinking things through out loud, was essential to survival and success.

Bell called up a larger-scale chart. "Check this out, Captain. The two cables are almost parallel, but not quite. They slowly draw closer together, as they run north away from the Rocks."

Jeffrey saw what Bell was getting at. "They intersect *here*." He touched a spot on the map near the Azores and used Bell's joystick to move a cursor. He clicked on the Rocks, then clicked again when the cursor hit where the two cables met. He read off the distance that popped on the screen. "One thousand one hundred nautical miles."

"That's a long way off."

"I know. At flank speed that would take us over twenty hours. . . . And at flank speed our best sonars would be half deaf, and *von Scheer* might hear us coming from a hundred miles away or more."

"It's an awfully big area to search," Bell said.

"The convoy forward elements are closer than that already. That cuts down the area somewhat. It'll keep on shrinking even if we don't do anything more ourselves."

Bell nodded. The convoy was moving south, generally toward the Rocks and away from the Azores.

Jeffrey pondered. "The closer the convoy gets, the more the search area narrows. But the closer the convoy gets, the more it moves in easy range of *von Scheer*'s missiles."

"Use our active sonar, sir? While there's still time?"

"Without knowing who's winning or losing on the Rocks, the SEALs or the kampfschwimmer, we don't know how much time we really have. Active sonar used too soon might hurt us more than it helps. . . . It's time to commit to another strategy step."

"Sir?"

"Helm, slow to ahead one-third, make turns for seven knots."

Meltzer acknowledged.

"Sir?" Bell asked again.

"If we can't be rushing all over the place, we go for the other extreme. We lurk in one spot until the situation clarifies."

"Should I show you the large-scale bottom terrain?"

"You just read my mind, XO."

Bell typed again. He windowed a map of the seafloor, in that key slice of ocean between the two old phone cables.

Jeffrey and Bell studied the nautical chart—its area reached far beyond the maximum range of their gravimeter, which could see out only thirty-five or forty miles from *Challenger*.

"The eastern foothills of the Mid-Atlantic Ridge," Jeffrey said. "Rugged and rolling terrain, all the way from here to the convoy and past. All deep, but well within a ceramic-hulled submarine's operating envelope."

"Yes, Captain. For both us and for the *von Scheer*."

"I can think of several things we might do next, XO. But I don't like any one of them."

"Sir?"

"*Von Scheer* has to come shallow to launch her missiles. We know it, and Beck knows we know. That's his one real weakness."

"That's why I suggested active sonar, Captain. If he rises out of the bottom terrain, we'll make contact. He'll use out-of-phase acoustic masking, but our arrays and signal processors are probably smart enough to not be fooled. Especially if we get an echo off the slats at the back of his pump jet."

"*Or,* he'll hear us prematurely and not come up from the bottom terrain. He'll either shoot nuclear torpedoes at us, which is bad enough, or he'll sneak quietly away. If he shoots, we get *some* idea of where he is, and we shoot back and maybe at least we damage his ship. But if Beck sneaks away, we're left empty-handed. Until he launches . . . He'll be thinking what we're thinking. So he'll know his best choice is to sneak away, once he either gets what he wants from the kampfschwimmer or knows they lost on the Rocks. Time is on *his* side, not ours."

"Understood, sir."

"Sonar," Jeffrey called.

Kathy Milgrom turned her head. "Captain?"

"Anything at all of *von Scheer* on passive sonar?"

"No contact on *von Scheer* whatsoever. My men would have reported it instantly, sir." Milgrom gave the captain just enough of a *look,* as if to say, *And* you *know they would have too.*

"Very well, Sonar." Jeffrey stared into space.

"But there's Orpheus, Captain," Bell said.

"Two hours or so from now, XO, unless we slow down even more or change our course, we'll be too far north of the Rocks and we'll lose the acoustic link with the minisub. From there we'll be on our own. No more help from Orpheus on getting *von Scheer*'s location and course and speed so we can move to intercept her smartly, whatever her actual distance from us right now. It all hinges on that fixed anchor station. . . . But if Beck does sneak off north, he'll unwittingly lie masked between those two cables until he's too far off for us to put a stop to him, and we won't even know it. In that case, us lingering here and depending on Orpheus will have done more harm than good." *It's like we can't win either way.*

Bell looked at the map for a very long time. Jeffrey let him think; he knew there were many moving parts to this tactical problem, and he didn't want to rush Bell. Undersea warfare was in some ways like a grand-master chess tournament. You had to think several moves ahead. You had to consider a lot of different strategy choices and trade-offs. And you had to try to take account of what your opponent would think and feel and do.

But unlike chess, the stakes here aren't prestige or money. The stakes are life and death for hundreds, even thousands of people.

Bell looked up abruptly. He seemed emotionally unsettled, but he'd clearly made up his mind. "We have to nuke the Rocks ourselves, Captain, *now*."

Jeffrey raised his eyebrows. *"Why?"*

"We can't afford for Estabo to loose his battle. If the kampfschwimmer win, and we guessed right about their purpose, they'll send good targeting data to *von Scheer*."

"And if we nuke the Rocks we kill everybody, so that way the Germans can't win?"

Bell nodded, but seemed doubtful when he heard Jeffrey put it so bluntly out loud.

Jeffrey shook his head. "First of all, I'm not intentionally killing friendly troops. Second, the blasts would cause so much noise and aftershocks we'd lose the acoustic link to Orpheus, assuming the mini even survived."

"I agree, sir. I just felt I had to offer the option."

"Good. Keep it up." But Jeffrey felt halfhearted when he said it. The *von Scheer* was out there, somewhere tantalizingly close—unseen but real. She must weigh something like twenty thousand tons submerged, and have well over a hundred men in her crew, but even so she'd vanished. For all the brainstorming with Bell, Ernst Beck's mind remained opaque to Jeffrey. The German captain held the initiative, and Beck's ship remained invisible.

Jeffrey felt frustration. The taste of failure began to rise inside his gut like bile.

"Captain!" Kathy Milgrom called.

Jeffrey turned, his train of thought broken. *"What is it?"*

Milgrom didn't flinch. "New contact on acoustic intercept . . . Multiple contacts on acoustic intercept." The acoustic intercept array was specifically designed to detect another active sonar pinging.

"Range? Bearing? *Classification?* Come on, give me a proper report."

I'm starting to lose my grip here. Chill out, buddy. Your people don't need such abuse.

"Contact rough bearing is north, sir, picked up through

the deep sound channel. Range approximately four hundred miles. Contact classification, tentative, is airdropped active sonobuoys."

Jeffrey brightened.

"Another cluster of sonobuoys, Captain. Closer to us, by maybe fifty miles."

"Can you identify the sonobuoys?"

"Definite American and British manufacture, sir. Some are SSQ-seventy-fives." That model of sonobuoy could descend to sixteen thousand feet or more.

"Okay, Sonar. Good. Thanks. Keep the info coming. . . . XO, plot these contacts on the large-scale nautical chart."

Marks for the rough location of the sonobuoys began to appear on the chart on Bell's console.

"What do you think, XO? Antisubmarine search by the convoy's forward aircraft screens?"

"There's a trend to the patterns they're dropping," Bell said. "They're not probing along the relief convoy's base course through the Narrows, Captain."

"Hmm . . . Let's just watch for a minute. . . . Helm, steady as you go."

"Aye aye, sir. My course is zero one five."

"Captain," Bell said, "something strange is happening here." He pointed at the map.

Jeffrey looked at the map. Minutes ticked by. Precious minutes. Then he saw it, and in a flash all his second-guessing and worries vanished.

"That brilliant son of a bitch," Jeffrey exclaimed. "He figured it out!"

"Captain?" Bell said.

"The sonobuoys, XO! They're all being dropped between the two phone cables. Admiral Hodgkiss figured it out! Our radios are jammed so we can't talk to him, but still he sees the same things we've been seeing, thinks the same things we've been thinking. . . . He sent us air support, XO. Those planes are coming at us at almost five hundred knots. Unless Ernst Beck has stronger nerves than I do, he'll *have* to move

out of the way, east or west, or an SSQ-seventy-five will hit
him on the nose and then a big nuclear depth bomb'll hit him
hard right in the head."

Jeffrey walked over to Milgrom's console to watch as
more and more data came in. A solid carpet of sonobuoys
was saturating the bottom terrain between the convoy and
the Rocks, between the two old telephone cables. The leading edge of the carpet inched south steadily.

The number of sonobuoys expended was truly prodigious.
Jeffrey knew that, at this rate, soon the carriers and even their
underway-replenishment-support auxiliary ships would exhaust their entire inventories.

Jeffrey was very glad that he'd decided to stay shallow
and not rush away farther north. Otherwise, those constant
pings might've bounced off *Challenger*'s hull and given her
away to the *von Scheer,* or—worse—might have subjected
him to friendly atomic fire.

"Captain," Bell called out. "New Orpheus contact. Positive Orpheus contact! *Von Scheer* is moving due east, *here*.
Her speed is thirty knots."

*Thank you, Admiral Hodgkiss! You flushed Beck for us af-
ter all.*

Jeffrey turned to COB—it was time to hunker down for
the fight. "Chief of the watch, relay by phone talkers shipwide, rig for nuclear depth charge."

COB acknowledged smartly. Jeffrey returned to Bell.

"We've got him, XO. *We've got him.*"

"Yes, sir." Bell gave a feral grin.

That suddenly, the entire mood in the control room altered. The crew, which had been sensing Jeffrey's growing
despair, sensed instead his confidence, and their own confidence skyrocketed.

"Helm, right thirty degrees rudder. Make your course zero
nine zero." Due east.

"Right thirty degrees rudder, aye. Make my course zero
nine zero, aye."

Estabo and his men will have to fend for themselves for now.

Challenger banked steeply into the turn. The readings on analog compass circles, and digital gyrocompass displays, spun rapidly, then steadied. "My course is zero nine zero, sir."

"Very well. Helm, ahead flank."

"Ahead flank, aye!"

The ship began to accelerate. As she topped forty knots, flow turbulence began to cause a harsh hiss on the sonar speakers and a constant shaking in the control room. As *Challenger* topped fifty knots, the engineering plant worked *very* hard. Immense power was being put through the propulsion shaft to the pump jet.

The vibrations grew heavy. Consoles squeaked as they jiggled in their shock-absorbing mounts. Light fixtures in the overhead bounced on their springs. Mike cords swayed and everyone held on tight. *Challenger*'s speed was steady now at just over fifty-three knots.

"Sir," Bell said, "you told us before that at this speed we'd be blind, and noisy as a freight train."

"Except for one thing, XO. Now we know where *von Scheer* is. And *now* we use active sonar."

CHAPTER 23

Ernst Beck watched the data on his console in disbelief as his ship fled east to escape the barrage of enemy sonobuoys. "So many SSQ-seventy-fives," he said mostly to himself. "I didn't know they even *had* that many SSQ-seventy-fives."

Von Loringhoven looked disturbed, even irate. "Everything is going wrong. *Everything*. First our men on the Rocks encounter U.S. Navy SEALs. Now their carrier planes are searching bottom terrain at our crush depth. The SEALs, that could be explained in other ways. But the deep-capable active sonobuoys, in such heavy quantities, there can be only a single explanation. They suspect the *von Scheer*'s presence. They suspect it, or they *know* it."

"Baron, I concur," Beck said. "But there's little good in belaboring the obvious."

Von Loringhoven opened his mouth to say something, but to Beck's gratitude, Stissinger smoothly cut him off. "Captain, recommend clearing baffles." The *von Scheer* was moving too fast to trail a towed array. Aft of her stern, she couldn't hear a thing.

"Very well, Einzvo. Pilot, slow to ahead one-third, turns for seven knots. Starboard ten degrees rudder."

Von Scheer slowed and began to turn in a circle. Her sensitive side-mounted wide-aperture arrays began to listen keenly to the water outside as the arrays swung with the ship in a wide arc.

"New passive contact on the starboard wide-aperture array!" Haffner shouted. "Bearing two seven zero true." Due west. "Range is forty thousand meters." Twenty nautical miles. "Contact is submerged! Confirmed! Contact gaining, *contact speed is over fifty knots!*"

"The *Connecticut*?" Stissinger asked, referring to the sister ship of the USS *Seawolf*. According to Imperial German Naval Intelligence, the *Seawolf* was way up near Iceland, but the *Connecticut* might be escorting the convoy.

"Negative!" Haffner yelled. "Strong tonals now . . . Not, repeat *not*, a *Seawolf*-class." Then the sonar officer gasped. "Contact is USS *Challenger*! Confirmed, definite match of flank-speed tonals to prior data in our library! Contact is USS *Challenger*!"

Man, this is worse than hell itself. Felix scrambled over a charred inhuman landscape beneath an absurdly clear and balmy blue sky. Other black figures swarmed on the Rocks, grappling with each other or spitting muzzle flashes, like warring parties of fire ants.

Felix cursed when he almost tripped on loose rock. He shouldered his MP-5 and fired another three-round burst at a glimpse of an enemy kampfschwimmer. He missed—the nine-millimeter rounds everyone carried weren't meant for accurate sniping over long distances.

Felix gasped for air. He was almost drowning in his own perspiration—it couldn't evaporate within his protective suit, because his body sweated faster than the special layered material could breathe—and Felix roasting from built-up body heat. His mouth was so dry that his tongue was glued to the roof of his mouth and his lips were chapped and cracked and bleeding. He had a headache and felt nauseous—definite signs of early heatstroke.

It was so bad he was starting to seriously consider taking his suit helmet off, radioactivity be damned.

Stay focused. Don't be stupid. You're the man in charge.

Felix ducked as another German bullet cracked by, frighteningly close. The boulder he chose for his next bit of cover was black and slimy, like all the rest, and the outside of his suit was smeared with toxic goo.

At least he could see through his faceplate better. The inside of the plastic had started fogging up, but now heavy droplets of condensation ran down to streak the fog. It was like driving a car in the rain with no defroster.

Seeing his chiefs make frantic hand signals, he broke cover and picked up the pace.

The deadly contest for the cargo-ship hulk was down to the final sprint. Because of the place where the first and then reinforcing teams landed on each of the Rocks, SEALs and kampfschwimmer were sandwiched in the most bizarre tactical setup Felix had ever seen. The rate of fire was low because everyone on both sides was fast running out of ammo. Felix's MP-5 was empty, and now he held his pistol in one hand, continuing to fire at fleeting targets of opportunity. It seemed that his men had a razor-thin positional edge overall—Felix's reinforcements had landed on Northwest Rock, by chance the one closest to the hulk.

Felix dashed along a narrow shingle beach. On one side of him was a slope and on the other was the ocean. Surf broke as he panted along the beach. But around a bend too small to be called a headland, the minuscule beach petered out, ending in a sudden drop from the upslope into the water—a sheer cliff. Felix decided to run, not swim; swimming was much too slow.

Felix started up the slope toward the spine at the top of this Northeast Rock. A German carrying a pistol came over the slope, and the two of them almost collided. Felix and the German fired their weapons at the same time, aiming two shots dead-center chest by instinct—but both pistols only fired one shot, then were empty. Both men staggered backward as the bullets hit outer-suit Kevlar and thudded hard against their Draegers' casings inside. Both men recovered instantly. They holstered their pistols and swung their MP-5s as clubs.

The German was taller, nimble and quick. But Felix was also good. Each man kept trying to smash the other's skull, yet every thrust was parried, every blow deflected away.

Felix changed his tactics, trying not to telegraph his next move. He bent for his K-bar fighting knife, intending to rise with a slash at the enemy's face: the clear plastic was the only vulnerable point of the suit. But the German had picked up a big piece of stone. He and Felix locked eyes for a moment, knife versus rock. There was a mix of hate and admiration in that German's eyes, and Felix felt the same.

The man threw the rock at Felix's head, perfectly aimed and hard enough to kill. Felix was forced to duck. By the time he got up, the German was halfway down the slope. He went right into the water and dove out of sight.

Felix turned. His tunnel vision from that man-to-man contest cleared. Then it registered on him that the German had been wearing a tactical radio headset under his protective hood. He'd shouted something as he threw the rock, something authoritative, into his mike. The other surviving kampfschwimmer were withdrawing into the sea.

That guy was their leader, their officer. They're conceding the Rocks, for now. They'll retreat into their minisub while there's still time. . . . They know we came by submarine, just as they did. They know what's coming next, too: atomic-torpedo warhead blasts.

Felix ran down the opposite slope and splashed through the filthy shallows. His two chiefs and their teams already had climbing ropes set up, reaching to what was left of the main deck of the cargo hulk.

Felix realized that most of his men were dropping on their

feet by now. They helped one another as much as they could as they climbed. Two men were wounded; the dead had to be left where they fell, until later—if there was a later.

Both wounded SEALs had broken limbs, where German bullets had hit arms or legs and only the Kevlar had kept the slugs from penetrating—but the impacts weren't cushioned by any trauma pads like a flak vest. The other SEALs used one rope with a double bowline tied at the end to lift these two men onto the hulk.

Felix helped from below; he insisted on being last. He took a running jump and climbed the rope hand over hand. He used his aching, trembling leg muscles too, because his arms burned and felt rubbery—his body had very little left. Clambering over the rusty, pitted gunnel onto the even more corroded, crumpled deck, he took stock of the hulk.

His men held the viable high ground. The only problem was, they had barely any ammo left to repulse another kampfschwimmer attack—and the kampfschwimmer might reload from stocks in their minisub.

First problem first. This hulk needs to become our bomb shelter, against close-by bursts in a tactical nuclear undersea duel.

The cargo ship was a mess. Blast and heat had wrecked the steel of her superstructure. Massive cargo-hold covers and cranes had simply vanished, blown off or blown apart, and the hold contents were burned to ashes and heaps of twisted metal.

One hold held what once had been dried meat products. The ashes were soaked with seawater sloshing and slapping through cracks and tears in the hull. The mess was revolting to look at. Then Felix reminded himself that outside his suit there was also a smell.

The deck was perfectly steady in the moderate surf on the east side of the Rocks—the hulk was hard aground.

Felix told his exhausted men to move into the dented and mangled superstructure. Inside was better protection, and also shade, which gave some relief from the dangers of heatstroke. Even so, now that the immediate struggle had died down, several of Felix's men passed out. Their fellows had to hold their Draeger regulators in their mouths and prop their jaws shut, by reaching through the softness of their hoods. Other SEALs just lay on their sides, staring into space numbly, to relieve their chests of the weight of their front-worn Draegers.

I must maintain team discipline, even now.

Felix posted lookouts to cover every quarter of approach to the Rocks and the hulk. In dark corners, by the sunlight that streamed in through cracked and sooty portholes, he could make out human remains.

During his disaster-diver recovery training, earlier in his career, he'd been told never to look at the faces. But Felix had superb peripheral vision. He could see that most of these remains didn't even have faces.

He spoke to the wounded SEALs. Both were in great pain, but they coped bravely. Their broken limbs were dressed with field-expedient splints, made from MP-5s and rope.

Felix glanced out a porthole, east. He wondered how high the tidal waves would be when they arrived here. He wondered if they'd wash right over the top of the hulk. He wondered if the hulk would capsize or shatter when the airborne shock fronts struck, after the undersea fireballs broke the surface. He wondered how much hard radiation those fireballs would still give off, in the seconds and minutes after the warheads' initial detonation, as mushroom clouds exploded into the air.

Jeffrey bounced against his seat belt as *Challenger* tore after *von Scheer* at flank speed. . . . Or at least after the place where Orpheus said the *von Scheer* should be.

She's down there somewhere, on the bottom, heading east. We're looking down at the seafloor terrain from thousands of feet higher up. The ridgelines here all run east-west, so von Scheer *won't be screened from us by bumps or cracks in the bottom. . . . Right now Ernst Beck can't hide.*

"Sonar, go active!" Jeffrey ordered. "Maximum intensity, *ping.*"

Challenger's bow sphere emitted an earsplitting screech, a burst of sonic power so loud it came back through the hull and nearly deafened most of the crew. The screech began to rise and fall in tone, like a whale call. It ended abruptly, with a sudden silence that seemed a portent of doom. Milgrom's people hunched over their sonar consoles.

The ping was on its way, a spreading blast front of pure acoustic power—a mix of changing frequencies to cut through ocean reverb, optimized by the most advanced signal processors known. Designed to pick out a target whether it was moving or still, to sense its speed and even give its size and shape and which way it was heading . . . Impossible for the stealthiest sub in the world to cloak itself entirely or suppress a telling echo.

Sound traveled through seawater at almost a mile every second, five times as fast as through air. Even so, it would take half a minute for any real target return to come back.

Jeffrey forced himself to keep breathing evenly. Next to him, as fire-control coordinator, Lieutenant Commander Bell looked prepared and eager to unleash the forces trapped within tiny atoms, and give birth to brand-new underwater suns, to destroy the *von Scheer* with unspeakable violence and kill every person aboard her.

The Axis started this, Jeffrey told himself. *Now it's our turn to help finish it.*

"New active sonar contact!" Milgrom shouted. "Bearing zero eight five, range thirty thousand yards! Course zero nine zero, speed thirty knots! . . . Depth eleven thousand feet, hugging the bottom!"

"Identify!" Jeffrey ordered.

"Contact consistent with Orpheus datum. I merge and designate the contact Master One. Master One identified as the SMS *Admiral von Scheer*."

"Fire Control," Jeffrey snapped. "Firing point procedures, Mark Eighty-eights in tubes one through eight, target Master One."

"Solution ready," Bell recited. "Ship ready . . . Weapons ready."

"At five-second intervals, match generated bearings and *shoot*."

"Unit from tube one fired electrically," Bell said. "Good wire to the weapon." The Mark 88s were wire guided.

"Unit is running normally," Milgrom reported. Sonar, by listening, made doubly sure the torpedo was running true.

"Unit from tube two fired electrically. Good wire."

"Unit is running normally."

And on and on the litany went as *Challenger* launched eight wide-body, deep-capable nuclear fish at the *Admiral von Scheer.*

"Reload all tubes, Mark Eighty-eights Mod Twos. Set warhead yields to maximum." One full kiloton each.

Bell, Weps, and their people got busy.

Jeffrey studied the tactical plot. *Challenger* had gained on the *von Scheer*'s projected position, but *Challenger*'s torpedoes were dashing ahead and gaining on the *von Scheer* much faster.

Without needing to be told, Bell had his weapons technicians spread the charging, fully armed weapons apart—to catch the *von Scheer* in a pincers and make it harder for her to evade or destroy Jeffrey's fish.

Jeffrey's eight reloads were all positioned by the tube breach doors, for him and Bell to enter their special weapons arming codes. Soon all tubes were ready to shoot another massive salvo. It was high time to update the firing solution. At flank speed, with *von Scheer* so quiet, Milgrom still held no passive contact on Master One.

"Sonar, go active."

The overpowering bow-sphere blast this time was like a

shout from an angry dolphin. The undulating whistles and clicks were designed to look past *Challenger*'s own noisy Mark 88s in the water and pound the *von Scheer*'s hull and sail and control planes and pump jet with an inescapable fist of pure sound.

Once more Jeffrey waited for the data to come back. While he fidgeted impatiently he brought up that picture he had of Ernst Beck and windowed it onto his now-crowded console.

You know I've got you cold, Herr Korvettenkapitan Beck. Watcha gonna do next?

———

Ernst Beck listened on the sonar speakers. The all-too-familiar engine noise of eight inbound enemy torpedoes bounced off ridges and escarpments and came in through his ship's hydrophone arrays. The other bounces of increasing, gaining noise, of *Challenger* herself tearing after *von Scheer,* emphasized the energy of Jeffrey Fuller's pursuit. The time for sneaking and guessing was over. There was nothing subtle about what was going on now, nor anything the least bit quiet or stealthy about what would happen quite soon.

"Inbound torpedoes are spreading out, Captain," Stissinger reported.

Beck watched his tactical plot. "As expected, Einzvo."

"Can't you go any faster?" von Loringhoven demanded.

"*Yes,* I could go faster. Thirty knots is our top quiet speed, Baron. More than that, we begin to make much more noise. We give *Challenger* a continuous passive sonar contact to track, which sharpens the enemy's firing solutions and takes away options from *us.*"

Just then an earsplitting whistle hit the ship, with palpable physical force—the control room was filled with the siren call of a determined and deadly opponent. The whistle was overlaid with piercing clicks, like stones hurled against the hull—a small hint of worse things to come.

"Contact on acoustic intercept!" Werner Haffner shouted by rote. "Unable to suppress ping echoes off our stern!"

"Very well, Sonar," Beck said, blasé—he surprised himself. He realized his newfound command persona was fast kicking into gear and felt rather pleased with himself. Even amid mortal threats from outside, and even in such close confines with the shaky nerves of his inexperienced crew, Beck was finding the inner strength to lead his men. *They need a father figure now above all else, to reassure them—like frightened children—that everything will be all right. . . . And being a good father is one thing I do know plenty about.*

Beck and Stissinger watched *Challenger*'s first salvo of torpedoes draw closer. Because of the ranges involved, even with the high-speed Mark 88s, it would be minutes before they got in lethal range.

"Noisemakers, Captain?" Stissinger prompted.

"Not yet."

"Launch counterfire?" All eight of the *von Scheer*'s tubes were loaded with deep-capable Sea Lion nuclear eels; *eel* was German slang for "torpedo."

Beck watched his screens. "Not yet."

"What are you waiting for?" von Loringhoven said. "We have eight atomic weapons on our tail!"

"Watch closely. You might actually learn something."

"Order flank speed! They're moving more than twice as fast as us!"

Beck shook his head.

"But—"

"Baron, if this game is too hard on your pampered constitution, I suggest you retire to your cabin for a nice lie-down and keep out of my way. I must warn you, though, don't expect pleasant dreams. The ride is about to become much louder and rougher than anything you ever imagined."

This time it was Beck who sneered—again he surprised himself. But now that battle was joined, the gap between atomic combat veteran Beck's sum total of experience, and the cushy life von Loringhoven had led, seemed truly unbridgeable. Beck considered ordering the baron to his cabin right now.

No, let him stay where I can see his fear and suffering. Let this be my revenge on him for the terrible things I must do later. Let my crewmen also see his panic and his sweat, as a portal through which to find their own bravery.

"Sir," Stissinger said, "we should launch our counterfire."

Beck gave no answer. His ship continued her fast but quiet thirty-knot course due east.

"Evasive maneuvers at least, sir? Make a knuckle in the water?"

Beck looked at the loyal but untested Stissinger. He'd never fired a nuclear weapon in anger, just in a simulator. He'd never been shot at for real, only in training drills.

The captain smiled. "Thank you, Einzvo, but I think not."

Stissinger was going by the textbook, and doing it well— but men like Beck and Fuller had thrown out the textbook months before.

Beck returned to observing the tactical plot. "Show me the enemy warhead kill zones against us."

"At what yield, sir?" Stissinger said.

"The maximum for Mark Eighty-eights. I'm sure he'll use the maximum."

"One-tenth kiloton."

Beck nodded.

Little disks appeared around each inbound torpedo symbol. They represented the radius within which their warhead detonations would inflict fatal damage on Ernst Beck's ship at her present depth. The disks still had some time before they were dangerous to the *von Scheer*. Though water was very rigid and dense, so that blast force traveled great distances, the warhead yields were small, and the *von Scheer* was very shock hardened. . . . And blast force in deep water died off inversely with the cube of the range: ten times as far from ground zero meant only one-one-thousandth the impact. Even a megaton hydrogen bomb set off in the sea could just kill a steel-hulled sub out to a dozen miles or so.

Beck was surprised at his own inner calm as he ran through these cold-blooded facts. But calm was one key part of his plan. He watched the icon on his display that represented *Challenger*. He listened to her noise coming over the speakers.

Who knows himself and the other man better, Captain Fuller, you or me?

Who remembers more from the last time we met? Who more clearly understands the crucial differences now?

And who learned the most from our previous battle? The victor or the vanquished, you think? I do believe that failure is a sharper, keener tutor than success.

————————

"Master One still maintaining constant course and speed, sir," Bell reported.

"No countermeasures? No decoys? No torpedoes launched?" Jeffrey was puzzled—a sensation he *really* didn't like.

"Negative, Captain."

"He *has* to have heard us pinging."

"I concur."

"So what's he up to?" Jeffrey's common sense set off alarm bells in his head. Beck *must* be up to something. The German's total lack of reaction to the surprising presence of Jeffrey's ship and then to *Challenger*'s aggressive pinging, and now Bell's full salvo of oncoming nuclear fish, was the last thing he had expected.

"Sir," Bell warned, "there's so little we know about the *von Scheer*'s design. He may have a nasty trick up his sleeve."

"Like what, XO?"

"He's much too quiet at thirty knots for that to be his flank speed. He's holding something back."

"You mean you think he might be faster than us?"

"Maybe."

"Sonar."

"Captain?"

"What's *von Scheer*'s stern look like? One propulsor or two?"

"One large pump-jet propulsor, sir."

"How many nuclear reactors?"

"Captain?"

"The Russians often use two on their bigger submarines, right? We know the Axis gets help on propulsion plants from Moscow. Does *von Scheer* have a single reactor, or two?"

"Wait, please," Milgrom said.

Jeffrey turned to Bell. "What's your guess?"

"He might have two."

"I know he *might* have two. I need a specific best guess."

"One big propulsor seems to suggest one single big reactor."

Jeffrey bobbed his head around as if he was thinking about what Bell said and wasn't sure if he agreed with his XO or not.

"Sonar?" he pressed. He felt worried and impatient.

"Impossible to tell number of Master One reactors on-line from the sound profile available."

Jeffrey looked at Bell. "So he may be running at whatever top quiet speed he can get out of just one reactor, with another held in reserve, idling in quick-start-up power range. He might suddenly throw both on-line at full power and zoom away from us."

"But from our *torpedoes,* sir?" Bell said. "The Mark Eighty-eights do seventy knots."

Jeffrey fought hard not to lose his temper as he went on: "And the Russian Shkval undersea rocket torpedoes do two hundred knots. And we know even back in the Cold War, the Russians worked on slippery long-chain polymers they'd squirt from the front of the bow dome to lower hull friction in order to help them outrun inbound fish."

Bell nodded reluctantly. "So at least for short periods, sir, the *von Scheer* might be able to run at seventy knots."

Something in Jeffrey's spirit sagged. "If that's true, we've already lost this contest. If Beck is waiting for just the right moment to shove all his throttles hard against the firewall, and he really is able to sprint that fast, we don't have a weapon aboard that can stop him."

"Our Tomahawks do hundreds of knots."

"You know they've all been loaded just for high-explosive land attack."

Bell stared at his screens. Jeffrey realized his XO had run out of useful ideas. He felt his own throat start to go dry; he had to pucker to summon saliva. A few uncomfortable minutes passed.

"Sonar, Fire Control," Jeffrey said, "any change whatsoever on Master One?"

"Negative, sir," Milgrom said. "No change in tonals, no mechanical transients at all."

"Contact's course and speed continue steady, sir. Due east at thirty knots."

Jeffrey looked at the tactical plot. His eight atomic weapons were drawing closer to the *Admiral von Scheer*. Very soon they'd be in lethal range, and Ernst Beck had to know it, and Ernst Beck wasn't doing anything to save himself.

Unless he has a way to sprint even faster than my torpedoes. Is he rubbing it in now, reading my mind, and showing me his contempt? . . . Or does he have a whole new secret weapon, and he knows that I don't know it, and he's not the least bit worried about me or my inbound fish?

Maybe Beck has something awful, an entire new technology—and he's about to deal with me and my torpedoes once and for all, the same way a horse would use its tail to swat down pesty flies.

For almost the first time in his life in the navy, Jeffrey began to feel genuine, gnawing, soul-crushing fear.

"I think we've toyed with Fuller's mind enough," Ernst Beck said, and cleared his throat. "*Achtung,* Einzvo, target one

Sea Lion at each incoming Mark Eighty-eight. Set all Sea Lion warhead yields to maximum, one kiloton."

"One kiloton, sir? Doctrine is to make defensive counter-shots at *lowest* yield."

Beck smiled again at Stissinger, then shrugged theatrically. "So I'm a nonconformist."

"Maximum yield, *jawohl*," Stissinger acknowledged.

"Load firing solutions."

"Loaded."

"Close all inner doors. Flood tubes."

"Closed and flooded, Captain."

"Equalize to sea pressure. Open all outer doors."

"Equalized and doors open."

"*Achtung,* tube one, *los!*" Go!

Stissinger relayed the firing command.

"Tube one is fired."

"Unit is operating properly," Haffner called.

"Tube two, *los!*"

"Tube two is fired."

"Unit is operating properly."

Beck fired all eight tubes. He glanced at the tactical plot. There were eight new icons, friendly torpedoes outbound. Once freed from the tubes, they looped around and headed back past *von Scheer*'s stern, aiming west under wire-guided control. One Sea Lion ran at each inbound Mark 88. The net closing speed of each interception was almost 150 knots.

Beck knew he had a key advantage over Fuller: unlike *Challenger*, the *von Scheer* could close her outer torpedo tube doors to reload without losing the wires to weapons already launched. In what Beck planned to do next, this would be crucial.

"Reload all tubes, Sea Lions, preset warhead yields to maximum."

Jeffrey listened as Milgrom and Bell reported that the *von Scheer* had launched countershots at Jeffrey's torpedoes.

"Finally," Jeffrey said. "He played that close."

"So he's using conventional tactics after all," Bell said. "We shoot, he countershoots."

Jeffrey nodded. "This fight'll be one really hard slugfest."

I mustn't tell the crew, but we hold a crucial advantage. We're expendable in a double kill, and von Scheer *isn't. That lets me be more flexible, more aggressive than Ernst Beck.*

"New mechanical transients on Master One!" Milgrom called. "Launch transients! One, two, three . . . Eight *more* torpedoes in the water!"

Jeffrey studied the tactical plot—there were now sixteen enemy weapon icons moving away from the hostile-ship marker.

"This new bunch is aimed *our* way," Bell said, pointing at the plot.

Jeffrey saw what he meant. Of Beck's second salvo of eight atomic torpedoes, four each were curving north and south of the wide arc formed by Jeffrey's own eight fish.

———

Beck watched the tactical plot with considerable self-satisfaction. "*Achtung,* Einzvo. Detonate all sixteen warheads *now.*"

"All *sixteen,* sir?"

"Sixteen. Please."

———

Jeffrey leaned forward with anticipation. Any second now it would be time to detonate his fish as they closed fast to lethal range of *von Scheer.*

Red warning lights flashed across Bell's console. "Lost the wires, all tubes!"

"What the—"

The signals through the fiber-optic guidance wires from

the torpedoes traveled at the speed of light—instantaneously. The blast force of undersea nuclear weapons took a little longer to arrive.

A tremendous crack resounded, a thunderclap that rattled the ship like the first impact of an unfolding earthquake. The warheads had detonated all at once, but from the geometries and distances involved, their shock fronts through the water got there one by one a few moments apart.

It was as if a giant's jackhammer began to smash at *Challenger*'s hull. Vibrations inside were so strong and so vicious, Jeffrey's vision blurred. He could barely see his instruments as standing crewmen were thrown from their feet. He was jolted hard against his seat belt and his headrest. The entire vessel shivered and rolled as conflicting turbulence from different bearings punished her amid unendurable shaking and ungodly noise.

The continuing decibel level quickly became so loud that Jeffrey lost all hearing. The scene of chaos and pain around him refused to relent, but now it showed itself in an otherworldly silence. He felt booms and rumbles deep in his gut, telling him what constant eruptions his eardrums were simply too overloaded to pass through the nerves to his brain.

Light fixtures shattered. Console screens went dark. Cabinets that were locked burst open; manuals, breather masks, laptops, and pencils went flying. Jeffrey ducked. He began to cough as the air was filled with choking dust from flaking paint and heat insulation.

Sadistic aftershocks hit, reflections of the original blasts off the surface and the bottom. Jeffrey held his armrests in a cringing white-knuckled death grip. The aftershocks sent grating tremors up his ass and tried to crush his spine. He stamped the deck with his feet involuntarily as his leg muscles forfeited any control and his lower limbs flailed about wildly.

Each of the sixteen atomic fireballs pulsated in a process Jeffrey knew too well. They started at the instant of fission at a temperature of a million degrees, swelled outward fast against the deep-sea pressure, then fell back as the pressure took charge. They rebounded outward violently, sending out a whole new shock front. The merciless throbbing happened over and over: the spheres of steam and vaporized weapon parts were buoyant. Each raced for the surface and rebounded outward again. Once more each reached a limit, then was squashed back in by the weight of the sea. Once more each sphere collapsed, only building up strength to rebound. Again each rebound threw off more concussive force.

Each new shock front reached for *Challenger,* hitting the ship and her crew with a seemingly conscious intent to shatter them. Sixteen separate fireballs did this, over and over without end.

Jeffrey's body grew numb from the ongoing punishment, yet the unforgiving ocean still raged and swirled. At last the fireballs broke the surface. There was one final series of tremendous jarring blows, and the fireballs leaped into the air.

Survival had to come first. When the kampfschwimmer made no rapid counterattack, after they'd withdrawn into the water, Felix decided he needed to change tactics. He regrouped his men deeper inside the cargo-ship hulk's superstructure. Additional layers of steel, he knew, would further block the impending gamma rays.

He also told his men to huddle in a circle, on one charred compartment's deck. Since the human body was mostly water, and water gave some shielding against gamma rays and neutrons, one SEAL's body could help to further protect another's. This huddling was a common-enough SEAL practice, but normally it was done for mutual protection against bad weather: wind and cold.

Well, we're on an atomic battlefield now.

Felix, as the officer in command, felt an obligation to maintain his situational awareness. He peered out the nearest porthole, which was almost totally black from caked soot and faced east. He had a hunch the action would happen in that direction. Africa was east.

Leaning against the bulkhead next to the porthole to help support the weight of his body and his equipment, he studied the spiderweb of cracks in the armored porthole glass. He felt horribly thirsty and hot. His mind began to play tricks, and Felix became obsessed with licking his own sweat off the inside of his protective-suit helmet. He knew this was the worst thing he could do: the sweat was not only salty, but held other bodily wastes, and to drink it would make him even more dehydrated than he already was. But it was very hard to resist taking at least a little lick.

Face it, we're in pretty desperate straits here.

Then Felix felt the thing he'd dreaded, a series of tremors through the deck of the cargo-ship hulk. He saw the surface of the ocean churn a foaming white.

The underwater shock wave always comes first.

There was a blinding glare from outside and he had to look away. He dashed toward where his men were sitting together and placed his body between theirs and the glare.

Soon the glare subsided and was replaced by an eerie quiet. Tremors continued to come through the water and rattle the hulk.

Felix was overcome by curiosity. He went back to the porthole.

Through the soot, he made out a staggering number of glowing golden-yellow fireballs. Each was rising higher and higher into the air. Beneath each widening fireball was a solid pillar of white. He knew this was water and steam—and fission by-products from the warhead itself, the worst form of nuclear waste. Felix knew the mushroom clouds would be horribly radioactive: neutron bombardment by the initial weapon flash while underwater would act on metals dissolved in the sea—sodium especially—transforming their atomic structure into unstable isotopes. Those isotopes would decay, giving off alpha and beta and gamma rays, and more neutrons.

The wind is from the east. That stuff is coming right at us.

Felix barely had time to form these thoughts when the airborne shock waves hit. They pounded the hull of the burned-out cargo ship, in a repetitive hammering action that was a result of the mushroom clouds being different distances away. The hulk rocked back and forth. The cracked porthole bulged inward. Rust and ash and blistered paint were shaken loose and drifted in the air like an infernal blizzard; it was harder to see inside the compartment where he and his men had taken shelter. Their suits were sprinkled and dusted by the clinging unholy black snow. Felix's well-trained eardrums felt the air pressure constantly change; his suit faceplate was squashed or made to swell as the overpressures and following partial vacuums plucked at his lungs. As each shock front passed over the Rocks, the compounded noise of all the explosions increased. The noise made talking impossible.

The noise makes thinking *impossible.*

Then Felix saw the thing he dreaded most. The thing his protective suit could offer no protection from. The thing from which the hulk's steel plates gave no real shelter at all.

In the distance, a long stretch of the horizon seemed oddly higher than before. Felix watched in morbid fascination as this strange phenomenon drew near.

It was the expanding tsunami, not a true seismic tidal wave but a huge wall of water kicked up by the force of the sixteen atomic blasts.

He yelled for his men to hold on. But there was little to hold on to besides one another.

Felix watched as the monster wave moved relentlessly closer.

When it came into shallower water near the Rocks, just as he expected, the wave began to pile up upon itself. It started to form an almost vertical churning, roiling wall. The wall climbed higher and higher, racing inshore.

Now Felix heard the noise of it, even above the continuing noise of the fireballs in the distance. The new noise was a terrible, deep-pitched roar.

He pulled himself from the porthole and, together with his men, cowered on the opposite side of the compartment. The noise became louder and louder. The wall of water was so close and so high, it blocked the sun from outside. The compartment grew totally dark.

The tsunami engulfed the hulk with a crash that made Felix's skeleton shake inside his body. The porthole was smashed and a solid column of water jetted in.

The hulk began to list, to lean over from the force of the wave.

"We're capsizing!" one of the SEAL chiefs shouted.

As water streamed in through every hatchway, down every ladder, between every crack in broken welds, the hulk leaned over more and more. There was a new sound now, of screaming metal, as weakened steel was further strained by the movement of the ship falling onto its side.

Felix and his team scrambled for their lives as the cargo ship tilted and seawater sloshed. In slow motion the deck became a bulkhead, and a bulkhead turned into the deck.

The hulk settled down with a teeth-jarring crash and sagged from its own redistributed weight. Felix knew the superstructure would collapse or break loose entirely, crushing him and his men under hundreds of tons of debris.

But at last the shaking and tumbling died down. The screaming of steel subsided into scattered moans and bangs. The roaring of the tidal wave receded into the distance.

Everything dripped. Sunlight came into the compartment again, through what was now acting as the overhead, the ceiling: the porthole Felix had looked out before. Yet another sound began, a whistling screech—*wind* was blowing through the mangled superstructure, a different sort of wind than before, as air was pulled in and upward toward ground zero, toward the cluster of ever-rising voracious mushroom clouds. Electric blue flashes flickered in the otherwise clear sky, followed by distant rumbles: the cooling moisture-laden mushroom clouds, with their heavy burden of static charges, were beginning to act like manmade thunderheads.

Felix was amazed that any of his men had survived the ordeal. The two men with broken bones were in great pain, and two others had suffered new fractures, including one of the chiefs. It made Felix feel guilty to know that others' bodies had cushioned his own as they'd all gone rolling and falling.

But he and his people were, first and foremost, U.S. Navy SEALs.

"You, you, and you," Felix said to the men who seemed in best physical and mental shape. "We have to find a way out of here, make contact with the minisub somehow, and then come back for the others. . . . Chief, stay put and take care of the wounded. You three with me, let's go. You see any Germans, remember. Head shots only."

———

Beck had expected the worst, but nothing could have prepared him and his men for the reality of what happened.

Sixteen nuclear torpedoes had gone off at once, at his command, in an arc like a scythe several miles across. His mind and body were still reeling.

He squinted and shook his head to try to get his vision to focus. The vibrations through the deck were so wild, the pitching of the ship so violent, Beck's knees kept buckling as he tried to stand. His organs felt as if they were flying apart inside his body. Many of his crew were in obvious pain from injuries.

But time was of the essence now.

Speech was out of the question as the noise of the tortured ocean continued to echo from all around, barely diminished by the thickness of the *von Scheer*'s immensely strong hull.

Beck struggled to the pilot's station. He made his intentions known by hand signals, by pointing at the pilot's controls.

Slow to ahead one-third, make engine revs for three knots. Hug the bottom, conceal the ship in terrain as much as you can. Right five degrees rudder, gently, steer due south.

———

All sonars were rendered useless by the endless reverb of nuclear bubble clouds. Jeffrey's only outside data came from the gravimeter—which fortunately still worked.

Jeffrey realized his ship continued making flank speed, heading east.

Good. Everything still works, then. We can't have serious damage.

But Jeffrey felt so addle-brained from all the sensory overload, he was having trouble thinking clearly much beyond that.

Then he realized that his ship was charging straight into the center of the watery maelstrom kicked up by the nuclear blasts. Her thick hull and shielded condenser pipes would stop the radiation out there, and clean seawater farther on would quickly wash external surfaces clean—but the maelstrom beckoned.

Meltzer, at the helm, seemed stuporous from a near concussion. COB kept blinking and shaking his head, in not much better shape. Bell appeared to be unhurt, but his console had gone dark. Jeffrey badly needed data, and needed to make some major judgment calls, but his thoughts moved like molasses, too much happening everywhere at once.

"Sonar!" he yelled at the top of his lungs. The noise from all around beyond the hull was impossibly loud.

Milgrom turned. Her face was pale, but her eyes were alert, and she showed no visible signs of serious injury. *"Captain?"*

"How many warheads went off?"

"I think all sixteen of theirs!"

Jeffrey was already getting hoarse from shouting, and the

cacophony from outside refused to diminish. He mouthed each word carefully. *"I need to know if any torpedoes are still running!"*

If only one had survived, and it found *Challenger,* they were dead.

Milgrom turned to her console.

Jeffrey yelled, *"Meltzer! COB!"* but it did no good.

Milgrom pinged on the bow sphere, over and over, to search for a torpedo somewhere in the trillions of bubbles swarming everywhere. Jeffrey knew the lingering heat of all those blasts made acoustic propagation paths impossible to decipher. This pinging might do more harm than good. It might just draw a live torpedo toward them.

Then *Challenger* entered the worst part of the wall of solid turbulence. She heaved and bucked and plunged in different directions. Jeffrey's stomach rose to his throat, or he was pressed down on his backside, with no letup. The ship's autopilot kicked in, since the computer sensed the lack of inputs from the helmsman. But there was just so much even the autopilot could do. Jeffrey was glad that *Challenger* had stayed shallow—a collision with bottom terrain would have been the end of everything.

Eventually *Challenger* came out the other side of the major turbulence. Meltzer and COB began to revive. Jeffrey shouted for them to slow to ahead one-third, in order to make a less noisy target, and maybe be able to pick up torpedo-engine sounds. But the passive sonars were useless in such a high acoustic sea state: The continuing noise, its primary source behind the ship now, drowned out any meaningful signal as it echoed and reverberated from all directions—off the surface waves and bottom terrain, and off the ocean's ever-present tiny biologics and organic waste that drifted everywhere.

Then a message from Engineering appeared on Jeffrey's screen, like an e-mail through the ship's fiber-optic LAN. He was glad to see the LAN was functioning, but he wasn't happy with what the message said. Lieutenant Willey strongly recommended avoiding any higher speeds until his men were able to check the propulsion-plant systems from top to bottom. Something might be on the verge of catastrophic failure, and a thorough safety inspection was vital. Jeffrey, disappointed but knowing exactly how valid Willey's caution was, typed him an acknowledgment. For now, Jeffrey's ship was almost immobilized.

He ordered Milgrom to ping again on the bow sphere, to search for *von Scheer*.

Nothing.

He told Milgrom to ping again. He waited for a good target echo.

Nothing.

Jeffrey turned to Bell. "I think you were right!" he shouted.

Bell seemed dazed. His face was ashen. *"Sir?"*

"He didn't want to sink us! He knew he couldn't win a stand-up fight if we traded blow for blow!"

"Yes, Captain!"

"He cared more about getting away! He raised that solid wall of atomic fireballs to block *von Scheer* from our view! Then he took off, east! Using twin reactors and polymer squirts and God only knows what else! He regroups with all the other Axis submarines massing near Africa, and takes another shot at the convoy from there!"

Bell nodded dumbly.

Jeffrey touched Bell on the shoulder to make sure the man was all right. He knew there'd be injured throughout the ship. Mess-management specialists, trained as the ship's paramedics, began to appear, making their rounds with first-aid kits.

Bell tapped Jeffrey's hand and nodded more briskly, less disoriented now. "We have to go after him, sir! Abandon the SEALs and the minisub if we must!"

Jeffrey hated that last part, but he had to agree. "Helm, make your course zero nine zero!" Due east.

Jeffrey picked up a mike for Engineering—he wanted Willey to hear the urgency in his voice.

"Give me flank speed now! Forget caution, the von Scheer *is getting away!"*

CHAPTER 24

Ilse Reebeck watched at her post in Admiral Hodgkiss's war room as the first stage of the Battle of the South Atlantic began. There was a frenzy of constant activity at desks and consoles all around, people yelling across the room, messengers running, senior officers talking into two or even three phone handsets at once. Reports came in from out on the ocean. Command and logistic decisions were made under terrible pressure. Hasty orders went out from Norfolk to major fleet units at sea. The shouting of SEAL Lieutenant Estabo over the radio, before he got cut off on the Rocks, hung in the air of the war room like a storm cloud. The news of contact on *von Scheer*, and then the huge burst of undersea atomic detonations, was electrifying and terrifying. In the worst scenario possible, escalation all the way to global thermonuclear exchange, the Norfolk naval complex would be high on Russia's target list; Ilse pitied civilians in any large city—in this war there was no such thing as being safe far behind the front lines.

Ilse was way too busy to be able to worry much more than that. Oceanographic data poured in to her desk from sensor platforms in space or in the air, and from other platforms on or under the water. All this information she helped to harness and massage, to render most meaningful other data cascading in to Norfolk, data relayed by satellite from ships and planes and helicopters: data from hundreds of active and passive sonobuoys.

Ilse was so intent on her work, she was startled to notice that Commodore Wilson was standing next to her. He nodded curtly, as was his manner; then glanced back and forth between her console displays and the huge TV screens on the wall. Ilse suspected the waiting must be difficult even for him, and he'd come to her for a measure of companionship.

On the surface-warfare plot, Ilse saw that the destroyers and frigates were tearing toward their new positions, well out ahead of the carriers. The carriers and cruisers themselves raced at flank speed to form up for the dash through the Narrows, and then for their suppression of Axis installations posing seaward threats from looming North Africa. The main air-warfare situation plot showed modified U.S. Air Force long-endurance midair refueling tankers were staging from bases in Venezuela to help keep carrier planes in the air far longer than the navy could on its own, and let them stay much farther forward deployed than the Axis would ever expect. B-52s with huge lift capacity and almost endless on-station time were also helping the navy—by dropping sonobuoys, not just air-to-ground missiles and smart bombs. There'd been very few air-to-air combat skirmishes yet with enemy fighters, but Ilse knew the modern Luftwaffe would be coming up in strength when it best suited *them*.

Just then the house phone on her console rang. The caller was Hodgkiss's senior aide, who wanted Wilson. Ilse gave the phone to the commodore. He listened, then said, "We'll be right there."

Wilson gave her back the phone handset. "The admiral wants us in his private conference room. Now."

Ilse quickly made sure the people on either side of her had things under control and could fill in while she was gone.

They were staffers from the navy's Meteorology and Oceanography Command—they knew their stuff.

Ilse followed mutely a step behind Wilson. They left the big war room, took a corridor, then cleared a security checkpoint and entered a windowless room, with a mahogany table and half a dozen nice chairs. Hodgkiss and his aide came into the room a moment later. Hodgkiss nodded to Ilse and then addressed Wilson. "They said it's an emergency. Beyond that I know as much as you do."

The director of naval intelligence entered. He was a vice admiral—a three-star. He and Hodgkiss exchanged looks of concern, and Ilse wondered what was going on. The DNI said hello to her; they'd met several times before.

A minute later, two new people walked in. Ilse was surprised and impressed. She'd met them both back in January at a formal debriefing after her first two missions on *Challenger*.

"Admiral," a tall and lanky woman said to Hodgkiss.

"General," Hodgkiss responded. They shook hands as Ilse watched. The woman was a retired U.S. Air Force general, now the national security adviser to the president. She had bags under her eyes, but seemed alert, if severe. She was elegantly dressed, and her eyes were hard and piercing. Her chin was chiseled and naturally jutting. Her lips were pursed in a permanent frown.

"Admiral," a short and rotund balding man said. He also looked rather tired, but very focused.

"Director." The man was the director of central intelligence—the DCI, the head of the CIA. Ilse knew he had a civilian background, in academia and high-power Washington think tanks. He wore a dark gray business suit, which seemed out of place amid the other people's uniforms. But the national security adviser seemed not the least bit out of place; she carried herself as if she still bore four general's stars on each shoulder.

Ilse noticed the director's attaché case was handcuffed to his wrist.

Hodgkiss noticed too. "This must be important if you came down here as the bagman, sir."

"Let's sit," the national security adviser suggested. Hodgkiss's aide left the room, locking the door shut behind him. Everyone else sat down without formalities; these senior people had bonded closely since the start of the war. Any politics or rivalry, Ilse noticed, was either nonexistent during the present national crisis or—as was more likely—it was suppressed to a level so subtle that it didn't show to someone as junior as her. She began to wonder why she'd even been invited.

The national security adviser seemed to read her mind. "I wanted you here as a stand-in for Captain Fuller."

"Yes, ma'am." *That again.*

"So what's going on?" Hodgkiss said. His tone put it somewhere between a question and an order.

The national security adviser sighed. She turned to the DCI. "Harry, you do the talking." The retired general herself was known as a woman of few words, at least when not ensconced in high-level meetings with the president—or while playing with her grandchildren.

The DCI cleared his throat. "The president told us to fly here instead of teleconferencing because he's very worried about enemy signals intelligence, and possible agents or moles in the White House or Pentagon. That brazen attack in the Capital has everyone stirred up about security."

"Which I'm sure was part of the Axis intent," Hodgkiss said rather sourly. "Gets us wasting time on mole hunts. Makes us scared to even use the phone."

"Yup. And with good reason." The DCI unlocked and opened his briefcase. "Most of you know that lately we've been increasingly concerned about Axis activity in South America."

Hodgkiss and the others nodded, but this was new to Ilse.

"Pieces of the puzzle seem to be falling together," the DCI went on, "and the picture looks ugly."

"Brazil and Argentina," Hodgkiss stated.

"The CIA, the Defense Intelligence Agency, and the National Security Agency have been working together on this one. That's giving us a good set of electronic reconnaissance assets and human intell sources too. In plainer language, satellites in space and spies and informers on the ground. We learned the hard way, ten or twelve years back, that we can't get by with one and not the other."

"Preamble heard and concurred with," Hodgkiss said. He seemed a bit impatient for the DCI to get to the point. In the official Washington hierarchy, both the DCI and the national security adviser outranked the commander, U.S. Atlantic Fleet—by several levels both inside and outside the military. But Hodgkiss was the battlefield commander, on the spot in more ways than one, and he knew it.

The DCI continued. "The recent incursion by Navy SEALs into northern Brazil gives us hard proof of strong Axis assistance to local insurgents in that area. Our conclusion is that the Axis presence there is a diversion, meant to draw Brazilian forces away from their front with Argentina way down on the other side of the country. And from what we see on roads and airfields, the diversion is succeeding all too well."

"Have you told Brazil that?" Hodgkiss asked.

"Only in the vaguest terms," the national security adviser broke in, "through our ambassador in Brasilia. Mention the SEALs and we admit we violated sovereign soil. Do that and we could end up in a three-way fight. Us against Brazil, Brazil against Argentina, and us against the Axis while the Axis aids Argentina."

Hodgkiss grunted. "Go on."

"We know a few things for sure." The DCI ticked them off on his fingers. "A reactionary political faction in Argentina would dearly love to topple the moderate regime now holding elected office, and seize total power for themselves. The reactionaries include some dinosaurs and fossils in high places, who still bear a grudge against the UK for the Falklands business thirty years ago, and don't exactly admire the U.S. either. And although the old Nazi refugees are dead of old age by now, their children in certain cases hold key financial and industrial posts."

"Jesus," Hodgkiss said under his breath.

"Also, Argentina and then Brazil recently mobilized all their reserves. This is a *very* serious step. Moving active-duty forces toward the short shared border was bad enough, but that could be dismissed as posturing, brinkmanship, as dangerous as such things are. Full-scale mobilization is *not* a good sign. It cripples both countries' already hobbling civilian economies, further destabilizing social conditions and adding to heightened political discontent. It makes war between Brazil and Argentina almost inevitable."

"Which is the last thing we need right now," Hodgkiss said.

"It all started with the disaster in the Indian Ocean last month," the national security adviser said. "Then the South Pacific atrocity, then Japan announcing that they're a nuclear power . . ."

The DCI nodded. "War hysteria gets contagious and feeds on itself, like Europe in 1914. We're sure Axis agents are behind the trouble inside Argentina, and also behind the trouble between Argentina and Brazil. Falsified provocations by paid agitators, shootings back and forth by unidentified gunmen who vanish, jingoist headlines in newspapers controlled by the pro-Axis groups, inflammatory speeches over TV and radio stations they own. And bombings, and orchestrated street riots. Some of this comes right out of *Mein Kampf*. . . . The Argentine president barely controls his own military, and what little control he has won't last. His party, the Populist Peronist Front, is tottering. . . . I know, that lingo makes him sound like some kind of latter-day Communist Fascist all rolled into one, but the language and the history involved are hard to convey succinctly. Basically he's middle of the road, and tries to stand up for the poor people. The opposition, who won some votes under their so-called Christian

Democrat banner, are in danger of starting an all-out civil war if they have to. They're anything but Christian in their values, and anything but democratic in their goals. And the Germans and Boers are secretly egging them on."

"What's the status of Brazil's nuclear-weapons program?" Hodgkiss asked.

"I was just coming to that," the DCI said. "And the answer is, we just don't know. They might, repeat *might*, have several weaponized devices. . . . But the president of Brazil is a pretty good guy. His Centrist-Pluralist Party is in solid control, and he definitely *is* the Brazilian military's commander in chief in every positive sense of the phrase. I don't see him being first to use atomic weapons, even if things went badly in a conventional war."

"And Argentina?"

"That's why we're having this meeting," the national security adviser said. "Harry?"

The DCI took over again. He removed a sheaf of papers from his briefcase. "These are transcripts of several intercepted telephone conversations. Translated into English by the best linguists we've got on the Argentina desk."

"How'd you get these?" Hodgkiss asked as he took the papers.

"The usual. Satellite eavesdropping, picking up the top lobes off microwave towers."

Ilse understood what he meant. Every antenna, no matter how directionally focused its main beam might be, always leaked some energy to the sides—side lobes—and also straight up in the air: the top lobe. These weak lobes could be detected, amplified by millions or even billions of times, decrypted if necessary, and listened in on. Nuclear submarines lurking offshore, at periscope depth, with an antenna mast raised, were often used to catch these invaluable side lobes. Spy satellites could do impressive things with the top lobes.

Hodgkiss whistled as he read. "You'd think that with this kind of dynamite, they'd be more careful."

The DCI nodded. "I don't believe they realize quite how powerful our capabilities are. A group of prowar ringleaders in Buenos Aires needed to talk to some of the old-guard elite hanging out at a ranch on the pampas. We believe this rich guy's cattle ranch is serving as a headquarters or safe house for the Axis sympathizers. They did use scramblers, but we were able to undo the scrambler routines."

"And before you ask," the national security adviser interjected, "the option of shooting a Tomahawk down their throat has been ruled out. The pro-Axis faction is too big, too well dispersed, too mobile. That sort of direct action would just give them martyrs, not to mention amount to an act of war, which we can ill afford under present diplomatic circumstances. And worst of all, it would tip our hand prematurely, that the U.S. is on to the conspiracy."

Hodgkiss nodded impatiently, half distracted as he read the papers. "These are literal translations?"

"Yes," the DCI said, "with Argentine slang, tones of voice, and inflection, it's all there in the transcript with annotations by our linguists."

Hodgkiss finished reading, then looked up. His face was very grave. He glanced at Ilse and Wilson, and at the director of naval intelligence. Then he glanced at the DCI. "Everyone here has clearance for this?"

The DCI nodded. "Of necessity. On the president's say-so."

Hodgkiss let out a long, deep breath. "This says the Argentine bad guys are expecting to receive a supply of atomic warheads from Germany. Soon. Very soon." He hesitated for a moment, his expression skeptical. "But this is just one source. It could be a ploy, a fake, a provocation."

"Yes," the DCI said. "And we have people on the ground at certain Argentine air bases. They say that several Argentine fighter-bombers have been modified, recently and in a hurry. From an interpretation by our experts of how our agents in-country describe the modifications, the refitted aircraft are each intended to carry, arm, and drop an atom bomb. There's your perfect independent confirmation, Admiral, humint versus sigint, with completely separate lo-cuses of origin." *Sigint* was "signals intercept intelligence"; *humint* meant "reports from human spies."

"Okay," Hodgkiss said. "It's bad, but it does explain how Argentine madmen might hope to win a war with Brazil, outnumbered four or five to one in conventional forces, start-ing on such a narrow front, with such a lousy road network to fight on, and with such a gigantic area to cover." Ar-gentina's population was forty million; Brazil's was almost two hundred million; heading north from their shared border between Uruguay and Paraguay, Brazil was shaped like a big triangle that got wider and wider until it reached a front as broad as the whole continental U.S. "Brazil would be an at-tractive target for conquest. Factory sites, mineral wealth, and other natural resources. Even forced labor. But where does Atlantic Fleet come in? We've got our hands full and then some with the Central African pocket. . . . And how are these atomic bombs supposed to get to Argentina? *Airmail?* Don't be ridiculous. And they aren't on a cargo ship; we've had *that* route of weapons infiltration locked down for years! The noose there's even tighter with this war."

"That's just it," the national security adviser said. "Atomic war in South America would create a tremendous mess in your rear, at the worst possible time imaginable, right? The worst time for *your* forces, and strategically for the whole Allied cause."

"It's a ploy, a diversion," Hodgkiss scoffed, "a clever fab-rication meant to befuddle us. You're falling into the trap, don't you see? With respect, General, don't pull me in there after you. . . . And don't tell me they're sending the A-bombs by U-boat. The South Atlantic weather's been too good. At this point, nothing, but nothing, could sneak past our open-ocean antisubmarine screens." The admiral ticked things off on his fingers. "Standing patrols by Allied subs well off South Africa, surface ships that slowly trail long towed arrays, and hydrophone nets on the bottom of the

sea—which is probably why the U-boats are massing in
Axis-owned African coastal waters."

The national security adviser and Hodgkiss locked eyes.
"Then where is the SMS *von Scheer*?"

Hodgkiss turned to Wilson. "Commodore?"

Wilson cleared his throat. "Last we knew, *Challenger* was
pursuing *von Scheer* east toward Africa."

"How positive are you of that?" the DCI asked.

Wilson told Ilse to have data from her console updated.
Ilse picked up a phone and called the lieutenant (j.g.) who
sat beside her in the war room. She asked him to patch the
audio signal, consolidated from the sonobuoys, onto the
line, then switched her end to speakerphone mode. Everyone
in the conference room listened.

A watery hissing and mechanical throbbing filled the air.

"That's *Challenger*," Ilse said, "making flank speed."

The sounds got lower in pitch, and quieter, until they became inaudible.

"She's slowing," Ilse said, "for better sonar sensitivity. . . .
Now she'll be listening on passive sonar."

A loud siren noise came through the speakers. The national security adviser looked startled.

"That's the ship's active sonar, ma'am. It does that to confuse enemy acoustic masking."

Everyone listened. Nothing more happened.

Then the sound of *Challenger* speeding up could be
heard.

Ilse lifted the phone and spoke to the lieutenant in the war
room. "No trace of torpedo noises?" The junior officer said
no. "What's her course?" He said due east. "Depth?" Four
thousand feet. "Okay, thanks." She hung up the phone.

"Captain Fuller is using what's called sprint-and-drift tactics now," Ilse said. "It's a method of searching for an enemy
target that balances covering distance fast with stopping to
listen for threats while own-sonar systems are optimized.
He's increased his depth significantly, into the deep sound

channel, to maximize his detection range against any enemy submarines. And going deep gives him greater protection against Axis antiship cruise missiles. His pings can probably be heard all the way to the African coast." Since Wilson didn't interrupt or seem at all disapproving, she added one more thought. "I would also interpret this to mean that Captain Fuller has become more cautious, because before, after crossing the wall of lingering nuclear bubble clouds, he was making flank speed continuously."

The national security adviser and the director of central intelligence looked at each other doubtfully.

The DCI turned to Hodgkiss. "What you're really saying is that *Challenger* has lost contact with *von Scheer*."

"Temporarily," Hodgkiss said. Ilse sensed his hackles were up. "*Maybe*. We need to try to see this from Captain Fuller's point of view."

"Why don't we just *ask* him?" the national security adviser said, verging on open sarcasm.

"With respect, ma'am," Ilse jumped in, "we can't. He's too deep for two-way comms."

The general ignored Ilse and glared at Hodgkiss. "Don't you have some kind of special radio?"

Hodgkiss shook his head. "It takes forever to send the simplest message, and it's *only one way*. He'd need to slow down and come shallow to answer, using frequencies impaired now by enemy jamming. . . . I won't micromanage Captain Fuller in the middle of an engagement."

Ilse could feel the interpersonal tension mount.

"Sirs," Ilse spoke up. "Ma'am. There's someone very important we're leaving out, besides Captain Fuller."

Ilse saw everybody turn in her direction and peer at her hard.

"The captain of the *von Scheer*."

Hodgkiss looked at the others. "This guy we've identified, Ernst Beck. What's *he* doing now, thinking now?"

"I can try to guess for you, Admiral, sir," Ilse said.

"You faced him before, didn't you, along with Captain Fuller?"

"Yes." Ilse was flooded by memories of a long and difficult fight. She remembered increasingly ruthless tactics used by both sides. She remembered a climax so violent it seemed a miracle *anyone* survived. . . .

Ilse stared at the polished mahogany tabletop, and rested her head in her hands, and concentrated.

"A battle happens on a specific time line, one that's very chaotic and compressed. A battle is a *vector* of events, a particular *sequence*, with order amid the disorder. One side or the other has the initiative, from moment to moment. Whoever has the initiative dictates both sides' very next move. Somebody there, *in* the battle, lives it from moment to moment, leading or being led around by the nose. . . . This intensity of focus colors their perspective heavily." Ilse pictured the entire battle by the Rocks again. She tried to relive it as if she were there on *Challenger*.

She looked up abruptly. It came to her so suddenly, the understanding, that it had an almost physical impact, as if she'd gone through a plate-glass door.

"Captain Fuller is heading east because he believes the wall of nuclear detonations was intended by the *von Scheer* to break contact so that *von Scheer* can continue east unmolested, closer to Africa. *We* know now that in the bigger strategic picture, the South American front is as important as, or even more important than, Africa. And the Germans have known it for some time. Presumably since before the *von Scheer* sailed."

"You mean—" the DCI said.

"*Yes,*" Hodgkiss said. "Now it all fits. *Von Scheer* was thwarted at the Rocks. . . . *Dammit*. Ernst Beck isn't going east. *That's* why Captain Fuller can't find him. . . . He's heading *west*, toward South America, this very minute. *That's* why Beck led Fuller on that merry chase, then raised his wall of detonations. And that's how the Germans intend to get the A-bomb warheads to their opportunist friends in Argentina."

Hodgkiss got up and went to the globe in the corner. He spun it until it showed the South Atlantic. He ran his finger along the globe, almost angrily.

"I see it, all of it." He made eye contact with the national security adviser. "Beck will cut two sides of a triangle as fast as he possibly can: the Rocks to Buenos Aires, then Buenos Aires across the South Atlantic to the Congo basin. Meanwhile our convoy will cut the third side of the triangle, see? Through the Narrows, past the Rocks, and straight for the Congo basin pocket . . . *Von Scheer* runs the errand to Argentina, *then* scoots over to take the convoy from the rear, completing the triangle and also creating the far end of a big pincers. The convoy gets sandwiched between the *von Scheer* on one side and the massed Axis U-boats and land-based forces on the other, the worst conceivable setup from our point of view. And the more time goes by, the more and more likely the German and Boer land offensive will open, too."

"Oh boy," the DCI said. "The *von Scheer*'s the perfect transport vehicle, isn't she? One missile tube could hold dozens of atom-bomb warheads, all nicely gift wrapped for the opposition faction in Buenos Aires. Then the Germans step back and wash their hands, and watch as Latin America explodes in our face, literally. Atomic war on land by Third World countries, an entire new front to America's south . . ."

"Something else just fell into place for me," the national security adviser said. "Even Germany wouldn't give nuclear weapons to a neutral country unprovoked. They'd know the connection couldn't be hidden forever, and history would be the judge, and the sick hypocrites are always outward sticklers for the letter of international law. . . . So Germany must know something we don't know. They must have their own proof that Brazil has the bomb."

Hodgkiss nodded slowly and soberly.

The national security adviser and Hodgkiss locked eyes. "We've absolutely *got* to keep the *von Scheer* from delivering," she said. "How do we warn Captain Fuller? Is he even the right guy to use?"

"*Challenger* is already tasked to prosecute *von Scheer*. She's still the closest sub we have to *von Scheer*'s probable track. She's by far the only one fast enough, deep-diving enough, stealthy enough, to get in range and kill *von Scheer* with adequate odds of success. To order a different sub after *von Scheer,* instead of Fuller, could be tantamount to sending good men to a useless death."

Hodgkiss grabbed the phone and reached his aide. "ELF message, override anything else in the queue. Recipient address is *Challenger,* confirm hull number seven seven eight. Message is the cipher block for 'Come to two-way floating-wire-antenna depth and trail the wire. . . . ' We'll just have to hope we can both burn through all the jamming."

Hodgkiss held the phone and turned to Ilse. "Might Fuller ignore the message if he thinks we're only distracting him?"

"He very well might," she answered honestly.

Hodgkiss spoke into the phone. "Append to message the cipher block for 'Imperative order, no recourse, Commander U.S. Atlantic Fleet sends.' "

The admiral almost hung up the phone, but then gave his aide more orders. "Get whichever carrier's closest now to send a medevac helo to the Rocks to pick up the injured SEALs from that cargo-ship hulk. Lots of ice and drinking water, electrolyte packs, the works, they'll be dropping from heat stress by now, even the guys without wounds. Get an Osprey to haul a mobile radiological decontamination unit. On an underfuselage sling. They can set the trailer down on the ruined lighthouse. . . . Raise *Challenger*'s minisub. Radio, signal sonobuoy, whatever it takes. Tell the mini to close on the Rocks and recover all able-bodied SEALs. Then they head south to deeper water and prepare to dock inside *Challenger*. . . . You see what I'm getting at. Take it from there."

Again Hodgkiss almost hung up, then spoke to his aide. "I want another Orpheus station established, on Ascension Island. Pronto, smartly, yesterday. The Brits own it; the Royal Navy liaison is in the building somewhere, track him down and get their help. Their Special Boat Squadron boys can make the hookups. Ascension has a decent cable net to help us monitor the South Atlantic for *von Scheer.*" The admiral hung up.

The director of central intelligence looked around the room. "What if we guessed wrong? What if it *is* a giant German trap, or double bluff, after all? What if *von Scheer* is still going toward Africa *now?* We're taking by far our most powerful antisubmarine asset, *Challenger,* our only ceramic-hulled sub, and we throw her away on a wild-goose chase to nowhere and beyond. The enemy gets the convoy and escorts in a pincers *soon,* with the U-boats and their land offensive on one side and *von Scheer* on the other. It'll be a perfect nutcracker, a bloodbath, with *Challenger* on a fool's errand to the wrong continent."

"We can't have things both ways at once, Director." Hodgkiss stared very hard at the globe. "If we guessed wrong, ladies and gentlemen, I think we just lost the war, and the Allies will have to offer the Axis an armistice. . . . But if we guessed right, and Captain Fuller fails and Ernst Beck sinks him off South America, we're looking at Armageddon itself."

CHAPTER 25

Two days later, off the east coast of Brazil, Jeffrey
Fuller sat in his control room, tense and exhausted.
The lighting was rigged for red. He'd set the main
menus on his console to feed his screens each status page in
turn, changing every ten seconds. The constant updating,
and the simple stimulation of such movement on his console, helped him stay awake.

Jeffrey had been awake for over forty-eight hours continuously—since before his two-way conversation with Norfolk, when Admiral Hodgkiss issued him new orders at the
Rocks, and the subsequent recovery of the minisub with Felix and a handful of SEALs.

Jeffrey was still pissed off at himself. Ernst Beck had gotten him completely confused and left him looking like a
fool, tagged as the weakest link in a complex and vital strategic situation.

This Beck is better than I thought.

Jeffrey turned and glanced at Bell sitting next to him. The
younger man looked fresh, rested, and recently shaved.

At least he's had the common sense to grab some sleep

and take a shower. I'm falling into old bad habits, trying to keep an eye on everything every minute during a hunt for our adversary. . . .

"I hope we're doing the right thing, XO," he said quietly. As he spoke he could tell how much his whole body and mind dragged from fatigue. His arms seemed much too heavy. His head felt as if it was stuffed with cotton.

"Captain?" Bell's voice was deep and confident, and the whole set of his face was different than it had been in the past. He seemed more mature but not worn down internally, more centered within himself, more evenly balanced as a person, than on previous deployments with Jeffrey on the ship.

"I tried to be unpredictable at the Rocks. Unpredictable for *me*. Look where it got us."

"Sir, it made the most sense at the time. Beck outthought us both. It's my job to backstop you, but instead I led you straight down the path Beck wanted you to take. *Seventy-knot sprint speeds*. What a bunch of hooey! It was all just mental smoke and mirrors. I fell for it too, Skipper."

Instead of answering, Jeffrey looked once more at the picture of Ernst Beck that he kept windowed on his console.

Then he studied the status screens. Eight nuclear fish were armed and ready in *Challenger*'s torpedo tubes. Her new towed sonar array, installed in New London dry dock, was deployed. Instead of electric hydrophones along a lengthy cable, this array had three separate parallel cables. And the acoustic sensors were thousands of tiny fiber-optic coils in line, each with its own built-in laser. The subtlest low-frequency signals hitting the cables distorted the coils by the slightest amount, and this altered the laser-light wavefronts' behavior by just enough to be recorded. The whole system was a quantum leap in performance ahead of even the most advanced conventional electric-based towed arrays. Kathy Milgrom and her staff were using it well.

Challenger was in the deep sound channel, listening for

whiffs of the *von Scheer* that even the quietest submarine had to give off. Infrasonic noises, disturbances with a frequency as low as only one cycle per *minute*—a sixtieth of a hertz—were caused by any sub's motion through the water, and by resonances of internal heavy machinery with the hull, and by slow and rhythmic flexing of the hull itself, all of which no known quieting mechanism could suppress.

Challenger was moving at top quiet speed, twenty-six knots. The ship's course was generally southwest. Though the shortest route from the Rocks to Buenos Aires ran straight down the long east coast of Brazil, Jeffrey had decided to swing wide into very deep water. The ship was between the landmass of South America and the rugged terrain of the Mid-Atlantic Ridge, over the vast abyssal plain that separated the two. Here, the bottom was at or below *von Scheer*'s and *Challenger*'s crush depths. Here, it would be much harder for Ernst Beck to hide. And here, so long as he stayed more than two hundred nautical miles from the neutral coast, the Joint Chiefs of Staff global rules of engagement let Jeffrey go atomic against an enemy target.

In the last two days, *Challenger* had left the convoy and its escorts and air support over a thousand nautical miles behind. Now no sonobuoys pinged anywhere near—they were being saved to guard the convoy, or for later, and their pinging might by accident give *Challenger* away. Now *Challenger*'s on-watch communications officer in the secure radio room listened for another ELF order telling Jeffrey to come up to two-way radio depth. If such a message did arrive, it could mean news of an Orpheus contact on *von Scheer*. By now the new listening station on Ascension Island might be up and running.

And now *Challenger*'s active sonar was secured. The foundations of Jeffrey's new tactics were stealth and surprise. The South Atlantic was huge—almost five thousand miles from Buenos Aires to the Congo-basin coast. *Von Scheer* could already be almost anywhere inside an arc with a total area of millions of square miles. Every hour, as Ernst Beck steamed at thirty knots—or whatever his maximum quiet speed actually was—that arc of possible locations expanded more.

Jeffrey's main advantage, he hoped, was that Beck didn't realize he was on his tail again—this was why Hodgkiss was holding back on surface warfare and air support: in order not to tip Jeffrey's hand, to make Beck think *Challenger* still searched for him near Africa. Another advantage, Jeffrey hoped, was that he himself could stay closer to Brazil, and hence take a shorter route to Argentina, because the *von Scheer* had more to conceal from Brazil—and thus more reason to hide—than *Challenger* did. Brazil's navy was not insignificant, and her coastal defenses were strong. And a third advantage, Jeffrey hoped, was that whatever devious route Ernst Beck might take, his ultimate destination was known: the pro-Axis, prowar faction waiting a few more days to the south. The geography was fixed, and for once worked in the Allies' favor: the coast of Argentina started south of the coast of Brazil.

"New passive sonar contact," Lieutenant Milgrom announced. "Transient contact." Jeffrey looked up, eager for news.

"Contact bearing zero five zero, range extremely distant, identified as underwater nuclear detonation, near the North African coast."

"Very well, Sonar," Jeffrey said. "Any trace of *von Scheer*? Hole-in-ocean contact?" The *von Scheer* backlighted by acoustic illumination from that nuclear blast. "Ambient sonar contact?" The echo of the blast off *von Scheer*'s hull.

"Wait please." It could take minutes for a quiet spot or echo far away to be detectable, and minutes more for *Challenger*'s signal processors to verify a genuine detection.

The wait seemed to drain the last of Jeffrey's energy. *The Battle of the South Atlantic just started with that nuclear shot. The battle started, and I'm not there to help.*

"Negative contact, Captain."

Jeffrey felt terribly disappointed.

"*New* passive sonar contact," Milgrom called. "Contact held on towed array."

Jeffrey's adrenaline surged.

"Contact bearing two eight two." West. "Contact is submerged." Jeffrey's heart leaped into his throat. "Contact distant, uncertain range . . . Correction, contact is over the Brazilian continental shelf. . . . Contact now held on starboard wide-aperture array. Contact classified as a snorkeling diesel submarine."

"Axis?" *Please, God, give me a target,* any *target so I can score a kill.*

"Infrasonic tonals indicate engines of British manufacture. . . . Contact tentatively identified as Brazilian Navy diesel submarine recharging its batteries."

"Very well, Sonar."

There was still no sign of the *Admiral von Scheer,* and no message from Norfolk.

Two hours later, Jeffrey almost nodded off as Bell stepped aft to use the head; Lieutenant Sessions came over from the navigation console to fill in for Bell.

Jeffrey watched and listened as COB, sitting at the ship-control station, spoke to the control-room phone talker. COB asked the phone talker to contact the maneuvering room and request Lieutenant Willey to come forward to discuss some engineering details. Jeffrey thought the details seemed minor, but he trusted COB implicitly—and he knew he needed to delegate, not interfere.

Jeffrey decided that his tight, aching stomach might be ready to handle more caffeine and asked the teenage messenger of the watch to get him a mug of hot coffee from the wardroom, loaded with milk and sugar. COB heard this and asked the messenger to wait. He said he'd go aft soon himself and he'd take care of it.

Jeffrey went back to staring at his screens.

Bell returned from the head; he resumed as fire control and general keeper-of-eyes-on-things. Willey arrived from aft, looking a bit puzzled.

COB stood up and stretched, glancing at his commander. "Captain, I think I want to go over this with you first, in private."

Since Willey was right there, and Willey was senior to Sessions, Jeffrey told Willey to take the conn in his place while Sessions retained the deck. The watchstanders acknowledged, and Jeffrey led COB aft the few paces to the captain's stateroom.

COB closed the door behind them.

"What's up?" Jeffrey asked. He caught a glimpse of himself in his dressing mirror. His face was haggard and drawn, and his beard stubble was heavy. As if to emphasize the point, his stomach picked that particular moment to growl, loudly.

"Skipper," COB said firmly, "there are times when I just gotta say what I gotta say."

"COB?"

"You need to eat and you need to sleep just like the rest of us."

Jeffrey opened his mouth to object but COB cut him off.

"Let's leave aside the question of who really outranks whom, a commander or a master chief. Someone needs to tell you this. Whatcha gonna do, *fire* me for it? Bust me to seaman second class?"

"COB, you know you always have my attention. You don't need to rub it in like that."

"See? You're even *touchy* now, and you're supposed to be the meanest sumbitch in town in any nasty fight. . . . Go to the wardroom immediately. Eat a decent meal and skip the coffee. Then come back here and lie down for a solid six hours at least."

"But—"

"Sir, we'll all be right outside! If something happens we'll get you!"

Jeffrey stood up straighter. COB had made his point. "Aye aye, Master Chief. Tell Lieutenant Willey he retains the conn. He knows the plan. He knows where to find me." Jeffrey looked at COB and smiled—with relief and gratitude. "You clever old sea dog you. Now I see why you brought the engineer forward."

————

Alone in his cabin, Ernst Beck prepared for bed. He welcomed the chance to escape, from his workload and from his overbearing passenger, Baron von Loringhoven.

Beck's sleep was troubled. He kept waking from vague but disturbing nightmares. He would roll over and fall asleep again, but only for a short while.

Then Ernst Beck had a different sort of dream. He was age ten, and home with his mother and father on their prosperous dairy farm in Bavaria, in the scenic rolling foothills of the mighty snowcapped Alps, near historic and cosmopolitan Munich. In the dream they were finishing dinner, time for dessert, and Beck's mother had baked a pie that looked and smelled delicious.

Ernst Beck woke in a cold sweat after this dream, soon enough to remember it very vividly. He felt homesick, nostalgic, almost heartbroken for that simple, innocent, and happy time forever lost in the past.

Throwing off the soggy covers, he began to get up; he knew that sleeping now was useless.

As his right foot hit the floor, Beck realized something and almost gasped. To make doubly sure, he rushed to open his laptop and called up a nautical chart. The SEAL setup on the Rocks that Shedler had described in some detail after the battle—the satellite dish and the cables running down into the water—was there for a *reason*. It couldn't be coincidence. It *had* to be cause and effect.

Beck now understood how the Allies, how *Challenger*, had located his ship near the Rocks in the Atlantic Narrows so easily and precisely. And he recognized what he had to do to keep them from finding him and his ship the same way again.

My unconscious mind took facts and processed them and made connections while I slept.

On the chart on his laptop screen he saw the St. Peter and St. Paul Rocks and the east-west ridge on which they lay. The chart also showed the undersea phone cables, as nautical charts usually did.

Through the LAN, Beck downloaded from stored data the exact pattern of the enemy SSQ-75 sonobuoys dropped north of the Rocks during the battle. He overlaid this on the nautical chart.

The fit was too perfect for there to be any other explanation. *They were trying to get me cornered between two cables, to force me to flee over one or the other.*

It was the cables. *It was somehow all about the* cables.

Beck knew the countermeasure was simple, now that he understood the danger. Whenever his ship neared another such old cable on a chart, he'd have to go shallow or go very slow. . . . Annoying, but a minor inconvencience to beat the Allies' high-tech trick.

CHAPTER 26

Jeffrey awoke refreshed from his long nap and took a very hot shower. He decided to use his privilege as captain and let the steaming water run for two whole minutes continuously. *No quick on-off conserve-the-water navy shower for me today.*

Then he shaved, an unpleasant business, as the razor snagged on two-days-plus worth of stubble. He donned clean khakis and checked himself out in the dressing mirror: he was transformed, in appearance and mood.

Now this *is how a warship's commanding officer is supposed to look.*

Jeffrey went into the control room with a much lighter step than when he'd left it eight hours before. Now, instead, the prospect of more cat and mouse with *von Scheer,* of more stalking and shooting with Korvettenkapitan Ernst Beck, excited him. A thrill of adrenaline rushed through his body.

The weapons officer, Lieutenant Torelli, had the deck and the conn. Jeffrey eyed a ship's clock. It was before midnight, local time. The watch was about to change, as it did every six hours around the clock, day in, day out, whenever the ship was under way but not at actual battle stations.

In the control room, which was rigged for red, Jeffrey greeted Torelli. Weps was fairly new to the ship, having first come aboard for *Challenger*'s previous mission the month before. Jeffrey found out fast, then, that he was a good department head, knowledgeable and yet eager to delegate, crisp and attentive to duty under fire, and great fun to share a beer with while relaxing in home port. Torelli was single, in his late twenties, from a suburb of Memphis, Tennessee. He came across as arrogant until you got to know him. He also seemed like a hard-ass toward his men, until you heard how he mentored them so well as individuals in private.

Jeffrey told Torelli he intended to take the conn once he familiarized himself with the ship's present status. He then wandered purposefully around the compartment, studying different men's console displays: sonar, weapons, navigating, ship control.

"Very well," he said to Torelli. "I have the conn."

"You have the conn." Torelli slid over and Jeffrey sat down.

"This is the captain. I have the conn."

"Aye aye," the watchstanders acknowledged. Soon the entire watch rotated. A talented lieutenant (j.g.) from Engineering came forward.

Jeffrey settled in at the command workstation conning officer's console. The lieutenant (j.g.) from Engineering sat next to him, serving as officer of the deck. The OOD's job was—among other important things—to oversee machinery operations and related procedures inside the ship. This left Jeffrey undistracted, free to monitor the larger picture and make the big decisions on how *Challenger* should fight.

Jeffrey scrolled through the digital log from the previous watch for the sonar department. The sonarmen had detected a number of loud explosions in the distance, back toward

North Africa. These were all identified as tactical nuclear detonations on and under the sea.

The battle between the relief convoy and Axis forces is definitely heating up. . . . Still no hint of a contact on the von Scheer.

Then Jeffrey had an awful thought. His feeling of being transcendently *alive* at the prospect of combat quickly wilted.

He turned to the messenger of the watch. He tried to keep his voice even. "Where're the XO and Sonar?"

"XO's sleeping, sir. Lieutenant Milgrom is using the enlisted mess to do a training drill for some of her people."

"Get them, smartly."

"Aye aye." The messenger, a very young enlisted man still pimply-faced from acne, hurried aft.

Milgrom arrived in seconds. Bell showed up a minute later, stuffing his shirttails into his pants. He fast went from drowsy to alert when he read Jeffrey's expression.

"People, we have a problem. I think it fell through a crack, all the way up the line."

"Sir?" Bell and Milgrom said together.

"The *von Scheer*. She's about the size and shape of one of our boomers?"

"So far as we know, Captain," Bell said.

"Or one of our boomers converted to SSGNs?"

Bell and Milgrom nodded reluctantly. They saw where the captain was going with this.

"So on ambient or hole-in-ocean sonar alone, we really can't tell the *von Scheer* from one of our own *Ohio*-class boats?"

"We'd need to get close enough to get good tonals, sir," Milgrom said, "to rule out that possibility. Yes."

"Not quite," Bell said. "We'd have their depth and speed. The *Ohio* ships can't go below about a thousand feet, and can't go past something like twenty-five knots, max. Anything deeper or faster has to be the *von Scheer*."

"But shallow and slow, a contact could be friend or enemy, correct?" Jeffrey said. "Shifting our operational area to South America throws a wrench in the works. We don't have any data on our own boomers' patrol boxes. We don't have up-to-date data on their or the SSGNs' en route safe corridors in this part of the ocean either."

"It would compromise security to give out too much of that info, Skipper," Bell said. "When we left Norfolk we didn't have a conceivable need to know. It's the same old thing, moles and spies and code breaking. This go-round, they might cost *us* the war."

"These are special circumstances," Milgrom said. "Perhaps if we made the request, Captain, Strategic Command would give us what we require."

Jeffrey frowned. "To ask, we'd need to radiate. We radiate, we make a datum that could get us killed. . . . And then there's the very real likelihood our request will be denied. . . . No, we can't risk it."

Bell worked his jaw, thinking hard. "So if we see something huge out there, moving slow and shallow, we need to get in really close to make sure it's the *von Scheer* and not a friend."

Jeffrey nodded.

"What about Russian boomers or SSGNs?" Milgrom asked. "They're very large."

"They're all in their bastions, way up north, playing pure defense. That's one problem we *don't* have."

"Would *von Scheer* really go shallow and slow?" Bell asked. "To fool us like that, Captain?"

"Beck can't hide in the bottom when the Brazil Basin's abyssal plain goes down twenty thousand feet or more in places. What's his next-best choice?"

Milgrom and Bell looked at each other. Milgrom said it for both of them. "Ape an *Ohio* to throw us off."

"And at eight hundred feet or whatever," Jeffrey said, "with the water so deep, Orpheus is useless. Even when he steamed right over one, Beck's hull and the telephone cable would be something like four miles apart."

Jeffrey saw Bell and Milgrom's faces fall as he made that last, unpleasant statement.

The intercom from the radio room blinked. Jeffrey picked up his handset. "Captain."

"Sir," the lieutenant (j.g.) communications officer said, "an ELF message now coming in with our address."

"What's it say? I'll hold."

Jeffrey glanced at Milgrom and Bell. "Another ELF message."

Bell got excited, then confused. "An Orpheus contact report? But you just—"

Jeffrey cut him off as the radio room had more.

"Come to floating-wire-antenna depth," the lieutenant (j.g.) read off the message's cipher-block meanings. "Do not radiate. Imperative; no recourse. Commander, Atlantic Fleet sends."

"Very well." Jeffrey hung up the mike.

"XO, take the conn. Bring us up to floating-wire-antenna depth. Then trail the wire. I'll be in the radio room." He ran his eyes over the tactical plot once more. "Have the messenger knock if you run into the slightest trouble out here."

Jeffrey went to the rear of the control room, to the radio room. The door was posted with dire security warnings—most of the crew were never permitted access. He punched in the combination to the lock and entered.

The compartment was small and crammed with electronic equipment and men. Here were all the transmitters and receivers *Challenger* could use, covering radio bands from deep-penetrating ELF extremely low frequency, up to SHF super-high frequency used for satellite communications. The radio room also contained *Challenger*'s encrypting and decrypting gear. This hardware and software, including one-time-use code keys and very advanced data-scrambling routines, were some of the most highly classified materials on the ship.

Despite the strong air-conditioning, the room was warm from the heat of electronics and tense men's bodies in such close quarters. The junior lieutenant in charge was young and green, and capable but nervous under his captain's impatient scrutiny. He was assisted by a senior chief—a mature man, cocky and confident of his skills.

Jeffrey read each word as the incoming message was received, then decoded, then displayed on a screen and spat out by a printer; reception was slowed by Axis jamming.

He read in increasing disbelief.

As soon as the last page was finished, he grabbed the hard copy. He left the radio room and made sure the door was locked behind him.

"Sonar, take the conn," Jeffrey snapped. "XO, my stateroom, now."

———

"No Orpheus contacts after all," Bell said. "So much for Ascension Island. So much for that." He sounded badly frustrated.

Jeffrey shook his head. "Admiral Hodgkiss sees it too. Beck must have figured something out, or been warned by radio from Berlin."

"How would Berlin know about Orpheus?"

"Like you said, code breaking or moles. Or both."

"Crud."

Jeffrey held up the radio message. "At least the good admiral had the presence of mind to warn us. 'StratCom indicates large contacts may be friendly.' The rest of that, Hodgkiss seems to be leaving to our imagination or guesswork."

"*Ohio* boats in our area after all . . . Which is the worst possible tactical picture for our side."

"*That's* not the worst of it," Jeffrey said. "Things in Africa and Europe are going from bad to worse."

"What do you mean?"

"We better sit down."

Jeffrey and Bell used the chairs by his desk. Jeffrey put the message papers on the desk and tapped them for emphasis. "It seems that as the fighting at sea nears Africa, and tactical nuclear combat has begun, and the Axis land offensive will get rolling any day, Israel has decided to play a trump card."

"Sir?"

Jeffrey knew Germany had made a nuclear no-man's-land when they nuked Tripoli in Libya, then invaded North Africa after overrunning Europe—while America was still reeling from the shock of the opening nuclear ambush off western Africa the previous summer. Now Egypt and Israel, as two of the Allies, formed a bulwark against German advances across the Suez Canal toward the Middle East oil supplies.

It's like Montgomery versus Rommel all over again. El Alamein, the Afrika Corps, Tobruk . . .

Except this time the no-man's-land is protected by Israel's nuclear umbrella.

Jeffrey took a deep breath. "Norfolk informs us that Israel made an announcement several hours ago. Issued an ultimatum, one that's causing a furor worldwide . . . Israel indicates that at some time in the unspecified past, they brought a dozen atomic warheads onto German soil, and concealed them just in case."

"My God."

"I'm guessing," Jeffrey said, "but I'll bet they did it when the Mossad worked with Germany in the War on Terror. While helping to close the borders to weapons of mass destruction, Israel sneaked in weapons of their own."

"What for?"

"As life insurance. When they say never again, they mean it."

"But—"

"Listen. It's hardly the first time the Mossad looked out for number one and didn't tell the U.S. everything. You and I know *that* firsthand."

"How do we, how does Germany, know it isn't a bluff?"

"The Israelis planned for that. They disclosed the location of one of the bombs. German internal security found it. They verified the bomb was in good working order. It had a detonator that could be set off from nearby through remote control."

"How do we know this last part?"

Jeffrey shrugged. "The CIA must have their ways. . . . The yield was estimated at twenty kilotons. . . . Some may even be in office towers, to go off as airbursts. City busters."

"That leaves *eleven* bombs in place?"

"Supposedly. They're all uranium gun-bomb designs, with very long shelf lives. Israel says they're well concealed in big German cities or major military sites, and the Germans will never find them in a million years. And Mossad agents are in-country, ready to set off the bombs. *If* Germany violates the no-man's-land in northeast Africa. Kablooey, and at the cost of the agents' own lives, *if* the Israeli homeland is threatened."

"So Israel has their own form of mutual assured destruction with Germany now. And the Germans know it."

"Pretty much."

"So what does this mean for *us?*"

"Just that things are getting more destabilized. The announcement, according to this message from Admiral Hodgkiss, has triggered riots in Buenos Aires, between pro-German and pro-Israel activist groups. There've been shootings and bombings already."

"Civil war in Argentina?"

"They're getting closer and closer to it. There are other suspicious signs of an organized influence orchestrating increasing chaos down there."

"Such as?"

"Chemical and biological warfare."

"My God." Bell looked ashen. "On land in Argentina?"

Jeffrey nodded. "Insidious, camouflaged, so the locals don't even know. That's the worst part. The Germans, or so the CIA and our own Centers for Disease Control are telling us, have expanded the envelope, broken the mold."

"You're losing me, Skipper."

"I'm starting to have the feeling I'm lost too. But here are the bare facts as we know them, according to this message. There's an outbreak of dengue fever in Buenos Aires."

"So? It happens now and then in that part of the world."

"*Except*. The outbreak started in several places at once, miles apart, and the strains of the germ are identical. The CIA got samples, and the CDC says this strain is the same exact one, genetically, that led to an epidemic in Guatemala seven years ago."

"That doesn't make sense."

"It does, if the germ was *cultivated,* cloned in a lab, and then released in Argentina *now,* as a stealth weapon."

"Why would anyone do that? Dengue isn't even all that contagious or lethal, if you get medical help."

"It's lethal enough to infants and old folks and the malnourished poor, XO. The purpose, the CIA conjectures, isn't to kill per se. It's to further undermine the government in Argentina, the president and the mayor of Buenos Aires, and the governor of greater Buenos Aires province. . . ."

"This really is total war, isn't it, sir? In a whole new form."

"There's more."

"Sir?"

"The shantytowns around Buenos Aires are also having a sudden epidemic of asthma."

"*Asthma?*"

"That combined with a dose of dengue is completely overwhelming their health-care system. And opposition factions are using this to call on the president of Argentina to resign. The place is ripe for a coup."

"How in heck do you *cause* an epidemic of asthma? It isn't even something you catch!"

"Chemical warfare, XO. Sneaky, almost invisible, by hid-

ing in plain sight . . . In a manner of speaking, you have to
admire them."

Bell sat there, waiting for details.

"Cockroach saliva."

"What?"

"There's a protein molecule in cockroach saliva which
happens to be the most allergenic substance known to man.
In purified form, in large-enough doses, it's deadly to people
with sensitivity. This message from Norfolk, the assessment
from the CDC, says it's powerful enough to debilitate
healthy adults who didn't even think they *had* asthma."

Bell shook his head. "I'm still missing something."

"Crop-dusting planes."

"Oh, Lord."

Jeffrey nodded. "The locals thought they were spraying
for mosquitoes. The shantytowns are mostly on low ground.
They get a lot of flooding in rainstorms. Puddles. Stagnant
water. Breeding ground for insects. Drug-resistant malaria
has become more and more of a problem. Only now, the
CIA is pretty sure, somebody with the right connections and
the wrong agenda imported a batch of artificial protein like
the one in cockroach saliva. They got it into the crop-duster
loads. And public health is collapsing."

Bell thought for a very long time. "In World War One,
the Germans gave us poison gas and the flamethrower. In
World War Two, they gave us V-Two rockets and V-One
buzz bombs. Now they're using germs and chemical
weapons on neutral civilians. In a way that no one in-
country can even tell, or ever be certain about. To bring
down a national government."

"Yup. Even if Argentina's legit regime tries to blame it on
some Axis two-pronged sneak attack, you think anybody
whose babies have died is going to accept that? You think
people lying feverish in their own body waste and gasping
for breath, untreated in the parking lot 'cause every hospital
in town is overwhelmed, are going to give a damn what the

government says? . . . The more the elected officials deny any blame, the more culpable they look."

"Again, Captain, what does all this mean to *us?*"

"The assessment from our national command authorities is that these are just opening moves, to lay the groundwork. Soon the atom bombs will be delivered by the *von Scheer*. Delivered to the pro-German fascist opposition waiting in Argentina. Waiting to seize control and wage atomic war on Brazil."

"So what's Brazil doing now?"

"Arming to the teeth. Expelling the Argentine ambassador and severing relations. Artillery duels have intensified along the border, way down south. The Brazilian Army is confiscating vehicles belonging to foreign citizens and businesses, apparently to augment troop and war-matériel transport. The government in Brasilia nationalized every railroad and port facility too, including ones that were foreign owned. They announced martial law in the border area. The whole city of Foz is being evacuated. That's a quarter of a million people. . . . They declared the two-hundred-mile limit as an exclusion zone for foreign warships. Then the leaders dispersed to hardened secret bunkers underground."

"What about U.S. citizens in-country, Captain?"

"State's told everybody to leave Brazil and Argentina. They're being shuttled across the Andes Mountains to Peru or Chile by air."

"What's the Brazilian Navy up to?"

"To put it in quaint terms, XO, they sortied the fleet from Rio." Brazil's main navy base. "The exclusion zone will be enforced by the *São Paulo* carrier battle group, apparently." The *São Paulo* was the former French Navy's *Foch,* refitted and sold to Brazil in 2001. "We have to watch out for her ourselves. Eighteen fighter-bombers plus eight helos. Her escorts are frigate types, some homegrown and some bought used from the Brits. . . . Fast patrol boats and missile craft are working closer in-shore. To prevent Argentine commando incursions, I think . . . Argentina responded in kind, declared an exclusion zone of their own. Not that they've much to hold it with." The Argentine Navy's largest warship was one secondhand British destroyer.

"And Brazil's atomic weapon status?"

"The CIA still doesn't know precisely. Circumstantial evidence strongly implies Brazil has the bomb."

CHAPTER 27

Twelve hours later, after a block of frequently interrupted sleep, Jeffrey was back at the conn. He listened as Sonar reported yet more atomic blasts off Africa. After hours in the deep sound channel, he was starved again for news of the outside world. At the same time he dreaded what another news report might bring.

His crew's search for the *von Scheer,* using passive sonar only, had still yielded nothing. Jeffrey's one remaining reliable secret weapon, *Challenger*'s new multiline fiber-optic towed array, had caught no clue at all to the enemy submarine's whereabouts. Whenever suspicious infrasonic tonals were picked up, Jeffrey—or the OOD who'd summon Jeffrey—would bring *Challenger* toward the contact. Milgrom's people—every time—identified it as a neutral diesel sub, or a ship on the surface.

Even Ernst Beck, audacious though he might be, would never run von Scheer *on the surface as a trick to deceive or elude me. The* São Paulo *and other surveillance platforms would find him in a snap. . . . No, at this point the battle might not open till we're close to Buenos Aires, where I'm forced to use high-explosive fish alone. That's probably Beck's intention. He'd be willing to use his nuclear weapons, with everything else going on, even close inshore, and I'll be at a big disadvantage. . . . The battle might not even open until von Scheer has delivered her goods, those crated warheads. If that happens, catastrophe in South America becomes inevitable, and with it comes new catastrophe for the world.*

Jeffrey's greatest quandary was that whatever choice he made, either lingering in one area to do a thorough search for *von Scheer* or zigzagging to check out more of the open ocean, would most likely just give Beck a better chance to draw irrecoverably ahead.

Challenger was already at her top quiet speed; to go much faster would make her noisy. To change tactics and ping, with no idea of the *von Scheer's* location, would also be counterproductive. It would ruin any chance Jeffrey had of surprise: Beck's acoustic intercept would pick him up going active, at four or five times the range that *Challenger* could first sniff any faint returning echo off *von Scheer*. The German captain would then have an easy job to maneuver to avoid.

There seemed nothing to do but keep steaming toward Buenos Aires, remain on high alert, and pray. Jeffrey was glum. He hated playing catch-up ball.

In the worst case, with *von Scheer's* advantage of four knots at what appeared to be her top quiet speed compared to *Challenger's*, Beck would be drawing ahead of Jeffrey by a hundred nautical miles a day. Three days south of the Rocks now, *Challenger* was nearing the latitude of Rio de Janeiro, Brazil. It was another thousand miles south-southwest to Buenos Aires, where the coastline of Argentina first began.

If Beck is indeed making a steady thirty knots all along, he'll be at Buenos Aires in another twenty-four hours.

To cut him off, if all of Jeffrey's estimates and hunches were correct, *Challenger* needed to increase speed.

He called up a nautical chart. For something this simple he didn't ask for the navigator's help—and Jeffrey wanted to keep these thoughts to himself.

Forty knots would just do it. Forty knots for twenty-four hours and we're right outside Buenos Aires same time as Beck.

But forty knots would make *Challenger* a much more vulnerable target. It would also reduce her sonar sensitivity, making the *von Scheer* that much harder to find.

And because forty knots was dangerously noisy, Jeffrey would need to use sprint and drift. That meant slowing down sometimes, to listen for threats. For part of every hour, he'd have to go even faster than forty knots and be even noisier.

I've faced nothing but bad trade-offs before. I've been in high-stakes stern chases before—both as pursuer and as pursued. But never have I been forced to choose between such unpleasant alternatives as the ones confronting me now.

The worst of it was, Jeffrey couldn't even savor the stimulant of imminent battle. The facts offered nothing but grinding uncertainty piled onto grinding uncertainty. The *von Scheer's* presence as a looming threat somewhere unseen—intact as a force-in-being—made her more frightening than any opponent he'd ever faced in head-to-head combat. The way Ernst Beck played with Jeffrey's mind and taunted Jeffrey's ego, simply hiding and doing nothing, felt like torture, a wounding insult to Jeffrey's pride.

He decided his best approach had to be: forestall the worst possible outcome. He gave his odds of betting right as less than fifty-fifty. To Jeffrey, this was a losing proposition already. But anything else he could do offered even worse odds.

He recognized that he was sinking back into a mental funk as he stared at the photo of Ernst Beck on his console. The German was way too good. He was winning the psychological warfare with Jeffrey hands down, and he hadn't even fired one shot that was really aimed at *Challenger* yet.

To Jeffrey this was completely unacceptable. He shook his head so vehemently he startled the young OOD.

At least I can try to turn this fight from Ernst Beck's call into my type of fight. Make it active, dynamic again . . . Up the ante and take greater risk. Raise my crew's lagging morale by substituting fear for mounting passivity.

When my people feel fear, they also feel purpose.

"Helm," he said in his most decisive voice, "make your depth fourteen thousand feet. Ahead full, make turns for forty knots."

As the surprised helmsman acknowledged, Jeffrey's intercom light from the radio room began to blink.

Crap. "Helm, belay the change in depth and speed!"

"Aye aye. My depth is four thousand feet, sir. My speed is twenty-six knots."

That was too close. If the helmsman had turned the engine order dial to ahead full, the maneuvering room would have cranked the steam throttles wide open. Reactor coolant check valves would have slammed into their recesses inside the pipes with a thunderous boom.

That unmistakable mechanical transient would've carried for miles.

His nerves badly strained by the stop and go, Jeffrey answered the intercom. Now a senior chief was the communications supervisor.

"Sir, we're ordered to two-way floating-wire-antenna depth."

"Two-way?"

"Affirmative, sir. Message includes code block for radiate on voice, imperative, no recourse."

"From *who?*"

"Atlantic Fleet again."

"Very well. I'll be there as soon as I can."

Will this be valuable info, or more bad news, or useless meddling?

Jeffrey thought it over very carefully. To listen to a radio message on his floating wire antenna was one thing. The wire was trailed underwater, and *Challenger* didn't transmit, so the whole process was pretty stealthy. But to *radiate,* to transmit, would give his position away to any halfway decent eavesdropper on the sea or up in the air or out in space. The risk involved was severe.

And what else is new? Last I heard the whole world was coming apart at the seams.

Jeffrey studied the tactical plot.

Most merchant shipping had headed closer toward the Brazilian coast to gain protection inside the newly announced military exclusion zone. But some ships continued on course.

Their masters may think this exclusion zone could backfire. They might feel safer far out at sea.

Which suits my purposes nicely.

Jeffrey picked the closest big merchant ship outside the zone. It was designated Master 153 on his plot. Master 153 was over thirty miles away to the south, but heading northward.

"Navigator."

"Captain?" Lieutenant Sessions sounded tired, but eager for something nonroutine to do.

"Give me an intercept course on Master one five three."

"Own ship's speed, sir?"

"Use our present speed, twenty-six knots."

"Aye aye."

And now, just in case . . .

"Chief of the watch."

"Sir?" a senior chief answered. He sounded as if, at this point, nothing Jeffrey said would surprise him.

"Sound silent battle-stations torpedo."

People in the control room played musical chairs, while others rushed smoothly hither and yon throughout the ship. The quiet of it all was the eeriest part.

———

Jeffrey listened on the sonar speakers as Master 153 churned steadily northward overhead. *Challenger* had met her and then changed course to keep station underneath. The cargo vessel, identified by Kathy Milgrom's people as an Iranian-owned container ship of Panamanian registry, might intend to put in farther up the Brazilian coast—at Salvador, for example—until the Atlantic Narrows were safer for a neutral flag to cross.

The vessel's diesel-electric engines growled and whined, and her screw props churned and burbled with a syncopated beat. There were also thrums and whirrs from auxiliary machinery, and a rhythmic hissing as her hull cut through the gentle swells.

Now and then Jeffrey could also hear a different, intermittent whine and sigh. He knew this was the ship's hydraulic steering gear, shifting the rudder slightly as her helmsman made small course corrections.

"Considering how mild the sea state is topside, Captain," Bell said, "this helmsman seems rather ham-fisted."

"He'll do," Jeffrey said dryly.

"My depth is one hundred twenty feet, sir," Meltzer called from the ship-control station. "My course and speed match Master one five three's. We are directly under Master one five three, sir."

"Very well, Helm . . . Chief of the watch."

"Sir?" COB responded.

"Trail the two-way floating wire antenna."

"Trail the two-way wire, aye."

COB flipped switches on his panel next to Meltzer's. The antenna began to reel out.

"The noise should be well masked by that container ship," Jeffrey said.

"Concur, Skipper," Bell said.

"My intention, as if you haven't guessed, is to make our transmissions appear to come from the merchant ship."

Bell nodded. "Understood. But I feel compelled to point

out, sir, that a hostile signals intercept would recognize our broadcast as some sort of Allied military code."

Jeffrey shrugged. "Precisely. And they'll mark the merchie down as a spy trawler."

"What if the Axis take a shot at her later?"

"I hate to sound callous, XO, but would you rather the enemy drew a bead and took a shot at *us?*"

Bell kept his thoughts to himself.

"Antenna deployed," COB announced. The two-way floating wire antenna was equipped with distinct transmitter segments. Special software cut through signal distortion as the antenna whipped around and bobbed beneath the waves—or twisted under a surface ship's wake.

"I'll be in the radio room," Jeffrey said. "XO, take the conn. Nav, you take fire control."

Jeffrey donned a headphone set and moved the lip mike in place. He stayed standing.

The first thing Admiral Hodgkiss did when he came on the line was tell him that the conversation was totally private. Jeffrey ordered everyone else in the radio room to leave. The second thing Hodgkiss did was yell at him for waiting so long to answer the ELF message.

"Sorry, sir. The tactical situation demanded I take precautions first."

Hodgkiss hesitated, just long enough to make Jeffrey sweat. "Explanation accepted." Then Hodgkiss hit him hard. "So where is the *Admiral von Scheer?*"

That made Jeffrey angry. For Jeffrey anger overrode self-doubt. "Sir, I do not know, and we need to keep this short." *Challenger* had slowed to the surface ship's speed—which was only twelve knots—and was steaming in the wrong direction, north.

"I have more news for you, and new orders."

"Admiral?"

"Some of this comes from the top. The *very* top."

"The Joint Chiefs?"

"Higher . . . The White House."

"I'm prepared to receive news and orders, sir. I still don't see why you need me to transmit."

"You will. . . . There've been bombings and attacks in Brazil."

"Sir?"

"The American ambassador to Brazil and many of his staff are dead or badly wounded. At the same time, our military attachés have been kidnapped or assassinated."

"By *whom?* Didn't we have *security?*"

"We suspect by Axis operatives. We suspect our security measures were penetrated in advance, or overwhelmed by sheer force."

"What does Brazil have to say?"

"That's just it. We, the American government, were trying to offer advice and aid to Brasilia. President da Gama kept refusing outside help. In a nutshell, he was suspicious of our motives. Said we just wanted free real estate to base troops and planes and ships on sovereign Brazilian soil. Said we'd do nothing good for Brazil except bring in social diseases and useless invasion scrip instead of hard dollars. Not to mention drag his peace-loving country into the war . . . Face it, Captain, our record of winning neutrals over to our side has not been good."

Jeffrey winced. "You're referring to Turkey?" In this war, not Gulf War II.

Hodgkiss sighed. "Look, you did your best."

"Didn't anyone try to warn da Gama about the *von Scheer?*"

"That's when he threw our ambassador out of his office. Da Gama went ballistic, said it was the stupidest thing he ever heard, an insult, expecting him to swallow a tall tale like that. Virtually accused us of inventing the *von Scheer,* said she didn't really exist, and even if she did she'd be over by Africa fighting the Allies there. Remember, he's a former Brazilian Army general, got a Ph.D. in foreign policy from Princeton University, thinks he knows all about America and war—and maybe he does, too well."

"Oh boy." Jeffrey could half picture the scene. He'd met da Gama during a long seminar at the Naval War College, when Jeffrey was stationed there in Newport, Rhode Island, months before the war. Da Gama had grown up in poverty, a genuine self-made man. He'd be a tough nut to crack if he disagreed with you.

"Our ambassador went back to our embassy to call the State Department for guidance. A car bomb got him before his vehicle could make it into the compound."

Jeffrey paused. "My condolences to his family, Admiral. And the other victims."

"*Later.* The point is, we need da Gama on our side, and everyone of consequence on our embassy staff or other advisers in-country are suddenly dead or wounded or missing. One thing da Gama did say, in an earlier meeting, is that his country does not, repeat *not,* have nuclear weapons. . . . Which is, by the way, undoubtedly why he sees Germany giving A-bombs to Argentina as so preposterous."

"The State Department, the CIA, they believe him?"

"Da Gama's a forthright man. Honor and integrity mean a great deal to him personally."

"No rogue faction behind his back?"

"Not in *his* administration. Or outside it." Hodgkiss sounded quite positive.

"Then isn't that good, sir? That Brazil doesn't have any A-bombs?"

"Use your head. It's *terrible.*"

Jeffrey tried to grasp Hodgkiss's point. "Does the Axis know? Do the Argentines know?"

"We have to assume they do."

"Then the prowar faction in Argentina can make a first strike and be sure they're immune to atomic retaliation."

"Affirmative. But if given the chance, they might have

made a first strike anyway, out of recklessness or grandiose ego. *Think,* Captain."

Jeffrey blanched. He saw it. "If the Germans know Brazil doesn't have the bomb, they must have some other way or excuse to justify giving the bomb to Argentina."

"You're catching on. . . . Now, it gets even worse."

"Sir?"

"The following is highly classified, but you need to know. Tell no one else on your ship unless *they* need to know, understand?"

"Yes, sir."

"Our Deep Submergence specialists for a while have been using robotically operated vehicles to inspect hulks after nuclear battles. To monitor contamination and apply sealant foam when needed if there's leakage from reactors or warheads."

"And for salvage?"

"Got it in one. To remove or neutralize cryptogear or other sensitive equipment, and recover atomic warheads whenever possible. Ours or enemy, as the case may be."

"Makes plenty of sense, Admiral." *So where is he going with this?*

"An *Arleigh Burke* wreck has been plundered by the Axis."

"Before our team could get there?"

"*Yes.*"

"What's the problem, sir? They got the codes?"

"*No.* They didn't get the codes. Those parts of the ship were vaporized, or left untouched."

"Left untouched by what?"

"The destroyer hulk was three miles down."

"That's deep, sir, even for our Deep Submergence people."

"Affirmative. But the vehicle they used to sniff around saw footprints in the bottom muck."

"*What?*"

"Most of them were wiped off, or disguised as the divers

withdrew. But the clincher, the real clincher, is that with all the waterlogged soot, the vehicle's cameras saw fresh *handprints* on and inside the wreck."

"That's impossible!"

"Nevertheless, it's a fact. Our scientists have suspicions how they did it, but that's irrelevant right now."

"Yes, sir."

"Needless to say, our people on the scene gave high priority to determining what had been taken. The vehicle lost both its miniprobes trying to peer far enough in the hulk. All they could tell was that an intact internal magazine, which held atomic warheads, had been entered. We have to assume they went in there to steal one or more of the warheads. . . . It's the only way they could have gotten those warheads. Gone inside and done it by hand using tools."

"And the isotope mix when they detonate would tell any competent nuclear physicist which country made those bombs."

"Got it in one. There's the provocation, the casus belli." The reason for war. "We suspect the *von Scheer* intends to somehow use those warheads to make it look like the U.S. gave atom bombs to Brazil and Brazil attacked Argentina with them. Then . . . Well . . . You get the picture. The *von Scheer* herself would have equipment to make the isotope analysis as a matter of course."

Jeffrey had to sit down. "That justifies the so-called foreign aid. That makes it tit for tat. That makes it look like Germany only reacted, and fairly, to an atrocity *we* pulled off." He thought about this hard. "But, Admiral, if the Axis frames us for a major crime, what's supposed to be our *motive?*"

Hodgkiss's voice grew sarcastic, bitter. "Snatch South America as Allied turf before the neutrals there can go with the winning side, the Axis. Grab a bastion on the west coast of the South Atlantic because we know we'll lose Africa soon. Do it on the cheap, use Brazilian troops and a handful of nukes, to not divert our own overstretched forces."

Jeffrey hesitated. "Sir, it *is* the myth of the ugly American pushed to the hilt. . . . But the people down there are conditioned by their politics and culture to believe it, aren't they? And the Allies occupied Iceland in World War Two, uninvited, to get there before the Nazis did. The Icelanders were *really* pissed, but we went in anyway. . . ."

"Given the status of our usable senior personnel inside Brazil—i.e., virtually none—and given da Gama's skeptical attitude, which may in part be due to Axis supporters there working against us—without da Gama knowing their true colors, I mean—our commander in chief sees only one recourse."

"Admiral?"

"The president needs to give da Gama absolute proof that we're telling the truth. The two of them go way back, even longer than you and da Gama do. They met at the Army War College when both were still in uniform." Such international relationship building was one main purpose of the war colleges; it was by design, not coincidence, that so many key players knew one another from peacetime.

"So?"

"Da Gama will know exactly who you are, and that'll count doubly with him because of all the publicity over your Medal, of which da Gama is well aware. You are ordered to serve as an emissary, president to president."

"*Sir?*"

"Brazil is a different culture, like you said. Ceremony and gestures of good faith count for a lot there. If you leave your ship just long enough to meet da Gama, you achieve several things at once. Understand?"

Jeffrey pondered this. "I can't leave my ship."

"You can, and you will. That's the whole point."

"Oh . . . From da Gama's perspective, applying the same sort of logic he used against our ambassador, the fact that I *am* where I am, right off the Brazilian coast, would be hard confirmation that I have good reason for being here. *Chal-*

lenger being in South American waters, not a whole ocean away near Africa and the convoy, helps prove the *von Scheer* must be real, and must be somewhere close by too. Otherwise, why would I be wasting my time anywhere *near* Brazil, thousands of miles from where the convoy action is and from where *Challenger* would do any good? . . . And if *von Scheer* is here, therefore not chasing the convoy, she must have other nasty business in Latin America now herself."

"We simply *must* convince da Gama of our sincerity. We simply *must* convince him that atomic war in his front yard is very imminent. And at the same time we *must* convince him we have a strong resource in place, able to intervene to help him. *You.*"

"And all the talk-talk and pictures of a sunken destroyer could be empty promises and simple fakes. But me speaking to da Gama, there in the flesh as he watches my eyes, would do the trick?"

"Vital national interests are at stake. . . . It's the best the State Department and the national security adviser and everybody else here can come up with, given the deadlines and the distances and travel times involved."

Jeffrey took a deep breath and let it out slowly.

"Sir, with respect, how am I supposed to get into Brazil, and keep *Challenger* meaningfully in the fight? How do I maintain stealth with Axis agents lurking everywhere and *von Scheer* on the prowl? How do I know there isn't a car bomb waiting for *me?*"

"Our communications between here and there have been spotty the last few hours, they're being tampered with or jammed. . . . We need to wrap this up quick, before some Axis hacker puts a cork in *this* conversation, Captain. . . . We have a plan that makes sense to me from the technical perspective, and da Gama is willing to go along, covertly. It keeps *Challenger* heading south, with your XO in acting command. *You* show your face to Getulio da Gama. Bond with the guy as much as you can. He's supposed to be an excellent judge of character. Your orders are to win him over. Convince him we're the good guys in this. Get him to perceive the actual threat, in real-time *today,* so he can take steps to try to fend off a nuclear holocaust. Get him to accept our help, and give us all of *his* help, to stop the maniacs in Berlin and Buenos Aires before it's too late."

"What sort of help from Brazil would make any difference? I'd much prefer to work on my own in international waters."

"No, no, *no*. Because of those stolen warheads, *everything* is changed. American involvement crosses the coasts. This thing is way too big to sneak in just a small commando team covertly. We need outright permission for staging recon drones, deploying Special Forces, getting logistics support, and we need it *fast*. Your trip had been given the code name Operation Mercury. This also comes from the very top. If you need something from us yesterday, help or backup of any kind while you're ashore, stick *Mercury* in the message header."

"Mercury, like the planet?"

"The swift messenger of the gods from ancient mythology. *Mercury*. Invoke his name and the bureaucratic Red Sea of tape will part before your eyes."

Jeffrey hesitated. "Sir, will I be asked to even the score, to give Brazil some of my nuclear weapons?"

"*Negative*. You will neither give any such weapons to Brazil, nor will you use atomic devices within the two-hundred-mile limit of the continent, under any circumstances whatsoever."

This complicated things by reducing the options, but even so, Jeffrey felt immense relief. "Yes, sir."

"I'm having my people here switch into digital mode. Details on how you get from points A to B to C will come through at your end in a text message once I sign off. We don't know where the *von Scheer* is, but we do know where she isn't. The routing instructions you'll get make use of that to play things safe. And the Brazilians promise to get you back to *Challenger* as rapidly as they can."

"Understood."

"Cheer up," Hodgkiss said. "I know about your private chat with the president. You did well, Captain. He's very impressed. Now's your chance to make it two for two."

"Yes, sir." Jeffrey felt doubtful inside. It seemed much more like double or nothing, a game he'd rather not play.

"It's just like the good old days. When ships' captains had to go ashore and act as diplomats. When the United States Navy was young, and the ink on the Monroe Doctrine was barely dry. Commodore Perry opening Japan. Teddy Roosevelt sending his Great White Fleet around the world . . ."

"That was a very long time ago, Admiral." *Hodgkiss is either supremely shrewd or exceedingly desperate.*

"Besides," Hodgkiss added as if he'd read Jeffrey's mind through the radio, "ever been to Rio de Janeiro?"

"No." Jeffrey's head was spinning.

"It's beautiful. You'll love it. . . . And this could be your last chance for a visit before the place gets nuked."

CHAPTER 28

Ernst Beck had the conn in the *von Scheer*'s hushed and crowded Zentrale. The steady rhythm of normal changes of watch, submerged in a pressure hull that hadn't seen the open air in days, gave him a feeling of intimate and cozy timelessness. The rising and setting of the sun, high affairs of state, trivial matters of human beings scurrying about on land in their teeming billions on different continents, all slipped into unreality. It was only the ship's chronometer set to Berlin time, plus some mental juggling, that let Beck know what hour, what date it might be up on the surface.

It was only the thought of his orders that prevented him from having complete peace of mind.

He eyed his console screens. The ship's depth was steady at 275 meters—900 feet. Her speed was thirty knots. She was over very deep water, drawing toward the South American coast. Conflicting ocean currents in what was called the Subtropical Convergence, where warm seas from the equator clashed with cold from frigid Antarctica, garbled local sonar conditions and greatly aided stealth.

Beck was pleased with his crew and with himself. There were no signs at all of enemy pursuit. The only sonar contacts were biologics, as *von Scheer* carefully stayed far outside civilian shipping lanes. Schools of shrimp, sardines, and tuna clicked and splashed and digested food in this less despoiled part of the ocean. Humpback whales sang hauntingly, evocatively as they migrated south—their normal seasonal movements rendered perhaps more urgent by the human battle erupting far behind.

Beck had even been able to sneak back to the Rocks in the initial acoustic confusion of the atomic skirmish with *Challenger* to quickly recover *von Scheer*'s minisub with all the surviving kampfschwimmer. Shedler and his men were vital for what *von Scheer* needed to do next.

As the German captain scanned through other screen pages using his console menu, track marble, and keyboard, he was surprised to see Stissinger enter the Zentrale from aft, accompanied by a messenger.

"The baron requests a meeting with you in your cabin, sir. At your convenience, he said." Stissinger rolled his eyes meaningfully. He obviously found the diplomat as tough to take as Beck did.

Beck sighed. "Very well, Einzvo. Now's as good a time as any. You take over here." Von Loringhoven *was* quite an annoyance.

"I have the conn," Stissinger said. He shot the captain a barely suppressed grin.

"You have the conn." Beck smiled too; he appreciated Stissinger's backstopping and support.

"This is the first officer," Stissinger announced formally. "I have the conn."

"Aye aye," the watchstanders acknowledged.

Beck followed the messenger aft toward his own cabin.

———

Beck saw von Loringhoven waiting for him in the passage-way. He opened the door and let the baron precede him, as the guest, then locked the door behind them.

"I suggest we sit first," von Loringhoven said.

Beck sat, leaving von Loringhoven to take the other chair, the one with its back to the door.

A small ploy, but let him feel slightly vulnerable. I have the power position, facing the door.

Von Loringhoven leaned forward and gave Beck one of his piercing eye-lock gazes.

Typical. Beck returned the gaze, impassive, not blinking. He waited for the other man to speak.

"I think this phase of our relationship has gone on long enough."

"Baron?"

"We will open the next envelope with your orders soon. But much of what it says, I prefer now to anticipate and tell you in my own words."

"As you wish."

"We will have the kampfschwimmer leader Shedler join us when the orders are opened."

"Fine. I suppose it's his job to deliver our cargo?" The crated atom bombs, which Beck, while in Norway, had naively thought were bound for Boer South Africa. *The bombs I learned at the Rocks, to my horror, are destined for Argentina instead.* The bombs to which he gradually recon-ciled himself by falling back on his unfailing concept of duty and discipline.

"No. I see you do not fully understand."

Beck tensed. Then he saw it, *all* of it.

A even worse atrocity. More *innocent blood on my hands.*

Beck felt his face turn purple with rage—at himself for his prior stupidity, at fate for putting him in such an insanely repugnant role, and at von Loringhoven for being the instru-ment of his moral self-destruction.

"That American warhead. It was never meant for intelli-gence purposes! You, *you . . .*"

Von Loringhoven held up both hands. "Captain, please. I did not make these decisions. I am under orders as much as you. Do you think I *enjoy* implementing the necessities of war any more than you do?"

"Frankly, yes! I think you enjoy it a great deal. I think you love power, and you find murder and destruction almost erotic. I've met your kind before."

"Your previous captain?"

"Among others."

"You hated him."

Beck looked back within his mind. The memories were unpleasant. "I suppose I thoroughly hated him."

"Yet you did your job very well."

"Of course!"

"You've no need to raise your voice. I read your formal patrol report. The one you filed after your rescue . . . The most brilliant tactical gambits played by your last ship were *your* ideas as einzvo, not your commander's."

"Please get to the point."

"You and I are tools of our government. We have our instructions, distasteful though they may be. We're participants, both of us, in the continuum of history. Our task is not to make value judgments. The distinction between military and civilian targets is specious. The distinction between war at sea and war on land is a fallacy. The whole purpose of seapower is to influence events on land. Even American naval officers study and memorize that overwhelming, inescapable fact."

"Then what exactly *is* our job, if we're indeed amoral instruments as you say?"

"While Shedler and his men emplace the American warhead, equipped with new timer and arming equipment, you hold *von Scheer* ready with the cargo of German atom bombs. I leave with the kampfschwimmer, to show my face to old friends and strengthen relationships with the faction that supports us in Argentina."

"And meanwhile I just linger offshore? Under combat

conditions? With atomic war about to erupt between adjacent countries hard on our bow?"

"We'll be in friendly waters. The Argentine Navy commanders are already behind us in secret. And as you know, there are no hostile contacts for thousands of miles, thanks to your subterfuge verging on genius in the Atlantic Narrows. . . . Since this is in large part a military operation, all the crucial orders must be issued by you yourself, as commanding officer of the kaiser's most powerful modern capital ship."

Beck felt heartsick. "What about our attachés right there?"

"We can't have divided command on such a crucial and ticklish venture. That's textbook military science, and it would be the road to disaster for Germany here. . . . Only *you* have been briefed on everything. For security. On a submarine at sea observing radio silence, there can't be careless talk or enemy spies. . . . And we dare not have our people based in Buenos Aires try to contact Berlin, to verify shocking instructions or shift the blame."

Beck thought it over, then nodded. Besides the risk of enemy signals intercept, he could easily picture embassy bureaucrats, when confronted with such aggressive escalation of the war, calling home to Germany for help, or stalling . . . or both. "You seem to know consulate habits well, Baron."

"This is what I do for a living."

"Where exactly are you going, then?"

"To a big house, on the pampas." The fertile prairies of Argentina.

"A big house? You make it sound like a children's story."

"Sorry, that's an expression in Spanish. It means a mansion, a villa. On a working cattle ranch. Owned by a native Argentine, a wealthy friend from when I was stationed in Buenos Aires. Outwardly, my visit is merely a gesture of friendship to a neutral being persecuted by a mutual enemy, the United States abetted by Brazil. The *foreign aid* you'll deliver via minisub, the German-made bombs, won't be sent ashore until long enough after our faked American blast that everything will appear as *fully legitimate*—so the scheme should make you feel better, Captain, not worse."

Beck nodded; he couldn't deny the awful logic of one appalling act designed to justify the other.

"By that time as well," the baron went on, "and through the selfsame enabling event of the pseudo-American blast, our local friends will have seized control of Argentina's armed forces and the central government."

"It's all so Byzantine."

"That's how these things work."

"If you say so." *Events are moving too fast.*

Beck knew his hesitation had to be obvious.

"Think how this will benefit your career," von Loringhoven said. "It can't be easy for you, as the son of a dairy farmer. Unless you achieve great victories in battle, and implement grand strategies so 'Byzantine' as you call them, you'll never earn a *von* after your name if the kaiser still smells cow manure beneath your fingernails."

"I don't give a damn about titles."

"Such titles are hereditary. Do it for your sons."

Beck sat and pondered. To go backward now would be cowardice and treason. To go forward might well bring prestige and great social advancement, but at the cost of countless innocent lives.

I need more time to deal with this.

"The time approaches," von Loringhoven said. "Let's open the envelope, shall we, and then get Lieutenant Shedler in here?"

Beck stood up. He felt something inside him yield and break. There was a terrible sinking in his stomach and chest.

But the feeling of falling inside himself wasn't endless. It rebounded swiftly, as if his innermost being had hit a core of hardened steel. "I'll go through the act, Baron. Only make no mistake."

"Yes?"

"I completely despise *you*."

"So long as we achieve what our country asks of us in

South America, you're welcome to detest me as much as you like."

"All this just rolls right off your back, doesn't it?"

"I take that as a compliment. No sarcasm intended. You have your talents and I have mine."

"Suppose this Jeffrey Fuller is smarter than you think? Suppose he's hunting for us, *here,* in these waters, *now?* What if they know we're giving atom bombs to Argentina? What if they even know we stole one of theirs from that destroyer hulk?"

"Lucky guesses, compromised codes, double agents are always threats. You think High Command are *amateurs?* Open your safe. Contingency plans for every scenario wait in there for you, and for your kampfschwimmer team. Sink *Challenger* off Latin America, *now,* so far from the convoy? Why, then that much the better for you and all your descendants, Captain *von* Beck."

CHAPTER 29

The sea was warm and sunlight dappled the surface overhead. Jeffrey—refreshed by another catnap— breathed underwater through his Draeger, embraced by the sea. Felix and a SEAL chief were his dive buddies. He watched for a moment as a large ocean turtle swam by above him, silhouetted by the sun; it paddled rapidly, as if it was in a great hurry. Jeffrey floated effortlessly, weightless, letting his body relax. He drew air in and out of his re-breather mouthpiece rhythmically and evenly. Felix did a last equipment check, gave him a macho thumbs-up, then unclipped the six-foot lanyard attached to Jeffrey's waist. Jeffrey looked down through his dive mask and watched. Beneath him was *Challenger*—from an angle, an aspect, he'd never seen before. The top of her sail was barely thirty feet beneath the surface. She was almost at periscope depth, as shallow as she dared go—just shallow enough for Jeffrey's pure-oxygen rig not to give him convulsions.

Felix and the chief swam down through the open upper hatch atop the sail. The lower watertight hatch was closed, of course, and would be opened only after the flooded sail trunk was pumped dry. The sail of a nuclear submarine was rarely used as a lockout chamber. But the capability was there. Doing it this way kept the main bulk of the ship as far beneath the waves as possible.

Challenger was a huge black shape, longer than a football field and more than forty feet in diameter. Jeffrey couldn't see as far as the bow or the stern. The water here was murky as he gazed down, alive with tiny organisms, clouded by their waste, and further obscured by silt from rivers swollen by the rainy season. As he observed her from outside, breathing through his Draeger, Jeffrey felt a mix of pride and concern. He remembered that more than ten dozen people worked inside that looming pressure hull. He prayed that they'd be safe, and he'd be reunited with them soon under favorable circumstances.

Challenger had come close inshore off the coast of Brazil, up on the continental shelf—the water beneath her keel right now was only three hundred feet deep. She was following a safe corridor arranged by President da Gama's senior naval staff, as laid out in the instructions from Admiral Hodgkiss. This side trip hadn't helped the schedule any, but the minisub lacked the required range and was much too slow to be of use. Jeffrey's ship, under Bell's command, was already running hours late; the atomic torpedoes in all eight tubes had been replaced with conventional ADCAPs.

Jeffrey saw the sail cockpit's outer streamlining clamshells swing closed. Even this nearby, his ears could register no sounds as Felix and his chief locked back into the ship.

Isolated so suddenly, left all by himself in a state that verged on sensory deprivation, he was struck by a surge of paranoia. *What if it's all a giant trap?* Challenger*'s pinned against the coast and the bottom, and now she's half disarmed.*

Jeffrey almost physically reasserted self-control and told himself to trust his chain of command, to have faith in their security measures. But it wasn't easy.

He allowed himself to drift slowly south just beneath the surface, riding the one-knot Brazil Current, saving his strength. COB and Meltzer kept *Challenger* on a perfect trim beneath the gentle swells. Now they moved the sub sideways, north, by engaging her auxiliary maneuvering units—again there was nothing but silence. They needed to get well away from Jeffrey before they went deeper and picked up speed, or he might be pulled down by the suction, with fatal results. Too close, he might even be drawn into the pump-jet propulsor intake. *Challenger* would be crippled, and her captain would be very dead.

Jeffrey watched with growing misgivings as his vessel shied away and disappeared. Soon he felt a firm jostling and suspected it was *Challenger*'s rudder wash as she turned.

The Draeger mouthpiece he had donned tasted rubbery, and the oxygen he breathed felt dry. But he knew his throat was dry for other reasons too. He rose to the surface and took a quick peek up into the air.

The sun overhead was deceptive. Not far off, eastward, threatening low dark clouds were massing, their undersides blurred by what Jeffrey knew was strong rain. As expected, as detected on passive sonar before, a squall line was forming, moving inshore. Then brilliant lightning sizzled, and unfettered thunder cracked—and a fuzzy gray funnel reached down to the sea.

Jeffrey realized he was near a waterspout, a tornado on the ocean. To a ship or swimmer, it was as deadly as any twister on land.

A seaborne tornado was *not* part of the plan, nor was a squall so sudden and violent. Jeffrey felt defenseless as the wind began to pick up. Lightning sizzled again, and hit the surface of the highly conductive sea. He knew Brazil had more lightning-bolt strikes per square mile each year than anywhere else on earth; someplace or other in the country received such a million-volt shock on average every half second. Jeffrey gripped his waterproof travel bag more tightly, as if that would help; it was attached to his gear belt by a lanyard, and also had a floatation bladder so its weight didn't drag him down.

He wondered how deep he'd have to dive to be safe from the lightning, and if the metal in his equipment would draw the terrifyingly sudden energetic bolts, even if he was submerged. He wondered as well if the Brazilians would cancel the pickup because of this squall—and leave him helpless, abandoned, with no radio and very little shark repellent and no drinking water at all.

Will they even be able to find me once the storm passes, assuming I survive? Delay of another hour could spell a disastrous loss against the *von Scheer*.

Then Jeffrey heard a powerful clattering roar and the whine of twin-engine turbines. A helicopter was approaching him from the north, skirting the forward edge of the oncoming storm. But the waterspout and the squall line were advancing rapidly too. It seemed a toss-up which would reach him first.

The helo-engine noise grew very loud and the aircraft passed right overhead, its rotor downwash lashing the surface into a rippling foamy white. Someone in the helo, standing in an open door, was searching the water.

The helo banked, turned back, and came in at less than twenty feet. Jeffrey recognized a Sea King, wearing Brazilian Navy insignia. It slowed. One after another, seven men in black wet suits and Draegers leaped from the door and into the water. The Sea King rushed back north.

Jeffrey ducked beneath the surface.

He activated a weak sonar transponder, worrying that the ultrasonic signal might draw sharks.

Soon six men were swimming toward him underwater. Their technique, their form, their team discipline, all were outstanding. Submerged, the men surrounded Jeffrey. He was unarmed except for his dive knife—an emergency tool, not a weapon. His instincts were to draw himself into a ball, but he resisted doing so.

One of the scuba divers took a quick look at Jeffrey through his mask. He tapped him on the shoulder and then pointed up.

Seven men had jumped from the helo. Seven men now swam in the sea, including Jeffrey. One of the "men" from the helo had been a heated rubber dummy, weighted to sink and stay down. The others were Brazilian Navy frogmen.

Jeffrey heard a new noise now, a screaming two-toned throbbing buzz. It came at him both through the air and through the water. The frogmen spread out in an extended line, leaving him in the middle.

Lightning sizzled again, very close, and hit the ocean with a blinding blue-white flash. The ripping thunderclap came almost instantly. The curving, whirling funnel of the water-spout seemed not to have moved.

Then Jeffrey saw that it *had* moved, it just hadn't changed relative bearing. It was bigger now, substantially bigger, and it was coming right for them. They could try to dive, but Jeffrey wasn't sure this would help. He had no idea how deep the suction of the big tornado might reach. He did know that much below thirty feet, his Draeger could kill him instead of helping him breathe.

One of the frogmen shouted something to him in Portuguese. Jeffrey didn't understand his words, but he sounded tough and confident. The frogmen spread out even more. The two-toned buzzing was very loud, and now it felt and sounded like a whooshing and a growl. It competed with the roaring of the waterspout.

As if out of nowhere, a big black air-cushioned hovercraft raced by in a cloud of spray, so close that the noise of its diesel was deafening. As it passed, its wake rolled over Jeffrey, and he was pummeled by the turbulence of the big airscrew that drove the vessel forward.

The hovercraft continued south, riding just over the water on a man-made wind blown out from under its air-cushion skirt, making at least forty knots.

There was another thunderclap. The sky above was dark now. It began to pour rain; heavy drops pounded the surface. The waterspout was closer and louder. Jeffrey started to hyperventilate. His Draeger air grew stale, and he forced himself to calm his respiration. But still his heart raced from raw fear. The tornado towered above him, much too close, bridging the gap between the clouds and the sea. Its vortex spun so fast it was impossible to make out details: wind and water revolving tightly at two hundred knots or more. When the twister caught him, it would sweep him high and tear him into pieces.

Another vessel came out of nowhere, a smaller one shaped like a race boat. It circled the line of frogmen, then slowed. Now Jeffrey could see someone in the low enclosed wheelhouse and another person at the open stern.

The man working aft leaned over the side and held out a big orange ring. The first Brazilian frogman reached and grabbed this hoop as the speedboat went by. The boat's momentum lifted the frogman out of the water and he rolled and tumbled bodily into the stern.

Soon it was Jeffrey's turn. Now his heart was in his throat. He reached up and tried to time everything just right.

The shock of connecting almost dislocated his arm. The world in an instant seemed to do a somersault around him. He thumped into the speedboat. A crewman gestured for him to hurry up and move aside. Almost at once another frogman came aboard. In moments the entire team had been recovered.

The boat turned north to skirt the waterspout and picked up speed. Jeffrey went into the small wheelhouse, his wet suit hood up and his dive mask on. He looked around inside. The speedboat had a crew of two. Both sailors were intent on piloting the vessel now. One of them pushed the throttles all the way forward.

The twin diesels growled and throbbed at over a thousand horsepower. The deck vibrated strongly and the ride became rough as the vessel skimmed and slammed through the strengthening windblown swells from the squall. White water creamed and splashed and sprayed from the long and sharply pointed bow. The wake behind was a fast-receding blur of churning white.

Rain pelted the forward windshield. Visibility closed in. All the noise made conversation difficult.

. The radar display glowed a reassuring green. The speed log on the boat's instruments said they were doing a solid forty-five knots. The vessel turned without warning, banking steeply and skidding and pounding hard. She leveled off. The gyro-compass showed they were heading 070 now, east-northeast.

Their next stop, Jeffrey knew, was Rio de Janeiro. The speedboat he rode was an ex–Royal Navy FIC-145 covert operations craft. Fifty feet long, its Kevlar-sheathed hull was a hybrid, with two hydroplane steps underneath. The frog-man training exercise had been a cover for picking him up.

The hovercraft that had headed south was also ex–Royal Navy, sold to Brazil. It was a Type 2000 TDX(M) and could maintain forty knots for a full three hundred nautical miles before needing more fuel.

That hovercraft was *Challenger*'s free ride south. The Type 2000's immense noise and her kicked-up wake would help disguise the sub's own acoustic and surface-turbulence signature as both made toward Argentina well inside Brazil-ian waters. At Paranaguá farther down along the coast, ac-cording to the orders from Admiral Hodgkiss, another Type 2000 would take over for the next leg of Bell's high-speed dash toward Buenos Aires.

Jeffrey settled back on a bench in the FIC-145's wheel-house. The frogmen cleaned equipment and mostly ignored him. He figured they were preoccupied by visions of im-pending war—war with Argentina, in which they'd play a central role and probably take losses. He thought these men looked ready, intense and well trained. They were Brazil's equivalent of U.S. Navy SEALs, an elite, and they knew it.

Jeffrey noticed the speedboat was armed with two .50-caliber heavy machine guns. But both were wrapped in can-vas shrouds, protected from the rain and corrosive salt spray. No one seemed to think they'd need them soon.

The frogmen showed so little interest in Jeffrey, now that he'd been safely retrieved, that he suspected they had no idea at all who he was. He thought it was interesting how this whole process had been compartmentalized.

Suddenly Jeffrey had to blink. The special-operations craft pierced through the squall's far side. The morning sun once more shone brightly. The radar display showed land approaching fast off the port bow. Soon he saw the tops of a line of tall hills. Even through the thin haze lingering just above the water, the hilltops shimmered a verdurous green.

Jeffrey watched as the special operations craft moved inshore. In quick succession they passed a series of scenic coves and headlands, islands, reefs, and lagoons. The vessel slowed to twenty-five knots and the frogmen began to examine the coast with binoculars. As they rounded a point, Jeffrey caught his first glimpse of greater Rio. A wide curving beach of glittering yellow-white sand stretched before him. Behind the beach spread a broad boulevard, backed by high-rise luxury hotels and apartment buildings.

"Copacabana," the frogman leader told him.

Jeffrey nodded. The sand, he saw, was dotted with people, a thick speckling of multicolored bathing suits, umbrellas, and towels. The surf was mild, but very few actually went in the water.

That squall was miles away. It hasn't rained here yet today. The sky was crystal-clear pale blue, flecked with scattered fluffy white clouds. The bright sun made the ocean sparkle, golden flecks against a deep blue shading to rich green closer to shore.

The frogmen continued to use binoculars. One of them handed Jeffrey a pair and helped him stand steady and zoom in.

Jeffrey focused. He spotted a big gathering of what looked like Japanese tourists sitting on beach chairs. All were fully clothed from head to foot, including wide-brimmed hats and dark sunglasses.

"Japanese? Nippon?"

The frogman nodded. He shifted Jeffrey's field of view to the right.

The new object of attention was a group of young Latino women sunbathing topless. Nearby were others wearing bathing suits so skimpy Jeffrey wondered why they bothered dressing at all. Then he saw people tanning themselves nude.

Copacabana soon fell behind. The speedboat closed on the entrance to the harbor. The vessel's green, yellow, and blue Brazilian flag snapped jauntily in the breeze. The frogmen, more relaxed now, chatted among themselves while Jeffrey listened. Their Portuguese didn't sound at all like Spanish. If anything, snatches seemed vaguely similar to Italian. The frogmen were very expressive, and talked constantly with their hands. The speedboat made a sharp left turn.

Jeffrey saw at once that Rio de Janeiro's Guanabara Bay formed a truly superb natural harbor. Volcanic formations jutted from the shoreline on both sides of the mouth of the huge upper bay. The tall granite features worked as ideal breakwaters. He recognized Sugarloaf Mountain, shaped like a gigantic cone, an unmistakable soaring landmark. Parts of Sugarloaf were densely overgrown with bushes and vines. The more sheer drops, of hundreds of feet, were stark naked rock—shades of brown and tan embedded with vertical seams of milky quartz. A cable car led to Sugarloaf's peak; it was running and its spacious cabs seemed crammed to capacity.

As the speedboat entered the main shipping channel into the port, Jeffrey passed lighthouses and buoys. The boat skirted Sugarloaf; the protruding hump fell behind. He noticed that both sides of the harbor entrance were guarded by ancient forts.

Now Jeffrey caught a sweeping panorama of Rio itself. On the left sprawled more modern buildings, of gray concrete, white masonry, and glass. He saw parks and marinas,

and the gilded domes and weathered copper steeples of
many churches, plus two airports along the water—one
small, then one large. Several miles ahead and to his right
were shallows, leading to mangrove swamps and stream out-
lets and housing projects and slums. In the middle of the bay
there were islands of all different sizes, and anchorages
where merchant ships were moored. Ferries plied between
opposite shores of the bay. There was also a bridge, under
which the speedboat passed.

Beyond the bay rose Brazil's great coastal escarpment:
more towering solid granite, only superficially weathered.
The mountainsides were covered with lush greenery, or held
clusters of dwellings for more of Rio's poor. Overlooking
the whole scene from just inland on Jeffrey's left soared another prominent summit, Corcovado, Hunchback Mountain.
At its 2,400-foot peak stood the world-famous statue of
Cristo Redentor—Christ the Redeemer—with arms out-
stretched, a hundred feet tall.

The motorboat turned left again and headed for a pier on
the mainland. A long enclosed shed covered the structure,
and the slip alongside was protected by an awning, for security; Jeffrey noticed armed guards.

The crew brought their craft under the awning and alongside the pier with skill. The frogmen and Jeffrey climbed
out, hurrying into the shed.

Inside, Jeffrey saw an armored personnel carrier—an old
M-113, a boxy thing that rode on tracks. Dating from the
Vietnam era, it could have been fifty years old. This one was
painted matte black. Yellow letters on the side said POLICIA.

The big rear hydraulic ramp hatch was down. Jeffrey and
the frogmen clambered in.

The odor of diesel fuel and exhaust was sharp and thick.
The ancient engine was idling roughly, and the whole vehicle shook. Headroom was low and Jeffrey had to stoop.

At the front of the troop compartment, on one of the passenger benches, dozed a man in civilian clothes. His right arm

was in an air cast and sling. The man woke up when he heard the frogmen take seats and raise the ramp hatch closed.

He looked at Jeffrey and was obviously glad to see him.

"Sorry, the painkillers made me drowsy."

"What the heck happened to you?" Jeffrey shook the man's left hand with his right.

"I'm the senior surviving military attaché. Lieutenant Colonel Chuck Stewart, United States Army Green Berets, at your service."

"What happened to your face, Colonel?"

"Shrapnel. It's nothing. They closed the wounds with surgical glue, then smeared on antiseptic." The colonel had long gashes on his cheeks and forehead, unbandaged.

Jeffrey nodded sympathetically. "I heard there were attacks."

The man's eyes clouded with anger and grief. "We're hardly out of the woods yet, not by a long shot. . . . Anyway, I'm supposed to be protocol and liaison officer for your visit."

Jeffrey hesitated. "In other words, my handler. Make sure I don't put my foot in my mouth in front of somebody important."

"Pretty much." Stewart patted the bench next to him. Jeffrey sat and put his travel bag in his lap. The lighting in the vehicle's interior was dim.

Some of the half-dozen frogmen opened their equipment bags and took out special warfare versions of the M-16. Jeffrey saw that the M-113 had viewports and firing ports cut in its sides. The men locked their weapons into the firing ports, slipped in long thirty-round magazines, and pulled the charging handles to chamber rounds.

The frogman leader yelled to the driver. The engine roared to life and the aged transmission slipped into gear. The armored personnel carrier lurched forward. It came out onto a road between drab warehouses, turned right, and picked up speed.

The engine and the worn tracks and sloppy suspension

made for a most uncomfortable ride; the tracks had rubber blocks in each link so they wouldn't tear up the pavement, but this didn't help much.

"Where are we going?" Jeffrey shouted.

"You'll see," Stewart told him. "Be careful what you say until you know we're secure. Then just be yourself. Do whatever it is your orders told you to do."

"When will we be secure?"

"When I say so. Your dress uniform in that bag?"

Jeffrey nodded.

"Change now. In here. You need to look the part when you arrive. . . . You were supposed to get an entry visa by radio."

"Got a printout with me, and my military ID card." The ID replaced a passport for U.S. servicemen and women on active duty.

"Fine," Stewart said. "Everything has to be by the book. Can't have you enter Brazil illegally."

Jeffrey unsealed the bag and began to take out his rolled-up full-dress uniform.

"You brought your Medal?"

"The ribbon for it."

"Good."

Jeffrey stripped off his soggy wet suit. He'd brought a bath towel in his bag, and he dried himself. He pulled on his clothing and shoes; the navy-blue uniform jacket came last. He combed his hair and wished he had a mirror.

"Much better," Colonel Stewart said. He threw Jeffrey a left-handed salute.

The stink from an exhaust leak somewhere in the M-113 got so bad that the frogman chief safed his weapon, then opened one of the vehicle's top hatches and climbed up and manned the machine gun there. Now fresh air and sunlight came in through the roof. The frogman swiveled the heavy machine gun around.

"This protection really necessary?" Jeffrey asked.

Colonel Stewart pointed at the gashes on his own face, and at his bruised and broken right arm. "These answer your question? . . . Cheer up. Take a nice look outside. Enjoy the tour." Then his face grew stern. "Wait. Use my sunglasses."

Jeffrey put them on. They were very dark, and wrapped around to cover the sides of his face. He slid to the bullet-proof viewing port vacated by the frogman who'd climbed up through the open hatch, and peered out at Rio de Janeiro.

He noticed that traffic was light, though a gaudy yellow electric trolley they passed was crowded with local people. The city had beautiful architecture, a mix of very old and very new. The ground floors of buildings that Jeffrey could see were open and airy, and bright colors were used everywhere. He knew Rio was mostly a resort city, and business was down with the war. But even so, the area had a population of about twelve million. Shops and food-vending carts were numerous and often frequented now that it was getting toward lunchtime. Most Brazilian men and boys were dressed in short-sleeve shirts and slacks or jeans. The women wore summer dresses, or blouses and skirts, and some wore jeans. Jeffrey saw bill-board advertisements, many with themes and celebrities from Formula One car racing, or soccer.

He noticed that the police were everywhere, and heavily armed. But the populace seemed largely unconcerned. Pedestrians glanced at the M-113 more out of curiosity than fear. Rio had a reputation for being a relaxed and friendly place. The vehicle passed lovely gardens, pillared mansions, bustling shopping malls.

Jeffrey noticed more Japanese tourists.

"The locals don't seem especially worried."

Stewart shrugged as best he could. "Most of them see what's happening with Argentina as saber rattling."

"And bombings in Brasilia? That's just saber rattling too?"

"Brasilia's five hundred miles away. Guerrillas and terror-ists of all ilks have been nipping at the edges of this society for decades. Remember, the whole place used to be a brutal dictatorship, within the memory of anyone much over age twenty-five you see out there. Death squads and secret police once stalked these streets with impunity. The locals learned the hard way to take things in stride, horrible things that to you and me are barely conceivable. . . . Besides, for them to show each other anxiety now would be taken as weak or unpatriotic. Brazilians are *very* patriotic."

"What about the Atlantic Narrows convoy battle?"

"To the degree they even know about it? That's *thousands* of miles away, and the prevailing winds don't get here from there."

Jeffrey began to wonder how much even Colonel Stewart was aware of the real situation. "Why so many Japanese?"

"With the war, travel from the U.S. and Europe has dried up completely, right? The Pacific Rim is booming, selling everything from oil to microchips to textiles to parts for battle tanks to America and our allies. And to the Axis. So the Japanese have big money again plus the leisure time to travel. And the Pacific Ocean air routes are fairly safe."

"But during a tactical *atomic war?*"

"I think that adds to the kick, the allure, for the Japanese. Remember, they're the ones who had two A-bombs dropped on them in World War Two. There's a perverse attraction for them to get close to where the action is now. A ringside seat, voyeurism, getting even vicariously, whatever."

"Weird," Jeffrey said.

"Yeah, weird. And double weird, since Japan announced they have their own nuclear weapons."

Jeffrey looked out the viewport more. They passed public squares with monuments or modern art, then an opulent cathedral, and for a short while rumbled over cobblestones. Moving through traffic circles, they went by delightful fountains and nice statues. Jeffrey saw people riding motorbikes, standing on street corners waiting to cross, chatting at outdoor cafés. The racial diversity was impressive. "I'm still surprised how everybody's just going about their daily lives. . . . I mean, I see fewer men of military age, sure, with the mobilization, and I heard a lot of cars and trucks were grabbed by the army."

"And you didn't see any warships sitting in port, did you?"

"No. Nothing big."

"Welcome to South America. The people here don't exactly think like you and me. So remember, in this meeting coming up? We're on *their* turf. *They* make the rules here, not us."

CHAPTER 30

The armored personnel carrier left downtown and got
on a highway, picking up speed. The tall hills on both
sides of the road were covered from top to bottom
with shacks, clinging to the slopes, piled one above another,
some sporting TV antennas or laundry drying on lines.

"They call them *favelas,*" Colonel Stewart said. "Vertical
shantytowns. Low-end service workers for all the restaurants
and condos and hotels."

"I thought President da Gama was *good* for the economy."

"You should have seen these places five years back. Then
very few people had full-time jobs, or even living quarters
with running water and electric power."

Jeffrey stared up at the teeming hillsides. The shantytown
districts seemed to go on and on, forever.

"The single best measure is infant mortality," Stewart
said. "It's a tenth of what it was when da Gama took office."

The M-113 drove north and then east. It turned into a security area, heading down a concrete ramp toward the base
of a mountain. The vehicle halted, then moved forward

again. It grew dark, and Jeffrey could see a low-ceiling over-head above the open top hatch now. Thick doors swung closed behind the M-113, and it grew even darker outside and in. Other thick doors in front swung open, and the vehi-cle advanced again. It stopped under harsh fluorescent lights hanging from springs. As the second set of doors swung closed, the frogmen lowered the troop compartment's rear exit and the driver shut the engine off.

"This is where we get out," Colonel Stewart said. "You can leave your wet-suit stuff here."

Jeffrey helped the injured Stewart from the vehicle. He noticed the colonel favored one leg as he walked. The man also looked very pale now, probably drained by the effort of talking during the ride, and by discomfort from his wounds as the pain drugs wore off. But even so, Stewart's bearing was dignified, soldierly.

A Brazilian Army officer came up to Stewart and Jeffrey and saluted. He said something in Portuguese and Stewart replied. The three of them went to another door inside the heavily guarded cavernous space. This door led to an eleva-tor. They took the elevator down.

"This is a hardened command post," Stewart told Jeffrey. "The geology here is ideal. They built it four or five years ago, after that war scare in Asia. Aboveground they have laser sparklers and dazzler strobes to throw off homing smart bombs."

Jeffrey nodded—since Axis hackers distorted the Global Positioning System signals too, underground bunkers re-gained some real protection against nonnuclear ground pen-etrator rounds.

Waiting at the bottom when the elevator door slid open was a man in a purple sport jacket, orange suede slacks, and scuffed leather loafers. His shirt was lime green, and his polyester tie had red and yellow polka dots. Jeffrey figured nobody in their right mind would dress that way except on purpose—as some sort of distraction from his face, or as a disguise by its very conspicuousness. It was working, too: the man's clothing clashed so badly it was almost painful to look at him.

He nodded to Jeffrey and Stewart. "You can call me Mr. Jones. They're ready for us." He was obviously American.

Things were moving a little too fast. "Who are you, or should I say *what* are you, Mr. Jones?"

"I work for Langley." Langley, Virginia—CIA headquarters. "Come. We can't keep these people waiting."

"Mr. Jones" led Jeffrey and Colonel Stewart into a conference room. The furnishings were bare and functional, except for the video and communications equipment, which were state-of-the-art.

Two Brazilian generals and an admiral jumped to attention when Jeffrey entered the room. The generals snapped him salutes.

Jeffrey braced to attention, in acknowledgment. This was standard courtesy. Even senior officers saluted someone junior who wore the Medal of Honor. And the U.S. Navy never saluted indoors. The proper etiquette for Jeffrey was to brace to attention instead of saluting someone from a different branch of the services—American or foreign.

I don't need a protocol officer to tell me that much.

The Brazilian top officers welcomed Jeffrey. They all spoke English fluently. Colonel Stewart murmured to one side with Mr. Jones, who nodded. Stewart told Jeffrey the room was secure.

"Come," the most senior of the Brazilians, an army general, said. He guided Jeffrey to a chair at one end of the table. Stewart and Jones sat on Jeffrey's left and right. The Brazilians also took seats. The chair at the other end of the table was empty.

The tabletop was spotless and bare: no writing tablets, no pitcher of water, no coffee service, nothing. Jeffrey wondered what this might signal in the language of diplomacy.

"We want to show you something," the general said.

The Brazilian admiral turned on a digital video player,

and a flat-screen TV monitor on the wall came alive. Jeffrey shifted his chair for a more comfortable view; he was stiff and achy from the pounding ride in the speedboat and the rough ride in the M-113.

"This is infrared," the general said, "from one of our reconnaissance drones."

At first Jeffrey saw nothing.

"The altitude is three thousand meters. The location is about fifty miles outside the Rio de la Plata estuary." The la Plata estuary, Jeffrey knew, was a wide bay and tidal basin, a sharp indentation of the South American coast, between southern Uruguay and northern Argentina. Outside its mouth, on one side, stood Mar del Plata, an Argentine beach resort and Argentina's primary naval base. At the inner end of the estuary, where major rivers met the sea, stood Buenos Aires, Argentina's capital. . . .

Jeffrey saw an aircraft enter the picture. It looked like an old transport plane, a DC-9 or something.

"The aircraft is Argentine."

"When was this taken?" Jeffrey asked.

"Last night," Mr. Jones said.

"With respect, how do we know this is genuine?"

"Good question, Captain," Jones said. "President da Gama gave permission for an AWACS to make overflights of Brazil. For purely humanitarian reasons, of course. To supervise the evacuation of Americans into Peru . . . None of us want to see a planeful of women and children fly into a mountain in the Andes in the clouds."

"The AWACS held radar contact on this?" Jeffrey pointed at the plane on the TV.

Jones nodded. "From takeoff to landing, at an airfield near Buenos Aires. Just watch."

A door in the side of the Argentine plane popped open. Objects began to drop out, over the ocean from high altitude in the dark.

The recon-drone camera zoomed in.

The objects were *people,* and they were being *thrown* out.

Jeffrey watched in horror, his heart pounding. One by one twenty victims cartwheeled and flailed in the air as they fell from the transport plane. It seemed to take forever before each made a gigantic splash in the sea.

Jeffrey was grateful when the recording stopped.

"This has been going on almost every night for most of a month," the Brazilian general said.

Jeffrey took a deep breath. He made eye contact with Stewart and then Jones. "Okay. Who were they killing?"

"Mostly journalists and teachers," Jones said. "Clergy too, priests, nuns, rabbis, ministers, anyone who is speaking out for peace in Argentina, against fascism and the Axis."

"So it's another Dirty War."

Everyone in the room nodded.

Jeffrey turned and stared at the now-blank TV screen. "Why are you showing me this?"

"Isn't it obvious?" a new voice said.

Jeffrey glanced over his shoulder, startled. A stout, bearded, dark-skinned man had just entered the room. Jeffrey recognized President Getulio da Gama—older than last time they'd met, but then Jeffrey must seem older to da Gama too. The Brazilian president wore a gray pinstripe business suit.

Everybody jumped to attention again. Jeffrey joined them.

Da Gama came up to Jeffrey and shook his hand very hard. "It's good to see you again, Captain. Thank you for coming."

"Yes, sir," was all Jeffrey could think to say.

"Sit, everyone, please." Da Gama took the seat at the other end of the table, facing Jeffrey. Everyone else sat only after the president did.

"This is why you insisted on me coming here, isn't it, Mr. President?" Jeffrey said. He gestured at the video player.

"I wanted you to judge for yourself who the true aggressors are." Da Gama's English was impeccable.

"I thought it was you who wished to be convinced of certain things."

"That too, Captain. Your presence already has me largely convinced of your sincerity. But I had another selfish agenda. Do you see it?"

"Sir?" Jeffrey noticed Stewart and Jones were keeping quiet, as were the Brazilian brass. This exchange was strictly between Jeffrey and da Gama.

An exchange, or a face-off?

"What did you think of Rio, Captain?"

"A beautiful city, Mr. President."

"A city is nothing but buildings and roads. I speak of the *people,* the citizens. They are the true heart of Rio."

"Friendly, happy, thriving, from what I could tell."

"That described most of my country, until a short while ago."

"I understand, sir. I wish I didn't have to be here."

"I wanted, *needed* you to be here. To see some things for yourself, in flesh and blood. So they would not remain as mere abstractions, but could come alive in front of your eyes, to compel you to perform the work you must do with the utmost skill . . . Including what the fascists are already doing to those who oppose them in Argentina. The new wave of disappearances."

Da Gama turned abruptly to Mr. Jones. "How much does Colonel Stewart know?"

"Nothing of the latest problem, Mr. President."

"Very well," da Gama said. "Then let me summarize. Captain Fuller, you tell me if you feel I'm mistaken."

"Yes, sir."

Da Gama turned to his commanders. "The Americans would have us believe that a German nuclear submarine is off our shores, heading for Argentina, for the specific purpose of starting atomic war on land between Brazil and Argentina. The Americans tell us this submarine carries a supply of atomic warheads for the pro-Axis faction plotting to take over in Buenos Aires. They also tell us the Germans have stolen one or several American atomic warheads, which they intend to detonate themselves to create an atrocity to make the war appear to be Brazil's and America's fault."

The Brazilians remained impassive; Colonel Stewart looked shocked, aghast.

"Is that essentially correct, Captain Fuller?" da Gama said.

"Yes, Mr. President."

"Have you made any recent detection of this supposed German submarine? Any indication, other than your own surmisings or fears, as to its whereabouts?"

"No, sir," Jeffrey said reluctantly. "Only supportive circumstantial evidence, plus a lack of negative proof to the contrary."

"What do you mean by the latter?"

"That the German submarine—"

"The *Admiral von Scheer*?"

"Yes, sir. That the *von Scheer* has not for days attacked the Allied convoy to Africa, although she is designed primarily for that purpose and has had every opportunity to make such an attack."

"I have other problems with your theory," da Gama said.

"Mr. President?" Jeffrey thought the best way to be convincing would be to listen first.

"Admiral?" Da Gama gestured.

The admiral worked the video player again. A map of Argentina appeared on the big screen.

"Where would the fascists detonate an American warhead so as to serve as adequate provocation?" da Gama asked.

Jeffrey studied the map.

"You needn't answer," da Gama said. "My staff have been studying the issue. This is where my understanding is stymied. If they set off the bomb, or bombs, in a wilderness area, the detonation lacks military value from our perspective, and thus begs the question of our practical motive or goal, if we truly were the culprits. Such a blast also has little effect on Argentina as a whole, except for possible fallout, which is quite invisible to the average citizen. So it would hardly serve to incense the Argentine people, and therefore would not help the fascists much."

"I have to agree," Jeffrey said.

"Yet to detonate the bomb on an Argentine military facility, or on a major Argentine urban center, while certainly making Brazil look like a great villain, also does terrible harm to the Argentine fascists themselves and to their supporters. . . . Most of the population of that country is concentrated right around Buenos Aires. The fascists might wish to dispose of the shantytowns, or of the Jewish quarter, but to use a nuclear bomb would do massive damage to other people and establishments the fascists would want to protect. And again, it raises the problem of credibility for the entire ruse. Why would *Brazil* want to kill people in Argentina who oppose the fascists?"

Jeffrey saw that da Gama was making very telling points. He began to wonder himself if he and his superiors had misjudged the entire basis of Axis intent, and began as well to better understand how da Gama had earned his reputation as a charismatic and spellbinding orator and debater. Da Gama also displayed his trademark combination of working-class pragmatism and ex-army skills as organizer and administrator. No one could have poked holes in the American arguments with greater clarity or fewer words.

But Jeffrey *was* utterly convinced of his own position. He *knew* the *von Scheer* was out there.

"I don't want to put you on the spot unfairly, Captain," da Gama said. "I have no doubt that Argentina verges on a fascist coup. I have no doubt they would welcome support from the Axis. And I don't question that an attack by them from the south would be a distraction and a nuisance to Brazil. But they couldn't possibly defeat us, given the correlation of forces and the distances involved and the mounting logistic difficulties for them as they advanced."

"Sir, that's just it. If the Argentines had atomic weapons, the correlation of forces would be very different, wouldn't it?"

Da Gama frowned. "Yes."

"And a fabricated provocation of *some* kind, as an excuse for Germany to give the Argentines a supply of such weapons, would be consistent with their history. German history."

Da Gama nodded. "The Nazis dressed concentration-camp inmates in Polish Army uniforms, then shot them outside a German radio station on the border. They said, 'See, Poland has attacked us.' Then they invaded Poland. Yes, it's in every history book. . . . But that was many years ago. And the current regime in Germany aren't Nazis."

Mr. Jones cleared his throat. "We seem to be at an impasse."

"The impasse may be irrelevant," da Gama said. "Captain Fuller, if we come right to the point, assume *von Scheer* and the latest German plot are real, what would you have us do that we aren't already doing?"

"Warn your people and evacuate main cities."

"And cause tremendous panic while attempting something that our own computer modeling and traffic analysts have shown cannot be done?"

"Sir?"

"The people living in and around Rio de Janeiro, and our business and commercial center in São Paulo, and the new capital city Brasilia, total close to fifty million. The best roads in the whole country connect these three cities only to one another. How do we evacuate fifty million people? Where do we send them?"

"What about the trans-Amazonian highway?"

"Largely a daydream from our era of dictatorships. Hardly comparable as a civil defense asset to America's interstate system, or as a military conduit network to Hitler's Autobahn. Parts of this so-called highway through the Amazon are nothing but mud holes in the rainy season; they aren't even paved. And many paved parts get washed out every time the Amazon floods, which it does each year as part of the normal seasonal cycle. . . . Please, Captain, be realistic."

"Then the only option, Mr. President, is interdiction."

"Captain?"

"Help us interdict the Germans when they try to bring the atom bomb ashore."

"How much more help can we give? Do you think we don't know that half of the tankers sent to refuel your AWACS in midair are really electronic warfare reconnaissance planes? And that your AWACS aircraft's orbit is suspiciously close to the Argentine border? Not to mention, shall we say, today's varied naval activities? . . . To work directly on Argentine soil, or in their territorial waters, would constitute an invasion itself, an act of war. We'd start the very thing we all seek to avoid."

Jeffrey glanced again at Jones and Stewart and saw that neither man had anything to say. Figuring he held the momentum himself, he kept talking.

"Give us permission, Mr. President, to stage our assets from your soil. More sophisticated reconnaissance drones of our own and Special Forces."

"For what purpose?"

"To be better poised to halt the German detonation of an American atom bomb. It's only fair we be allowed to reclaim our dangerous stolen property. Our transterritorial right of hot pursuit."

"You would cross the border into Argentina yourselves, staging from Brazil?"

"It's the least evil of the unattractive choices available, sir."

"*How will you even track this warhead?* Don't tell me your AWACS or your ECM planes or drones can see a shielded tactical nuclear warhead from such a vast distance away. The Atlantic coast of Argentina is fifteen hundred miles long!"

"Sir, I'm honestly not aware of our true capabilities there. I do know my superiors believe such staging access, if you grant it, could make some difference."

Mr. Jones cleared his throat. "I think I can add something here."

Everyone turned. Jones took an object from his pocket and put it on the conference table.

"What is that?" da Gama said.

The Brazilian generals passed it to their president.

Da Gama looked at it. "This is a *bottle cap?*"

"Mr. President," Jones said, "how often have you walked by one of those on the sidewalk and paid it no mind? Ignored it altogether? Not even noticed it?"

"Why, I don't know. There must be millions of bottle caps strewn everywhere each day." South American bottling companies used and reused glass much more than aluminum cans.

"Precisely," Jones said. "Only this isn't really a bottle cap."

"What is it?" Da Gama turned it over in his hand.

"It's a gamma-ray detector. With a built-in radio transmitter. The microbattery is recharged daily by solar power."

"And . . . ?"

"These have been strewn, as you put it, sir, all around the waterfront of Mar del Plata, and Buenos Aires, and other ports of possible infiltration into Argentina such as Bahía Blanca farther south."

"I'm impressed," da Gama said.

"Can I see?" Jeffrey asked.

Da Gama slid the bottle cap along the table. Jeffrey looked at it carefully. *Probably has a loop antenna built into the rim.* "What's the range of the radio link when this thing decides to sound the alarm?"

"I don't know," Jones said. "That's above my clearance level."

"Mr. President," Jeffrey said. "Everyone. I think the way to break our impasse is to stop thinking in terms of certainties when we face so many unknowns. We need instead to consider scenarios. One possible scenario is the one we've all described, that the *von Scheer* is real and close and will deliver an American warhead, intending to detonate it as the excuse to then present German warheads to Argentina."

Da Gama looked at Jeffrey. "Have you considered, Captain, that this whole train of thought we've been following is a very clever Axis trick to dupe us all and have us do their work for them? That, in fact, the Germans want us to think just this, and then an American incursion on either Brazilian or Argentine territory presents the Axis with sufficient excuse right there? That *we,* gathered here in this room, by holding this meeting and making the decisions that Captain Fuller presses us to make, may very well create the provocation for war?"

Jeffrey blushed. He hadn't thought of that.

Da Gama is smart. Scary smart. But Jeffrey would not be put off, even by such powerful rhetoric.

"Mr. President, viewing everything as a whole, I think we need to take the risk."

"I appreciate more and more why your head of state sent you, Captain. You've been in nuclear combat several times."

Jeffrey nodded.

"You've dealt and taken atomic blows. You've seen and felt the horror firsthand. An envoy, a diplomat, an embassy man I could dismiss too easily as a mere theoretician. You, however, speak to me with total credibility."

"Yes, thank you, Mr. President."

"I know you do not urge active involvement upon me lightly. But still I must reject your premise of risk. I begin more and more to consider the opposite view. That to *act,* with no harder information to go on, would be our gravest possible error. I must think of my own people first, Captain, and not get caught up in adventures based on American whim. Brazil is a democracy, and I cannot on my own either perform or condone what amounts to a declaration of war, especially not at the behest of a foreign power, the United States. My people, our congress, they know nothing of the threat of nuclear fighting on this continent. To convince them, to have any constructive effect, seems an impossible task when I'm not convinced myself."

"Sirs," Jones broke in, "may I suggest we take a short recess?"

Da Gama nodded curtly. He got up to leave the room, followed by his officers. Once they were gone, Colonel Stewart and Mr. Jones came over to Jeffrey, who remained seated. He felt exhausted and beaten by the verbal fencing that had gone nowhere.

"Well, at least you're trying," Stewart said.

"Be careful," Jones said in an undertone. "We have to assume this room is bugged, and they're recording everything we say."

"Fine," Jeffrey said. "We don't have anything to hide, do we?"

Stewart and Jones shook their heads.

Jeffrey walked up to the map of Argentina. He studied it from top to bottom.

Where would the American warhead come ashore? Where would they detonate it? How can Estabo's SEALs effectively interdict a kampfschwimmer team? How best could Challenger *intercept von Scheer? . . . What if* von Scheer *landed her warheads too soon?*

He began to form a plan. "Colonel Stewart? Mr. Jones? Either of you know how to work this map-displayer thing?"

"What do you want to see?" Jones asked.

"A different area. Run from Mar del Plata up to Paranaguá."

"Remind me where's Paranaguá."

"South of Rio. On the coast."

"And?"

"Go inland enough to show Buenos Aires, and all of the border between Brazil and Argentina too." The border stretched about three hundred miles.

Jones played with the controls. He cursed once or twice, but soon had the new map on the screen.

Da Gama and his men returned to the room.

Da Gama saw the map had changed. "What are you looking at, Captain?"

"We need to see this more from the German point of view. We know time is critical for them because of *Challenger*'s presence."

"Are they sure your ship is nearby? We took great precautions bringing you here."

"They have to at least make allowances for the possibility."

Da Gama nodded. "They too must look at different scenarios."

"When transporting anything, time interchanges with distance, and distance with time."

"Of course."

"The Germans knew from the beginning that they wouldn't have forever, or even very long. . . . Their target needs to be somewhere on this map, I think. Somewhere within easy range of Mar del Plata, which stands out as the closest port or naval base to wherever the *von Scheer* might be."

"Easy range by what means?"

"If the target isn't either Mar del Plata or Buenos Aires themselves—for all the various reasons we discussed and agreed on before—it has to be someplace inland to make any sense."

"Transport by truck, or plane, or helicopter," da Gama stated.

"Yes. All of which can be tracked by one of our airborne reconnaissance platforms."

"So, Captain?"

"Our mistake before was fixating on the map of Argentina alone, thinking of Argentina in isolation. I think the target's going to be somewhere on the *border,* close to the *border.*"

"There's nothing there but jungle and swamps. We already moved the civilians out of Foz, with great difficulty."

"Foz. That's near the Triple Border, where Brazil and Argentina touch and both also meet Paraguay?"

"Yes."

"Okay. Scratch that, then. But there are troop concentrations *all* along the border, right? All the way south from Paraguay to Uruguay?"

"Yes. On both sides, ours and Argentina's. We're running low on artillery shells already. . . . So are the Argentines, from what our intelligence sources indicate."

"Then *that's* it," Jeffrey said decisively. "They'll set off the American bomb somewhere just on the Argentine side of the border. Kill some of their own troops, but not damage any primary fascist assets. Make it look like Brazil brought the bomb to the border from *your* side, Mr. President, and snuck it across, and *you* set it off as prelude to a breakthrough assault through the hole you punch in Argentina's shaken defensive front lines."

Da Gama stared at the map for a very long time. Finally, he nodded. "Our paradigm, our perspective, was wrong. They don't intend to use the stolen device as a weapon of terror. They plan to use it as tactical nuclear arms were designed to be used, on a military battlefield. . . . It makes their scheme to implicate Brazil and the U.S. wholly plausible to world opinion this way. . . . What do you want us to do?"

"When the hovercraft change shifts at Paranaguá, while they escort my submarine south, I want my SEAL team to sneak off *Challenger* and come ashore at Paranaguá. That'll put them in better striking distance of anywhere on the border, hours sooner than otherwise."

"Why SEALs, Captain?" da Gama said.

"The border is mostly defined by major rivers in full flood."

"Yes. The Iguazú. The Uruguai. The bridges were blown and the ferries burned, days ago now."

"That makes the warhead recovery a riverine operation, sir. That's one thing SEAL teams do. It's our warhead; let it be our people who fight to get it back or disarm it."

"I'm not sure."

"If there must be a border incursion, Mr. President, it should be by Americans. Later you can deny you'd ever approved—in order to defend Brazil's neutrality."

"We have our own troops on the border. The core battalions are very well trained. Professionals. I'm hardly the only one who studied with your U.S. Army."

"Sir, no slight on your men is intended, or implied. But my team have recent live experience on an actual nuclear battlefield. They've gone up against kampfschwimmer hand to hand and they did well."

"Yes?" Da Gama sat thoughtfully. "It does make sense the Germans would use kampfschwimmer to plant the bomb. . . . Very well, I give you my permission."

Jeffrey wondered how much da Gama knew about the Rocks.

"I'll get on that for you, Captain," Colonel Stewart said. "I'll help get the commo links set up, here and in the States, and we'll get your orders to *Challenger* by low-frequency radio."

"And Mr. President?" Jeffrey said.

"Captain?"

"Can you have a long-range transport helicopter put on alert at Paranaguá, please, for use by my SEALs? Their lieutenant's name is Felix Estabo. He and his men are all Latino, fluent in Portuguese or Spanish or both. They won't arouse suspicion. They'll blend in."

"And then what?"

"If nothing more happens, then nothing, and your country is blameless. Or at least subjected to no more possible blame beyond right now."

"Yes."

"If the American warhead does come ashore in Argentina, sir, we need to lock on by aerial recon and track it and the kampfschwimmer carefully. Send my SEALs in your helo on an interception course, on the Brazilian side of the frontier."

"A race to meet, and fight at close quarters? . . . It doesn't sound like very much to go on."

"I know, Mr. President. . . . We need a way to harass and distract the bad guys. Something that intimidates, confuses, but nonlethal and without a premature border violation . . . If I understand the mind-set of the Argentine rebels, sir, their leaders are rash, incautious."

Da Gama nodded.

"I want us to put more pressure on the Argentines and Germans. Breathe down their necks and let them know it, bad. If they start to worry that we're catching on to them, it might force our opponents to rush and make hasty decisions, maybe even commit some revealing mistakes. . . . Less time to work with also heightens the dangers for our side. It's a risk we'll have to accept. . . . Mr. Jones, how far up the Rio de la Plata estuary do international waters go?"

"The twelve-mile limit? Pretty far up. It's a hundred miles wide at its mouth."

"And what platforms monitor your gamma-ray detectors?"

"I'm guessing we have operatives in Argentina, or across the estuary in Uruguay, with proper equipment. Out on the water in boats, on top of mountains, I don't know."

"Okay . . . Colonel Stewart, invoke the code name Mercury, and use that to make some drones available, fast. Predators, Global Hawks, whatever. And a U.S. Air Force B-One-B bomber based from Venezuela, something really conspicuous but well able to defend itself. It can follow a dogleg course out over the ocean, we don't need to think about overflight rights. It's supersonic, it can be at the estuary very quick. Have it fitted with a recon sensor pod. Visual and infrared especially . . . And have the bomber loaded with active sonobuoys; don't worry about the receivers, this part is just for effect, to slow *von Scheer* and her minisub."

"I'll make the request Flash Immediate, route it through Atlantic Fleet so Admiral Hodgkiss can press his support."

Jeffrey nodded. "Can the B-One break the sound barrier at sea level?"

"I think it can manage a thousand knots or so."

"Have it do that a few times in the estuary. Make big noises at Mar del Plata, rattle windows in Buenos Aires, get on the enemy's nerves and keep them wondering why it's there."

Jeffrey turned to da Gama. "Is this acceptable to you, Mr. President?"

"Yes."

"And Colonel Stewart, if you don't mind acting as my executive assistant for the duration of this, add a summary of our intentions for Atlantic Fleet, with informational copies to whoever you think makes sense. Do it in my name, and say up front 'Unless otherwise directed.' Then we go into motion and hope nobody upstairs screams."

Stewart nodded, his wounds forgotten now.

"And Mr. Jones. I don't want to take any chances your local people might be compromised or neutralized. Call Langley *now*. Get technical specs to the air force, pronto. Make sure that B-One's avionics include a black box that can listen for those bottle-cap things to go off. The magic word is *Mercury*."

CHAPTER 31

Beck was startled out of his sleep when a messenger knocked on his cabin door. He pulled on a robe and answered.

"Sir, the communications officer sends his respects, and he has received this over our floating wire." The messenger handed Beck a sealed envelope.

"Did the Einzvo see this?"

"Yes, sir. I gave him a copy at the conn. He awaits your further instructions."

"Very well."

Beck sat at his desk and read.

Berlin—with help from Moscow—was seeing a suspicious pattern to Allied radio communications and aircraft flights to and from Brazil and near Argentina. Axis High Command believed that the enemy might be aware of *von Scheer*'s plans. The timetable was therefore being moved up aggressively, with support by added information-warfare attacks and jamming.

That's easy for them to say, but my ship even at flank speed can't work miracles. We've a very long way to go to reach Mar del Plata.

Beck read on. The kampfschwimmer team and von Loringhoven were ordered to leave *von Scheer* immediately, using Beck's minisub, along with the one working U.S. atom bomb. Once Beck and *von Scheer* proceeded farther south, the minisub was to ping on the frequency commonly used by Argentine diesel subs. Sonobuoys being dropped from an Argentine seaplane would thus locate the minisub by triangulation, a simple process. While a two-man crew stayed aboard the mini per standard procedures, everyone else would swim out and deploy a rubber raft to the surface. The seaplane would pick them up and return with them to Mar del Plata as if they were Argentine submariners or commandos on an exercise or an emergency personnel transfer. Then the mini would return to the *von Scheer* covertly, and Beck would wait beyond the continental shelf.

Beck grew concerned that the Allies might indeed be on to the plan. If so, with the enemy forewarned, able to take active countersteps or even just prepare a firm and persuasive-enough denial, the Axis scheme might begin to unravel. Beck appreciated now why Berlin saw the need to hurry. He dressed.

Beck left his cabin and knocked on von Loringhoven's door.

———

President da Gama left the room to attend to other duties—Jeffrey reminded himself the man had an entire country to run.

Lunch was brought in. Jeffrey and Colonel Stewart made small talk with the two Brazilian generals. The admiral and Mr. Jones were working in another part of the underground bunker.

Jeffrey let Colonel Stewart set the tone, but the inconsequential chitchat was driving him crazy. Every neuron in his brain tingled for news of the stolen warhead, and every nerve in his body screamed for him to get back to his ship.

The Brazilians said they were having communications and mechanical difficulties making final arrangements for Jeffrey's clandestine departure.

Jeffrey exerted tremendous self-control to master this latest lesson in command and diplomacy: patience.

But his self-control only went so far. He couldn't help glancing often at the TV screen on the wall. Now it was set up to show a master status display. Estabo's team had landed at Paranaguá and were airborne, heading west toward the inland border in a Brazilian helo; another Brazilian Navy hovercraft was dashing south, presumably with *Challenger* making forty knots right under it; the U.S. Air Force B-1 bomber launched from Venezuela was over the Rio de la Plata estuary now, its supersonic dogleg sprint out past the coast of Brazil complete.

Mr. Jones burst into the room. "The warhead's come ashore!"

CHAPTER 32

Adrenaline surged through Jeffrey's body, and he fought hard not to ball his fists in frustration. The generals were very apologetic, but there were continuing snags getting Jeffrey away. They hinted darkly at message jamming, even sabotage, by Axis agents inside Brazil.

In the meantime, Jeffrey could do nothing but watch. He was stuck deep underground, yet ironically had a bird's-eye view of the action.

The data from several of the CIA's bottle-cap gamma-ray detectors was conclusive. According to other intelligence— of some undisclosed kind but probably visual recon—a group of men had carried the suspect package from a flying boat onto a small corporate transport jet at Mar del Plata. Now powerful radars on the B-1 and the AWACS were tracking that jet as it neared Buenos Aires at over four hundred knots. The B-1 and AWACS were also tracking Estabo's helo, which was making for the border at barely half that speed.

The map showed that it was 720 nautical miles from Mar

del Plata to the middle of the Brazil-Argentina border—with Buenos Aires as a way point a third of the distance along the route. It was half that far, coming from the opposite direction, to get to the border from Paranaguá.

Half as far, but barely half the speed.

It was a toss-up whether the bomb or the SEALs would reach the border first.

Jeffrey, Colonel Stewart, and the Brazilian admiral were getting all the information they could as to where that flying boat at Mar del Plata had come from. All that was known was that it first appeared on radar miles out at sea on a course due west. Jeffrey was sure the flying boat had somehow rendezvoused with the *von Scheer* or her minisub. This was his first datum of any kind on the German submarine since the encounter at the St. Peter and St. Paul Rocks days ago. Jeffrey was busy working backward from what he knew—using clues about the flying boat and time elapsed and the maximum range and speed of German minisubs—to pin down a circle on the nautical chart where the *von Scheer* had to be.

Everything's coming to a head at once. . . . I need some way to warn Bell.

And Christ, I must *get back to my ship.*

An aide rushed into the conference room. In heavily accented English he told Jeffrey that Admiral Hodgkiss was calling. He handed Jeffrey a cordless phone, whose shielded signal was patched into the bunker's main communications center.

"Commander Fuller speaking. Yes, sir."

"Captain," Hodgkiss said from distant Norfolk, "we're having a lot of trouble keeping in touch. It's not just radio jamming. Our basic communications-management software is under information warfare attack. We're fighting back, but it's as if the Axis can find and block our most important voice and data links. I may lose you soon."

"Yes, sir."

"Captain, I want you to—"

The line went dead.

"Admiral? Hello?" Nothing. *I said before, "Unless otherwise directed." He wants me to do* what? *Or* not *do* what?

Jeffrey gave the phone to the aide. "Thank you. See if you can reestablish the connection quickly, please."

"Look!" Colonel Stewart pointed at the TV.

From a control room in the bunker, a technician was feeding in live video, windowed in a corner of the wall screen.

"This must be coming from the B-one," Stewart said, "from its long-range visual-observation sensor pod."

The main status plot showed the B-1 at the inner edge of international waters in the estuary off Buenos Aires. The angle of the view suggested it had ascended to very high altitude.

Jeffrey saw an aircraft that looked like a Learjet or a Gulfstream putting down on a civilian airfield at La Plata, a town right on the water forty miles southeast of central Buenos Aires. The tarmac and hangar areas held a number of other small planes. He figured these were corporate jets, or aircraft Argentina's rich elite used for pleasure flying.

The jet with the kampfschwimmer and warhead aboard slowed at the end of a runway, turned onto a taxiway, and met a refueling truck. As Jeffrey watched, another truck drove up to the plane.

Several men got out of the plane and began removing bulky packages from the back of the truck, carrying them onto the plane. The packages looked like rectangular canvas sacks. Another man got out of the plane and climbed in the back of the truck and stayed there, out of sight.

"Argentine liaison, probably," Jeffrey said, meaning the man who wasn't returning to the plane.

"Uh-oh," Stewart said. "I think those sacks are parachutes."

"You mean in case they're shot down?"

"No," Stewart said sourly. "That's *not* what I mean."

Then Jeffrey understood. Kampfschwimmer, like SEALs, were airborne qualified. "With chutes they can deploy just about anywhere with the warhead, by jumping right out of that plane."

Jeffrey looked at the map, unfolded on the conference table, of airfields on the Argentine side of the border. The paved ones, long enough to handle a corporate jet, had been circled with a red marker by someone on the Brazilian staff. "I guess we won't be needing this now," Jeffrey said with concern and disgust.

An hour later, Jeffrey watched the status display on the TV screen on the wall in the underground bunker. The tension of waiting with nothing to do, and yet with so much at stake, was having a physical toll on him. There was just so much adrenaline his body could handle. He felt as if tiny buzz saws were tearing up and down his spine and countless scalpels were stabbing him in the heart and intestines. The only consolation was that he knew everyone else in the room, in his own way, must also be feeling the strain.

Contact with Admiral Hodgkiss, or anyone else in Norfolk, hadn't been reestablished. No one could reach the U.S. Army's Southern Command, headquartered in Miami, either. Communication satellites appeared to be going haywire. When the technicians in the bunker tried to relay a message by radio through the AWACS or the B-1 bomber, Axis hackers somewhere on the ground inside the U.S. interrupted the connection almost immediately. Mr. Jones said that even attempts by some of his people to call the U.S. by telephone, from their offices or homes or public pay phones in Brazil—to the White House or special CIA unlisted numbers or even an innocuous public library picked at random in Idaho—just kept giving "busy circuits," and no one could get through. The tattered remnants of the war-torn Internet were no help either: international server links had been broken on purpose months ago, as the ultimate firewall against unstoppable, incurable worms and viruses.

The enemy has prepared very well for whatever it is they plan today. But by such a systematic and widespread attack, these hostile information warriors reveal their methods and algorithms. Their routes of infiltration can be traced. Pentagon and FBI experts will find some of them, and Axis operatives will be compromised or captured or killed. The Germans must feel the sacrifice is worth it. . . . The implications of that alone are scary. The damage they're doing will certainly be worked around or repaired, but will it be soon enough? Tomorrow, or even tonight, may be too late, and the Germans know it.

Jeffrey watched the situation plot; communications inside Brazil remained mostly intact—and he wondered how much longer *that* would last.

The helicopter with Estabo's team was near the middle of the border between Brazil and Argentina. They were orbiting in a holding pattern, waiting for further instructions.

Everything depended on what the plane with the Germans and the American bomb did next. The AWACS had a solid radar lock and followed its every move. So far, it kept heading north.

"Something doesn't make sense," an exhausted Colonel Stewart said. "They aren't slowing or turning. They're heading into Paraguayan airspace." The American diplomat sounded worried and confused—Paraguay and Uruguay were neutral, both in the larger conflict and in the impending fight in South America.

The Brazilian generals began to show signs of agitation. "Might we have followed the wrong plane?" one of them said. "Did we fall for a deception, and that isn't even the bomb?"

An oppressive, uncomfortable silence suddenly filled the room.

Jeffrey turned to Mr. Jones, who now looked deadly serious despite his outlandish garb. He'd taken off his jacket and loosened his tie, and there were spreading marks of sweat on the armpits of his shirt. Jeffrey, in contrast, thought the conference room was too cold, and his hands felt like ice cubes.

"Can we get that aircraft's flight plan?" he asked Jones.

"On such short notice? I doubt it. There's nothing says they filed one, or if they did they could've lied."

Jeffrey grunted. He knew Jones was right, but what the man said, the way he said it, couldn't help but sound defeatist.

The generals now seemed paralyzed by doubt or indecision.

Jeffrey reminded himself that these men vastly outranked him, and this was *their* country—but they had no experience at all of total war, while *he'd* been fighting and outsmarting Germans for months. He realized that he'd better show some initiative and interpret his fragmentary orders from Admiral Hodgkiss—plus the existing assent from President da Gama—in very broad terms. *I don't know if the White House or Pentagon ever meant for Operation Mercury to go nearly this far, but I can't stop now. These times demand strong leadership from the bottom up.*

Jeffrey was in his element.

"We have to work with what we've got. Let's look at a detailed map of the northern part of the border. And somebody, tell the chopper with the SEALs to start heading north." The Brazilian admiral nodded and left the room.

Someone handled the map-viewer controls. Jeffrey now saw the tongue of Argentine land that stretched north between Brazil and Paraguay.

"That's the Triple Border," Stewart said. "I thought we ruled that out."

"Maybe we were wrong," Jeffrey said. "Look." He stood up and pointed at places on the map. "If they cut through Paraguay, they gain protection from Brazilian antiaircraft fire until the last possible moment."

The generals nodded. "But that would severely limit the area they can attack," one of them said. "When they turn east from Paraguay, they'll only have access to a short fringe of the shared frontier. If our army attacked Argentina from *there*, our ground forces would be canalized into a narrow front aiming south, and it adds two hundred fifty kilometers to the route to Buenos Aires! I thought they were faking a breakthrough by our army going through the *center* of their lines."

Jeffrey stared at the map. "Can we get President da Gama in here?"

One general rose wordlessly and went out. In a few minutes da Gama preceded him back into the room. The admiral returned with them.

As the Brazilian president took in the situation plot, Jeffrey pointed at a place on the map that was marked with a cluster of standard military icons that represented heavy antiaircraft artillery.

"Mr. President, what are these ack-ack guns protecting?"

"That's the Itaipu Dam."

"What is it, *exactly?*"

"It's the biggest hydroelectric dam in the world. Enough steel for four hundred Eiffel Towers. Plus fifteen million cubic yards of concrete and cement." Da Gama was obviously proud of the dam; he rattled off the figures like a tour guide.

"All this blue here is the lake built up behind it?"

"Yes. The dam is seven hundred feet high, and altogether almost five miles wide. The reservoir is something like a hundred twenty-five miles in length."

"That's one huge head of water, sir."

"I think the visitor brochures say it's a trillion cubic feet, behind that dam."

Mr. Jones whistled.

"The dam spillways drain south?" Jeffrey asked.

"Yes, into the Paraná River." Da Gama sounded impatient now; he obviously thought the American questions were distracting, even irrelevant.

Jeffrey was undeterred. "And the Paraná goes where, Mr. President?"

"It runs south through Argentina, then drains just north of Buenos Aires into the Rio de la Plata estuary."

"The dam might be their target."

"But it's on *our* side of the border."

"Just barely, from what this map seems to say."

"Yes. But the dam is owned by *Brazil*. . . . Paraguay sold us their shares during their latest banking crisis."

"Don't you see? Brazilian ownership just gives you better, easier access, sir, to implant an American bomb. . . . Nuke the Itaipu Dam, and where does that gigantic radioactive tidal wave go? Whose border troops are wiped out or cut off from reinforcements? Which capital's shantytown suburbs get flushed by the surge of contaminated water, laced with so many tons of vaporized and neutron-activated concrete and steel?"

"Argentina. Argentina. Argentina."

"Now, Mr. President, would *anyone* believe you didn't nuke the dam just because you *own* it? Could *anything* cause more widespread harm and outrage in Argentina? And could anything give the Germans better reason to help the Argentines nuke your country in revenge a dozen, a hundred times over?"

"You know the answers to those questions, Captain."

"Sir, you must order your antiaircraft batteries to fire into Paraguayan airspace to protect that dam at all cost."

CHAPTER 33

D a Gama had left the room again to issue more directives as commander in chief.

Jeffrey's further thoughts were sharply interrupted: an American electronic warfare plane held radio intercept contact on communications from the aircraft bearing the kampfschwimmer and the bomb. Jeffrey listened to it all on a speaker while one of the Brazilian generals, who understood Spanish, translated. It gave Jeffrey the creeps to hear the enemy conversing—confirming all his best guesses and raising all his worst fears.

As everyone in the Rio bunker expected, the Argentine corporate jet reported to its headquarters that it was now taking heavy flak from gun emplacements protecting the Itaipu Dam. The Brazilian antiaircraft artillery was even firing across the border, violating Paraguayan airspace, in an effort to knock the jet down.

Jeffrey's suggestion to da Gama had been turned into a presidential order, and now that order was being carried out.

Over the speakers came the hard crack of antiaircraft

shells bursting near the plane, picked up by the enemy pilot's microphone as he talked.

The Brazilian general leaned toward Jeffrey. In an undertone he said, "Someone is telling them to arm the timer on
the bomb and fly over the dam and just parachute the bomb
into the water. The pilot is saying the flak is too intense,
they'll never make it close enough. . . . A different voice is
telling the pilot to shift to the secondary target."

"What secondary target?" Mr. Jones said in confusion.
Colonel Stewart looked ashen.

Everyone rushed to study the map of that part of the border.

"This," the Brazilian general said after a pause. "Now that
we know how they're thinking, from the Axis point of view
it's the next best thing." He tapped a spot a few miles southeast of the dam.

"What's *this?*" Jeffrey said.

The general looked at him grimly. "The Iguazú Falls.
Massive, horseshoe-shaped, exactly on the Brazil-Argentina
border."

"I need to get new orders to my SEAL team, redirect them
to the falls."

The general nodded and picked up a phone; it was quickly
done.

From opposite directions as Jeffrey watched the situation
plot, the corporate jet and the chopper converged on the
falls. The general explained what little the map itself didn't
make clear: The mighty Iguazú River drained the central
Brazilian highlands, then plunged off the escarpment of an
ancient earthquake uplift fault. Below the plateau lay
Brazil's southern geological depression.

A few miles past the falls, the Iguazú fed the Paraná River—
the same river that was fed by the Itaipu Dam, the same river
that flowed through Argentina all the way to Buenos Aires.

Felix Estabo caressed his MP-5 submachine gun tightly in both hands as the helicopter flew along the border. He looked down at the top of the Brazilian jungle as trees raced by beneath the chopper's skids. They were over the southern highlands, following the Iguazú River as it flowed west. The river was wide and fast-running, and the water it carried was reddish brown from silt—to Felix it looked like the color of drying blood. Then, in the distance ahead of the aircraft, he saw a giant rainbow arcing across the entire sky.

Beneath the rainbow swirled a cloud of billowing mist.

Beneath the mist, the land and the river seemed to end abruptly. Water poured over the edge of the plateau, between and around hundreds of small wooded islands and moss-covered rocks—from there a deadly maze of stepped and layered cataracts of foaming angry water plunged in stages straight down three hundred feet. Every foot of the way, that reddish-brown water gained speed and momentum, until it pounded without end onto boulders below. From there, it collected itself and raced on, barely diminished in power and energy.

The entire waterfall complex was two miles across. It dwarfed Niagara and Africa's Victoria Falls combined. Near its center was a maelstrom where river branches converged from three directions into a vortex of terrible violence and overwhelming force. Countless tons of water slammed into this area every minute. The locals, Felix knew, called the vortex Garganta del Diablo in Spanish; it was Garganta do Diabo in Portuguese. It held both names because it sat precisely on the border between Brazil and Argentina.

Either way, the words were apt. They meant the "Devil's Throat."

Through his earplugs, even over the noise of the engines and rotors of the helicopter, he could hear the thunderous roar of the falls.

Direct orders from Captain Fuller, relayed in code in Portuguese from Rio, had told him to be ready to dive down seven hundred feet behind the Itaipu Dam—using mixed-gas scuba rigs the Brazilians would supply—to retrieve the bomb and disarm it at all costs. Every second was vital, and Captain Fuller's grim but unquestionable orders told Felix and his men to risk a fatal case of the bends to get the bomb up and away from the dam.

Felix gripped his MP-5 even tighter. *A fast return ascent from seven hundred feet down, with no time to pause for decompression stages, is a guaranteed death in pure agony. . . . In the Iguazú Falls, in the Devil's Throat, I can think of ten more awful ways to die.*

———

Jeffrey and the others sat mesmerized. Technicians in the bunker had patched another radio link—between the AWACS and the SEAL team's helicopter—into a speaker-phone on the conference-room table. Now he heard two separate airborne conversations at once.

Jeffrey listened to the AWACS vector the pilot of Felix's chopper toward the Argentine corporate jet. The flight director in the AWACS and the pilot of the Brazilian Army helicopter both used English—the international language of air-traffic control. The TV-screen map on the wall tracked their movements.

"Are you taking ground fire?" the AWACS director asked.

"Negative! Negative! No sign of troop activity below."

Da Gama ordered his units pulled back, to avoid a friendly-fire tragedy and save lives when the stolen warhead blows. . . . The Argentine commanders might have done the same on their side.

Ground-to-ground howitzers shooting from now on might hit the wrong Special Forces team, or have an unintended bad effect when the SEALs and kampfschwimmer collide face-to-face.

But the Brazilian antiaircraft fire continued. The Argentine corporate-jet pilot's voice became so high-pitched that he sounded like a woman. He screamed things in garbled Spanish that Jeffrey knew must be bad news. Jeffrey heard straining engine noises and other jagged sounds and shouting, picked up in the background over the pilot's open mike.

"They're at the secondary target," the Brazilian general translated. "An engine fire, loss of hydraulics, he can't control the plane much longer."

Jeffrey heard the word *kampfschwimmer* amid the chaos of whistling, screeching noise, and yelling from the aircraft.

"Visual contact!" the chopper pilot shouted. "Bandit is trailing smoke! It's losing altitude!"

Badly damaged by ack-ack from the dam.

"I see chutes! Four good chutes! One more, big, an equipment container!"

The warhead.

"Four more chutes! . . . That's it. The bandit is going down."

The screeching noise from the corporate jet grew louder, edgier, ominous, and the pilot's voice shot up another octave. He was cut off by a sudden very hard smash. From that speaker now came only heavy silence.

"Impact! Impact!" the Brazilian helo pilot shouted over the speakerphone. "I see smoke and fire!"

"Status of the parachutists?" the AWACS director asked. His voice was calm and cool, involved but impassive.

"They're in the jungle, on the highlands, on the Argentine side of the falls! . . . Navy SEAL team is fast-roping down from my aircraft! . . . SEAL team is on the ground. I am egressing the area."

An aide came into the conference room, breaking Jeffrey's concentration. "Captain Fuller, your transport back to *Challenger* is ready now."

CHAPTER 34

Felix listened as the noise of the chopper receded into the distance. That sound always caused him to feel mixed emotions, which flowed in a predictable stream. A sense of being abandoned in hostile terrain. A nostalgic, wistful longing to still be on that aircraft and heading for safety. A powerful feeling of duty. A strong drive to get on with the job. Then his instincts to lead and achieve would kick in, and he wouldn't look back until his work was complete.

He did an immediate sensory recon.

Felix's team was down on the ground, through the triple-canopy overhead cover. In the murky lighting of late afternoon, amid the squawk and chatter of parrots and toucans and monkeys and the languid chirping and croaking of insects and frogs, everyone geared up. The heat and humidity were only slightly less severe than at the equator, but this heavily wooded area wasn't true rain forest. The trees weren't quite so tall, and the canopies weren't so dense. Felix had noted this firsthand—as he slid down the rope that led from the chopper to the jungle-penetrator weight that had lain in the mud at the rope's end.

For the most part the men, including Felix, were equipped as they had been during his intelligence raid into northern Brazil days before—the raid on which the SEALs' lieutenant was killed.

Now I'm the lieutenant. Terrific.

The team had silenced MP-5 firearms and ammo and ceramic flak vests and helmets in anticipation of action against the kampfschwimmer team with the bomb. Each man—including Felix—also bore a heavy rucksack on his shoulders, with his Draeger in a cover on a load harness worn at his hips. The differences now were that one man carried a bipod-mounted light machine gun and another a thick-barreled sniper rifle. And everyone, again including Felix, wore draped around his shoulders and torso a roll of one hundred yards of spun-monofilament climbing rope, plus belts of extra ammo for the machine gun. Festooned and overburdened this way, Felix thought they looked like a bunch of bandit outlaws spoiling for a fight.

At least they didn't have to wear those oppressive antiradiation suits like on the St. Peter and St. Paul Rocks.

Either the stolen A-bomb goes off or it doesn't. If it does, at this range, no amount of protective clothing will do my team any good.

But having learned a lesson on the Rocks about the need to identify friend or foe when everyone wore the same garb, the SEAL team all had subdued black and yellow versions of the American flag patched onto their composite jungle-fatigues-and-wet-suit sleeves.

Using hand signals, Felix formed his men up for a hurried approach march to combat: he set flank protection, rear security, and assigned a seasoned man as point. He knew from watching the chutes that the kampfschwimmer had landed on the other side of the Iguazú, in Argentine territory. Even so, he wasn't taking chances and kept the team's chief with him, in the center of the eight-man formation, so they could go over tactics and exert all-around control. He kept the radioman and combat medic near him too.

Felix quickly took stock in this pregnant moment before the clutter of tree trunks and underbrush all around them began to block the team from his easy view.

The men were pumped and excited; once they'd hit the ground, their repressed fear and visible nervousness gave way to eagerness for action. Each of them knew what his country was asking: for the next few minutes, or hour, or however long it took, the fate of the world would hinge on their courage and skill against a hardened enemy kampfschwimmer team. But all of Felix's men were battle-tested veterans by now, volunteers since their earliest days in the SEALs; superb team players, they were also fiercely competitive.

As cold-blooded as it sounds, as dangerous as this mission task might be, every one of my guys is thrilled to be here. Something like this is what they trained for, lived for, for long and tough years. High pressure and high stakes is what they thrive on . . . and it doesn't come higher or better than this.

Most other SEALs, all over Navy Special Warfare, would sell their grandmothers to be in their place.

Felix himself felt privileged, and proud. On a practical level, he was satisfied with whom and what he'd been given to work with.

He ordered the team to move out.

———

Felix set a blistering pace for the approach march toward the Iguazú Falls. He was sweating and breathing hard already. He and his men eyed their surroundings very carefully, watching for signs of booby traps or mines—and constantly scanning for dips and hollows that might give them the slightest cover from incoming fire. Plants of various species intermingled. Some tree trunks were red, others gray and smooth like newly poured concrete, and some had primeval-looking wrinkled green-brown bark like dinosaur hide. Strangler vines had grown around one tree in a killing embrace—all that remained was the fused skeletal framework of the vines; the tree itself was long gone, decayed away. Fungus and lichens were everywhere.

The atmosphere was thick with the usual fermenting stink of the jungle, but soon a different smell began to coat Felix's throat: a poisoned sweetness, the stench of rotting flesh. The team cautiously approached a more sunlit area, where the canopy cover was open. Soon Felix saw the reason for the smell. Fresh bright scars of naked raw wood, and snapped or shattered tree limbs dangling down or lying broken in the mud, showed where howitzer shells had hit and gone off in the air.

Four shells, looks like, 105s, Felix thought appraisingly: 105mm rounds. *One quick salvo, a battery of four guns . . . Tree bursts like this—when you have no solid overhead protection like sandbags and logs—are a real bitch.*

The stench of putrefaction was even stronger: Brazilian soldiers recovered any of their dead comrades between artillery duels, but dead animals lay where they fell.

The team skirted this unnatural open area to avoid surveillance from the air. They hurried on. On slightly higher ground, closer to the bank of the Iguazú, they passed a forward Brazilian Army observation post, deserted now. The dug-in bunker was made out of rails and ties taken from the nearby tourist railroad. Once, Felix knew, before the border troubles began, that narrow-gauge line had brought visitors to the falls. Back then, buses ran from the city of Foz do Iguazú, fifteen miles northwest—but now Foz had been evacuated, and Felix was very glad. Buses had also run from the Argentine city of Puerto Iguazú, twelve miles off to the west, where the Iguazá fed the Paraná.

Some scattered—now empty—hotels were the closest civilization. Beyond that, the falls lay in the middle of national parks, on both the Brazilian and Argentine sides.

The parks were supposed to be nature preserves. Lizards darted along the ground. Beautiful white and lavender wildflowers bloomed amid the brush and thickets, and colorful orchids grew on the trees, nurtured by the ceaseless "plant-mister spray" from the nearby but still unseen falls. Lianas and hanging vines of different lengths and thicknesses bridged between tree branches and the ground.

Toucans used their huge, specialized beaks to pick fruit from the trees. A band of inquisitive coatis, reminding Felix of raccoons except that they had more pointed noses and were active during the day, approached the team to beg for food with their striped tails raised high in the air. The SEAL chief waved his arms to chase them off.

The rushing noise of the river and the roaring of the falls was growing louder by the minute. The air was much moister and water dripped from the trees. Felix began to see swarms of butterflies. Above him, over the triple canopy, he heard the raucous cry of hawks.

His route-march formation pressed on.

Again the smell of festering carcass grew strong. Felix heard a powerful feline growl, then caught glimpses of graceful, menacing movement between the trees: something big, orange-brown fur, mottled with round black markings. *A jaguar, scavenging, determined to guard the remains of a deer killed by a mortar shell or shot by a nervous sentry.* Felix made more hand signals, and the team gave the jaguar a very wide berth.

The sky grew dark, and lightning flashed and thunder cracked. Felix and his men all cringed reflexively against incoming cannon or rifle rounds. The usual afternoon rainstorm began.

————

The thunderstorm passed through quickly, leaving the wet trees and vines and brush even wetter; the reddish mud was more slippery; puddles took up added space between the

soaring trunks and the protruding roots on the ground. The
birds and butterflies became active again. Felix and his men
were soaked, but they hardly noticed or cared. Felix and his
chief exchanged quick glances, and the mixed emotions on
their faces let them read each other's mind.

*We're in a race against the Germans. They have the ad-
vantage since they're the ones with the bomb. But they know
they've lost the element of surprise: the Brazilians' dam defenses fired on their jet while it was still over neutral
Paraguay. The alerted kampfschwimmer must have seen my
chopper from the jet, and they probably saw us fast-roping
down while they hung in their parachutes.*

Felix wasn't sure which side held the edge. But a lot of his
tactics depended on what he saw the Germans do.

*I guess that means they're the ones with the initiative . . .
and that's not good.*

Captain Fuller had told him by radio in the chopper that
the kampfschwimmer would almost surely emplace the
shock-hardened, pressure-proof American atom bomb
somewhere against the base of the falls, with its arming device on a timer. This way they'd achieve almost the same
amount of outrage and damage as if they'd blasted the Itaipu
Dam itself: detonated against the bottom of the escarpment,
in the center of the horseshoe of the falls, the warhead
would vaporize millions of tons of rock and silt-laden water.
The whole flow of the river would suddenly stop. Then
more massive chunks of the escarpment would collapse, and
the atomic shock front that held back the river flow would
dissipate.

The mighty Iguazú River would resume, its pent-up force
released as a major flash flood. Neutron bombardment
would make elements like silicon and calcium in the rocks
and clay become intensely radioactive. The mess would rage
down toward the Paraná River, then pound its mad way south
until it passed by Buenos Aires. The Germans would have all
the excuse they could possibly need for the *von Scheer*—
wherever she was lurking—to hand over Axis atomic war-

heads in bulk to the Argentines. The scenario that would unfold from there surpassed Felix's worst nightmarish visions of Armageddon.

Felix signaled his men to move faster.

Navigating by compass, the team neared their first phase line. Felix could tell they were at the proper way point by using his ears and his nose.

The team was moving onto the spit of land that projected into a wide oxbow curve of the Iguazú River. Here the river turned south, went around a giant bend, then came back north, before resuming its course due west. At the narrow base of the spit, Felix could hear the rush of the river on both flanks as his men headed south. The Iguazú Falls were in the middle of this oxbow curve. The roar of the falls lay directly ahead—but so did commanding ground, where the SEALs could interdict the Germans by long-range fire.

On the Brazilian side of the highlands plateau, overlooking the falls, were an old hotel and two tourist observation towers. This much Felix knew from his map and his hasty briefing notes. The odor of smoldering wreckage and rotting flesh grew very strong.

The team's point man reached the edge of the jungle cover. He signaled, and Felix crawled forward.

Argentine artillery had blasted the hotel and observation towers. Then Brazilian Army engineers had dynamited the remains as they withdrew just hours before. Everything lay in ruins. Places deep in the rubble—sheltered from the daily rain—still burned. A horrible stench told Felix there were bodies trapped deep in that rubble too.

"Let's get our base of fire set up," he whispered to his chief in Portuguese. The man nodded. He had the team spread out along the verge of the jungle. Felix felt everyone's blood pressure rise. Each man drew in a few deep breaths despite the smell. On a signal from Felix they dashed all at once across the open ground, and gained cover and concealment amid the rubble of the hotel.

Felix gave more orders, and the men worked their way

gingerly forward, hugging the east side of the collapsed and burned-out structure. Felix rounded a pile of shattered masonry and brick, and the view took his breath away.

Arrayed before him, in all their deadly majesty, were the vast and always plunging, smashing, boiling cataracts of the Iguazú Falls.

As before, like from the chopper, the water was an incongruous reddish brown.

That color comes from topsoil, erosion from the highlands because of years of clear-cutting forestry mismanagement. Every new rainfall washes away a little more of Brazil's future—assuming Brazil even has a future, after today.

Across the river, atop the escarpment on the other side of the falls, lay the ruins of another hotel, of more modern and solid construction.

That hotel sits in Argentina. Militarily—with this sweeping, split-level terrain—it's as pivotal to the kampfschwimmer as the ruined Brazilian hotel is to me and my team.

Lying in shadows under a slab of shattered flooring, careful to avoid broken glass and twisted, jagged steel and sharp-edged aluminum, Felix turned to his chief. "The range look right to you? Three thousand yards?"

The SEAL chief nodded.

Felix and the chief picked good spots to set up their .30-caliber machine gun and their .50-caliber sniper rifle, choosing voids in the rubble that gave them the widest possible arcs of fire. Everyone passed their belts of machine-gun ammo to the men who worked the gun. The sniper said he saw an even better place to hide. He and his spotter shifted their positions.

The range was extreme, but now their weapons threatened the wreckage of the Argentine hotel, plus the wreckage of the stairs and walkways that led from the Argentine side toward scenic overviews of the falls, or out onto the upper river itself for even closer views, or down the steep escarpment toward the bottom of the falls.

Felix used his binoculars to survey the opposite side of

the falls for any signs of kampfschwimmer movement. As he huddled in the stinking, smoking rubble of the Brazilian hotel, he began to grow very worried.

The Germans couldn't have picked a better secondary target, once driven from the dam. And the next move is theirs.

He hated having to wait, and desperately wanted to seize the upper hand. He considered telling his machine-gun team to rake the Argentine hotel or the jungle behind it—a reconnaissance-by-fire might provoke the kampfschwimmer into acting prematurely.

But Felix glanced at his watch, and up at the afternoon sky. The sun was already getting low, and in just a few more hours it would be dark. If he told his men to open fire now, the kampfschwimmer would need to keep their heads down only till after sunset.

Whichever way you cut it, my tactical situation sucks.

Felix's heart almost stopped, then leaped for joy, as he saw steady muzzle flashes from inside the Argentine hotel. Shrapnel bursts the size of rifle grenades began to pelt the rubble he and his men were using as shelter.

The kampfschwimmer know we're here. They want us to keep our heads down. Why?

Of course! They're working to a forced schedule. They need the mushroom cloud and flash flood during daylight. Both have to be seen to do the most good, soaring high into the sky and inundating helpless Argentina from evil Brazil.

The SEAL chief crawled up to Felix. As incoming small explosive shells pounded the ruined hotel and shrapnel whizzed and zinged and little new fires broke out, the chief shouted, "That's a German objective crew-served weapon, sir!"

"I know." Both men cringed as a round hit very close.

"We're outgunned! We just have a thirty-cal!"

"I know," Felix said.

"Return fire?"

"No. Save the ammo belts till we have targets. That hotel's on high ground, too far back from the river. I doubt they'll leave the bomb in there."

"Sir?"

"The falls. They need to break cover and get to the falls. They want to set off the bomb right under the falls."

For a moment the chief looked horrified. "Understood."

"Tell the sniper and gunner, weapons tight till they see men in the open. Then kill them all. If they see a big package, that's the bomb. Shoot it to pieces!"

"Sir, won't that make it go off?"

"Not in theory!"

The chief looked very doubtful.

"It's not like we'd feel anything," Felix yelled.

The chief crawled off to issue orders.

No, we won't feel anything. Our brains won't even have time to register our own catastrophic failure.

The German machine cannon ceased firing, and Felix waited for the kampfschwimmer to make their next move. Nothing happened. He scanned the falls and the escarpment, and the river below, with his naked eyes and with his binoculars. Watching the water cascade over the edge of the cliff became hypnotic. He made himself look away.

Fixating on the view of flowing water had played nasty tricks on his brain. When he looked at the enemy hotel again, it seemed to be rising steadily *upward,* into the air. Felix needed to blink and shake his head, to make the optical illusion stop.

This is not a good beginning.

The German machine cannon started firing again. The flashes were coming from a different place in the rubble of concrete and I-beams.

They waited for us to react to their initial burst of fire, then shifted the gun's position.

Then Felix caught glimpses of motion outside the hotel. Kampfschwimmer were dashing for the ruined walkway that led down to the base of the falls.

His ears ached as his men opened fire. The .30-caliber
light machine gun used short and steady bursts, punctuated
by the booming crack of the heavy .50-caliber sniper rifle.
But it was hard to aim accurately from a mile and a half
away. Updrafts of wind caused by the crashing of water
under the falls made good marksmanship even more difficult.

The kampfschwimmer took cover, unhurt. Felix's gunners adjusted their fire, and it became more effective. The
kampfschwimmer began to rig climbing ropes on the edge
of the escarpment. One rope unrolled and jiggled as it hung
down to the far bank of the river below the falls. But now the
Germans were pinned down.

Their objective crew-served weapon fired again. With its
laser range finder and adjustable explosive rounds, it began
to probe the rubble, searching for the SEALs with the light
machine gun and the sniper rifle. Both crews were forced to
pull back and seek new positions, and the Germans knew it.
The kampfschwimmer broke cover, and another anchored
climbing rope uncoiled down near the first.

*They're going for the bank on the other side. From there
they can use old tourist catwalks to get under and behind
parts of the falls. . . . We can't let them do that.*

Felix shouted for his men to open fire.

A German began to rappel fast down the side of the escarpment on a rope. The SEALs' machine gunner and sniper
pursued him with fire. Through binoculars, Felix could see
their rounds chip rock from the brownish, grayish cliff face
near the rappelling German garbed in black.

Suddenly the man was hit. He lost control of his rate of
descent and plunged two hundred feet to the base of the cliff.
He bounced once, then lay still. His helmet rolled away and
fell in the river.

Felix heard scrambling and scraping as his shooters
rushed to different hides within the hotel's debris.

The German machine cannon fired again, as if in revenge.

The SEAL machine gunner and sniper knew better than to return the fire—they'd reveal their newest positions and invite quick death.

We're in a standoff. We've proven they can't get down the cliff . . . but if they can't, neither can we.

Felix saw another blur of movement, on the high ground near the Argentine hotel. Kampfschwimmer were heading toward the upper falls.

The SEAL gunners fired at them, but the line of fire crossed closer to the precipice face of the falls, and the powerful updraft of mist and wind threw off the trajectory of the rounds. The SEALs missed. The German objective crew-served weapon immediately retaliated. Felix heard a scream rise from the rubble of his hotel. The sniper's spotter crawled up from behind. He said the sniper was dead, and the .50-caliber sniper rifle was smashed.

Whoever's commanding the kampfschwimmer team is good. He timed the rhythm of those latest moves just perfectly. I'm sure he even used the wind from the falls to give his men better protection.

Now what the hell are they doing on the upper *end of the Falls?*

Felix's chief crawled up. "Sir, I think they plan to drop the bomb down the falls!"

Felix stared through his binoculars and thought hard. "No, Chief! Not drop it! *Lower* it!"

"You mean—"

"Yeah. Underwater they're protected from our machine-gun fire. Right?"

"Uh-oh."

"Tell the thirty-cal crew to duel with that cannon, just enough to keep it occupied and distracted. Everyone else into Draegers."

"Sir?"

"Take all the climbing ropes we've got. We're going into the water after the Germans."

At the edge of the river on the upper escarpment, just above the falls, Felix briefed his men. He had to shout constantly to be heard over all the noise. Felix pictured working in the falls.

"It's just like a beach recon under enemy fire! It's just that the beach is incredibly steep, and there's an ungodly tidal rip!" A riptide, an undertow.

Felix could tell his men were nervous, frightened, scared. *So am I.*

"Look," he yelled over the steady roaring and pounding sounds of the river and the falls. He tried not to think what those sounds really meant in terms of sheer destructive energy. But the panorama spread before him and his men could leave no doubt. "It's just as hard for the Germans. Use your submachine guns, or knives. Kill them any way you can."

The chief and the four enlisted men with Felix nodded.

"Watch out for logs and other debris in the river," Felix added. "The flow looks stronger since it rained."

Again the men nodded, grimly.

Felix shared their fear, but he tried not to let it show. SEALs trained hard and realistically to work in water, under fire. *But nothing, absolutely nothing, could have possibly prepared us for a situation like this.*

Felix looked out across the choppy surface of the rushing, murderous river. Small islands covered with bushes and palm trees dotted the upper edge of the falls where the river suddenly disappeared into space. Rock outcroppings coated with green moss also jutted from that menacing horseshoe-shaped drop-off. All these split the water into narrower adjacent falls, the whole series of which together made up the mass of the Iguazú Falls. Some of these subcomponent falls were so large they even had names of their own, such as Floriano or Santa Maria.

Felix could see fragments of the upper tourist walkways,

constructed in parched dry seasons when the river flow was weak, then damaged in previous record-breaking El Niño rainy seasons—or broken up more recently by artillery or demolition charges.

From both the Brazilian and Argentine side of the river-banks, the islets and rocks and fragments of walkway con-verged on the central vortex of the falls, the Devil's Throat. There, a gigantic vertical fracture indented the face of the escarpment, and water poured in and plunged down from three sides.

Way off on his right, Felix heard the chatter of automatic-weapon fire. To his front, he caught a glimpse of movement on the farther riverbank. Two Germans dashed behind a truck-sized boulder on the water's edge, carrying a heavy package.

American machine-gun bullets found the range and windage, and began to chip at the boulder. Through his binoculars Felix saw white rock dust fly from the near face of the boulder; roundish light tan patches spread amid the mossy green. *Too late.* For now, the Germans with the bomb were behind good cover.

CHAPTER 35

Jeffrey changed from his dress uniform into dirty gray overalls. He was sneaked out of the underground command bunker near Rio in the cab of a garbage truck, which sped toward Rio proper. While it made another pickup of commercial trash at a shopping mall, he sneaked into the mall's covered parking garage. There he climbed in the back of a windowless, unmarked van. The van headed south, into a tunnel through the hills that separated Rio from some outlying beach resorts. Once it was in the tunnel, policemen inside halted traffic. Jeffrey pulled on a black ski mask, of the sort SWAT teams might wear, grabbed his waterproof bag with his wet suit and uniform, and a satchel with some other things, and transferred to one of two other identical white vans. He noticed even their license plates were the same.

Traffic resumed, with Jeffrey going back north toward downtown Rio. His original van continued south, as if he were still in it, with a policeman in back in his place. The third van followed the one he was currently riding in, then peeled off and took the highway toward the international airport. Jeffrey's van went into an office park, where a corporate helicopter sat on a helipad. Jeffrey left the van still wearing his overalls and mask and took the service entrance into a building, where he changed to a dark green flight suit and helmet. He pulled down the helmet's sun visor and used a different exit. He climbed into the helicopter. It took off and went south, following the hills along the coast to Paranaguá.

The view was breathtaking, but Jeffrey couldn't enjoy it. Instead his head was filled with nautical charts, with curves and lines and ranges and bearings. In his mind, over and over again, he pictured that Argentine flying boat landing at Mar del Plata.

Somewhere out there, way down south, out beyond Argentina's continental shelf, Ernst Beck and von Scheer *are waiting. To strictly comply with the Axis rules of engagement for handing German atomic warheads to the Argentines, so far as our naval intelligence understands them, he'll need to stay at least two hundred miles from the coast. . . . Probably a bit farther, since exactly two hundred miles would be too obvious. That would put Beck out beyond the far edge of the continental slope, in water as deep as his—or* Challenger's—*crush depth.*

Then there's the whole other question, how fluid and changeable those Axis ROEs might be depending on what unfolds in the next few hours. It's total war now. Nothing's guaranteed.

At Paranaguá, the helicopter landed at a small civilian airport. A troubled Jeffrey went into a hangar and got into another van. During the short ride, he changed into his wet suit—which someone in the Rio bunker had kindly hung up to dry while he had met with President da Gama.

The van let Jeffrey out at a auxiliary naval installation. There, he boarded a Brazilian Navy transport helo. In the helo were open-circuit conventional scuba compressed-air tanks, secured for the flight with bungee cords and nylon strapping.

Jeffrey found this security shell game of clothes and cars and helicopters dizzying. He hoped it would be at least as confusing to the enemy, if they even realized he was in Brazil.

As he buckled in tight, he could see out a window on the starboard side of the aircraft. The helo took off, and Jeffrey continued his fast journey south, to catch up with USS *Challenger*.

He'd chosen the starboard side so he faced inland. From the helo he kept staring, preoccupied, at the distant horizon to the west.

The Iguazú Falls are three hundred miles away, in that direction. Will I be able to see a flash from here, when the atomic warhead goes off?

———

In the silt-obscured deafening water above the falls, the current tugged at Felix frighteningly. Only the first length of climbing rope, anchored to a thick treetrunk onshore, kept him and his men from being swept away. If the rappelling buckles on their weight belts failed and they couldn't grab the neutrally buoyant rope and cling by hand, they'd go over the edge and fall hundreds of feet into the torrent to be bashed to pulp on the rocks below. Each man had a collapsible, lightweight metal river-crossing stick to help him gain some purchase against the bottom—but the sticks had not been designed for any river crossing like *this*.

As team leader, Felix went first and took the greatest risks. He kept below the surface as much as he could, using his Draeger. To raise his head to see what the Germans were doing always drew fire—not from the hotel, but from kampfschwimmer who'd already made it partway out into the river and had cover on a small island.

A continual hiss and rumble assaulted his ears underwater. The river made noise as it scoured the bottom and pelted past obstructions. The hard impact of the falls at the base of the cliff sent heavy vibrations back up through the rock, and this noise too came through the water from the rock.

Felix knew he was coming to the end of his rope, literally. He had to find an anchor point. The water was so thick with silt, it was impossible to see. If he wasn't careful, the magnitude of its flow could tear the dive mask off his face into oblivion.

All things considered, it wouldn't make much difference. I might just as well work with my eyes closed anyway.

Felix dived a few feet deeper. He tried to find the bottom again as the submerged riverbank sloped down. The farther out he moved the more insistent the surging current force became. Any moment, an uprooted tree weighing tons could wash down the river and smash right into him. As he whipped around in the turbulent flow near the end of the anchoring rope, he might be impaled on a steel rebar projecting from a broken concrete abutment of the now-damaged upper tourist walkway. There were hidden reefs and rocks, which might knock him unconscious to drown. Felix decided he'd better let some gas out of his buoyancy compensator to make himself heavy and gain more traction.

Submerged in brownish darkness, he touched the pebbled bottom with his flippered feet, standing in a low crouch sideways to the current to minimize his water resistance. The pressure in his ears told him he wasn't dangerously deep. The men tried to steady him by steadying their parts of the rope—they certainly couldn't see him from even a few yards away, and could only guess at what he was trying to do from minute to minute. The anchor rope, the lifeline, was his sole connection to the team.

Felix kept his river-crossing stick upstream of him, slanted down into the flow as he leaned into it. The stick helped break the current, while the pressure of the current lodged the stick against the bottom and levered its high end down on his chest. This gave him firmer footing and added stability as he inched along. Felix began to search the bottom blindly, systematically, by touch alone. Sometimes he used the stick instead to cast about in order to give himself greater reach. He became afraid of losing all sense of direction, and wandering unknowingly right over the edge of the falls.

Finally he found what he was looking for before it found and pierced or fractured *him*. A subtle back swirl in the feel of the current just downstream was his guide. He'd located the remnants of one of the walkway support piers. To work, Felix now required both hands. He collapsed his crossing stick and wrapped its lanyard tighter around his wrist so he wouldn't lose it. The intense flow of the river still dragged at him constantly, and its hiss and rumble were relentless in his ears. No sunlight penetrated from the tumultuous surface above.

Felix took a free end of the coil of rope draped over his torso and deftly secured it to the bent steel bars that jutted from the concrete of the pier. Using this new length of rope as his safety anchor now, he secured the end of the first rope to the pier, then tugged a signal, which told the team that the far end of their rope was secure, and he was ready to advance another hundred yards. Keeping himself on a short leash for the moment, he let more gas into his buoyancy compensator.

Felix popped his head above the surface; he had to squint in the sudden brightness. He could barely make out the cluster of boulders that was his next objective. The noise of the falls was much louder with his ears out of the water. He kicked with his swim fins to try to lift his head high—the waves that were created as the river converged on the falls, and split into channels between all the islands and rocks, made it hard to see far.

Small splashes raised up all around him. Felix ducked below and heard the impact of the bullets against the surface. Those German MP-5s weren't accurate for long-range sniping, but one lucky hit from a spray of rounds would still have high velocity, enough to kill any man it struck. Felix knew his team had to reach that cluster of boulders soon, and leave a man behind there temporarily in order to give the rest of them covering fire.

───────

Felix was growing tired. His team had reached a flat little island on the very edge of the falls. It was covered in thick green underbrush, and he used this for concealment as he crawled forward. His men followed.

For a moment Felix paused to rest and gave hand signals for his team to do the same. Here, the noise of the falls was overwhelming. Speech was out of the question.

Felix lay on his back, supporting his Draeger with his arms, and glanced up at the sky. Streaks and fluffs of white cloud drifted peacefully far above. Butterflies swarmed, in amazing numbers, immune to any sense of danger; some were vivid turquoise with wingspans of four inches. He sighed and rolled over onto his elbows and knees, fighting the weight of his Draeger, then crept to the side of the island for a broad field of view in order to judge the enemy's progress. The Germans had a head start and a clearer plan, but he hoped their pace would be slowed by the weight of the bomb.

Felix felt his way gingerly through the underbrush. Suddenly he felt nothing in front of him at all. He crawled forward inch by inch, very carefully, and peeked between the leafy ferns and branches.

He was on the verge of a gaping precipice two miles across. Curving wide around both sides of him, literally hundreds of waterfalls poured down. Brown water churned into white as he watched. Droplets turned into foam that turned into spray. Thick sheets of water ran over the edge in unimaginable quantities, as if the supply would last for all eternity. The waterfalls in most places fell in steps, where smaller and lower plateaus jutted out from the face of the main escarpment. Everywhere water plummeted and smashed; in some spots the drop went straight to the bottom, thirty stories below. When islands on the edge were big enough to block the flow from wide patches, the entire cliff face beneath was covered in unbroken greenery. Mist like plumes of smoke rose up from where water ceaselessly impacted at the boiling base of the cliffs. Down there the river recovered itself and rushed on, in fast-flowing white-water rapids that disappeared around a broad bend to the west. Birds darted high and low, safe from the power of the falls, feeding on insects that flew through the swirling clouds of foggy vapor. Updrafts drenched Felix's face. A rich and vivid rainbow framed the entire awesome, magnificent scene.

Felix felt as if the waterfall complex and rainbow were reaching to wrap around and embrace—or crush—him bodily. He began to suffer vertigo, gazing down into this all-encompassing deluge powered by unforgiving, unrelenting gravity. He asked himself if the vista reminded him more of heaven or hell. He tried to imagine what it would be like here in the first few seconds and minutes after a nuclear weapon went off.

Then bullets tore through the bushes above his head, and Felix remembered he and his team had a job to do.

———

Felix and his men struggled through always-tugging water, saved from doom only by their anchored climbing ropes. They crawled over islets and rocks under enemy fire. The alternate up and down, the going in and out of the river—using Draegers one moment and shooting their MP-5s the next—became increasingly taxing both physically and mentally. The SEALs were getting closer to the Germans, which meant they were closer to the bomb. But the Germans were getting closer to the Devil's Throat with the bomb, and the return fire from their submachine guns was growing progressively more accurate. At least the German machine cannon wasn't shooting their way, not yet. *It must be busy arguing with my light-machine-gun crew.*

Then Felix felt total despair. He watched as kampf-schwimmer on a fragment of walkway near the Devil's Throat began to lower the bomb, at the end of a rope, straight down into the vortex. He ordered his men to try to stop them with sustained fire.

The SEALs' silenced weapons coughed and sputtered, burning through magazine after magazine. Kampfschwimmer on or near the walkway returned the fire just as viciously. Both sides began to take losses.

Felix saw one kampfschwimmer pitch headfirst off the walkway, then snatch up short on a rope that had secured him to a fragment of the railing. Right at the edge of the Devil's Throat, his body twirled like a rubber doll in the torrent. More bullets flew in both directions.

Other kampfschwimmer kept playing out the rope attached to the bomb. Finally, with a triumphant toss, the man Felix guessed to be their leader threw the free end of the rope into the vortex, after the bomb. The end of the rope vanished instantly. The dead German continued to twirl, as if grotesquely mocking the SEALs.

The kampfschwimmer began to withdraw, back the way they'd come.

The SEAL chief crawled up next to Felix. He had to shout in Felix's ear. "We've lost, sir!"

That was exactly how Felix felt, but hearing the other man say it out loud helped him find new courage from somewhere deep inside himself.

"We haven't lost until the warhead blows! We have to go down after it!"

"Down *there?*"

Felix nodded. He looked around. One of his men was dead, hit by a round that had pierced the base of his neck as he lay prone. Felix assigned their combat medic to stay and aid another enlisted SEAL who was wounded, seriously but not mortally.

Something in the sky caught Felix's eye and he looked up. It was a Global Hawk surveillance drone. These were new and each cost millions. Felix guessed da Gama had given the U.S. Air Force permission to launch the unarmed drone—Jeffrey Fuller's negotiating with da Gama must have succeeded completely.

The Global Hawk possessed sophisticated sensors, including live color video imagery relayed back to its portable ground-control station.

Knowing that people were watching, that they cared, that he had an audience, gave Felix more renewed strength. He told the chief the two of them would have to work as a team.

Using the same techniques as before, moving underwater held by ropes and leaning on crossing sticks—and transiting islands on their bellies—they worked their way to the Devil's Throat. They ignored the dead kampfschwimmer as they rigged the last of their climbing ropes to this anchored, isolated stretch of damaged walkway. Each rope, three hundred feet long, ought to be just enough to get within range of the bottom of the furious vortex, if they were lucky.

Surviving kampfschwimmer saw what they were doing and began to shoot.

"I'll stay," the SEAL chief yelled, "tie myself to an abutment in the water for better cover! I'll keep the Germans from coming back!"

"Thanks, good, perfect!" Felix said. *If the Germans can fight their way back to the walkway while I'm still on my way down, they'll untie my rope and I'll fall inside the vortex and I'll die.*

He waved to his two remaining men in the distance, the wounded SEAL and the man who was caring for him. They signaled they understood: lay down a base of covering fire.

Felix gave the chief all of his ammo and his own MP-5. It would do him no good where he was going.

"Good luck, Chief!"

"Good luck, sir!"

Felix was now on his own. The maw of the vortex beckoned before him. The way river channels crashed into one another, and creamed into waves that piled high before suddenly vanishing, reminded him of a demon foaming at the mouth.

Felix went underwater and played out the rope through his harness belt's rappelling buckle. The turbulence here was exceedingly strong. It tried to turn him over and over and pound him against the final margin of the rocky riverbed. Visibility was zero again. The overwhelming noise had a very strange quality. It came at him from every direction at once, as if the cauldron were trying to swallow him whole.

Felix scraped over a hidden submerged outcropping and lost one of his swim fins. He gripped his Draeger mouthpiece even more tightly between his teeth. The pure oxygen tasted stale, laden with carbon dioxide he was exhaling. Never had he hyperventilated so rapidly. Never had he felt such raw fear. What he was attempting, he knew, was utter madness. Each cubic yard of plunging water weighed almost a ton. There was no way he could survive.

Suddenly Felix was over the edge, dangling straight down. The water tore off his dive mask, and seemed to tear at his flesh.

The tension of the rope against the buckle was so great, Felix needed to exert all his strength to make some slack to let it pass through the rappelling harness. For the first time since the battle began, he was using the rope and buckle for their intended purpose: to go *downward*. But never had the equipment been meant for use inside a raging waterfall. Felix began to tire.

He made himself go on. He kept his eyes tightly closed as water bashed at his face and his shoulders. His other swim fin was torn from his foot. He came to a ledge in the cliff face. Felix forced himself to move sideways, first right and then to the left, to make sure the bomb wasn't lodged here.

He continued down. Felix had no idea how much time was

left on the atom bomb's timer. He hoped the SEAL chief and the enlisted men could hold off the kampfschwimmer long enough. At any moment his rope might be untied and he'd go into free fall—and have just enough time to curse his fate before he hit the rocks and got killed. The rope was supposed to be unbreakable—impervious to chafing, or cutting by knives. Felix knew, today, he was putting the supplier's claim to the ultimate test.

Coming to another ledge, this one eroded into the cliff face by a backwash, and sheltered from the main force of the vortex flow, Felix once again checked for the bomb. Nothing. He allowed himself only a moment to rest. His arm and leg muscles felt like they were on fire. He was almost asphyxiating inside his Draeger, so heavy and rapid was his heartbeat and his breath.

Felix continued to struggle to play out rope. Down he went, blindly, as roaring water cascaded at him from three different sides at once, inside the chasm in the escarpment face that made the Devil's Throat. The plunging water whirlpooled and caromed and then recoiled against itself, all as it raced for the chasm floor. The wild crosscurrents inside the vortex threatened to tear him limb from limb.

Felix went down even farther. Here the water had accelerated, just as a falling body would. It slammed into him and then streamed past with terrifying speed. The noise of it was louder, both above and below. It echoed between the walls inside the narrow chasm too, building even more intensity.

Felix felt like the water was flogging his back, like it would strip off his wet suit and then strip his skin. His head was ringing, his ears hurt from the incredible volume of sound.

He knew it would only get worse. To go downward, along with the flow of the water, was one thing. To reach the base of the cliffs—where that water punched into rock and changed direction to horizontal with unspeakable violence—was beyond the human body's ability to endure.

Felix struggled to *think*.

To avoid being crushed by the weight of falling water, he

had to find a place where the river under the vortex was least shallow—a hidden pool between the house-sized boulders—so the fluid mass of the river itself would help cushion the constant impact from above. There had to be such places: eons of blasting by water laced with abrasive silt would have carved out pockets in the riverbed at the foot of the escarpment.

With his eyes gritty and stinging, even though he'd scrunched his lids tightly closed for many minutes, Felix did his desperate search by feel in the wet and the dark. He prayed for the guidance of Providence.

Felix hit deep bottom on slippery stones. Water punished him from every direction. It poured down from above and rebounded from below and he was caught in a maelstrom of total chaos. It hurt badly each time he breathed through his Draeger mouthpiece, and he was sure he'd broken some ribs.

Even so, he was still alive, and still had a job to do.

He reached the end of the rope, underwater in the deep pool, but couldn't find the bomb. Felix struggled through more-sheltered portions of the vortex, tightly hugging the cliff face, searching for quieter spots where the bomb in its hardened casing might have come to rest. Nothing.

He crawled over and between rocks while submerged, relying only on feel. Some of the stones were polished smooth, while others were newly fallen and jagged. He banged his head and smacked his elbows and knees. He searched systematically with arms whose muscles were worked to their very limits. Nothing.

Felix had no choice. He had to let go of the rope, and let the water take him.

I've followed pretty much the same path as the bomb. Here I'd let myself loose at about the same point where the Germans let the bomb casing loose from above. My last chance is to hope the water carries us both in the same direction.

Felix was surprised his brain still worked enough to form rational thoughts.

He tried to position his body in the torrent feet first, with his legs held tightly together and slightly bent. This way he might guide himself, and soften any collision. He released the rope and used his rubbery arms to protect his unhelmeted head.

The Devil's Throat was aptly named. Felix felt himself propelled through Satan's own water slide. He bumped and scraped along, totally blind. He tried to stay deep, where he knew that water resistance with the bottom would slightly slow its velocity. But this only increased the risk of hitting a waterlogged dead tree, or a boulder, or the wreckage of some boat that had gone over the falls.

Felix's legs smashed hard into something solid. The force of the river kept his body moving forward, and he did a somersault over the obstruction, underwater. His right foot caught on something; he was jerked to a stop and his hip joint almost dislocated. He was stuck, trapped. He began to panic.

He'd lost his crossing stick sometime before—he had no lever. He almost lost his mouthpiece, and without it he'd surely drown. He managed to open the valve for the Draeger's emergency oxygen bottle, because the carbon-dioxide absorber was totally useless by now.

Instantly, Felix's air supply became deliciously fresh and his mind cleared, but he was still held firmly by his left foot, by something heavy on the bottom.

Felix had to do a whole-body crunch against the force of the water to reach his foot to try to free it. He grunted from the effort, and gritted his jaw so hard he feared he'd crush his Draeger mouthpiece or crack his teeth. The muscular pain in his abdomen and chest were excruciating. He slowly bent himself double against the flow. His aching hands touched something.

He'd guessed right all along. His ankle was caught in a carrying handle of the casing for the bomb.

Felix got a firm grip on another carrying handle and worked hard to give his foot some slack. He freed his foot and grabbed the handle with his other hand.

Felix used the bomb now as a moving anchor. Again, so close to the infernal object, he wondered how much time was left until it blew. In spurts, as his dwindling reserves of strength allowed, he lifted and shoved the bomb along the bottom of the river. Slowly he worked his way toward the shore. He began to drag the bomb up the slope of the bank, underwater. Here the force of the river was less strong.

Felix raised his head. He could see above the surface. The shore was very near. This gave him new hope. He dragged the bomb out of the water, onto a narrow gravel beach, strewn with shattered driftwood, that fronted a solid wall of jungle growth.

He was just below the falls. The view was stunning, sublime, but Felix was so numb it barely registered. He bent double, hands on knees, drawing in natural air raggedly, at long last not needing his Draeger, catching his breath.

Then he looked up at the sky. He saw two drones above him. One was the Global Hawk, from before. It was maneuvering oddly, swooping and then turning, as if its controller pilot was trying to tell Felix something.

The other drone was an older type, a Predator. Felix thought it must be Brazilian: he knew they owned a couple.

But the stealthy Predator seemed to be sneaking around behind the Global Hawk. He realized it was the enemy.

The German plotters must have brought one into Argentina—maybe broken down and disguised as different parts before the war.

Beneath the wings of the Predator were two missiles.

Felix panicked again, fearing the Predator would kill him before he could disarm the bomb.

But the missiles were long and thin, meant for air-to-air combat only. As Felix tried to wave a warning, the Predator fired one and then the other missile. The first streaked at the Global Hawk and detonated in a loud and sharp hot-orange flash. Fragments of the drone and burning fuel rained from the sky. The second missile flew through the cloud of debris formed by the first, and kept going into the distance, leaving a trail of dirty yellow-brown exhaust smoke.

Felix ducked as metal bits fell. Liquid fire hit the river, then the flames were washed away.

The Predator came closer, and watched Felix on the ground.

Someone in a black wet suit rushed toward him. Felix thought it was his chief.

He must have somehow made it down the vortex, just like I did.

But the figure wore no American flags on his sleeves. Then Felix recognized the man. They'd been face-to-face before, on the St. Peter and St. Paul Rocks; that time both had worn protective suits. It was the leader of the kampf-schwimmer team.

Either he followed me down the vortex, or his automatic-cannon team silenced my light-machine-gun crew—and the German came down the easier way, using ropes and parts of the stairs along the dry parts of the escarpment face. One way or the other, he lost his MP-5.

But the German was armed with a knife. Felix reached for his K-bar fighting knife. It was gone, lost in the falls. He felt for his survival knife; it too was gone, ripped off by the vortex. He went for his titanium dive knife, his final hope, and felt its reassuring haft fit into his hand.

The German obviously recognized Felix; he drew his lips back in an animal sneer. *A rematch.*

The German held every advantage. Felix was burdened by his Draeger—which out of the water weighed three dozen pounds. He was far beyond exhaustion, into a realm of grim exertion for which he knew no name.

But Felix Estabo would be damned if he lost the contest now.

He crouched to use his Draeger as a shield and forced the German to come at *him.* Memories flooded back, of another knife fight twenty years before. Felix fingered the old, ugly scar along his cheek, caressing it, and flaunted it at the German, to tease him, egging him on.

The German was taller, so Felix stayed low. The German wore a flak vest, so Felix planned to aim low.

The German lunged and Felix leaned away. The German's knife struck him on the collarbone. The blade deflected up and cut deep into the top of his shoulder bone. Felix felt an icy agony there, and the agony gave him power. Instantly he drove his knife deep into the German's belly. He lifted and dug and twisted with the knife in his right hand. With his left arm, already covered with blood from his wound, he parried clumsily as the German's right arm flailed around.

Felix shoved the German backward and thudded squarely on top of him, Draeger rig and all; he almost screamed from the pain of his broken ribs. His face was inches from the German's. He could smell the man's breath, feel the warmth of his body. The kampfschwimmer opened his mouth, silently, and Felix could see down his throat. Still he dug his knife inside the German, seeking his liver and the major blood vessels below his heart.

Blood exploded from the German's mouth. Felix was almost blinded, but the German was definitely dead. By the time he thought to look the man in the eyes, the corneas were glazed and cloudy.

Felix quickly washed the blood from his face at the edge of the river. His left arm was nearly useless. He saw no arterial spurting, so dressing the wound would have to wait.

One-handed, he undid the hasps that sealed the shock-hardened, pressure-proof casing of the atom bomb. He lifted the lid. Felix, like all SEALs since the war began, had received basic training in atomic-weapon-arming techniques, but he was no expert. He saw the physics package, the hollow sphere of fissile metal surrounded by implosion lenses. He saw a battery power supply, arming circuitry, and the readout of a timer. The blurry numbers on the timer said the bomb had less than five minutes to blow.

Felix registered now that he'd been suffering from a split-ting headache, and his eyes had trouble focusing. *I've got a concussion. I got it in the falls.*

It seemed as if hundreds of thin wires ran from the arming circuitry to tiny components embedded in the implosion lenses.

Felix had no idea if the thing was booby-trapped. He doubted he had the time or strength to pull all the wires away from the high-explosive lenses—some were under the physics package where he couldn't reach. His addled brain did know that if even a few wires were intact when the deto-nation signal came, the bomb would fizzle, but it still might have a small yield, or could explode just strongly enough to send ten pounds of carcinogenic plutonium dust right into the river, upstream of Puerto Iguazú and many other cities and towns.

Felix did the only thing he could. With both hands he grabbed thick cables that ran from the power supply. He pulled with all his might; in his battered rib cage every breath was torture. The cables wouldn't budge.

Felix felt in the mud and blood for where he'd dropped his dive knife. It was meant for emergency cutting like this. He sawed away at the cables as the bomb's timer ran down. With only seconds to go, he cut through two cables at once—sparks flew from the positive terminal and a painful electric shock ran up his arm. The digital timer went blank. Felix waited for what seemed like forever.

Nothing happened.

Again he glanced at the sky. The Predator was still up there, watching him. Felix realized that he'd become disori-ented before. Looking at the river, he saw that it ran from his right to his left. Felix was on the *Argentine* side.

Cursing, he closed and locked the casing of the disabled bomb. He grabbed it and instinctively reached for the body of the dead German, put his Draeger regulator in his mouth, and wearily went back into the water.

He was barely in time. Enemy troops, whether German or Argentine, began to fire into the river after him.

Felix worked his way along the bottom of the chocolate-colored torrential Iguazú once more, zigzagging at an angle to the current. As before, he used the weight of the bomb as a safety anchor in the darkness. Unlike before, he was burdened by the German corpse, and his shoulder was badly cut. The corpse—his trophy and a possible intelligence prize—kept wanting to rise to the surface. This would give his location away and draw an Argentine mortar round or grenade.

Ghoulishly, Felix elbowed the corpse's solar plexus—below the sternum and flak vest and above the gaping wound in the guts. In a motion that aped CPR, he forced the German's lungs to draw in water. This made the body heavy, so it sank.

But between his own unbandaged wound and gore from the dead kampfschwimmer, Felix knew he was in yet another race against time, an extremely personal one: piranhas frequented this part of the river. Though they were normally benign, a whiff of blood would draw them in hordes and trigger a feeding frenzy.

Felix struggled toward the far bank underwater as fast as he could, working blindly and in terrible pain, expecting at any moment that his strenuous efforts would cause a broken rib to puncture a lung. Before he got much farther he heard repetitive pounding through the water and he felt it through the upslope of the riverbank. Brazilians with heavy machine guns had converged on the scene. They were holding off the Argentines. Felix saw the water change color, streaks of livid green. He realized the Brazilians were releasing piranha repellent into the river.

Felix clambered up the bank to the welcoming arms of Brazilian soldiers. They grabbed the bomb and the German's body while heavy machine guns continued to rake the far bank with crisscrossing red tracer fire.

Felix ran out of absolutely everything and collapsed.

Brazilian medics stripped off his gear and loaded him onto a stretcher, then carried him behind good cover. They started to bandage his wounds and inserted an intravenous plasma drip; they checked his pupils' reflexes with a flashlight and seemed satisfied. Away from the machine guns, Felix could hear the noise of friendly helicopters. The enemy drone was gone.

He tried to talk but a medic told him to be quiet. The medic congratulated him for his man-to-man victory against the German. Felix desperately wanted to ask about his men, his *team*. He tried to rise from the stretcher, but grimaced as his torso muscles flexed against his ribs. Someone pushed him gently back. He felt a different jab in his arm. Felix drifted away on the irresistible bliss of a morphine shot.

CHAPTER 36

Beneath the helo, on the surface of the sea, Jeffrey saw a Brazilian Navy hovercraft. But instead of going at over forty knots in a plume of spray, it was barely moving and black smoke issued from the diesel exhaust. He knew the engine trouble was fake.

The helo approached the hovercraft, and dropped off Jeffrey and a Brazilian Navy specialist. Then the diving gear and spare parts were handed down.

Jeffrey went into the soundproof wheelhouse of the hovercraft. The repair specialist who'd come with him had been picked for the job because he spoke passable English and had a high security clearance.

The navy chief in charge of the hovercraft was very excited to see them. Jeffrey remembered the ticking atom bomb.

But the chief seemed happy, delighted even, not angry or scared. He and the specialist spoke in Portuguese, the latter translating for Jeffrey as best he could. Over the radio, they'd learned that Felix Estabo had disarmed the stolen bomb, and retrieved it. He was wounded but safe, in a good Brazilian hospital.

Jeffrey was very proud of Felix. As the news sank in, he felt elation and almost giddy relief, but he forced himself to refocus. He knew he still had some very big problems.

Jeffrey and the repair specialist donned their scuba gear. Together they entered the water and dove under the hovercraft, supposedly to fix a broken part.

Jeffrey swam deeper. There beneath him was *Challenger*'s sail. A pair of divers waited, in scuba gear like his own. Since they were right under the hovercraft, the extra bubbles the four men's rigs gave off wouldn't show on the surface.

Jeffrey traded places with someone from *Challenger*. He was an enlisted man, one of the ship's qualified safety divers, selected by COB because his height and build were similar to the captain's. Jeffrey was sure he'd be crestfallen to be left behind when the ship was going into combat, but security needed to be maintained: two men in broad daylight had dived under the conspicuous hovercraft, so two men had to come up. To cheer the departing crewman, Jeffrey patted him on the shoulder and shook his hand underwater. He gave the young enlisted man an encouraging thumbs-up; if all went well, they'd be reunited in New London soon enough.

The enlisted man swam up and out from under the hovercraft. Jeffrey swam down and joined the other diver from *Challenger*. Together they closed the clamshells and went through the hatch and dogged it. The sail's lockout trunk was drained dry. Jeffrey opened the bottom hatch and climbed down into his ship.

His XO, Bell, was standing below the hatch, with a broad smile on his face. He welcomed Jeffrey warmly. "We were so shallow, Skipper," he said, "we heard a call through our on-hull VLF antenna saying to trail the wire. The call came from the Brazilians, and then they told us all about Lieutenant Estabo and the bomb."

Jeffrey nodded. "It's real good news, XO. It makes our life much simpler. Now we head south and go after the *von Scheer*."

The two men walked through the control room. Lieutenant Torelli, Weps, had the deck and the conn.

Gratified to see how happy everyone was to have him back, Jeffrey went into his cabin, pulled off his wet suit, and took a shower. He decided to reward himself and let the steaming hot water run over his body delightfully. His stiffness from tension and travel loosened up, and he began to feel refreshed.

Now that he was alone in the phone-booth-sized stainless-steel stall, everything sank in more. He felt a wave of elation bordering on ecstasy.

My excursion was a smashing success! Met a foreign president, won his and his armed forces' covert support, deployed a winning SEAL team under my orders, saved a continent from nuclear war . . . Talk about your joint and combined operations, and projecting seapower on land!

Dad, you'll be just thrilled. This'll look so *good in my service jacket. Did I get my ticket punched today big time, or what?*

Jeffrey came back to earth and calmed down. He dried off, shaved, combed his hair, and put on fresh khakis. He checked himself in the dressing mirror.

Well, Ernst Beck, who's got the upper hand now?

I respect you, and I'm gonna kill you.

Jeffrey went to the control room. The mood there continued to be celebratory. Bell seemed especially charged up, both from having held independent command of *Challenger,* if only for half a day, and also from anticipation of combat with *von Scheer.*

Jeffrey let Torelli keep the conn.

Then he cleared his throat and tried to assume a more levelheaded demeanor. "We'll give the people up there a few more minutes to go through the motions." He pointed at the overhead, meaning the fake repairs to the hovercraft. "Sonar, put it on speakers, please."

"Yes, sir," Lieutenant Milgrom said.

"Navigator," Jeffrey said, "bring up a chart that goes from here to two hundred miles south of Mar del Plata, and extends from the coast five hundred miles at sea."

"Aye aye," Lieutenant Sessions said.

Over the sonar speakers, Jeffrey heard banging and clanking. Then he heard a muffled clatter and roar as the Brazilian helo returned to pick up the two-man "repair crew."

The helo noises changed pitch and then diminished. Milgrom's sonarmen and Torelli's fire-control technicians tracked the departing aircraft. Jeffrey saw its icon moving away on the tactical plot.

"Sonar speakers off." The hovercraft would be loud enough as it was, once it got going. Right through the hull, Jeffrey heard the rumble and growl as the diesel engine revved toward maximum power. Torelli issued helm orders.

Meltzer used his engine order dial to hold *Challenger* under the hovercraft as both vessels picked up speed. Meltzer and COB had their hands full controlling the ship, as her speed topped forty knots up on the shallow continental shelf. The slightest error in trim could cause a collision with the hovercraft, or with the muddy bottom studded with new and old wrecks.

The renewal of risk and responsibility helped Jeffrey sober up more. *It's time to practice my primary trade.* His mind-set switched to envisioning undersea warfare tactics.

CHAPTER 37

Much to Ernst Beck's distaste, but as had been planned all along, Rudiger von Loringhoven was back on the *von Scheer*.

He was happy enough to stir up nuclear war on another continent, but he lacked the intestinal fortitude to linger once the plan unraveled.

The baron's return to the ship had been simple enough: While friendly Argentines sent out the flying boat as a diversion, von Loringhoven flew in an old army transport plane in a different direction. The baron used a parachute that opened at low altitude to land in the sea and get picked up by the *von Scheer*'s minisub.

Although showered now and freshly dressed, von Loringhoven was fuming exactly as much as he'd done when he'd first gotten back. U.S. Navy SEALs had foiled the plot to set off the stolen American warhead. A German-supplied Predator drone had seen the entire thing while von Loringhoven watched from the mansion on the grounds of his Argentine friend's ranch.

The secure radio room called Beck on the intercom. A

message was coming in on ELF, courtesy of the transmitter owned by the Kremlin. Beck listened, then hung up. He turned to Karl Stissinger, sitting next to him in the Zentrale.

"We're ordered to bring the ship to floating-wire-antenna depth in listen-only mode."

"More local news developments?" Stissinger asked. He didn't look happy. The baron paced about, still enraged. To himself, Beck had to admit that he wasn't entirely displeased that the nasty scheme had failed.

Beck issued the piloting orders to come shallower, then had the antenna wire deployed—if the ship was too deep the wire couldn't properly reach near the surface.

The radio room copied a much longer message. Again Beck listened on the intercom, then hung up. He was suddenly rather dismayed. The broader situation was distressingly in flux and unstable. *No one can predict, from the clean and tidy plans made in advance, how the people who made those plans will behave when things come unglued in the heat of action.*

"Berlin says, pending clarification of events in Argentina, that the delivery of our supply of nuclear warheads is on hold."

"On hold, *not* canceled?" von Loringhoven demanded.

"We're to remain well outside Argentina's Exclusive Economic Zone." An EEZ was the farthest type of beyond-the-coast jurisdiction recognized by global treaties. This two-hundred-mile limit also happened to coincide with Argentina's declared war exclusion zone. "Brazil announced that USS *Challenger* transported the SEALs that disarmed the bomb, and Jeffrey Fuller played a significant part on land in planning that operation." Beck heard von Loringhoven sputter in disgust, and hesitated. "We're told to stay on alert regarding certain new contingency plans."

This delay increases the danger that Challenger *and Jeffrey Fuller might find us—he obviously wants me to know he's here.*

It also puts off my return to the Central African front to destroy the Allied relief convoy before it makes the shore. At least that battle fits the professed Axis operational doctrine, of clearly limited tactical nuclear war at sea .

And worst of all, this message raises sinister new possibilities just when I thought our purpose near Buenos Aires had collapsed.

"So we still might be ordered to deliver the crated warheads," von Loringhoven stated. "Good. *Very* good."

Beck was angered but not surprised by this reaction.

"Baron, it's one thing if we're seen publicly as the defenders of the downtrodden, once America and Brazil are labeled as dastardly aggressors here. But for *us* to be exposed as the actual culprits in a premeditated provocation, and then *even so* we give bombs to local fanatics? . . . It would negate our new regime's most fundamental ideology, that we're resisting America's single-superpower tyranny and restoring social order in Europe and at the same time saving countless lives in Africa from AIDS and starvation and tribal slaughter. It would escalate the war beyond any means of further control!"

Von Loringhoven stared coldly at Beck. "It's the *victors* who write the history and sculpt future public opinion. Ideological doctrines serve the purposes of empire, *not* the other way around. A smashing success here forces a rapid armistice, and possible escalation is quenched. These knife-edge calculations have propelled our New Order forward from the start. The outcome now remains to be seen. . . . You say the message refers to contingency plans?"

"Yes . . ."

"Stop being evasive."

"We might be ordered to transfer the crated bombs soon so our local supporters can start an offensive before the elected Argentine government suppresses the pro-Axis coup." Beck knew he sounded very uncomfortable.

"Then we yet have a window to regain lost ground and achieve our initial objectives, if we're told to act decisively. Go on."

"I'm reading between the lines, the message is vague. But I do have considerable knowledge of what it means when naval orders are phrased, or not phrased, in a particular way."

And I may be projecting my own dreads into the minds of those in charge in Berlin ... some of whom, I suspect, are wilder extremists than even the baron.

"I *said,* stop being evasive."

Beck walked up to von Loringhoven and stood nose to nose with the arrogant man, right there in the Zentrale. "You really want to know what I think, or guess, or conjecture? I think High Command in Berlin is split into factions right now. I think some influential people there aren't willing to accept defeat in Argentina so readily. I think they might even order us north of the Rio de la Plata estuary ourselves, to give the tottering coup leaders a boost by fait accompli. We cut the locals out of the loop, pretend that we're one of their submarines, and launch nuclear cruise missiles at Brazil from *von Scheer.* Fifty million people could be dead before midnight."

Beck saw Stissinger blanch; his own guts were twisting; most of the crewmen around him seemed truly horrified for the first time. Beck's grim statement of the stark outcome they might together bring to pass by their own hands stripped away any last chance for detachment with harsh rapidity.

The captain turned back to von Loringhoven and jabbed a finger angrily in his chest. "Does *that* thought make you happy, Baron? It scares the hell out of *me.*"

———

Alone in the captain's stateroom, Jeffrey and Bell discussed the latest situation, what little they knew of it. The lack of further information was wearing. Since da Gama—at Jeffrey's urging—had agreed in advance to make a big announcement if Felix succeeded, accusations and counteraccusations would be flying thick and heavy between Brazil and Argentina, and inside Argentina too. Bell speculated— accurately, Jeffrey thought—that dozens of other nations must be looking on in amazement or shock. The opinions of many neutrals, and the decisions of some to choose sides, hung in the balance these next few hours.

What was going on in Berlin now was anybody's guess, and half of that was Jeffrey's fault by design, because he really wanted to get Beck's goat.

Privately Jeffrey dearly hoped he'd sink the *von Scheer* very soon. *Some of what I did in Rio, I went over about sixteen admirals' and joint chiefs' and service secretaries' heads. It could all backfire, if any German A-bombs still get sent ashore. If so, given the ways of the navy, everything will be on my head—and I can kiss a promising career good-bye. Retribution from above will be swift and cruel. . . . I might even be court-martialed, assuming there's enough of civilization left to care.*

Jeffrey had another surge of guilt. If he'd sunk the *von Scheer* at the Rocks as he was supposed to, none of this would be happening. He'd be busy protecting the convoy, with the Imperial German Navy minus its new ceramic-hulled submarine. *I might even be court-martialed for that failure, if we somehow get through this crisis and there's enough of a stink about it on Capitol Hill that the navy feels they need a fall guy—me. The convoy is suffering added losses because I'm heading for Argentina and not near Africa now—and I'm not near Africa because I didn't sink Beck earlier.*

Jeffrey could see that Bell was confused by his odd silence, and by the play of emotions across his face. He apologized, then returned to business. "You see what I'm trying to do here, XO?"

"Captain?"

"Remember what Admiral Mahan said a hundred years ago. 'The purpose of seapower is to influence events on land.'"

Bell nodded. Mahan's writings were classic, revered, though sometimes misunderstood. He'd taught at the Naval War College late in his life, and tried to make sense of the lessons of previous centuries of naval history.

"I'm playing it backward," Jeffrey said. "Trying to use events on land to influence seapower."

"Captain?"

"Turn poor old Mahan on his head . . . By heightening the disarray on land in Argentina, we helped pin down our seapower opponent, *von Scheer*, near Mar del Plata, to increase our own ship's safety from her as a threat."

Bell got it. "And then by taking away the *von Scheer*'s reason for being here, by wrecking their stolen-atom-bomb charade, and helping unmask the Argentine fascists and hopefully getting them all put in prison or shot, you completely remove Beck's reason for being near South America."

"We force him back toward Africa under time pressure."

Bell hesitated. "You don't think he'll go for the Falklands? Nuke them while he's over here? The Royal Navy base, Berlin might see that as a legitimate target."

Jeffrey shook his head. "It wouldn't be a decisive stroke, and would take him much too far out of his way. He needs to get back to Africa while our relief convoy is still at sea and vulnerable."

"I wish I knew how they're doing."

"So do I, XO. Believe me."

Bell thought. "Okay. Captain, so you turn Mahan bass-ackwards, if all goes well."

"*If* all goes well. For the moment what happens is beyond our control. I feel like we're caught in a giant tidal rip. You know, that dangerous place where the ocean meets the coast? Where the undertow can grab you and people drown?"

"Understood. And tides can flow in either direction, and so can tidal rips. . . . But if all *does* go well, and peace prevails in South America, and *von Scheer* turns back toward Africa, how do we ever find her before it's too late and she launches at the convoy? There's a symbolic tidal rip on the other side of the South Atlantic too, Captain. We struck out completely on the way over here. After the Rocks we never once made contact on Beck's ship. . . . How do we keep the same thing from happening twice, going back east?"

"I haven't figured that out yet."

"What if Berlin loses it, goes completely nuts, and orders *von Scheer* to attack Brazil directly? They're mentally committed, and politically badly embarrassed, and to maintain power at home the German High Command might go that far. Your Mahan twist is a kick in *their* teeth too."

"I know it, XO. You're giving voice to my worst fears."

"What then, Skipper?"

"If they accept what amounts to my brinkmanship double dare, and order Beck to push the button, then God help us all." *It's not like I had any choice, or could only go halfway. To drive Beck off I needed to test every last inch of the risk envelope. I also had to try to badly rattle the German captain's nerves.*

"God helps those who help themselves," Bell pressed.

"That's why we're heading toward Argentina."

"Minutes count. We're hundreds of miles away from the *von Scheer*'s probable location, sir. Other fast-attacks as reinforcements couldn't get here for hours or days."

"Yeah."

"So how do we find Beck and stop him in time? Play out the worst-case scenario, sir. Play it out. If he's told to nuke Brazil it'll come very soon. On their own, Brazil would be wide open. They've got no serious air defense, not to track and knock down supersonic cruise missiles. How do we stop Beck *then*?"

"XO, I honestly wish I knew."

———

Ernst Beck sat alone in his cabin, brooding and waiting for further word from Berlin.

To him the original plot had made some sense. He knew from reading his earlier set of orders that the number of atom bombs to be supplied to the Argentines would be limited. To use a bomb required complex arming codes that applied only to that particular bomb—and the Axis would parcel these codes out to the Argentines in small doses. The purpose was to shock America into suing for peace, not start World War III, by using a decisively harsh and brutal act the Axis wouldn't be blamed for: a full-scale demonstration of tactical nuclear warfare waged on land. The fault would appear to lie with America; even U.S. civilians might not believe their own government's denials. Such a modern *credibility gap* was one major Axis goal.

But now, because he knew the plot had failed, the sheer hypocrisy of it all was the most appalling of many things that bothered Beck. He saw too late the naked truth: He'd been a willing player in this hypocrisy from the start. To sail around with kampfschwimmer and send them off for this or that was glamorous. To provoke some banana republic into open revolution was enjoyable in a voyeuristic way. To have these people killing one another unbidden by him, so eagerly, yielded a brief but almost sexual thrill. Beck began to understand von Loringhoven better. He now saw parts of von Loringhoven beginning to grow, or fester, inside himself.

Still he waited for word from Berlin. Should he deliver the crated atom bombs? Would he be told to fire the missiles from *von Scheer*?

Beck knew that if he was ordered to pretend to be an Argentine sub and launch a handful of missiles at Brazil, then, duty-bound, he'd obey. If he was imaginative enough of a naval officer to conceive the possibility, there could be people in High Command who would at least consider it too.

Step-by-step the moral stakes had risen, as the moral standards fell. At each step Beck resisted, then gave in. Every time, he went from horror at his orders—or possible orders—to keenly and cleverly planning how he and his crew would help carry them out.

The ugly truths of the larger situation began to manifest

themselves more clearly in his mind. He knew his own complicity, and duplicity, could no longer be repressed or denied.

To sneakily set off a stolen American bomb as an outrageous lie, and then give more bombs to Argentina for them to use against Brazil, was supposed to be okay. But to shoot such bombs at Brazil directly from von Scheer *is for me somehow* less *okay?*

Beck shook his head. How could he have been so self-deluded as to believe that he held some special sort of ethical high ground? He waited and waited for a messenger to knock, or for his intercom light to blink, with news from headquarters.

Beck felt himself sinking deeper into gloom.

If God truly existed, and He really respected my trust in Him, then why has He allowed me to be caught in this situation? It's certainly not to test my faith. That's cruel theological nonsense. And it's not to challenge my moral commitment, because cowardice and treason, mutiny or suicide, are the only exits now and these are the ultimate immoral acts.

For a warrior to kill in war is not immoral. . . .

Hell is just a fantasy, a story to scare little children. I am a grown man, a blooded soldier fighting for my country, as other German soldiers have fought for generations past. They never questioned their duty or their destiny . . . and neither will I. They sought only to do their duty well and face their destiny with clear and confident eyes . . . and so shall I.

Beck opened his laptop and turned it on. He brought up a map of Brazil. To pass the time constructively, he began to pick what he thought would be high-value targets in the country, just in case the order came to launch his nuclear cruise missiles. Growing bored with that, he studied a chart of the South Atlantic, and planned his campaign against *Challenger* and the convoy.

———

Jeffrey let the Brazilian hovercraft rush on ahead alone, as a diversion, while *Challenger* changed course to leave the continental shelf. *Challenger* continued moving south at top quiet speed out in deep water, off southern Brazil. The local time was three A.M. in Buenos Aires and Rio. Jeffrey knew this was late, even for urban middle- to upper-class South Americans, who tended to stay up well past midnight every day of the week.

He and Bell sat in the captain's stateroom again, struggling over tactics for their fight against the *von Scheer*. Nautical charts and diagrams were windowed on his laptop screen. The display looked impressive enough, but Jeffrey knew that in reality he and the XO were going in circles and getting nowhere. They decided to take a break and went to the wardroom for coffee—Jeffrey locked his door, for security. In a short while they returned.

Jeffrey's laptop sat there, with the same busy mess on the screen.

"Let's get back to work," Jeffrey told Bell. "This is what they pay us the big money for." He sat down heavily.

Bell joined him, and many minutes passed. The two men still got nowhere. Jeffrey felt himself becoming irritable. That strong black coffee, instead of perking him up, had left him with acid reflux and a bitter metallic aftertaste in his mouth. The caffeine, the adrenaline, the long day of hard work and harder travel, the late hour and all the tension, were giving him a weird sensation—as though his head were stuffed with wool or wasn't quite attached to his body.

Someone knocked on the door. Jeffrey, startled, jumped in his seat.

Much more of this pulverizing wait for news and I'll really lose it.

A messenger informed him that Sonar was picking up

Brazilian airdropped signal sonobuoys in the acoustic-tone code Jeffrey prearranged with Rio.

"We'll be right there," he told the young man tiredly, then slid his door closed again for a moment and fought to regain some composure.

Bell, still sitting, looked up at him, obviously torn between hope and dread.

Lieutenant Willey, the engineer, had the conn; Sessions was acting as fire control; the ship had been at battle stations now for seven hours. This was grueling, draining, extreme, but Jeffrey deemed it necessary—*von Scheer* might appear from nowhere at very short range, and then every second would count.

Sessions had already decoded the sonobuoy signal relayed by Sonar. "Captain, message says, 'Come up to on-hull ELF antenna depth.'"

"ELF depth?"

"Yes, sir. That's what it says in the codebook from that diskette you brought from Brazil."

"But Brazil doesn't have an ELF transmitter." Such installations were miles across and hugely expensive. "Sonar, are you sure about what you got from the sonobuoys?"

"Yes, Captain. Quite certain this is the tone sequence they sent us."

"Somebody there made a clerical error?" Bell suggested.

Jeffrey frowned. "We'd better find out." He took the conn and Bell took fire control. Jeffrey ordered *Challenger* shallower.

Soon the radio room called on the intercom.

"ELF message with our address says to come to floating-wire-antenna depth and trail the wire, Captain. Imperative, and do not radiate. Commander, Atlantic Fleet sends."

"Hey," Bell exclaimed. "Our comms are working again!"

Jeffrey, very exhausted, was more cautious. "Either our information warriors defeated the Axis viruses for now, or this is all a fake and we'll be led into a trap."

"What do we do?"

"Watch real good for threats as we go shallower. Copy the message and see if the authenticators validate. If they do, we see what the message says. If they don't, we launch noise-makers and fire a decoy and run for our lives."

———

There was jubilation in *Challenger*'s control room. Some crewmen grinned from ear to ear, while others simply managed a smile for the first time in days. The more outgoing chiefs slapped one another on the back. Jumping high fives were exchanged among the enlisted men—one of whom was so carried away he banged himself on the overhead, then laughed. Lieutenant Sessions combed his hair and tucked in his ruffled shirttails as if he wanted to look his best for the special occasion. Bell took the picture of his wife and baby out of his wallet and kissed them. Jeffrey watched all this serenely.

The message from Admiral Hodgkiss was valid; the Axis computer virus assaults had indeed been beaten back—in the heaviest information warfare battle ever known.

"Read it aloud," Bell said, beaming. "Skipper, let's hear the whole thing."

Jeffrey cleared his throat dramatically. "I quote loosely as follows: 'Anti-Axis truth-based propaganda, founded on Lieutenant Felix Estabo's success, has foiled the Germans completely. Forestalled by aggressive warnings by President de Gama to his chief-executive counterpart in Argentina, an attempted coup in Buenos Aires has utterly collapsed. Military units that were revolting shortly before have switched back to their elected head of state.' With cynical rapidity, I might add." Jeffrey chuckled. " 'The ringleaders have been arrested or they killed themselves, or first were arrested and *then* killed themselves. More were beaten to death in the streets or lynched from lampposts by angry loyalist mobs. A few of the culprits,' alas, 'managed to flee for now into neutral Paraguay.'"

Crewmen mimicked hissing and booing the villains.

"'Separately,'" Jeffrey continued, "'reliable up-to-the-minute intelligence sources in-country confirm no German nuclear warheads are on the loose. . . . ' God be praised for *that*."

There was a chorus of sober *amens*.

Jeffrey cleared his throat again, and held up the message at arm's length as if it were a formal proclamation. "'The Brazilian Congress, meeting in special session, has unanimously approved President da Gama's request for a declaration of war against the Berlin-Boer Axis. Brazil is now one of the Allied Powers. The western side of the Atlantic Narrows is solidly in friendly hands. . . . Argentina remains neutral, at least for now, while taking active steps to fully restore democratic order and good public health. Her troops on the Brazilian border are standing down.'"

"This is just fabulous, Captain," Bell exulted. "We whupped the Axis decisively in the whole South American theater!"

"Let's not take too much credit, XO." Jeffrey glanced around his control room. "You did great, people. But remember, plenty of others played a big part too. And we still have unfinished business. *Major* unfinished business."

"*Von Scheer*."

"We've taken away Beck's purpose for being near South America. We need to do one more thing here now, XO."

"Sir?"

"Give him a *very* compelling reason to go somewhere else."

"Besides the convoy?"

Jeffrey nodded. "He needs to first make very sure he *reaches* the convoy undamaged. . . . Sonar."

"Captain?" Milgrom said.

"If we ping on maximum power in the deep sound channel, say at a depth of five thousand feet, how far off do you think the *von Scheer*'s acoustic intercept might hear us?"

"Let me run a calculation, sir."

"And if we move south at flank speed, could *von Scheer*'s signal processors know it from the Doppler effects of multipath sound-ray traces and reverb and so on? Could they tell our depth, within a thousand feet or so?"

"I'll assume their capabilities are similar to ours." Milgrom worked her keyboard. The senior-chief sonar supervisor looked on. He suggested some tweaks to the modeling. Milgrom glanced up from her console. "Six hundred miles, at least, Captain. And yes, if we're making fifty-three knots at five thousand feet when we ping they'd know."

"Good. Then they'll have no doubt whatsoever we're really *Challenger*." Jeffrey double-checked the nautical chart windowed on his console screen. "That should be more than enough to do it." *And we'll be safely outside the* von Scheer's *missile range.* "Ping once now in normal search mode, just in case there's a U-boat around, or an Argentine diesel sub that didn't get the word the Buenos Aires coup is off."

A high-pitched screech went out through the water. Jeffrey waited for possible target echoes to come back.

"No submerged contacts," Milgrom stated.

Jeffrey gave helm orders to Meltzer.

"Ahead flank, aye," Meltzer acknowledged in his thick Bronx accent. "Make my depth five thousand feet, aye." He turned his engine order dial. "Maneuvering answers, ahead flank, sir." He pushed his control wheel forward gently. *Challenger*'s bow nosed down, then leveled off. "My depth is five thousand feet, sir." *Challenger*'s speed continued mounting steadily.

"Very well, Helm . . . Now we let the *von Scheer* know we're coming, in no uncertain terms. Sonar, make some noise."

The sonarmen got their equipment reconfigured. Soon an almost deafening deep rumble, like a foghorn, pierced the hull from the big sonar sphere at the bow. It made the deck and the very air in the control room seem to hum, above the vibrations and shaking *Challenger* always made at flank speed. Jeffrey's toes tingled, and his clothing rippled oddly against his skin.

"No new sonar contacts, Captain," Milgrom reported routinely after a while. "All active surface contacts within our detection range already held on one or more passive arrays."

"Very well, Sonar. Keep it up." Low-frequency sound waves had the longest range before the underwater signal died off. Jeffrey's intent was not to find Beck but shoo him away with finality—before Berlin could do something insane.

Between the powerful blasts, Jeffrey turned to Bell. "XO, back to my stateroom for a minute . . . Nav, take the conn."

Sessions acknowledged.

"Chief of the watch," Jeffrey told COB with immense satisfaction, "secure from battle stations."

———

Ernst Beck sat alone in his stateroom with the doors locked, both the one into the passageway and the one into the head he shared with von Loringhoven.

On his desk was the latest ELF message from Berlin. Like all ELF messages, it was short. The alphabetic cipher blocks conveyed, in essence, "Proceed at once Africa. Attack enemy convoy soonest possible."

Beck was greatly relieved, but his relief went only so far. He was trading one form of Armageddon for another—the battle against *Challenger* would be violent, high-risk.

But he now had to inform his guest, the baron: *Von Scheer* was ordered away from South America immediately, leaving that whole continent untouched by nuclear fire.

Before Beck could stand to go talk to von Loringhoven, his intercom light blinked.

"Captain."

"Sonar, sir," Werner Haffner said. "Distant acoustic intercept contact bearing north. Extreme detection range, source submerged. Depth and speed of contact confirm positive identification, USS *Challenger,* heading our way at flank speed."

Beck rushed into the Zentrale, took the conn, and issued helm orders to turn due east and evade.

———————

Jeffrey and Bell sat down, and Jeffrey turned his laptop on again. This time he called up a large-scale nautical chart of the whole South Atlantic, with the bottom terrain highlighted.

"I have a search plan, XO. It's simple. I'm completely changing tactics."

"Tell me more, Skipper. More ass-backward Mahan?"

"No. Ass-backward Jeffrey Fuller."

"Huh?"

"You said it yourself before. Searching for *von Scheer* on the way over here, we struck out completely."

"Yes."

"Now that Sonar's making doubly sure the *von Scheer*'s on the run, you realize, don't you, XO? We've scored a strategic and tactical victory against her without ever firing a shot. Without ever even holding sonar contact once in this theater . . ."

Bell gazed at the overhead for a moment, digesting this, then tapped his fingers to his lips, digesting it more. "You know, Captain, you're right! This has to be one for the history books. A masterstroke of thinking outside the box!"

Jeffrey *was* feeling rather pleased with himself. As he gradually had time to reflect on it, the magnitude of what he'd accomplished was almost frightening.

I've also made some key people in Berlin extremely angry at me, in a different and worse way than ever before. . . . Those people have long memories. This frightened Jeffrey too.

He took a deep breath, and let it out. "Anyway, here's my new search plan."

"Keep going active as we transit east?"

"No. We already played that particular hand at the St. Peter and St. Paul Rocks, and you see where that got us against Ernst Beck. Ditto for searching on passive with our fancy triple fiber-optic towed array."

Bell nodded. "Shot nerves and ulcers for a week. Empty hours of worry for the safety of our families back home."

Jeffrey smiled. "Now we intentionally avoid all contact with the *von Scheer* as we cross the South Atlantic. We waste no time on search tactics during the transit. Instead we make flank speed as much as possible, and hide in the bottom terrain on the way. In the meantime, I'm making you command duty officer." Effectively, acting captain. "I'll be on vacation."

"Sir?"

"For the next two days I plan to relax. Catch up on sleep, eat regular meals, watch a movie or two in the enlisted mess, and hang out with the crew. Maybe even sit in on one of the training classes, pick up some of the nuts and bolts to broaden my mind, who knows? There's a cool book I want to finish, something Felix recommended, by this famous surreal Argentine writer, Borges."

"Reasoning behind all this, sir?"

"My intention is to swing north well away from *von Scheer*'s probable track, and do an end around, and ambush him from in front when I'm nice and refreshed."

Bell looked at the laptop. "But the Mid-Atlantic Ridge is huge, sir! There must be two thousand miles of broken terrain he could hide in, running north-south, to take the relief convoy from the rear from almost *anywhere*."

"Except with the geography, that isn't what he'll do."

"Sir?"

"*He* needs to move carefully, to be on the lookout for *us*. Since he seems to know how Orpheus works, he'll also have to go *very* slow, or go very shallow, whenever he nears an old phone cable. All this will limit his mean speed of advance, correct?"

"Correct. But Beck will be bitterly furious now, and ruthlessly driven to score big kills and get in his last licks!"

"By the time he'd reach *that* part of the ridge starting from Argentina, the convoy would be much more than five hundred miles beyond it. His supersonic cruise missiles won't have the range. . . . So he'll have to head *here*." Jeffrey tapped the map with a pencil. "The Walvis Ridge. A lengthy undersea offshoot of the Mid-Atlantic Ridge. Mountains and fissures that slice up toward the southern flank of the Congo-Basin pocket like a dagger."

Bell looked at the map and worked his jaw. "I *think* I see what you're getting at, sir."

"Both sides of the Walvis Ridge are very deep and wide and flat. The Cape Plain just to its south, the Angola Basin right on its north. So the Walvis is narrow and straight. All this'll channel Beck quite nicely for us as he chases the convoy."

Bell pondered. "The overhang of Saharan Africa corrals the convoy from one flank. You're saying he can't go for the convoy's rear, that with the time and distance involved it's too far north from Buenos Aires? So he'll go for its southern exposure, closest to friendly waters off greater South Africa? . . . I concur. The way the Walvis slants northeast, it'll let Beck make up for lost time and bring him in good missile range of all our ships, right outside the two-hundred-mile limit. He goes nuclear and plasters our convoy hard at the very last minute."

"*If* Beck gets that far. We'll be waiting for him at the southwest end of the ridge, where it first branches off from the Atlantic's central tectonic spreading seam. *Here*." Jeffrey touched the exact spot on the chart. "South of this flyspeck of land, the tiny Tristan da Cunha Island group. This is where we cut the *von Scheer* off. *This* is where we fight the endgame, deep and using nuclear fish two thousand miles from Africa."

CHAPTER 38

J effrey's vacation at sea had come to an end. He was
marking its close with a long hot shower, after a final
good night's sleep. Jeffrey thought back on the past two
days, during which he'd forced his mind to stay in low gear
and mingled with his crew—doing things for once in spite
of the war, rather than because of it.

One high point had been that, by coincidence and because
of the lull, two of his enlisted men finished their qualifica-
tions: they'd earned their Silver Dolphins. The presentation
to the honorees, by their captain, was a cherished tradition—
and always a festive occasion too. Jeffrey had most of his
crew, including available officers and chiefs, crammed into
the enlisted mess for the ceremony. He gave a speech, read
passages from the stirring memoirs of great submariners
from times and wars past, and urged everyone on to bigger
and better efforts as a team.

The occasion, and his vacation in general, were marred
for him by only one thing, and it came from outside the hull.
The closer *Challenger* got to Africa, the more clearly and
loudly passive sonar picked up the noise of the convoy bat-

tle. Some blasts could be identified as nuclear torpedoes. Bigger ones were airdropped atomic depth charges. Others, milder, were cruise-missile airbursts, their energy passed through the water.

There was no way for *Challenger* to judge who was winning. The convoy escorts or the U-boats? The land-based antiship cruise missiles, or the naval and air-force suppressive counterstrikes against the mobile launchers and their radars and command-and-control? All Jeffrey and his people knew was that the fighting was growing more vicious, more destructive, as the convoy drove unflinchingly closer to land to relieve and reinforce the beleaguered Allied-held Central African pocket. But the convoy formation was surely more and more ragged, the escort ships increasingly worn down. The sudden arrival of a super-stealthy SSGN fresh on the scene, with a massive salvo of nuclear-tipped supersonic cruise missiles attacking from the convoy's vulnerable southern flank, might tip the balance decisively—in the wrong direction.

Certainly, if I fail to protect the convoy from the von Scheer *here and now, not only will the war effort suffer badly but I'll be personally finished, disgraced—prior Medal or not.*

The navy was Jeffrey's chosen profession, his livelihood, his calling. He also knew that even if he survived this war and the Allies won, dealing with the aftermath emotionally would be difficult. The best way, for him, to make sense of the chaos and sacrifice and slaughter, to heal the mind-tearing randomness of who lived and who died, would be to stay on active duty. The best way he knew to honor those who'd fallen would be to carry on in uniform himself, on their behalf. Yet all that might be ripped from him by brutal Washington politics, his career truncated by factors beyond his control. He'd be cast up on the beach forever, bereft, just as his father, Michael Fuller, had cautioned. The thought of that pained Jeffrey far more than the thought of being killed.

Jeffrey knew the stakes were just as high, both strategically and personally, for Ernst Beck as they were for him. The enemy captain had failed off South America. As Bell warned Jeffrey two days ago, the German would be fired up, red-hot, burning for achievement and revenge—and he would make very sure that this time he *didn't* fail.

Jeffrey said one final heartfelt prayer that he'd guessed right, that the *von Scheer* would come along the Walvis Ridge. Then he turned off the shower and toweled dry. As he dressed he glanced at his bed.

Depending on how things go, the next sleep I ever see might well be my and my entire crew's eternal rest.

Jeffrey remembered what Admiral Hodgkiss had told him in the beginning: In a one-for-one exchange against the *von Scheer,* to defend the convoy and assure the relief of the Congo-Basin pocket, *Challenger* and all aboard her were expendable.

———

Jeffrey had his ship at battle stations. All compartments reported manned and ready in record time. Everyone in the control room shared the electric feeling, a mix of excitement and stress: the final showdown was about to unfold, in an ongoing clash with the mighty *von Scheer* that already was *Challenger*'s longest continuous engagement during the war—and probably with the highest stakes the crew had ever fought for.

Jeffrey called his weapons officer, Lieutenant Torelli, to take the conn. He asked Lieutenant Willey, the engineer, to send one of his junior officers forward to act as fire control.

"XO, Sonar," Jeffrey said, "join me and Lieutenant Sessions at the navigation plotting table. It's strategy time."

Bell and Milgrom gathered with Jeffrey and Sessions at the back of the control room. They grouped around the desk-high digital navigation console. The assistant navigator, a senior chief, worked with the enlisted men on the vital task of tracking the ship's exact position and warning of navigational hazards.

"Show me a chart of everything," Jeffrey said, "from the whole west coast of Africa out to the Mid-Atlantic Ridge."

The assistant navigator worked his keyboard. The chart appeared on a wide-screen display. Land edged the top and the right side of the picture—there was an upside-down L-shaped bend in the very long African shoreline, at Cameroon. Jeffrey and his officers leaned closer to study the chart; these caucuses always helped his people bond.

The ship was at a depth of ten thousand feet, in the foothills of the Walvis Ridge. The control room was rigged for red. Preparing for an attack, the compartment was crowded. Almost two dozen people manned every console seat or stood in the aisles. There was a heavy sense of expectation, a strong drive to contribute to the larger fight. Noise came over the sonar speakers, amplified from in the distance.

"*Listen* to that," Sessions said.

Far to the north, the convoy battle raged. Dozens of cargo ships and warships of every type—and navy auxiliaries ranging from deep-draft fleet-replenishment oilers to ammunition carriers—churned and throbbed and growled their way through the sea. Active sonars on the hulls of frigates and cruisers pinged from the surface. Dipping sonars lowered from antisubmarine helos probed above and below the thermal layer. Almost countless SSQ-75 active sonobuoys pinged from deep on the ocean floor. Friendly fast-attack subs worked hard too, unheard and unseen. The air battle over the ocean, and inland past the African shore, Jeffrey could only guess at and try to picture in his mind. The shattering fear and stark terror of all the combat, the fury and the agony, he could only project from memories of his own exposure to war.

"The antisubmarine searches are intensifying," Milgrom said.

Jeffrey tried not to think about the suffering of troops and civilians, trapped in the pocket for almost nine months. Malnourished, wounded, badly short of medical supplies, ravaged by emerging new strains of Lassa fever, O'nyong nyong fever, hemorrhagic fever, cholera, those people needed help soon. The eastern flank of the pocket was protected by natural barriers: the Great Rift Valley was the best antitank trap in the world. The north-south string of Lake Tanganyika, Lake Victoria, Lake Turkana, and lesser lakes, halted any major enemy troop advance.

But the western flank of the pocket, anchored on the lowlands of the South Atlantic shore, was vulnerable and exposed in the face of modern combat bridging equipment and armored vehicles—based on the Russian model—designed for crossing rivers under fire. If the coastline was pinched off, hospital ships would lose friendly harbors in which to moor, and their guaranteed safe passage at sea would be useless.

A distant rumble sounded through the water, rising to a crescendo that died off abruptly—a nuclear blast. Then another crack of thunder pulsed through the sea, and then another.

"I never get used to that sound," Bell said.

Somewhere out there, ships and aircraft and subs and enemy subs continued their battle of attrition, wearing one another down, inflicting and taking losses. Modern Axis U-boats prowled and risked death to score kills. Equipped with air-independent propulsion, or even with nuclear power, and armed with atomic torpedoes, they posed a deadly threat. Sometimes the port wide-aperture array, aimed toward the battle as *Challenger* steamed northeast, detected other active pings: U-boats, cornered in end-stage melees, sacrificing themselves to try to sink an Allied ship that cost twenty times as much to build and held a hundred, two hundred times as many people aboard.

Another sharp crack sounded, seeming closer than the others. Jeffrey saw his crewmen flinch, more from sympathy or concern, or out of hate.

Jeffrey felt the pressure of command leadership on his shoulders. It seemed to rival the pressure outside, squeezing *Challenger*'s hull: two tons for each square inch.

"They need our help," he told the control room at large in

his best, most steely voice, "and I intend to see they get it. A swarm of *von Scheer's* missiles coming over the horizon would spoil the rest of their day. I intend to see the *von Scheer* never lives to launch her missiles."

There was a murmur of agreement, of readiness among the crew. They began to merge their identities into one collective whole. The enlisted men, in their blue cotton overalls, began to act as what they called themselves with pride: "blue tools," well-trained cogs in Jeffrey's machine. Each officer was now an extension of the captain's own combat mental process, honed to his or her duties by endless drills and indoctrination, tempered in previous battles with Jeffrey acting as their boss. The chiefs, the down-to-earth and salty foremen of the ship, the guys who "had the answers," supervised their sections and made very sure all orders were translated into concrete and well-executed tasks.

Jeffrey cleared his throat and pointed at the northern part of the large-scale chart, at the ocean south of North Africa. Bell, Milgrom, and Sessions listened carefully.

"This line of seamounts up here slants down from the Bight of Biafra all the way to St. Helena. Most of those peaks are shallow enough for a U-boat to use to hide. The range of subsonic cruise missiles launched from the overhanging North African coast covers the whole Gulf of Guinea and extends way down to *here*." Jeffrey traced his index finger along a red arc on the chart, a thousand miles below the enemy-occupied shoreline that ran left to right—west to east—from Liberia past Ghana to Nigeria. "Those cruise missiles happen to cover the Bight of Biafra seamounts and almost reach St. Helena. That gives important air support to the U-boats. It creates a bastion for them, subject to real risk only from our fast-attack submarines."

Bell, Milgrom, and Sessions nodded.

Jeffrey went on. "We know the convoy's steaming in a broad hook south of this red arc, staying out of range of those missiles as long as they can." He glanced at the assistant navigator. A broad blue arrow popped onto the map display, aiming at the right side of the chart, to mark the route of the convoy. The arrow lay over the very deep Angola Basin. "As the convoy turns northeast, and rounds the home stretch to the friendly-held shore from Gamba to Luanda, along *here,* the massed U-boats will come down and try to savage their left flank." Jeffrey gestured at the chart with his hands. The Angola Basin abutted the middle of the north-south part of the African coast, and ran up to the outlet of the Congo River itself. "Other U-boats are probably lurking southeast of *us* somewhere, basing out of South Africa, to squeeze the convoy's *right* flank." He gestured again at the bottom part of the map.

As if for emphasis, another nuclear blast went off in the distance. Jeffrey looked at the sonar speakers. *Every one of those detonations sours possible Allied success. The ocean ecology and food chain here are hurting. At least prevailing winds and currents carry the fallout away from land.*

"Sir," Sessions asked, "what about the two-hundred-mile limit?"

"Yes, I was coming to that." Jeffrey pointed at the blue—friendly—chunk of Central Africa. "For better or worse, the Allied pocket's share of the coast is just about four hundred miles. We can only hope the Axis keep to their own rules of engagement, to not use atomic weapons within two hundred miles of U.S.-held turf." He spoke to the assistant navigator, and green arcs marked the outer edge of this hoped-for safety zone against Axis nukes.

"Sir," Bell said, "based on what we just went through in South America, I'm not sure how much we can count on Axis ROEs."

"Agreed."

"There's also the broader matter of the Axis land offensive," Milgrom said. "The pocket's coast may get pinched off. The convoy's landing might have to be an amphibious combat assault. The losses would be heavy, even against conventional arms."

"I know."

"The danger," Sessions said, "is that since the nuclear shooting has started at sea, and the U-boats are in hot pursuit of our surface ships, the atomic combat may run on momentum unbroken, straight through the two-hundred-mile limit and onto the land."

Jeffrey nodded. "A paramount Axis strategic goal is the German and Boer armies in Africa linking up at all costs. After what just did and didn't happen in South America, we can't tell what volatile mood Berlin and Johannesburg are in right now. There are some pretty scary wild cards here. They all emphasize the vital importance of *Challenger*'s mission. Sink the *von Scheer* . . . My concept of operations against the *von Scheer* is very simple. Before that, are there any questions on what we've covered so far?"

There weren't.

"Assistant Nav, plot the great circle route from the Tristan da Cunha Island group to the Congo River outlet." Once more the senior chief typed—a great circle route meant the shortest distance between two points on the globe. Another red line came on the screen.

"As you all can see, the *von Scheer*'s quickest final approach from South America to the convoy and the pocket lies exactly along the Walvis Ridge. The Angola Basin on one side and Cape Basin on the other both are deeper in most places than our and the *von Scheer*'s crush depth. For example, eighteen thousand feet along here, and here." Jeffrey touched spots on the chart. "The Walvis Ridge itself is an underwater mountain range that rises one to three miles off the surrounding ocean floor. In a few spots seamount peaks almost reach the surface. Questions?"

No one spoke.

"As Sonar told us two days ago, the deep sound channel functions perfectly in either basin. Active and passive detection and counterdetection ranges there would be long. The Angola Basin is heavily bathed in sound. So is the Cape Basin, less so, by SSQ-Seventy-fives presumably dropped on Norfolk's orders in our support. These sounds give the basin waters good acoustic illumination for ambient and hole-in-ocean sonar search modes. You all know what that means, tactically."

"Whichever of us sticks our nose out of the Walvis first," Bell said, "*von Scheer* or *Challenger,* can be seen by the other vessel while still in good hiding terrain in the ridge. The guy who's hiding gets off the first shots, and wins."

"Correct," Jeffrey said. "So we'll *use* that. Ernst Beck has to work his way along while hugging the ridge, and he doesn't have forever. He has to get in position to fire his missiles while the convoy is still out at sea. Once it reaches harbors or good beaches and unloads, him sinking cargo ships and troop transports is a somewhat hollow victory. The carrier groups would be freed to concentrate on self-defense and their own mobility, and they'd be much harder for him to hit as well."

"So what's the plan, Skipper?"

Jeffrey touched the own-ship icon on the navigation chart. "At the moment we're in the foothills approaching the Wust Seamount, on a base course zero four five." Heading northeast. "Just beyond that seamount is a sort of mountain pass through the Walvis, where the ridge terrain is broken by a flat path leading north-south. That path is very deep, right around fifteen thousand feet, about as much as I want our hull to have to take. But this mountain pass, if we can call it that, has a wide-open view to the north and the south." The pass was a few miles long, the same way the prominent ridge terrain was a few miles wide from north to south.

"Everyone, back to our stations. Let's get to work."

———

Jeffrey studied the gravimeter. Then he hardened his voice. A jagged, very steep, extinct volcanic pinnacle soared up close by the ship to starboard. "Helm, maintain nap of seafloor cruise mode. Come right and hug the east face of the Wust Seamount." He touched his console screen with his light pen—the mark repeated on Meltzer's displays, relayed through *Challenger*'s data-distribution network. "At this designated way point, Helm, all stop. Then rise on autohover, make your depth three thousand feet."

Meltzer acknowledged. *Challenger* banked into a gentle turn to starboard.

Jeffrey called up his weapons-status page. "Fire Control, pull the Mark Eighty-eights from tubes five and six and replace with high-explosive Mark Forty-eight Improved ADCAPs."

Bell relayed commands. "Sir, why ADCAPs? Their punch is weak and their crush depth is shallow."

"Two reasons, Fire Control. In this ridge terrain, first-detection and engagement ranges might be very short. We need the option to shoot without a self-kill from our own atomic warheads. Hence the high-explosive fish. And the *von Scheer* needs to go shallow to launch her missiles." Jeffrey glanced at the photo of Ernst Beck he still kept windowed on his console. "That's Beck's Achilles' heel. Shallow, we can use ADCAPs."

"Understood, sir."

Meltzer reported he'd reached Jeffrey's designated way point.

Jeffrey eyed a depth gauge and the gravimeter. *Challenger* began to rise, on a level keel and with no forward speed.

"Fire Control, pull the Mark Eighty-eights from tubes seven and eight. Replace with Long Term Mine Reconnaissance System units." The LMRSs were unmanned undersea vehicles—remote-controlled off-board probes; they could be fitted with various specialized black boxes. "Mission-configurable load-out is to be modules for antisubmarine passive sonar. I intend to use them as early-warning detection aids against the *von Scheer*. For stealth, control both units by fiber-optic tether." The probes could use an acoustic link instead, but the digital bursts might be heard by a sophisticated enemy.

"Understood, aye aye," Bell said.

Jeffrey watched his weapons-status screen. The color coding for tubes five through eight changed from green—ready to fire—to red: not ready. Then tubes five through eight had their outer doors closed and the seawater drained. The inner-tube-door icons popped open. The Mark 88s were disarmed by the torpedo-room crew, and pulled from the tubes and placed on the storage racks by the hydraulic autoloader mechanisms. ADCAPs, and off-board probes, were presented to the tube breach doors. The new units slid into the tubes, and the inner breach doors closed.

"Sir," Meltzer said, "my depth is three thousand feet."

"Very well, Helm. Fire Control, make tubes seven and eight ready in all respects including opening outer doors."

Bell acknowledged. He relayed orders to flood and equalize the pressure in the tubes. The outer doors slid open.

Jeffrey used his light pen. "Position the two probes here, and here." He marked places to the north and south of the seamount peak. "Hold them at a depth of three thousand feet." That was their crush-depth limit, and also put these listening outposts near the sweet spot of the deep sound channel.

"Data preset."

"Very well, Fire Control. Firing point procedures, LMRS units in tubes seven and eight."

"Ready."

"Tube seven, shoot."

"Tube seven fired electrically."

"Unit is running normally," Milgrom reported.

"Tube eight, shoot."

"Tube eight fired electrically."

"Unit is running normally."

"Very well, Sonar, Fire Control . . . Helm, on autohover, make your depth five thousand feet."

Meltzer acknowledged. Jeffrey watched his screens as *Challenger* descended beside the stark and jagged basalt face of the seamount. Meanwhile, on the tactical plot, the icons for the probes moved toward their designated places. COB took control of both probes from his console.

"Helm," Jeffrey ordered, "on auxiliary maneuvering units, rotate the ship onto heading two two five." Southwest.

Meltzer acknowledged. The auxiliary thrusters were mounted at bow and stern, and helped the ship navigate in tight quarters. Safely below the two probes, *Challenger* gently pivoted while the fiber-optic tethers to the probes continued playing out. Jeffrey did *not* want to break the tethers to those probes.

"Helm, back one-third, make turns for four knots."

Challenger eased away from the seamount face and the probes, keeping her bow—and her torpedo tubes—aimed in their direction.

"Helm, all stop. On autohover, take us to the bottom."

The tension in the control room rose as *Challenger* went much deeper. Jeffrey watched as a gauge showed the outside pressure increase more with every foot.

"Hull popping," Milgrom reported at nine thousand feet.

It couldn't be helped. The ridge terrain should help mask the ship from *von Scheer*—Jeffrey hoped. "Very well, Sonar."

"Hull popping," Milgrom said again at eleven thousand feet.

"Very well." The rote of standard reports and acknowledgments always went on, *especially* entering combat. Crisp and clear two-way dialogue, with no chance for awful mistakes or missed information, was indispensable.

Nearing fifteen thousand feet, Jeffrey felt the deck under his feet begin to buckle slightly as *Challenger*'s ceramic-composite hull was compressed. COB worked his console to maintain the ship's neutral buoyancy because as she was squashed in from all sides, she displaced less water and acted heavier. COB expelled water from the variable ballast tanks to lighten the ship. At such great depth, the hardworking pumps made noise. *This too can't be helped.*

Dust and crumbling heat insulation fell from the squeezed-in overhead as *Challenger* descended more. Extra damage-control parties were already waiting in key places throughout the ship, since *Challenger* had been at battle stations and rigged for deep submergence for some time. Even so, crewmen squirmed. People brushed the dust and insulation off their consoles and their clothes. Jeffrey did this too, as casually as he could, to set an example. But he knew that, three miles down, the slightest leak could be catastrophic. He saw some people sweating despite the cold air used to cool all the ship's electronics. Everyone grew very hushed, speaking in whispers if they spoke at all, and moving as little as possible: the hull compression so deep forced deck sound-isolation rafts and machine-vibration damping mounts to make hard contact, spoiling much of *Challenger*'s normal quieting.

Jeffrey realized his own hands felt ice-cold. He ordered the air circulation fans turned off—his excuse to himself was to quiet the ship even more. Quickly the compartment grew stuffy and humid, from so many overexcited bodies in close proximity.

"Sir," Meltzer reported, "my depth is fifteen thousand feet."

"Very well, Helm . . . Fire Control, Sonar, now we wait."

CHAPTER 39

Ernst Beck's ship was at battle stations and the Zentrale was rigged for red. Karl Stissinger, the einzvo, sat beside the captain at the command console. Baron von Loringhoven stood in the aisle, observing.

"My intention," Beck stated, "is to let the tactical situation itself reduce uncertainties. Since it must be clear to Fuller that we're approaching along the Walvis Ridge, we can expect to meet him there. His best strategy is to sit in ambush at ultraquiet and force us to remain on the move, giving him the sonar advantage. He has to be somewhere ahead of us, to stay between us and our missile launch point against the target convoy." Beck used his light pen on the nautical chart and gravimeter display on his console. His markings were reproduced on Stissinger's screens, and on the digital displays on the forward bulkhead used by the pilot and copilot.

"*Challenger* will almost certainly wait at this prominent terrain feature *here*. A deep pass leading north-south through the ridge just east of the Wust Seamount. He'll expect us to come past, and then he'll pounce."

"Understood," Stissinger said.

"What are you going to do about that?" von Loringhoven asked.

Beck turned to von Loringhoven. He tolerated the baron's presence out of self-interest: it was better to have him as a political friend than a political enemy. Since their defeat in South America, the baron's presence aboard had become superfluous. But Beck was wise enough to know that both he and von Loringhoven would have to close ranks and work very hard to save their reputations and careers when they returned to Germany.

Sinking Challenger *and devastating the Allied relief convoy will be my route to professional salvation. Having von Loringhoven here as a high-ranking objective witness will corroborate my claims when I draft my after-action report.*

Beck's newfound value system, the pseudotheology of the classic Germanic warrior ethic, inspired him and infused him with eagerness for the hunt.

I'm conscious of this transformation within me. I'm grateful for the moral load it took off my mind.

Beck smiled a predatory smile. "Baron, we're going to send Captain Fuller a little surprise."

"Torpedoes in the water," Milgrom shouted. "Two, three, *four* torpedoes in the water at our depth, passing below our northern off-board probe! Four *more* torpedoes in the water under our southern probe!"

"Torpedo headings?" Jeffrey snapped. "Weapon *types?*"

"Torpedoes now rounding north and south faces of Wust Seamount at seventy-five knots. Torpedoes inbound at *Challenger.* Torpedoes are Axis nuclear Sea Lion units!"

Hostile inbound weapon icons popped onto the tactical plot.

Shit. Beck knew I was here. He's smarter, more aggressive than I thought.

He'd supposed to act like a boomer captain, hiding and protecting his ship till it's time for him to launch.

But he's fighting like a fast-attack commander, a good one—sneaky, hard-hitting, outpsyching me from the start.

The gravimeter told Jeffrey he was badly boxed in: Immediately behind *Challenger,* a cluster of seamount peaks rose straight up almost three miles high.

"Inbound torpedoes now held as direct path contacts on both port and starboard wide-aperture arrays!"

Beck had *Challenger* caught in a vise. There was no place Jeffrey could run: seamounts in front and behind, four atomic torpedoes charging at him fast from the right and four more from the left. Noisemakers were useless this deep, strangled by the weight of miles of seawater pressing down. *Challenger*'s brilliant decoys had a crush depth similar to her off-board probes—at fifteen thousand feet they'd implode in the tubes the moment the pressure was equalized.

In the control room, Jeffrey felt many pairs of eyes glance his way. Those faces showed everything from panic to dependency, to an almost childlike faith that the captain—their father figure in a crisis—would find some way for them to survive.

All these thoughts and glances happened in fractions of a second.

"Fire Control," Jeffrey rapped out, "firing point procedures, nuclear Mark Eighty-eights in tubes one through four. Set warhead yields to maximum." One kiloton each.

"Preset!" Bell shouted.

"Snap shots, tubes one through four, fan spread, due north, *shoot.*" A snap shot lacked a firing solution, but launching fish this way, unprogrammed, saved precious time.

Four Mark 88s dashed from the tubes and into the sea. "Tubes one through four fired electrically!"

"All units running normally!"

The four Mark 88 fish ran through the mountain pass, toward the Angola Basin, trailing their guidance wires.

"Helm, *ahead flank.* Thirty degrees right rudder. Make your course due north."

Meltzer acknowledged. *Challenger* turned north and gained speed.

"Fire Control, aim one Mark Eighty-eight at each of the inbound Sea Lions to the north. Set them to blow by timer within kill range of those enemy weapons."

"The weapons may try to evade."

"Not in this narrow pass. They've got no more maneuvering room than we do."

"Lost the wire, LMRS from tube eight," a fire-controlman yelled. *Challenger*'s hard turn north had overstrained the fiber-optic tether to the probe that Jeffrey had holding to the south side of the Wust Seamount.

"My course is due north, sir!" Meltzer shouted.

"Very well, Helm!"

The ride became rough as *Challenger*'s speed built up toward fifty knots.

"Sonar," Jeffrey snapped, "any more torpedoes inbound? Any contact on *von Scheer*?"

"Negative," Milgrom said. *"Negative."*

"Shut the outer doors, tubes one through four and seven and eight."

"Lost the wires, all empty tubes!"

"Fire Control, tubes one through four and seven and eight, reload, nuclear Mark Eighty-eights!"

Bell relayed commands. Jeffrey pictured everything as below, at the special-weapons control console and inside the huge but cramped torpedo room itself, Lieutenant Torelli and his men were hard at work. He prayed there were no malfunctions or mistakes.

Jeffrey eyed the tactical plot. Four torpedoes were coming straight at him from directly ahead. His own atomic fish charged in their direction at a net closing speed of almost a hundred and fifty knots. Jeffrey charged after his own fish, doing fifty knots himself. Four enemy torpedoes gained at him from behind, at a net closing speed of twenty-five knots.

This'll be close. The timing has to be perfect.

"Units from tubes one through four have detonated!" Bell shouted.

The signals, through the fiber-optic cables, moved at the speed of light. The noise and shock force, Jeffrey knew, moved only at the speed of sound in water. The ranges were so short, his time to live or die so fleeting now, that the fiber-optic signals beat the blast fronts on their race to *Challenger* by much too little time to think.

Four one-kiloton nuclear blasts went off at once ahead of *Challenger*. An all-consuming demon of painful decibels and shaking smashed at the ship from every side. *Challenger* continued her hard sprint forward, into the midst of Jeffrey's self-made thunder in the deep. Noise battered the ship in every octave, and vibrations tore at her with every resonance period from high to low. They made Jeffrey's feet and buttocks jar and ache like pins and needles. They made his teeth chatter as *Challenger* shook, and his skeleton seemed to rattle inside his body. *Challenger* rose and fell like a roller coaster as Meltzer and COB fought to regain control.

Crewmen's arms and legs flailed as they tried to cover their ears and open their mouths—to relieve the pressure against their eardrums from the cacophony outside.

Then the aftershocks and blast reflections began to hit.

The four fireballs pulsated as they plunged for the surface. Each time they collapsed and rebounded, more noise and more hard punches were thrown at *Challenger*.

More noise and pounding reflected off the seamount walls to right and left. The roller-coaster ride went on. The deck—alive with buzzing and humming that came right up through Jeffrey's legs and into his genitals—seesawed as the ship's nose bucked.

"The *gravimeter*," Bell shouted.

Jeffrey forced his eyes to focus. Gouges and scars appeared in the seamount walls to either flank. *Avalanches,* triggered by the forces of the blasts.

Above all the other noise and shaking, Jeffrey felt sharp, hard blows. *Falling boulders, bouncing off our hull. One hit on our vulnerable stern parts and we're finished.*

The vessel shimmied and yawed. *Sloshing ocean, kicked up by the avalanches.*

Damage reports poured in, and repair crews went to work as best they could—so far, nothing fatal to *Challenger*'s ability to fight. But reloading the tubes was slow going.

"Assess enemy inbound weapons from north destroyed!" Bell shouted above the continuing racket. "Four torpedoes to the south still closing! . . . Inbound torpedoes have gone to active search!" The surviving Sea Lions had started to ping.

Jeffrey checked the speed-log gauges—the digital readings and backup analog dials agreed. *Challenger*'s speed was fifty-three knots, everything she had.

Torelli signaled he was waiting.

Jeffrey and Bell entered their special-weapons arming codes.

"Make tubes one through four and seven and eight ready in all respects including opening outer doors."

Jeffrey ordered the Mark 88s in tubes one through four fired as countershots against the weapons to the south.

The fish dashed from the tubes, spread out, changed course, and ran off back behind *Challenger*.

Jeffrey pondered his options. He was about to enter the wall of tortured water ahead of the ship, where her first four torpedoes had gone off. Four more were about to detonate behind him, unless those inbound Sea Lions got *Challenger* first—which was a very real risk since the engagement distances had grown so tight.

"Firing-point procedures, nuclear Mark Eighty-eights in tubes seven and eight! Set warhead yields to maximum!"

"Ready!" Bell acknowledged.

"Snap shots, loop north of the Wust Seamount and then course two seven zero." West. "Preset units for active search when steady on two seven zero." The units would ping with their own built-in target homing sonars.

"Preset!"

"Shoot."

"Tubes seven and eight fired electrically!"

"Units running normally!"

These two fish will hunt for von Scheer, *give Ernst Beck something to worry about.*

"Units from tubes one through four have detonated!"

My defensive countershots, against those four torpedoes closing from the south.

The blast forces hit at once from directly behind, while the brutality of the first four blasts ahead had barely diminished.

The awful punishment renewed: noise, vibrations, crew injuries, ship damage. Pitching, rolling, yawing, heaving.

Jeffrey was nearly deaf already, but the shocks and after-shocks and blast reflections never let up. There was terrible pain in his ear canals and a silvery whistling and ringing in his head—it got worse and worse as the punishment went on. Still, he forced himself to *think.*

"Helm! Right ten degrees rudder, make your course one eight zero!"

Meltzer turned his head toward Jeffrey as his bloodless hands gripped the control wheel. His lips moved, but Jeffrey couldn't tell what his own helmsman said—the noise, the deafness, were winning. Jeffrey realized both men simply could not be understood verbally.

Jeffrey used sign language. He mimed holding the control wheel, then mimed turning it right. He held up all ten fingers. *Ten degrees.* He pointed at a gyrocompass and held up one finger, then eight, then touched index finger to thumb to form a zero. *Course one eight zero.* South.

Meltzer nodded and went to work.

In the churning, surging, hellish Jacuzzi now swirling in the deep-water pass—between crumbling seamounts and opposite walls of million-degree atomic bubble clouds and multikiloton turbulence—*Challenger* altered course. The ship banked into a turn to the right, as sharply as Jeffrey dared at flank speed. *Challenger* swung back the way she'd just come, still moving as fast as she could.

Jeffrey leaned toward Bell. He had to bellow at the very top of his lungs. "Reload tubes one through four and seven and eight, Mark Eighty-eights!"

Bell nodded. The wait seemed endless; at last the reloading was done.

Jeffrey issued more orders. He sent two more snap shots after his two already in the water: north and then west around the Wust Seamount again, to also hunt on their own for *von Scheer*.

"Why not south for those two?" Bell shouted. "Pinch him from both sides like he just did to us?"

"You'll see."

"Aye aye!"

"Sonar!" Jeffrey yelled.

Milgrom didn't respond.

Jeffrey unbuckled his seat belt and struggled toward her. He gripped stanchions on the overhead to steady himself. Aftershocks and body blows came as each throbbing fireball finally broke the surface far above; hard pounding continued from avalanche rocks and viciously stirred-up water. The pummeling almost threw him from his feet. Sharp console edges and metal equipment seemed to beckon for his head and for his groin.

Jeffrey grabbed the back of Milgrom's seat as *Challenger* rolled and bucked yet more. "Any inbound torpedoes?" he yelled in her ear.

"Impossible to tell!" she shouted back.

Meltzer turned toward Jeffrey. Meltzer pointed at a gyrocompass. His course was steady on one eight zero, due south.

Jeffrey forced his way back to his seat. He ordered Bell to reload tubes seven and eight, and make tubes one through four and seven and eight ready for snap shots.

Jeffrey watched the gravimeter and the confused, outdated tactical plot. He had *Challenger* heading straight for the wall of acoustic and hydrodynamic chaos from his own most recent atomic Mark 88 blasts.

Jeffrey used his console keyboard to send a message to Engineering through the ship's LAN. "Push the reactor to one hundred fifteen percent." The control-room phone talker was lying on the deck, stunned and with a bloody nose—and conversation through the sound-powered phones or intercom was impossible anyway.

A quickly typed message came back: "115%, aye." The ship picked up a few tenths of a knot.

"Helm!" Jeffrey shouted.

Meltzer turned.

Jeffrey pointed up. He gave hand signals for one, then two, then zero, then zero, then zero. *Make your depth twelve thousand feet.* He needed to take *Challenger* away from so close to the seafloor terrain.

Meltzer pulled back his wheel, and *Challenger*'s bow nosed up.

She charged into the curtain of reverb, countless collapsing bubbles of steam, invisible whirlpools, and monstrous thermal and turbulence updrafts and downdrafts.

Sitting beside him, Bell pointed at Jeffrey's waist. Jeffrey remembered to buckle his seat belt just in time.

Challenger twisted and turned like never before. She needed every foot of added clearance from the bottom. The noise was now so loud it no longer registered. The ship's instruments showed that the vibrations and flexing of the hull itself, and inside, were stronger than ever. But Jeffrey was so physically numbed it hardly seemed to matter. He eyed the gravimeter carefully and gave thanks it didn't care about the noise. He gave thanks to God and the contractors that the device was still even functioning.

At the proper moment he issued more helm orders. This time he typed and sent them through the LAN. But he had trouble holding his hands to the keyboard. His vision was so blurred he could barely see the keys. He had little control of his fingers as he tried to type. Finally he hunted and pecked a barely intelligible message: "left10° rudder.Curs 030." He hit ENTER.

Challenger turned left as she rounded the south edge of the Walvis Ridge, where the deep-water pass let out onto the Cape Plain. She headed hard almost north-northeast, along the ridge.

The mountain pass and all its noise and buffeting quickly fell behind. Conversation was possible again. Jeffrey ordered Meltzer to bring the ship back into the ridge topography quickly, and resume nap-of-seafloor cruising at the ship's top quiet tactical speed, twenty-six knots. Trailing a towed array in such broken terrain was impractical—it would get snagged and ruined or lost. But Jeffrey ordered Milgrom and her people to use the wide-aperture arrays and bow sphere to search passively for any signs of enemy subs or their torpedoes. He had the photonic sensors at bow and stern activated in passive-image intensification mode to help Meltzer and Sessions navigate amid the uneven, unweathered volcanic crags and ravines—and also to help the fire controlmen scan for possible mines. Glows and flashes from riled biologics gave barely enough light to see.

Milgrom reported intermittent contact on a clutch of *von Scheer*'s Sea Lions, rushing belatedly south through the pass and continuing on into the Cape Basin. They were pinging, and eventually turned back north toward the ridge, but *Challenger* was well shielded by intervening terrain. Bell said these Sea Lions posed no threat.

Bell was also busy handling damage control and crew injury reports. There were several broken bones, concussions, and very bad cuts; the corpsman and his assistants were swamped with patients on the wardroom operating table and in the enlisted mess triage and treatment area. A number of systems—mechanical and electronic—were down or impaired, but backups or bypasses were covering the major problems.

Jeffrey waited for Bell to take a pause in the assessments he was making and the orders he was issuing—he didn't want to distract his XO—and meanwhile he allowed his own head to clear up more.

"That was a close one," he said when Bell was free for a moment; he was too shaken up and relieved to keep such strong emotions bottled inside.

"Why did you send all your offensive fish north, Captain?"

"I wanted Beck to think I was using them to screen us as we came up through the pass that way."

"That's why you turned back south?"

"I thought it would be what he'd least expect, and would pull him north away from us."

"Why didn't you stand and fight? Go back west and search for Beck and engage him?"

"We're in a weird role reversal, XO. As an SSGN captain, he's supposed to be the hunted. But he came hunting *us*. Instead of him mainly needing to preserve his ship as a force in being, *we're* the ones who have to favor self-preservation for now."

"Captain?"

"The one thing we *can't* afford to do is let him get past us alive, between us and the northeastern terminus of the ridge. His top quiet speed is faster than ours, and in such rugged terrain we might never be able to find him again. Then he'd have a clear shot at his most high-value targets. Even if he exposes himself by going shallow to launch, we can't count on being precisely there to sink him in time."

"I only half follow you, Skipper. I did remind you last week he came to *von Scheer* fresh from being first officer on a ceramic-hulled fast-attack. And also fresh from a long-running battle with *you*, so he knows your style."

"Yeah. And you were right, XO. Absolutely right . . . So I need to be more unpredictable. . . . We can afford to draw things out a bit, I think. We *need* to, for now."

"How does that help us, sir?"

"Trade space for time and get the feel of Beck and his ship. See better how *he* likes to fight . . . We know Beck has to work his way northeast along the ridge. He's got hundreds of miles to cover before he's close enough to the convoy to launch. Meanwhile let's act like we're feeling defensive, cowed."

"What do we do?"

"Retreat. In the only direction we can. Northeast along the ridge toward Africa."

CHAPTER 40

S till no sign of *Challenger* or her wreckage," Stissinger
said two hours later.

Instead of responding, Ernst Beck studied the live-
feed laser line-scan video coming in from his off-board
probes. He'd sent them ahead of *von Scheer* as expendable
scouts in case Jeffrey Fuller survived and was waiting in
counterambush for him nearby.

Beck saw piles of freshly broken boulders, a result of the
avalanches triggered inside the Walvis Ridge mountain pass.
The water was clouded with sediment and rock dust, kicked
up by the nuclear blasts. He also saw fragments of dead sea
creatures drift through the field of view from the probes:
shredded deep-sea jellyfish, broken body parts from strange
siphonophores—snakelike beings covered with thousands
of stinging tentacles for capturing prey and dozens of small
translucent stomachs for digesting. Some of the stomachs he
saw were still intact and held food. Beck noticed a colony of
blackened starfish, all unmoving on the bottom, charred by
the radiant heat of the blasts. He saw demonfish, naturally
black, with hideous faces and huge fangs that made them

look like something out of a horror movie. Except the luminous barbs near the mouths of these demonfish didn't glow, and they floated upside down—dead.

Von Scheer came out of the pass heading south. Beck gave helm orders to turn the ship northeast to avoid the antisubmarine perils of the wide-open and almost bottomless Cape Basin. He had the copilot use the remote-controlled probes to search the ridge terrain just northeast of the seamounts that guarded that side of the pass.

The wait for some report was tense and frustrating, but necessary.

Von Loringhoven came over. "You realize, don't you, that if he decided to run, he's getting away."

"It isn't about him, Baron. It's about us. Whether we get to launch our missile salvos soon enough. If we've scared Jeffrey Fuller off, and we can get in range of the convoy safely and then make a good escape, so much the better. We'll be free to concentrate on hunting and killing *Challenger* after that."

"Agreed," von Loringhoven said.

"But none of that has happened yet."

"So what do you intend to do?"

"We need to continue up the ridgeline at a good pace. Let me show you what I mean. . . . Einzvo?"

"Captain?"

"Have Sonar take the conn for a moment. Join me and the baron at the navigation table."

Young Werner Haffner took Beck's seat. He seemed honored to have the duty at such an important time. Beck smiled to himself. Haffner's boyish enthusiasm was a welcome tonic.

As he matures, if he survives, he'll make a good submariner indeed.

Stissinger paced aft and stood with Beck and von Loringhoven at the plotting table. Beck explained to the navigator what he wanted to see.

A display appeared of the now-familiar land and undersea terrain in this theater: the western African coast, the Walvis Ridge, the Angola Basin, the Bight of Guinea–St. Helena chain of seamounts to that basin's north, and the Cape Basin to the Walvis Ridge's south.

An animation appeared, showing the convoy moving toward the shore of the Allied pocket in the Congo Basin.

Beck cleared his throat. "The convoy's base course is roughly east. Our own base course, because of the ridge, has to be more like northeast. To converge on the convoy before it's too late, we need to better the convoy's average speed by almost fifty percent."

The animation began again, with the convoy moving at twenty knots and the *von Scheer* making the same twenty knots. The icon of the *von Scheer* closed the range to the convoy as it moved up along the ridge on the chart—but not fast enough.

The animation repeated, with *von Scheer* doing thirty knots. Now a red circle around the own-ship icon showed the range of her Mach 2.5 cruise missiles—five hundred miles; a green line marked the atomic rules-of-engagement two-hundred-mile limit from land. At thirty knots, the red circle enveloped a big part of the convoy before the convoy reached the two-hundred-mile limit.

Von Loringhoven watched all this. "Very clear explanation. It seems at thirty knots, which I believe is your top quiet speed, we should achieve our goal."

"It isn't quite that simple. We need to allow extra time for appropriate caution and self-defense. And we need to allow for the flight time of our missiles. Even at Mach Two point five, hugging the wave tops, it takes about fifteen minutes to achieve their maximum range. Baron, in fifteen minutes a nuclear-powered supercarrier going all out can cover ten or more sea miles, wider than the lethal burst zone of our missile warheads. So we have to build into their flight paths autonomous searching-strategy patterns, unless we can receive good and accurate targeting data in advance. And those patterns looping and zigzagging after their prey use up even more time."

"So why don't we get the data?"

"We'd need a high-baud-rate radio link. To download firing solutions for a hundred-plus missiles is a complex and painstaking task. To get that link established, without a kampfschwimmer team on an island and an acoustic connection into the water to us, we'd have to come to periscope depth and raise a mast ourselves, well in advance of when we launch. The Allies already know we're somewhere in the Walvis Ridge, thanks to the mushroom clouds above the surface marking our skirmish with *Challenger*. It'll be bad enough with the datum we make as our missiles all take to the air."

"You're saying we need to fire our missiles half blind, to have the best chance to survive to fire them at all?"

"Yes. Thus we need to get as close as humanly possible to the convoy, and that burns up even *more* time."

"What is your intention now?"

"I know Fuller well enough to know he won't give up until one of us is destroyed. . . . Navigator, overlay the Subtropical Convergence."

The navigator typed some keys. A broad and fuzzy yellow ribbon snaked along the map. It crossed the Walvis Ridge at an angle, three hundred sea miles northeast of the mountain pass that *von Scheer* had just left behind. Beck pointed to that spot, where the Subtropical Convergence intersected the Walvis Ridge.

"Fuller has the same information we do. He can read the same maps. His natural impulse and best strategy is to set up another ambush for us, *here*." He tapped that spot on the chart. "The same confusing sonar and oceanographic conditions we used to our advantage as we crossed the South Atlantic from the Rocks to Mar del Plata apply at this point equally well." In the hemisphere-girdling zone where frigid currents from Antarctica clashed and merged with warm ones from the equator.

"If he hides inside the convergence," Stissinger said, "we might be able to sneak past him."

"So he'll either wait for us in front of the convergence, or behind it," von Loringhoven said.

"The question is which," Beck said, "in front or behind? Fuller needs to slow us down as much as possible. He knows, so far, that each of our direct encounters has been indecisive, a draw. The Rocks, and then this Walvis pass. Therefore, he'll wait in the ridge terrain for us *behind* the convergence."

"Why behind?" the baron asked.

"May I?" Stissinger said.

Beck smiled and nodded. He noticed that Stissinger had been following his lead for the past few days, accepting the baron's presence without rancor—and allowing their passenger-guest to join in some command discussions as a useful third voice.

Stissinger really is the perfect einzvo: loyal and very capable, yet also keenly adaptable to changing conditions on the ship—responsive without being prodded as my own political thinking and the social dynamic evolve.

"If *Challenger* waits for us on the closer side of the Subtropical Convergence, Baron," Stissinger explained, "Jeffrey Fuller runs a serious risk. If we break contact for just a short while, say using the extreme acoustic sea state of torpedo blasts, the convergence gives us sanctuary. It's an ideal place for confusing sound-propagation qualities to offer us excellent cloaking, even from active pinging by a desperate *Challenger*. We'll have gotten between Fuller and the convoy. *But,* if Fuller seeks to engage us next on the *far* side of the convergence, that sanctuary becomes irrelevant. If we try to use it then, we run the wrong way, *farther* from our priority target, the Allied convoy. And we still have to come back and fight our way past Fuller all over again."

"Your logic seems inescapable," von Loringhoven said.

Beck patted Stissinger on the shoulder. He had a selfish motive here, besides giving his XO well-deserved praise. He was showing the baron he ran a skilled and talented crew—and again, it was best for them all to close ranks in front of their seniors in Berlin about the South American mess. Von Loringhoven seemed to get the point: his aloofness and his arrogance appeared to be finally gone for good.

Stissinger continued. "So long as *Challenger* is believed to have survived, Allied antisubmarine forces are hobbled. In the difficult terrain conditions within the ridge, they dare not attack any very deep contact, lest it be Fuller and not us."

"You mean," von Loringhoven said, "so long as Fuller is alive, that keeps us safe from Allied bombardment?"

"Precisely," Beck said. "We use Fuller's mere existence for our own purposes, for now."

"And *then* what's your intention?"

"Move quickly to the convergence. Turn Fuller's ambush plans against him yet again, from there."

———

It was ten hours later. Jeffrey released the crew from battle stations a few at a time so they could use the head, drink coffee, and eat. He had black coffee and a ham sandwich brought to him at the command console. He thanked the messenger, gulped everything down while the youngster stood there, and handed back the empty mug and plate.

Jeffrey returned to his harrowing vigil, waiting for the *von Scheer* to pierce the Subtropical Convergence as Beck moved his way along the Walvis Ridge.

He glanced at the picture of Ernst Beck on his screen.

Well, buddy. Soon one of us is gonna die. I intend for it to be you.

The crew around Jeffrey were tired and tense. But they all knew well from training drills, and from at-sea full-scale tactical exercises fought against U.S. or Royal Navy subs before the war, that waiting at battle stations—doing nothing yet not relaxing for hour after endless hour—was sometimes a vital part of a submariner's job—even if the submarine he was on was called a fast-attack.

Jeffrey flipped through his menu screens. His last two offboard probes were positioned to the southwest, one on each flank of the Walvis Ridge, to listen for *von Scheer* to emerge from the sonar forest formed by the Subtropical Convergence. Jeffrey had *Challenger* hovering, with her bow also aimed southwest, to launch his fish in Ernst Beck's face with the least possible delay.

Bell cleared his throat to get Jeffrey's attention.

"Yes, XO?"

"Why don't we send a few fish out in front, to loiter and get a better first crack at him?"

"Not a bad idea, but their fuel only lasts so long. And even loitering their engines make noise. We'd just waste ammo, or give ourselves away."

"Understood."

"A good question to ask, though," Jeffrey said. He stretched. "Overall, I do like this setup. As you said, XO, I need to do the unexpected, be unpredictable for *me*."

"How does this accomplish that, sir?"

"I'm using the exact same tactic as before. Ambushing Beck from behind a major hydrographic feature. Before it was that mountain pass. This time it's the convergence. Doing the same thing twice, especially when the first time failed, is what Beck will least expect."

Jeffrey and Bell returned to their waiting game. More hours passed.

"Torpedoes in the water!" Milgrom screamed. "Four inbound torpedoes held by passive sonars on each off-board probe!"

"Range? Bearing? Speed?"

"Range ten thousand yards from *Challenger*." Five nautical miles. "Bearing two zero five." South-southwest. "Closing speed seventy-five knots! *Sea Lions, Captain!*"

"They came right out of the convergence, sir," Bell said. "*Von Scheer* guessed where we were all over again." He sounded dismayed.

All over again is right. Jeffrey was really angry with himself.

Jeffrey ordered nuclear snap shots launched in self-defense from six tubes. He had the tubes reloaded, with more Mark 88s armed. He ordered more nuclear snap shots—some against the inbound torpedoes, some into the convergence to find the *von Scheer.*

He knew that scoring a hit against the *von Scheer*—inside the convergence eddies and conflicting currents and chaotic temperature and salinity horizontal layers and vertical cells—was unlikely.

More Sea Lions could come tearing at him any moment.

"Beck suckered me good," he said under his breath.

"Captain?"

Jeffrey needed to make a rushed decision. For his ship to take much more punishment, and suffer serious damage, would leave the convoy wide open to devastation by the *von Scheer.*

Supplies of crucial spare parts, and layers of systems redundancy, were severely depleted in the previous skirmish. More of this abuse, and something Challenger *can't do without will break beyond repair—and then we've had it.*

Jeffrey ordered Bell to retarget his latest salvo entirely for self-defense, and set them to blow by timer in case he lost the wires to those fish. He wrote off the last of his off-board probes. In the edgy silence before all his fish would blow, Jeffrey ordered Meltzer to turn *Challenger* onto course zero three zero: north-northeast. He called for top quiet speed.

Once more *Challenger* retreated, farther up the ridge.

Behind her Bell's snap shots detonated. The ocean erupted as it had before. Blast forces from aft arrived and punished the ship. Noise and shock fronts bounced off terrain to the sides and in front of *Challenger,* and punished her more. The ride was terribly rough, acoustic conditions impossible. More damage reports poured in, jury-rigged emergency repairs were made in haste, and Jeffrey fretted. *My ship's margin for survival is wearing too thin. . . . The con-*

*test with Beck is as much about good damage control as it is
about smart fighting tactics.*

Still fleeing northeast, up the Walvis Ridge toward Africa,
Jeffrey ordered flank speed. *Maybe Beck is better than me.*

———————

"No sign of him, sir," Stissinger reported. Off-board probes
had scouted well ahead and thoroughly.

"He retreated again." Beck knew he was stating the obvious.

"What now?" von Loringhoven asked.

Beck rested his head in his right hand, with his upper lip
cupped in the crook of his thumb and forefinger. His elbow
leaned on his console top, taking the weight of his forearm
and head. He stared into space and thought over everything
he knew.

"He has to stand and fight sooner or later. The closer to the
convoy we get, the more all the time pressure passes from us
onto him. He obviously used my own trick from the Rocks.
A wall of nuclear blasts as a screen to mask his escape."

"What if he used *all* of our tricks?" Stissinger said. "Including doubling back? He might be behind us now, planning to take us from the rear."

"We'd've heard him," Beck said. He had *von Scheer* holding between the convergence and the nuclear disturbance
near Fuller's last hiding place. As ordered, Haffner's sonarmen were pinging on low power to both sides, where direc-
tional acoustic paths were clearest. This ensured that
Challenger didn't do what Stissinger said she might do.
"No, Einzvo, he ran ahead again."

Beck called a nautical chart onto his console. He had it repeat on Stissinger's screen. "The next significant terrain feature is here," Beck said. As von Loringhoven leaned over his
shoulder, he used his light pen. "The Valdivia Seamount
complex. Seven or eight major peaks all grouped together,
after a long stretch of very deep ridge terrain. That's . . . an-

other three-hundred-sea-mile leapfrog ahead. Some of these seamounts are so shallow, their tops are only fifty or a hundred meters deep. The way they're clustered, the paths between them form a maze."

"Is that good?" von Loringhoven asked.

"For us? Yes. In the maze we can try to get lost. Fuller can't afford that. He also can't afford an action somewhere between there and here. The odds of him succeeding in a one-on-one, in deep water where neither ship has a terrain or sound-propagation advantage, are around fifty-fifty."

"You think he won't gamble the convoy with odds of fifty-fifty?" Stissinger asked.

"No. Not even to be unpredictable. Not even to take us by surprise just for the purpose of surprise. The convoy is simply too important for him to risk on the flip of a coin. . . . So, his next move will be to hit us just before the Valdivia Seamounts while he gets concealment on their edge and we have to come at him through open water."

"Head for the Valdivia Seamounts?" von Loringhoven asked.

Beck nodded.

CHAPTER 41

Six hours later, Jeffrey felt as if his ship had been at battle stations forever. *Challenger* worked her way along a stretch of the Walvis Ridge that was very rugged but deep. A depth gauge read 9,850 feet. Even so, the basins to both flanks plunged quickly to 16,500 feet; Jeffrey was hugging the Walvis at more than a mile above the surrounding ocean floor.

Sometimes, when old volcanic extrusions or ledges didn't block the path of sound, the port wide-aperture array could clearly pick up noises from the continuing convoy battle. The battle seemed slightly less violent than before. Jeffrey suspected this was because of the reduced number of platforms on both sides that had survived to keep up the fight. The convoy still had a long way to go to reach its destination and achieve its crucial strategic purpose. But in the meantime it was serving another use: as flypaper for the U-boats and enemy land-based antiship threats.

Because major reinforcement of the Central African pocket would be a big setback for the Axis, they had to do everything possible to prevent the convoy from getting through. This meant the Axis High Command could not preserve their war-fighting assets as a force-in-being, in order to menace the Allies indirectly or reduce the Allied side's options; those assets had to come out and fight. In the bigger picture, this was good, so long as the military value of the U-boats sunk equaled or exceeded that of the convoy ships and escorts sunk—where the measure of value included human lives and weapon stocks. If the trade-off went the other way, and the value of U-boats lost was much less than the damage they inflicted, the Allies would suffer adverse attrition at sea, apart from the question of the fate of the Congo-basin pocket. Even now, with the passage of time having allowed Sonar and Fire Control to assemble more data, Jeffrey didn't know who was winning and who was losing.

There's a definite possibility, that the slaughter on both sides will be so extreme that in the end neither can claim to have won.

All this put Jeffrey in a black mood. He still needed to stop the *von Scheer* somehow. That ugly thought recurred: *Maybe I just have to face the fact that Ernst Beck is better than me.*

Jeffrey eyed the gravimeter. The Valdivia Seamounts loomed a short distance ahead, clustered like a drowned archipelago. Somewhere behind him, he knew, the *von Scheer* was coming his way—Beck could read the same charts.

"What gambit this time, Captain?" Bell asked.

Jeffrey forced himself not to sigh. "If we try the same thing three times in a row, I don't know if that's what Beck will expect or it isn't what he'll expect."

"You mean, he might think you'd never pull the same tactic thrice when it didn't work twice?"

Jeffrey nodded. "The point is the tactics *didn't* work, *twice.* Both times *von Scheer* got closer to the convoy, and we risked irreparable damage with nothing to show for it but fewer weapons left in our torpedo room and more injured crew. I can see some other choices, but I like all of them even less."

"Captain?"

"I prefer to keep my own counsel for now." Jeffrey felt terribly alone, brooding over crushing facts he couldn't escape.

"Sir, with respect, I need to understand your intentions."

Jeffrey hesitated. "Okay." He had other officers take the conn and fire control. He led Bell aft to his stateroom. They went in and shut the door.

Jeffrey glanced at himself in the dressing mirror. His eyes were sunken, with dark bags under them. His eyelids drooped, as if he'd been up late drinking or had a serious case of the flu.

Worse than either of those. I've been through two tactical nuclear skirmishes. My head hurts worse than from any imaginable hangover. My body aches worse than from any known flu.

"This'll be easiest for both of us if we make it quick. You know I had a private session with Hodgkiss before you picked me up?"

Bell nodded tentatively.

"He told me we're expendable in an equal exchange with *von Scheer* to protect the convoy. . . . More normal tactics now, with two ships and captains so evenly matched as we've seen, it's a toss-up who'd win. The odds are unacceptable that the winner would be Beck. If Beck wins, the convoy loses."

Bell looked at the deck and pursed his lips; Jeffrey proceeded. "A forced one-for-one exchange may be our only remaining alternative. We *can't* let him get past us. In a regular fight, the odds are fifty percent we're dead already anyway."

"Trade the remaining half, the odds we survive, for a hundred percent odds that Ernst Beck dies? Mutual *suicide?*"

"I hate to use that word. But basically, yes. A knowing self-sacrifice in the line of duty, for greater good . . . Sometimes the calculus of war is very cruel."

"There's just one thing. Your combat tactics in the past. They've been extremely risk oriented, sir. They sometimes bordered on suicide, or you intentionally mimicked suicide, to defeat an enemy captain emotionally and then tactically."

"Right. And we know Beck knows *that* firsthand."

"The danger is you're becoming predictable again."

"There's one important difference, XO. This time I mean it. This time I'm not bluffing. This time I think we really need to make the one-for-one exchange."

Bell went ashen. "Sacrifice the ship to save the convoy?"

"Those were my orders if I deemed it necessary in the last extreme. The Axis land offensive along the coast is a ticking time bomb. It's a whole other issue besides the *von Scheer*. We eliminate *von Scheer*, at least we halve the problems for our seniors in command. It'd be a damn shame to lose *Challenger*, but the consequences if we put our own survival first . . . If we lose the pocket, then the Germans and Boers own all of two continents, and they grab a quarter-million U.S. and coalition POWs. With nukes in play and escalating, we'd never dislodge the Axis then. America would have to sue for an armistice, a dishonorable peace on enemy terms. We can't let that happen, XO."

Jeffrey glanced at the picture of his parents on the wall. *I wish there was some way I could at least say good-bye.*

Jeffrey thought of that photo of Bell's wife and kids he'd seen him take from his wallet. Bell must be horribly torn inside. Never had the burden of command been so heavy. Jeffrey blinked and fought off the wetness that tried to gather in his eyes. Bell stared at the deck, lost in contemplation, regret etched on his face. At last he looked up and met Jeffrey's gaze heroically.

"Sir, if you offer a one-for-one exchange with Beck and act suicidal, he'll assume it's one of your tricks. You'll gain the ultimate advantage, because *we* know it *isn't* a trick. It's just, well, it's just an ironic way to choose to become unpredictable."

"Tragic, you mean." Jeffrey had trouble talking; there was

tightness in his throat. He thought of the 120 people in his crew he'd condemn to die. He thought of the widows and orphans they'd all leave behind.

Then he remembered the tens of thousands of people he'd be protecting, and the tens of millions he'd bring closer to release from under the boot of Axis tyranny. *One side of the balance scale vastly outweighs the other: the unforgiving calculus of war. . . . I know what I must do.*

"I'm—I'm with you all the way, sir. . . . What about our people?"

"They'll do what we tell them to do. *This* is private."

"We better get back to the control room, Captain."

"One more thing. I'll skip the corny crap; you know what I'd say and I don't need to say it. Just make sure, for everyone's morale, we don't go in there like we're on death row."

———

Jeffrey was surprised how, once he'd made the decision, his mind cleared and he felt much less morose.

Sure, now I know I have no worries beyond my next encounter with von Scheer. *No growing old and prostate trouble or arthritis, no more doing my income taxes, no endless hard work and competition as I try to climb the navy ladder. No more regrets I never married and never had kids. No on-and-off strange and strained relationship with Ilse Reebeck.*

No more dentist appointments squeezed in between long months at sea. No more weekly haircuts in spit-and-polish assignments in the Pentagon. No more anything at all.

Jeffrey's intercom light blinked.

"Captain."

"Radio room, sir. ELF message with our address." Each entire sentence was conveyed by a very short letter-group cipher. "Come to two-way floating-wire-antenna depth. Imperative, no recourse. It says that last thing twice."

Jeffrey acknowledged and hung up, then turned to Bell. "We're ordered to two-way floating-wire-antenna depth."

"Last-minute change of orders?" Bell asked.

Jeffrey could see the needfulness in Bell's eyes.

"We have to find out," he said noncommittally. His own emotions were swinging wildly too.

Jeffrey studied his charts. He gave Meltzer helm orders to bring *Challenger* shallow enough. Since he intended to remain acoustically stealthy, and also stay masked by the bulk of the seamounts around him, he told Meltzer to rise on autohover and pivot the ship to face south-southeast. This would aim *Challenger* into the Benguela Current, which ran up from South Africa.

Jeffrey told Meltzer to order just enough turns on the main pump-jet propulsor to hold the ship steady against the one-knot current. He told COB to play out the two-way floating wire antenna and let it stream behind the ship, into the current.

Jeffrey gave Bell the conn. He went into the crowded and dimly lit radio room.

The communications officer—the lieutenant (j.g.)—and the senior chief were in charge, as usual at battle stations.

"We have a message relayed from Norfolk, sir," the senior chief said. "Authenticators check out. Commander, Atlantic Fleet, wants to talk to you."

The lieutenant and senior chief seemed worried, and confused. *Challenger* was being ordered to break radio silence in the middle of a major battle. Jeffrey didn't like it either.

Have the people in Washington or Norfolk lost their minds? Has some unified commander or carrier-battle-group admiral with no grasp whatsoever of the realities of undersea warfare made an insistent but stupid request? Jeffrey felt disgusted, betrayed—but orders were orders, to the last.

He put on a communications headset and positioned the

lip mike. There was a switch on the wire, past the alligator clip meant to attach the wire to his belt. If he pressed that switch, he'd be live on the air, transmitting.

Jeffrey heard Admiral Hodgkiss's voice in his earphones. The voice was flat and scratchy from the encryption processes, and there was heavy background noise—hissing, sirens, buzz-saw sounds—because of attempted enemy jamming.

"*Challenger,* respond," Hodgkiss ordered impatiently.

Jeffrey pressed the switch. "This is *Challenger,* over."

"I'll make this fast and you aren't going to like it. The Axis land offensive to pinch off the pocket shoreline has begun. The Boers are making a strong drive up the coastal strip, with armor. Our exhausted troops will soon be overrun."

"Why do I need to know this, Admiral?"

"The situation is desperate. The convoy is taking a beating. The escorts and the air force are running very low on high-explosive land-attack cruise missiles, and from their current positions the transit times to launch and impact would be too late. I think the Boers know this too; that's why they're doing what they're doing where and when they're doing it. . . . With Lieutenant Reebeck's help, we've been following your tactics and actions, and watching the string of mushroom clouds between you and the *von Scheer.* We knew you'd be in the Valdivias now. Your location is ideal, you're much closer to the crisis area than our forces guarding the convoy from farther north. Your conventional-warhead ammo load-out is perfect. You are hereby ordered to conduct an immediate Tactical Tomahawk strike against the advancing Boer forces. . . . You're our best hope."

"Sir, this will completely compromise my stealth."

"The survival of the pocket has to come first. Warships exist to inflict loss on the enemy by taking risks. The Valdivias put these emergency coastal targets well within your Tomahawks' fifteen-hundred-mile maximum range."

"The *von Scheer* will hear my launch datum."

"The same way the convoy is lure for other U-boats, *Challenger* is bait for *von Scheer*. You absolutely *must* stop the *von Scheer*. Beck might not have figured out where you are. This will bring him to you, positively. I'm *trying* to do you a favor. . . . And we simply *can't* let Boer tanks break into the pocket."

"Yes, sir."

"I remind you that your ship is expendable in an equal exchange with *von Scheer* as a last resort. You have very little time to launch your Tomahawks and sink the *von Scheer*. Fail, and everything in this theater will come apart at the seams. Let that happen, we've lost the war. Good luck to you, Captain. Out."

Jeffrey went back to the control room. He ordered Meltzer to bring the ship to periscope depth. He told Bell to stand by for a Tactical Tomahawk land attack. The XO was speechless.

"Everything's happening together," Jeffrey said. "The pieces interlock. Convoy, *von Scheer*, land offensive—they're all part of one whole. For now we play network-centric warfare." Firing weapons using real-time targeting and sensor data from distant platforms.

Meltzer called out when *Challenger* reached periscope depth. Jeffrey ordered COB to raise a photonics mast; mounted above the optical scanners on the mast was a small passive signals-intercept antenna. Bell quickly reported no visual threats on imagery coming down from the mast; the outside world showed on monitors in the control room. Via the sigint antenna, the Electronic Support Measures room gathered data from the ether above the surface, and analyzed it with special receivers and software. New contacts came onto Jeffrey's tactical plot, showing the range and bearing to far-off hostile radars. *Safe enough.* Jeffrey told COB to raise the two-way high-baud-rate antenna.

The digital handshake was made with a command vessel in the convoy escort group, via satellite. Data began to pour

in. Detailed targeting information and route way points were
sent for every Tomahawk launch. The data gave precise
three-dimensional mapping of land topography each missile
should follow by using its built-in look-down radar. The data
also included visual and infrared video of the targets,
whether tanks or artillery batteries or formation-headquarter
vehicles or hasty bunkers. It all took many megabytes. . . .
The download was complete.

Jeffrey ordered the antenna mast lowered. Bell and Torelli
went to work with the combat-system specialists to preprogram each missile for the emergency strike. *Challenger* had
twelve high-explosive Tomahawks in small individual silos
in her vertical launching system, built into the forward ballast tanks. She had eight more in the torpedo room on the
holding racks. One Tomahawk was quickly loaded into each
torpedo tube. *Now comes the scary part.*

Jeffrey decided to fire the torpedo room's missiles first.
They could all be in the air in less than two minutes. They
would make a god-awful racket, and be utterly conspicuous
as they launched. Each was subsonic, as fast as a jumbo jet,
with a range of about fifteen hundred miles—this put Jeffrey
in striking distance of the African coast, even though *von
Scheer*'s faster but shorter-legged supersonic missiles
couldn't yet reach the convoy at sea.

Jeffrey issued orders to shoot. He watched a periscope
monitor. One by one, the missiles broached the surface, riding a solid-fuel booster rocket. The flame was bright yellow
against the blue sky. The exhaust smoke was dirty brown.
The rocket noise came through the hull.

The first cruise missile's wings unfolded. The rocket got
the missile up to speed, then dropped away. A jet engine in
the Tomahawk took over. Bell called out every step of each
launch. Soon all eight Tactical Tomahawks disappeared beyond the horizon. They could be redirected in flight by other
Allied platforms, such as fighter-bombers or recon drones or
satellites, via radio. Enemy units on the attack, on the move,

would thus have much more trouble decoying or spoofing the warhead final-homing sensors.

Now for the vertical-launch-system salvo.

The launch noise was louder now. One by one, twelve more Tomahawks rocketed into the air, dropped their spent boosters, and transitioned to level flight. When the last one was away, before it even reached the horizon, Jeffrey ordered the photonics mast lowered. Torelli and the fire controlmen expressed proud satisfaction in their work despite the risks involved: that everything should have gone just right, that twenty out of twenty missiles made fully successful takeoffs, said much about the Weapons Department's months of training and constant hard work on equipment maintenance. Jeffrey gave them a heartfelt "Well done." Cluster minelets, fuel-air explosives, bunker busters were all on their way to the enemy. *And now we reap what we have sown.* "Helm, emergency deep."

Meltzer acknowledged and down the ship went, fast. Jeffrey needed to dodge the supersonic cruise missiles he was sure would be inbound from *von Scheer*. Her passive sonars had to have heard those Tomahawk-missile launches. From the first launch, enough time had passed for Beck to order *von Scheer* shallow in relative safety, enter good firing solutions, and send nuclear missiles after Jeffrey at Mach 2.5. Those missiles would have plunging warheads, designed to survive a hard impact with the surface and go off underwater.

Then there was the unknown factor: In what form would retaliatory fire come from other Axis forces on land or at sea? Cruise missiles, subsonic or supersonic? Torpedoes from diesel U-boats?

Jeffrey ordered evasive maneuvers among the seamounts in desperation.

But nothing happened.

He realized the Axis forces must have other priorities, or were afraid they'd damage the *von Scheer* by mistake, or were simply out of position for an effective counterattack.

"Why didn't Beck shoot?" he asked Bell after a while.

"Protecting his stealth? Saving all his missiles for the convoy, maybe? Figures he can get us with Sea Lions alone?"

"He's an awfully confident SOB if he thinks that."

"There's one other factor, sir."

Jeffrey nodded. "Missiles could easily miss, and badly muddle acoustic conditions in this whole area. Beck wants good clear water for his final tangle with us."

CHAPTER 42

Ernst Beck listened in disbelief as Werner Haffner reported a series of cruise-missile launches directly ahead, shallow, amid the Valdivia Seamounts. "Is it some kind of trick?" he asked. "A new type of noisemaker, to act as a decoy?"

Haffner replayed the recording of the launch noises on the sonar speakers. Beck listened to each set of watery whooshes and rumbles, each booster rocket suddenly cut off, the diminishing whine of each jet engine as it receded into the distance, and the final hard splash as each discarded booster hit the surface at hundreds of knots. He counted a salvo of eight torpedo tube launches, then twelve vertical-launch-system shots.

An ELF radio message from Berlin soon confirmed that radio transmissions had been intercepted from the launch location right before the launches, on two different bands. One transmission suggested a two-way floating wire antenna in use. The other was a high-baud-rate antenna—presumably a handshake and an error check.

"I can't imagine any decoy that can do all that," Stissinger said.

"Concur," Beck said.

"Could it be a different submarine, not *Challenger*?" von Loringhoven asked.

"I don't think so. The Allies would give *Challenger* a clear playing field, to avoid sonar contact confusion or any risk of friendly fire. And we expected *Challenger* to be in the Valdivia Seamounts by now."

"Then why would they launch missiles when they must know we're very near?"

"Baron, I'm sure they were ordered to from above. The course of the missiles, toward the southern flank of the Allied pocket, suggests the land offensive has opened and the Allies are in dire straits. The convoy is still very far from landing any reinforcing troops or tanks or ammo."

"That's good to hear." Von Loringhoven smiled.

Beck nodded. "Let's take care of Jeffrey Fuller once and for all."

———

Beck glanced at his chart and at the gravimeter. The closest edge of the seamounts was almost in maximum Sea Lion range. But even at seventy-five knots, it would take a Sea Lion half an hour to cover those thirty-five sea miles from the *von Scheer*.

Beck decided to wait to get closer. He intended to use more off-board probes to feel around for *Challenger*. If that didn't turn up anything, he would fire Sea Lions from closer in, to force a response. The same seamount maze that *von Scheer* could use in order to disappear from Jeffrey Fuller might just as nicely serve as a way to box Fuller in.

Let me see. Eight Sea Lions approaching the Valdivias from different bearings . . . Yes, he'd have to shoot back or go to flank speed, or both, and either way I've got him.

I've got him because I hold one decisive advantage. Challenger *cuts her guidance wire to a weapon every time she shuts the outer torpedo tube door to reload.* Von Scheer *has*

*better tube architecture. We can fire repeated salvos through
a tube and not cut any wires. . . . Our fire-control systems
are designed to control more eels in the water at once than
we can even fit aboard. And our technicians are highly
trained in handling such a weapon-rich environment. It was
hard for Beck to not feel smug.*

"Torpedoes in the water," Haffner screamed. "Eight torpedoes in the water, inbound at our depth and pinging! New
sonar contact, submerged, flank-speed tonals, *Challenger*!
Challenger's relative bearing is steady, range is closing
fast!"

Beck watched his tactical screens in shock. Mark 88s
were coming at *von Scheer* in a wide fan spread, converging
from every point on the compass between east and northwest. The Mark 88s were attacking at seventy knots. *Challenger* was charging at Beck, right behind Fuller's torpedoes.

"Hydrophone effects!" Haffner yelled. "*More* torpedoes
in the water. One, two, three . . . six, *eight* more torpedoes in
the water, pinging!"

———

Jeffrey gripped his armrests as *Challenger* made her rough
flank-speed vibrations. The final death ride had begun.

His plan was very simple. Hodgkiss's orders pushed
Challenger into another odd reversal of roles: it was *she,* not
the *von Scheer,* who had needed to come shallow to conduct
a missile launch. Forced to make lemonade from this unexpected lemon, Jeffrey saw a way his Tomahawk strike could
help him trap the *von Scheer:* such a conspicuous datum, exactly as Admiral Hodgkiss said, would make very sure Ernst
Beck knew precisely where Jeffrey was. Rather than have to
think up some credible ploy of his own, the missile launch—
under the present strategic circumstances—was believable
by itself. The datum would strongly confirm Beck's likely
hunch about Jeffrey's next tactic, that *Challenger* would
make a stand amid the Valdivias. Beck's recollection of Jef-

frey's final gambit the last time they clashed, before Christmas, would work to Jeffrey's advantage now.

Then Jeffrey, his ultimate commitment already made in agreement with Bell, threw the whole rule book away. *Whether or not it's true, Ernst Beck, keep thinking I'm predictable and—as captains going head-to-head—you're better than me.*

The *von Scheer* had been moving slowly, for tactical caution and for stealth. *Challenger* built up full momentum, with her reactor pushed to 120 percent—by hiding just beyond the north side of the Walvis down on the very bottom. This gave Jeffrey good acoustic masking until he was ready to turn and rush up over the top of the ridge. He used the active pinging by his first fish to find the *von Scheer*, then ordered Meltzer to bear down on her relentlessly.

Now that he'd caught the *von Scheer* by surprise, his salvos of Mark 88s would force Beck south, out of the protection of the Walvis Ridge and into the Cape Basin, where there was nowhere for either ship to hide.

Jeffrey smiled. *To hell with caution. To hell with stealth. Just keep on believing I'm bluffing, Beck. And then I'll see you in hell.*

———

Beck ordered salvos of Sea Lions fired at *Challenger*'s torpedoes in self-defense. Even with the Mark 88 guidance wires cut, their active pinging would let them home on Beck's ship.

Beck fired other Sea Lions at *Challenger*, but Fuller already had more weapons in the water. Still Fuller charged right at *von Scheer*.

Beck ordered the pilot to turn the *von Scheer* south and make flank speed. He needed to buy space and time in order to give his defensive countershots enough room so they wouldn't take *von Scheer* with them when they blew.

Challenger's bow sphere went active. It must have been

set on maximum power. A strident screech pierced the water and the *von Scheer*'s hull. The noise sundered the air in the Zentrale, rising and falling in pitch, setting Beck's nerves on edge as if fingernails had dragged on a blackboard. It made it hard for him to think.

He wanted to retaliate, but *Challenger* was coming at him from behind, in that arc where his own bow sphere was useless.

Fuller has to have planned it this way.

He's using his active sonar as a psychological weapon.

The worst of it is, it's working.

The sonar noise was drowned out only when atomic torpedo warheads began to detonate. The *von Scheer* was kicked hard in the stern. Now Beck began to understand what Fuller and *Challenger* had gone through back in the mountain pass. Warhead concussions and fireball pulsations, bounces of shock fronts off the surface and the bottom and the ridge, pounded the *von Scheer* like the Roman god Vulcan working at his forge.

Still heading south into very deep water, Beck knew he had to continue to flee. The massive blasts and aftershocks did more than deafen his crew and damage his vessel. They blinded all his sonar arrays. It became impossible to know what was happening back behind the ship.

One leaker, *one* Mark 88 making it through Beck's Sea Lion defensive barrage, could catch the *von Scheer* and put her on the bottom in pieces.

Still the blasts and hammer blows went on. The port-side torpedo autoloader jammed. Broken parts sprayed flammable hydraulic fluid, and firefighters raced to smother the fluid with foam before it ignited.

Overhead light fixtures shattered. Cooling-water pipes cracked. Consoles went dark, and software systems crashed. The control room filled with the burned-plastic reek of smoldering electronics. The crewmen raced to don their emergency air-breathing masks. Beck and Stissinger glanced at each other worriedly through their masks. A chief helped the fumbling von Loringhoven get his mask on properly and plugged its hose into the overhead supply pipe.

"He's going to kill us all!" von Loringhoven shouted. His voice was muffled through his mask, and he was barely audible above the noise.

"No!" Beck yelled. "I know him! That's what he *wants* us to think!"

Von Scheer had reached flank speed, over forty knots. But Beck knew *Challenger* was ten or twelve knots faster, and he realized by now that her warhead yields had been upgraded to a full kiloton. *We're in a stern chase, and he's gaining . . . assuming he's still back there at all.*

Beck ordered the pilot to turn east, just enough so the port wide-aperture array could hear back the way *von Scheer* had come.

Haffner and his men worked hard to filter out the noise and clean up the signals. The hissing and whooshing of air-breathing masks, including Beck's own, added to the other noise and made the scene seem mad. But Beck knew the lunacy was all too real.

Beck waited for a report from Haffner. *Challenger* had probably turned away, to continue the cat-and-mouse stalking as the acoustic catastrophe outside the hull died down. If Fuller got too close, he wouldn't be able to fire at Beck—his own weapon explosions would fracture *Challenger*'s hull right along with *von Scheer*'s. Three kilometers down, Beck knew, Fuller's only high-explosive torpedoes, his ADCAPs, were far below their crush depths.

"Flank-speed tonals and flow noise, Captain! *Challenger* still in pursuit!"

Beck cursed; Fuller was gaining on him. He ordered another salvo of Sea Lions fired. They had to run out in front of the ship and then loop behind to reach their target. This cost him precious space and time.

More Mark 88s went off. They had been set on lower

yields, probably a tenth of a kiloton, to knock down Beck's Sea Lions without damaging *Challenger* too badly.

Beck ordered the pilot to turn slightly, again. Immediately Haffner reported eight Mark 88s in the water, tearing after *von Scheer* at almost thirty knots net closing speed. *Challenger* resumed her brain-shattering sonar harassment.

Beck ordered the pilot due south. He ordered Stissinger to launch eight more Sea Lions. Stissinger yelled that the work was badly slowed because of the jammed autoloader and slippery firefighting foam, laced with oily hydraulic fluid, that was sloshing on the torpedo-room deck.

Beck ordered Stissinger to the torpedo room to take charge and steady the men. More A-bombs went off. The intercom circuits failed; the phone talker said his line had gone dead; the on-board fiber-optic LAN went down. The lights dimmed suddenly—and Beck was out of touch with the rest of his ship.

Soon a messenger came forward from Engineering, breathless from running in a heavy compressed air pack. He said an auxiliary turbogenerator was on fire and the main propulsion-shaft packing gland was leaking. The engineer requested permission to use the main batteries to drive the firefighting pumps and bilge pumps aft. Beck knew that to draw current from the main propulsion turbogenerators would slow the ship, the last thing he could afford. And draining the battery ran the risk that *von Scheer* might not be able to restart her nuclear reactor, in case the reactor scrammed because of blast shock or an electrical problem.

Beck began to think he was losing the fight. Jeffrey Fuller seemed fixated on taking both crews to their graves.

And Beck realized that, from a strategic point of view, it did make sense, like an exchange of queens in a grandmaster chess tournament.

An even trade. The balance of power of undersea forces, Allied versus Axis, is maintained—at a lower level for both sides—but the crucial Allied relief convoy is spared my salvo of missiles.

It was then that Ernst Beck knew for sure that, this time, Jeffrey Fuller wasn't bluffing.

The lights were dim; smoke filled the air and everyone wore their air breather masks. *Challenger* had taken a terrible beating, but still the speed logs all read 53.3 knots—and still she was gaining on the *von Scheer*.

"New mechanical transients, Captain." Milgrom projected her voice through her mask. "Assess as firefighting and bilge pumps running on *von Scheer*."

Jeffrey turned to her. "Could it be faked?"

"Negative. We're in their baffles. They don't have an array to project false sounds in this direction."

"What else?"

"Heavy banging and clanking, sir, as if crewmen are making numerous hasty repairs."

"Very well, Sonar."

Jeffrey turned back to Bell. They met each other's eyes through their masks.

"We've clobbered them good," Bell said.

"They're still making flank speed," Jeffrey said. "They still have nuclear weapons aboard. They're a functional fighting machine, XO. Our duty is to destroy them. If we back off now, we regress to our previous tactics, trading blow for blow from a distance. We need to get so close Beck's own defensive Sea Lion blasts would kill his ship if our shots fail. That's our only formula for guaranteed success."

"Understood."

Even through the mask, he heard infinite sorrow and regret in his XO's voice. "Reload another full salvo of Mark Eighty-eights," Jeffrey ordered.

Ernst Beck racked his brain for a way to survive this suicide charge by *Challenger*. The fire and flooding in Engineering were serious, even if the influx past the main shaft packing gland was muted by the fail-safe design of the seals. *Von Scheer*'s torpedo room was still in bad shape, even with Stissinger down there helping.

Only a lucky shot would get through *Challenger*'s defensive Mark 88 salvos—and the range between the two ships was getting so short that soon a single atomic torpedo from either one would kill them both for sure. It seemed that only some other lucky stroke, such as a major breakdown on Fuller's ship, could save Beck's own.

And right now I don't feel lucky. Then Beck had a desperate idea.

"Pilot, forty degrees up bubble. Make your depth nine hundred meters."

Von Scheer's nose soared for the sky. If Beck looked straight ahead, he saw the deck and not the forward bulkhead now. He was forced back against his headrest, and the ship went shallower fast. Because she was neutrally buoyant, literally floating while down in the sea, this rise toward the surface required no fight against gravity: unlike an airplane, a submarine could pull up hard without sacrificing forward speed.

"*Von Scheer* has pulled a steep up-bubble," Bell yelled.

"Collision alarm! Forty degrees up-bubble, smartly!"

The alarm was a shipwide warning for the crew to grab something, fast. Meltzer pulled back hard on his wheel. The control-room deck became a hillside. Jeffrey and Bell were tilted steeply in their seats.

Bell turned to Jeffrey and yelled, "What is he doing?"

"Going shallow enough that his noisemakers and decoys work! And so his high-explosive Series Sixty-five torpedoes can function!"

"But we can stop his Sixty-fives with our antitorpedo rockets if we go shallow!"

"Maybe not! And shallow relieves his rate of flooding!"

Jeffrey tried to put himself in Ernst Beck's shoes.

What manner of man is this guy? How driven is Beck to succeed and survive? How far out on the risk-taking envelope is he truly willing to go to accomplish his mission? . . . How willing is he, really, to die?

"Sonar!"

"Captain!"

"Status of mechanical transients on *von Scheer*?"

"Bilge and firefighting pumps! Hammering noises, and power tools now!"

"He's leveling off!" Bell shouted.

Jeffrey eyed a depth gauge: 3,000 feet—900 meters. "Helm, zero bubble! Make your depth three thousand feet!"

Before he could shoot, *von Scheer* launched four more Sea Lions. They looped around and charged at *Challenger*.

Jeffrey ordered Bell to fire four Mark 88s to destroy them, and four more at the *von Scheer*.

"He's still full of fight, sir."

"So am I, but him I'm not so sure. Watch what happens now."

The four inbound Sea Lions spread out. Bell had his men direct one Mark 88 at each inbound weapon. Bell had the warheads set at lowest yield, and blew them barely outside lethal range of *Challenger*. Beck made defensive counter-shots too, also at low yield, and they detonated a split second after *Challenger*'s.

Challenger was punished hard. A wall of noise and bubble clouds stood between *Challenger* and *von Scheer*.

"Helm, all stop!"

"Sir?" Bell yelled as the ocean outside fulminated.

"We don't know what's on the other side of that curtain now! With noisemakers and decoys, and up-close conventional Series Sixty-five shots, and with all the atomic reverb as distracting background noise, he can start a game of hide-

and-seek and maybe get in a lethal sucker punch!" Jeffrey drew deep breaths inside his mask.

"Our job is to destroy him!"

"Our paramount job is protecting the convoy! If we stay on this side of the wall of new blasts, we do that! We've *already* done that! We go through there blind, with Beck having all these new options, we stand to lose both *Challenger* and the convoy!"

"But—"

"If he *wanted* to accept the double kill, he'd've doubled back at us and it would all be over by now! He wants to *live*. Nuclear blasts to blind us, then noisemakers, decoys, to get us all confused about his location and course and depth so he sneaks away!"

"And then goes after the convoy?"

"*No*. We can easily stay between him and the convoy! We're faster and we're less damaged! He could see and hear all that for himself! . . . We've forced him so far south he's much farther away from his missile launch point than before! He *has* to know he'll never get past us like this!"

"Why don't we keep shooting at him with nukes?"

"Every time we tried, it was a draw! We're low on ammo! We don't know what else we might face as we head for the convoy!" Then Jeffrey saw it with total clarity. "The Golden Bridge, XO!"

"*What?*"

"Sun-Tzu! He said always give your enemy a Golden Bridge, a way to back down but save face, so you avoid mutual annihilation!

"So where's the Golden Bridge? Who built it for whom?"

Jeffrey worked his keyboard and called up a nautical chart. "There!"

"*South Africa?*"

Jeffrey nodded. "He'll limp there for repairs! Think politically, XO! Beck built the bridge for *himself,* to cover his backside with Axis High Command! . . . We won the psychological fight! We've beaten him strategically! We've got him on the run, retreating for real!"

———

"Why are you turning away?" von Loringhoven demanded.

"Baron, our best choice now is to preserve *von Scheer* as a force-in-being. If we make it to the Boers' underground pens at Durban, we can put in for repairs. We can also get liquid hydrogen there. Remember, we still have those two Mach Eight missiles in our silos aft. They're useless without fuel. *With* fuel, they're unstoppable."

"But you're accepting defeat. You're letting *Challenger* and the convoy get away!"

"Baron, be realistic. Fuller *has* defeated us. We're a floating wreck and he knows it. He's faster, he has a better rate of fire because of the damage he inflicted, his ship is in much better shape because of the damage we *didn't* inflict or he repaired, and he's between us and the convoy. If we head north past the acoustic wall we forced him to help us make, we're dead for sure. If we stay on this side of the wall, he'll hesitate to pursue because he won't know what might smack him in the face."

Von Loringhoven was torn.

Beck went on. "We're in extremely deep water, ideal for antisubmarine detection. He planned that part too. Look at the nautical chart. Except for a couple of isolated seamounts which Fuller can easily send a brace of Mark Eighty-eights behind to flush us, there's no bottom terrain we can hide in most of the way from here to the Cape of Good Hope! He hasn't come through the bubble clouds yet because we're shallow, and we can use our non-nuclear Series Sixty-fives point-blank. . . . We need to get away from here while we can, before Allied planes with atomic depth-charges close in."

"Durban?"

"You can blame it all on the sabotage in Norway. The convoy might have gotten through intact enough in *spite* of our Mach Two point five missiles. By withdrawing and staying alive, we buy ourselves time. We also tie down major Allied forces, who have to stay on high alert simply because we exist. With two Mach *eight* missiles ready to fire, we'll be a far, far more dangerous threat than now. You can put all that in your report. Say we led Fuller on a merry chase all over the South Atlantic, and kept him from guarding the convoy directly. Say we allowed our other U-boats to get in closer and score more kills because *Challenger* couldn't be there. Say that from Durban we can threaten the Allies anywhere: the Atlantic, the Indian Ocean, the Pacific, the Arabian Gulf. Say we outsmarted HMS *Dreadnought* sneaking through the G-I-UK Gap. . . . Say anything you want to save our careers! *You're* the diplomat!"

———

Two hours later, Jeffrey had his ship sneak east of the lingering bubble clouds and noisemakers and the decoys that sounded like *von Scheer* but were too small to really be her. The air was clean enough now that the crew were out of their air breathing masks.

With no more off-board probes in stock, Milgrom and her people did a careful search on passive sonar. Nothing. Jeffrey ordered her to ping on maximum power, a final raucous screech to find Ernst Beck and say good-bye and really rub it in. *He's good, but I beat his ass decisively.*

Milgrom reported a faint detection on the real *von Scheer*. Beck was far to the south, and heading east to hide under Boer land-based air support.

"Looks like he used his Golden Bridge, Skipper," Bell said. "A bridge *you* forced him to build, and take." He grinned.

Jeffrey was too lost in thought to respond. He had believed that he would certainly die along with his ship and his crew; to suddenly find himself reprieved by his own tactical skill and cold psychological calculation was stunning. Jeffrey had faced mortality before, often in combat. But never had he believed he'd really have to make the chilling word *expendable* come true. . . . And yet it *hadn't* come true. . . .

This was no time to get maudlin or philosophical, or congratulate himself either.

"XO, we've got a convoy to help protect."

"Aye aye, Captain." Bell was crisp and lively now.

"Helm, make your course due north. Ahead full, make your depth ten thousand feet."

EPILOGUE

Two weeks later

The relief convoy made it more or less safely to shore, and the Central African pocket was strongly reinforced. The Axis land offensive was beaten back, and the German and Boer armies failed to come even close to linking up. And tactical nuclear fighting stayed confined far out at sea. *Challenger* was ordered to the Newport News Shipbuilding Yard, near Norfolk, Virginia, for repairs and upgrades.

Jeffrey, rested and formally dressed, now sat in front of Admiral Hodgkiss's desk, facing the admiral alone in his office. His patrol report sat on Hodgkiss's immaculate desktop.

Hodgkiss, that man of birdlike build and iron will, peered at Jeffrey intently. It was impossible to read his face, and this made Jeffrey very nervous.

"I wanted you all to myself," Hodgkiss stated, "before you start through the debriefing mill."

"Yes, sir," Jeffrey said politely. He fought to keep his voice even and neutral.

Hodgkiss picked up Jeffrey's patrol report, weighed it in

his hand, and dropped it back onto his desk. The report was long and heavy, and landed with a thump.

The thump seemed to echo in the pregnant silence that followed. Jeffrey waited for the admiral to speak, to pronounce sentence on him, to inform him of his fate.

"I told you to show some initiative, Captain, but good Lord!"

"Sir?"

"All your machinations in South America caused some heavy political flak in Washington. You practically started a war between State and SECDEF!" The Department of State and the secretary of defense.

"A war for my head, sir?"

"Still such a direct lad, aren't you?"

"I did what was needed at the time, Admiral."

"And then there's the matter of the *von Scheer*."

Jeffrey grew crestfallen.

"You performed brilliantly."

"Admiral?"

"I didn't tell you to go out there and commit suicide. I told you to protect the convoy at all costs. And you did. The convoy was protected from the *von Scheer* as a direct result of your actions. Case closed."

"But the *von Scheer* escaped."

"Yes. On the one hand, you've left yourself more work to do about that, down the road. On the other hand, you're still alive and your ship is intact to conduct that work. And on the third hand, *Challenger* will be ready for sea again well before the *von Scheer*. At least, that appears to be the situation from what your report here indicates and what our sources in South Africa say. Net net, you increased Allied options at Axis expense."

"Temporarily."

"Temporarily can be like forever in a war of this kind."

"Yes, Admiral."

"Anyway, to return to the main point, you've presented us all with a quandary."

"Sir?"

"Ultimately, bending or disobeying orders, or interpreting them too creatively or aggressively, is judged by the results, not the ways and means or good intentions."

"I understand, Admiral."

Jeffrey waited for the reprimand.

"You're being awarded the Defense Distinguished Service Medal."

"Admiral?"

"We considered another Medal of Honor, but it didn't seem quite the thing. That's more for individual valor, conspicuous gallantry above and beyond the call of duty, blood and gore and that sort of thing."

Jeffrey kept his mouth shut.

"What you did showed broader leadership and judgment talents. Good communication and negotiation skills with an important new coalition partner, handled superbly under adverse and trying circumstances. And outstanding weighing of your tactical versus strategic alternatives in an important part of one of history's most decisive fleet engagements."

"Sir, I don't know what to say."

Hodgkiss peered at Jeffrey again. "You thwarted the Axis plans in South America completely, and turned a skeptical neutral into a friend. You helped maintain the status quo on land in Central Africa, when we were really on the ropes there for a while. . . . The Axis have reached their high-water mark. The last few weeks were like Stalingrad, or El Alamein, or Midway, in World War Two. The enemy threw everything they had at us, everything, set the sneakiest traps they could possibly think to invent. And we held the line, and made significant gains, and gave the bastards a bloody nose they'll never forget. The tide is starting to turn, thanks in part to your efforts."

"Thank you, sir." It was all still sinking in. *The Defense Distinguished Service Medal.*

Hodgkiss's phone rang.

He picked it up and snapped, "I said we weren't to be disturbed!" Hodgkiss listened. "Of the Naval War College?" He listened again.

Hodgkiss handed the phone to Jeffrey. "It's for you. The president of the United States."

Jeffrey stood up and took the phone. He almost dropped it, he was so flustered. "Commander Fuller speaking, sir."

"Welcome home, Captain," that familiar voice said from the other end of the line.

"Thank you, sir."

"I'm sure you're busy with all sorts of navy things down there, but can you come up to Washington the day after tomorrow?"

"One moment please, sir." Jeffrey put his hand over the phone. "He wants to know if I can go to Washington in two days."

Hodgkiss glared at him. "When the president asks you something like that, you say *yes!* Worry about juggling your schedule later!"

Jeffrey spoke into the phone. "Yes, Mr. President."

"Good. We're having a ceremony I think you should be at. That SEAL lieutenant who worked for you, Felix Estabo, is getting the Medal of Honor. And our new ally, Getulio da Gama, will be in town talking cooperative tactics."

"I'd be delighted to attend, sir."

"I already spoke to the secretary of energy. He's passed my invitation on to your parents."

"My parents?"

"Of course. We'll kill a few birds with one stone, and you'll get your new medal all in the same show."

"Thank you, sir."

They ended the call.

"Nice reunion in D.C.?" Hodgkiss asked.

"You knew about this in advance?"

"The gist of it. I didn't think he'd actually call you in *person*. . . . By the way, Lieutenant Reebeck did a very good job here on my staff. I might pull strings and keep her for a while. But both of you have leave due. Take it while you can."

"Yes, Admiral." Jeffrey was still standing. Now his head was spinning.

Hodgkiss came from around his desk and shook Jeffrey's hand, then escorted him to the door. "She's in the building somewhere. Go say hello. She's very good at reading your mind long distance. But I think you ought to renew the acquaintance face-to-face, before the telepathic connection wears off."

"Yes, sir." Jeffrey started out the door.

"Oh, one other thing."

Jeffrey braced himself. When an admiral threw in "Oh, one other thing" at the end of a meeting, it was usually a humdinger.

"That was absolutely terrific, Captain, the way you convinced Ernst Beck you really intended to sacrifice yourself and your ship to destroy him. That fabulous subterfuge was the pivot point in your confrontation with *von Scheer*. Once you got him to swallow that, the rest was smooth sailing. Beautiful work." Hodgkiss ushered him out of his office, and went back in and shut the door.

Jeffrey stood there for a moment in the anteroom, thinking. The admiral's aide and yeoman glanced at him quickly. They were used to people leaving formal audiences with the Great Man with big things on their mind.

Then it struck Jeffrey. *Hodgkiss, SECDEF, the President, they think I was* bluffing *in the battle with Ernst Beck. . . . Nobody here realizes I* was *willing to die to sink the* von Scheer.

GLOSSARY

Acoustic intercept: a passive (listening only) sonar specifically designed to give warning when the submarine is "pinged" by an enemy active sonar. The latest version is the WLY-1.

Active out-of-phase emissions: a way to weaken the echo that an enemy sonar receives from a submarine's hull by actively emitting sound waves of the same frequency as the ping but exactly out of phase. The out-of-phase sound waves mix with and cancel those of the echoing ping.

ADCAP: Mark 48 Advanced Capability torpedo. A heavyweight, wire-guided, long-range torpedo used by American nuclear submarines. The Improved ADCAP has an even longer range, and an enhanced (and extremely capable) target homing sonar and software logic package.

AIP: Air Independent Propulsion. Refers to modern diesel submarines that have an additional power source besides the standard diesel engines and electric storage batteries. The AIP system allows quiet and long-endurance submerged cruising, without the need to snorkel for air because oxygen and fuel are carried aboard the vessel in special tanks. For example, the German Class 212 design uses fuel cells (see below) for air independent propulsion. Some other systems burn high-test hydrogen peroxide, which has its own oxygen built in chemically.

Alumina casing: an extremely strong hull material that is less dense than steel, declassified by the U.S. Navy after the Cold War. A multilayered composite foam matrix made from ceramic and metallic ingredients.

Ambient sonar: a form of active sonar that uses, instead of a submarine's pinging, the ambient noise of the surrounding ocean to catch reflections off a target. Noise sources can include surface wave-action sounds, the propulsion plants of other vessels (such as passing neutral merchant shipping), or biologics (sea life). Ambient sonar gives the advantages of actively pinging but without betraying a submarine's own presence. Advanced signal-processing algorithms and powerful on-board computers are needed to exploit ambient sonar effectively.

ARCI: Acoustic Rapid COTS Insertion; COTS stands for commercial-off-the-shelf. The latest software system designed for *Virginia*-class fast-attack submarines (see below). The ARCI system manages sonar, target tracking, weapons, and other data, through an on-board fiber-optic local-area network (LAN). (The ARCI replaces the older AN/BSY–1 systems of *Los Angeles*–class submarines, and the AN/BSY–2 of the newer *Seawolf*-class fast-attack subs.)

ASDS: Advanced SEAL Delivery System. A new battery-powered mini-submarine for the transport of SEALs (see below) from a parent nuclear submarine to the forward operational area and back, within a warm and dry shirtsleeves environment. This permits the SEALs to go into action well rested and free from hypothermia—real problems when the SEALs must swim great distances, or ride while using scuba gear on older free-flooding SEAL Delivery Vehicle underwater "scooters."

ASW: Antisubmarine warfare. The complex task of detecting, localizing, identifying, and tracking enemy submarines, in order to observe and protect against them in peacetime, and to avoid or destroy them in wartime.

Auxiliary maneuvering units: small propulsors at the bow and stern of a nuclear submarine, used to greatly enhance the vessel's maneuverability. First ordered for the USS *Jimmy Carter,* the third and last of the *Seawolf*-class SSNs (nuclear fast-attack submarines) to be constructed.

Bipolar sonar: a form of active sonar in which one vessel emits the ping while one or more other vessels listen for target echoes. This helps disguise the total number and location of friendly vessels present.

CACC: Command and Control Center. The modern name for a submarine's control room.

CAPTOR: a type of naval mine, placed on or moored to the seabed. Contains an encapsulated torpedo, which is released to home on the target.

CCD: Charge-Coupled Device. The electronic "eyes" used by low-light-level television, night-vision goggles, etc.

COB: Chief of the Boat (pronounced "cob"). The most senior enlisted man on a submarine, usually a master chief. Responsible for crew discipline, and for proper control of ship buoyancy and trim at battle stations, among many other duties.

Deep scattering layer: a diffuse layer of biologics (marine life) present in many parts of the world's oceans, which

causes scattering and absorption of sound. This can have
tactical significance to undersea warfare forces by obscuring
passive sonar contacts and causing false active sonar target
returns. The layer's local depth, thickness, and scattering
strength are known to vary by many factors, including one's
location on the globe, the sound frequency being observed,
the season of the year, and the hour of the day. The deep
scattering layer is typically several hundred feet thick, and
lies somewhere between one thousand and two thousand feet
of depth during daylight, migrating shallower at night.

Deep sound channel: a thick layer within the deep ocean in
which sound travels great distances with little signal loss.
The core (axis) of this layer is formed where seawater stops
getting colder with increasing depth (the bottom of the thermocline, see below) and water temperature then remains at a
constant just above freezing (the bottom isothermal zone,
see below). Because of the way sound waves diffract (bend)
in response to temperature and pressure, noises in the deep
sound channel are concentrated and propagate for many
miles without loss to surface scattering or seafloor absorption. Typically the deep sound channel is strongest between
depths of about three thousand and seven thousand feet.

ELF: Extremely Low Frequency. A form of radio that is capable of penetrating seawater, used to communicate (one
way only) from a huge shore transmitter installation to submerged submarines. A disadvantage of ELF is that its data
rate is extremely slow, only a few bits per minute.

EMBT blow: Emergency Main Ballast Tank blow. A procedure to quickly introduce large amounts of compressed air
(or fumes from burning hydrazine) into the ballast tanks in
order to bring a submerged submarine to the surface as rapidly as possible. If the submarine still has propulsion power,
it will also try to drive up to the surface using its control
planes (called planing up).

EMCON: Emissions Control. Radio silence; also applies to radar, sonar, laser, or other emissions that could give away a vessel's presence.

EMP: Electromagnetic Pulse. A sudden, strong electrical current induced by a nuclear explosion. This will destroy unshielded electrical and electronic equipment and ruin radio reception. There are two forms of EMP, one caused by very high-altitude nuclear explosions, the other by ones close to the ground. (Mid-altitude bursts do not create an EMP.) Nonnuclear EMP devices, a form of modern nonlethal weapon, produce a similar effect locally by vaporizing clusters of tungsten filaments using a high-voltage firing charge. This generates a burst of hard X rays, which are focused by a depleted-uranium reflector to strip electrons from atoms in the targeted area, creating the destructive EMP electrical current. Other nonnuclear EMP weapons use bursts of microwaves emitted from special antennas.

ESGN: the latest submarine inertial navigation system (see *INS* below). Replaces the older SINS (Ship's Inertial Navigation System).

Fathom: a measure of water depth equal to six feet. For instance, one hundred fathoms equals six hundred feet.

Firing solution: exact (or best estimate) information on an enemy target's location, course, and speed, and depth or altitude if applicable. A good firing solution is needed to preprogram the guidance system of a missile or torpedo so that the weapon won't miss a moving target.

Floating wire antenna: a long, buoyant antenna wire that is trailed just below the surface by a submerged submarine, for stealth. Such an antenna can receive data at a higher rate (higher baud rate) than ELF radio (see above). Recently, floating-wire-antenna technology has been developed to the point where the wire is able to transmit as well as receive, allowing two-way radio communication while the submarine is completely submerged. (To transmit or receive radio data at a very high baud rate, such as live video imagery of a target, the submarine must come to periscope depth and raise an antenna mast out of the water—which might compromise stealth.)

Frequency agile: a means of avoiding enemy interception and jamming, by very rapidly varying the frequency used by a transmitter and receiver. May apply to radio or to underwater acoustic communications (see *gertrude* below).

Frequency power spectrum: a display of the relative strength of noise being detected by a sonar array at different sound frequencies. Such data can be valuable in locating and identifying passive sonar contacts, especially when tonals (see below) stand out within the display.

Frigate: a type of oceangoing warship smaller than a destroyer.

Fuel cell: a system for quietly producing electricity, for example to drive a submarine's main propulsion motors while submerged. Hydrogen and oxygen are combined in a chemical reaction chamber as the "fuels." The by-products, besides electricity, are water and heat.

Gertrude: underwater telephone. Original systems simply transmitted voice directly with the aid of transducers (active sonar emitters; i.e., underwater loudspeakers) and were notorious for short range and poor intelligibility. Modern undersea acoustic communication systems translate the message into digital high-frequency active sonar pulses, which can be frequency agile for security (see above). Data rates well over one thousand bits per second, over ranges up to thirty nautical miles, can be achieved routinely.

Halocline: an area of the ocean where salt concentration changes, either horizontally or vertically. Has important effects on sonar propagation and on a submarine's buoyancy.

Hertz (or Hz): cycles per second; applies to sound frequency, radio frequency, or alternating electrical current (AC).

Hole-in-ocean sonar: a form of passive (listening-only) sonar that detects a target by how it blocks ambient ocean sounds from farther off. In effect, hole-in-ocean sonar uses an enemy submarine's own quieting against it.

Hydrophone: an underwater sound listening device. In essence, a hydrophone is a special microphone placed in the water. The signals received by hydrophones are the raw input to passive (listening-only) sonar systems. Signal-processing computer algorithms then continually analyze this raw data to produce meaningful tactical information—such as a firing solution (see above).

INS: Inertial Navigation System. A system for accurately estimating one's position, based on accelerometers that determine from moment to moment in what direction one has traveled, and at what speed.

Instant ranging: a capability of the new wide-aperture array sonar systems (see below). Because each wide-aperture array is mounted rigidly along one side of the submarine's hull, sophisticated signal processing can be performed to "focus" the hydrophones at different ranges from the ship. The target needs to lie somewhere on the beam of the ship (i.e., to either side) for this to work well.

IR: infrared; refers to systems that make it possible to see in the dark or detect enemy targets by the heat that objects give off or reflect.

ISLMM: Improved Submarine-Launched Mobile Mine. A new type of mine weapon for American submarines, based on modified Mark 48 torpedoes and launched through a torpedo tube. Each ISLMM carries two mine warheads that can be dropped separately. The ISLMM's course can be programmed with way points (course changes) so that complex coastal terrain can be navigated by the weapon, and/or a minefield can be created by several ISLMMs with optimum layout of the warheads.

Isothermal: a layer of ocean in which the temperature is very constant with depth. One example is the bottom isothermal zone, where water temperature is just above freezing, usually beginning a few thousand feet down. Other examples are a surface layer in the tropics after a storm, when wave action has mixed the water to a constant warm temperature; and a surface layer near the Arctic or Antarctic in the winter, when cold air and floating ice have chilled the sea to near the freezing point.

Kampfschwimmer: German Navy "frogman" combat swimmers. The equivalent of U.S. Navy SEALs and the Royal Navy's Special Boat Squadron commandos. (In the German language, the word *kampfschwimmer* is both singular and plural.)

KT: kiloton; a measure of power for tactical nuclear weapons. One kiloton equals the explosive force of one thousand tons of TNT.

LIDAR: Light Direction and Ranging. Like radar, but uses laser beams instead of radio waves. Undersea LIDAR uses blue-green lasers, because that color penetrates seawater to the greatest distance.

Littoral: a shallow or near-shore area of the ocean. Littoral areas present complex sonar conditions because of bottom and side terrain reflections, and the high level of noise from coastal shipping, oil-drilling platforms, land-based heavy industry, etc.

LMRS: Long-term Mine Reconnaissance System: A remote-controlled self-propelled probe vehicle, launched from a torpedo tube and operated by the parent submarine. The LMRS is designed to detect and map enemy minefields or other undersea obstructions, and is equipped with forward and side-scanning sonars and other sensors. Each LMRS is retrievable and reusable.

MAD: Magnetic Anomaly Detection. A means for detecting an enemy submarine by observing its effect on the always-present magnetic field of the earth. Iron anywhere within the submarine (even if its hull is nonferrous or de-Gaussed) will distort local magnetic field lines, and this can be picked up by sensitive magnetometers in the MAD equipment. Effective only at fairly short ranges, often used by low-flying maritime patrol aircraft. Some naval mine detonators also use a form of MAD by waiting to sense the magnetic field of a passing ship or submarine.

Megaton: a measure of power for strategic nuclear weapons. One megaton equals the explosive force of one million tons of TNT. (A megaton also equals one thousand kilotons.)

METOC: Meteorology and Oceanography Command. The part of the U.S. Navy that is responsible for providing weather and oceanographic data, and accompanying tactical assessments and recommendations, to the navy's operating fleets. METOC maintains a network of centers around the world to gather, analyze, interpret, and distribute this information.

Naval Submarine League (NSL): A professional association for submariners and submarine supporters. See their Web site, www.navalsubleague.com.

Network-centric warfare: a new approach to war fighting in which all formations and commanders share a common tactical and strategic picture through real-time digital data links. Every platform or node, such as a ship, aircraft, submarine, Marine Corps or army squad, or SEAL team, gathers and shares information on friendly and enemy locations and movements. Weapons, such as a cruise missile, might be fired by one platform and redirected in flight toward a fleeting target of opportunity by another platform, using information relayed by yet other platforms—including unmanned reconnaissance drones. Network-centric warfare promises to revolutionize command, control, communications, and intelligence, and greatly leverage the combat power of all friendly units while minimizing collateral damage.

NOAA: National Oceanic and Atmospheric Administration. Part of the Department of Commerce, responsible for studying oceanography and weather phenomena.

Ocean Interface Hull Module: part of a submarine's hull that includes large internal "hangar space" for weapons and off-board vehicles, to avoid size limits forced by torpedo-tube diameter. (To carry large objects such as an ASDS minisub externally creates serious hydrodynamic drag, reducing a submarine's speed and increasing its flow noise.) The first Ocean Interface has been ordered as part of the design of the USS *Jimmy Carter,* the last of the three *Seawolf*-class SSNs to be constructed.

PAL: Permissive Action Lock. Procedures and devices used to prevent the unauthorized use of nuclear weapons.

Photonics mast: the modern replacement for the traditional optical periscope. The first will be installed in the USS *Virginia* (see below). The photonics mast uses electronic imaging sensors, sends the data via thin electrical or fiber-optic cables, and displays the output on large high-definition TV screens in the control room. The photonics mast is "non-hull-penetrating," an important advantage over older 'scopes with their long, straight, thick tubes that must be able to move up and down and rotate.

Piezo rubber: a hull coating that uses rubber embedded with materials that expand and contract in response to varying electrical currents. This permits piezo-rubber tiles to be used to help suppress both a submarine's self-noise and echoes from enemy active sonar (see *active out-of-phase emissions*, above).

Pump jet: a main propulsor for nuclear submarines that replaces the traditional screw propeller. A pump jet is a system of stator and rotor turbine blades within a cowling. (The rotors are turned by the main propulsion shaft, the same way the screw propeller's shaft would be turned.) Good pump-jet designs are quieter and more efficient than screw propellers, producing less cavitation noise and less wake turbulence.

Quieting: design techniques and technologies used to minimize the amount of noise a submarine transmits into the surrounding water. Since quieting is crucial to stealth, the most advanced methods are highly classified. Techniques include placing internal decks on "rafts" that float on springs or flexible pivot joints in order to isolate internal sounds and vibrations from the outer hull. Equipment may also be mounted on noise-insulating materials, such as rubber blocks or bladders filled with oil. Quieting can also include disciplined behavior by the submarine's crew, for instance not slamming hatches, not dropping tools on the deck, and not operating some devices or equipment at all when quieting is most essential.

Radiac: Radiation Indications and Control. A device for measuring radioactivity, such as a Geiger counter. There are several kinds of radiac, depending on whether alpha, beta, or gamma radiation, or a combination, is being measured.

ROEs: Rules of Engagement. Formal procedures and conditions for determining exactly when weapons (including "special weapons" such as nuclear devices) may be fired at an enemy.

SEAL: Sea Air Land. U.S. Navy Special Warfare commandos. (The equivalent in the Royal Navy is the SBS, Special Boat Squadron.)

7MC: a dedicated intercom line to the Maneuvering Department, where a nuclear submarine's speed is controlled by a combination of reactor-control-rod and main steam-throttle settings.

Sonobuoy: a small active ("pinging") or passive (listening-only) sonar detector, usually dropped in patterns (clusters) from an aircraft or a helicopter. The sonobuoys transmit their data to the aircraft by a radio link. The aircraft might have on-board equipment to analyze this data, or it might relay the data to a surface warship for detailed analysis. (The aircraft will also carry torpedoes or depth charges in order to be able to attack any enemy submarines that its sonobuoys detect.) Some types of sonobuoy are able to operate down to a depth of sixteen thousand feet.

SOSUS: Sound Surveillance System. The network of undersea hydrophone complexes installed by the U.S. Navy and used during the Cold War to monitor Soviet submarine movements (among other things). Now SOSUS refers generically to fixed-installation hydrophone lines used to monitor activities on and under the sea. The Advanced Deployable System (ADS) is one example: disposable modularized listening gear designed for rapid emplacement in a forward operating area. After the Cold War, some SOSUS data has been declassified, proving of immense value for oceanographic and environmental research.

Sound-ray traces: a display of the paths in which spreading sound waves will be bent and reflected underwater in a particular area. Ray traces are estimates, based upon calculations using information on local ocean temperature and salinity at different depths. Sound-ray trace information can be used to help a submarine find the best place to hide from enemy detection platforms. In addition, this information can be applied in interpreting noises detected coming through the water from an enemy submarine in order to help determine the hostile sound source's likely bearing, range, depth, and even its course and speed.

Sound short: a failure of a submarine's quieting (see above), in which noise from within the sub is transmitted into the surrounding sea. Sound shorts are very serious matters, since they can ruin stealth and lead to detection and attack by an enemy. A submarine's sonars are able to check it for sound shorts, and if any are found the crew will give a priority to correcting them. Often this can be done by repairing or replacing faulty quieting gear, or if necessary by switching off the machinery that is causing the unwanted noise—although the latter may put the submarine at a grave tactical disadvantage, if the errant machinery is needed for full war-fighting readiness.

SSGN: a type of nuclear submarine designed or adapted for the primary purpose of launching cruise missiles, which tend to follow a level flight path through the air to their target. An SSGN is distinct from an SSBN, which launches strategic (hydrogen-bomb) ballistic missiles, following a very high "lobbing" trajectory that leaves and then reenters earth's atmosphere. Because cruise missiles tend to be smaller than ballistic missiles, an SSGN is able to carry a larger number of separate missiles than an SSBN of the same overall size. Note, however, that since ballistic missiles are typically "MIRVed"—i.e., equipped with multiple independently targeted reentry vehicles—the total number of warheads on an SSBN and SSGN may be comparable; also, an SSBN's ballistic missiles can be equipped with high-explosive warheads instead of nuclear warheads. (A fast-attack submarine, or SSN, can be thought of as serving as a part-time SSGN, to the extent that some SSN classes have vertical launching systems for cruise missiles and/or are able to fire cruise missiles through their torpedo tubes.)

Subtropical convergence: the area in the South Atlantic Ocean where currents of warmer water from near the equator meet and clash with other currents of colder water from near the Antarctic. The result is a zone of unpredictable and confusing sonar conditions. The subtropical convergence does not extend across the South Atlantic as a well-defined straight line, but rather is a broad area that snakes across different latitudes in different places and varies over time.

Thermocline: the region of the sea in which temperature gradually declines with depth. Typically the thermocline begins at a few hundred feet and extends down to a few thousand feet, where the bottom isothermal zone is reached (see above).

TMA: Target Motion Analysis. The use of data on an enemy vessel's position over time relative to one's own ship in order to derive a complete firing solution (see above). TMA by passive sonar alone, using only relative bearings to the target over time—and instant ranging data where available (see above)—is very important in undersea warfare.

Tonal: sound given off at a single frequency, similar to a pure musical "tone" or note. Tonals are important in detecting and identifying passive sonar contacts. This is because different equipment—and thus different classes of friendly and enemy submarines carrying that equipment—have unique sets of frequencies at which they emit tonals. One example of the source of a tonal might be an item of equipment that rotates at a particular rate per second, such as a turbogenerator, a reactor cooling-water circulation pump, or even a food blender in the ship's galley (kitchen).

Towed array: a long cable equipped with hydrophones (see above) trailed behind a submarine. Towed arrays can also be used by surface warships. The towed array has two advantages: Because it lies behind the submarine's stern, aft of self-noise from the propulsion plant, it is able to listen in directions where the submarine's on-hull sonars are "blind." Also, because the towed array is very long (as much as a mile), it is able to detect very long-wavelength (very low-frequency) sounds—which smaller, on-hull, hydrophone arrays may miss completely. Recently, *active* towed arrays are being introduced. These are able to "ping" as well as listen at very low frequencies, which has significant tactical advantages in some sonar and terrain conditions. The next planned advance is a towed array with three or more separate parallel lines in which the individual hydrophones use fiber-optic coils and lasers. Tiny changes in the behavior of the laser light will result when the coils are influenced by sound waves in the surrounding ocean. Analysis of such data promises to greatly increase the sensitivity of the array to the presence of enemy submarines and other targets. (When not in use, the towed array is retracted by winches in the submarine's hull. Towed arrays often need to be retracted if the submarine is in close proximity to bottom terrain or surface shipping, or if the submarine intends to move at high speed.)

Virginia **class:** the latest class of nuclear-propelled fast-attack submarines (SSNs) being constructed for the United States Navy, to follow the *Seawolf* class. The first, the USS *Virginia*, is due to be commissioned in 2004. (Post–Cold War, some SSNs have been named for states, since construction of *Ohio*-class Trident missile "boomers" has been halted.)

Wide-aperture array: a sonar system introduced with the USS *Seawolf* in the mid-1990s, distinct from and in addition to the bow sphere, towed arrays, and forward hull array of the Cold War's *Los Angeles*–class SSNs. Each submarine so equipped actually has two wide-aperture arrays, one along each side of the hull. Each array consists of three separate rectangular hydrophone complexes. Powerful signal-processing algorithms allow sophisticated analysis of incoming passive sonar data. This includes instant ranging (see above).

If you enjoyed **TIDAL RIP,** you'll love
STRAITS OF POWER,
Joe Buff's new novel of nuclear war
under the waves, coming soon
in hardcover from William Morrow.
For a sneak preview, turn the page!

Chapter 1

At one small part of the sprawling U.S. Navy base in Norfolk, Virginia, Commander Jeffrey Fuller stood there waiting in the warmth on the concrete tarmac. He looked up at the very blue sky. Jeffrey told himself today was a good day for flying: sunny with almost no haze, easterly breeze at maybe ten knots, and a scattering of high, whispy, bright white clouds. Noise from helicopters taking off and landing assaulted his ears. Another helo sat on a pad in front of him, as its powerful twin turbine engines idled. The main rotors above the Seahawk's fuselage, over the passenger compartment, turned just fast enough to be hypnotic. Jeffrey, badly overworked for much too long, had to fight to not stare at those blades and abandon himself to be mesmerized, and let his mind go blank and drift away. It seemed so tempting. But the intoxicating stink of sweet-yet-choking helo exhaust fumes, mixed with the subtler smell of the seashore wafting from the mouth of Chesapeake Bay, stirred his gut instincts for combat, and helped him stay alert and on his toes.

Jeffrey glanced at his watch, then at the cockpit of the

matte gray Seahawk. He could see the pilot and copilot sitting side by side, running through their checklists. The helo should be ready for boarding any minute now.

Jeffrey was glad. Ever since he woke up before dawn this morning, for some reason he felt the loneliness and burdens of command with added poignancy. This seemed a warning of bad things to come, things he knew in his bones would happen soon—Jeffrey had learned to trust his sixth sense for danger and crisis through unforgiving, unforgettable experience. The ceramic-hulled nuclear submarine of which he was captain, USS *Challenger,* sat in a heavily defended covered dry-dock at the Northrop Grumman Newport News Shipbuilding yards not far from here, northwest across the James River. For several weeks now she'd been laid up and vulnerable, undergoing repairs and systems upgrades after Jeffrey's latest hard-fought battle, thousands of miles away, deep under the sea.

Jeffrey's rather young and clean-cut crew were working on *Challenger* around the clock, side by side with the shipyard's gruff and gritty men and women who applied their various union craft skills to Jeffrey's ship with a vengeance. Vengeance of a different sort was on everyone's mind, because this terrible war against the Berlin-Boer Axis—tactical nuclear war at sea that began with a brutal surprise attack and constantly threatened to escalate—was by no stretch of the imagination close to being won. Atomic explosions were devastating the Atlantic Ocean ecosystem, and stale fallout from the small warheads used did sometimes drift to settle in local hot spots even well inland. Gas mask satchels were mandatory for all persons east of the Mississippi; radiation detectors were everywhere. Some reservoirs, too contaminated, were closed until further notice; entire industries, including East Coast beach resorts, were wiped out, even as other industries thrived with the war. Only price controls, and price supports, prevented rampant hyperinflation or a regional real-estate market crash.

It all seems so unfair, but tyrants and madmen striking at America are never fair.

Then a messenger arrived, just as Jeffrey sat down to go over today's main progress goals with his officers. And here he was, thanks to that message, not in the wardroom on *Challenger* but standing by a helipad at barely 0800—8 a.m. Taken from his ship and crew on short notice, and ordered at once to the Pentagon without even the slightest hint why, left Jeffrey distracted and concerned. *My ship is my life. My crew is my surrogate family, and I'm the father figure to them all.* Jeffrey was a man who liked control of his destiny, and was addicted to adrenaline. *Deny me these and I'm almost half empty inside.* The ribbons on Jeffrey's khaki short-sleeved uniform shirt did little to console him. *I live for the present and future, not for the past.*

Even thoughts of his recent Medal of Honor, and his brand new Defense Distinguished Service Medal, couldn't disperse Jeffrey's mental funk. Strong as they were in traditions and symbolism, the ribbons were merely small strips of metal and cloth. They paled compared to the draining things that Jeffrey went through, and the awful things he'd had to do, to earn these highest awards from a thankful nation. The medals grated on Jeffrey's conscience too, because they made him be a hero and a national celebrity, but said nothing of those who'd been killed under his leadership. Jeffrey sometimes felt haunted by the faces of the dead; he had a keen sense of cause and effect, of the linkage between his actions and their consequences, and he remembered clearly every person who died while doing what he as captain had told them to do.

Who am I kidding? Part of me is stuck in the past.

Jeffrey perked up when a crew chief came out of the back of the Seahawk, carrying a bundle of head protection gear and inflatable life jackets. He handed them to Jeffrey and the half dozen others waiting a safe distance from the aircraft. Jeffrey put on the life jacket, zippered closed the front, and

fastened the straps around his waist and drew them snug. He
unfolded the collapsible helmet, with its built-in sound suppression earcups, and placed the thing on his head. He
closed the buckle of the chin strap and pulled that snug too.
He donned the big padded eye goggles last, and then picked
up his briefcase and his gas mask bag.

Conversation was impossible now. The crew chief told his
passengers what to do by using hand signals. The other passengers, junior officers and chiefs who were strangers to Jeffrey, seemed to know the routine. That Jeffrey was so much
more senior than all the others reinforced his suspicion that
something important was threatening. Otherwise, he wouldn't
be riding the shuttle in daylight—senior officers normally
used the Pentagon-bound helo after dark, for added personal
safety.

By privilege of rank and standard Navy etiquette, Jeffrey
got in last. He took the seat reserved for him among several
running down the center of the fuselage, facing sideways, so
he could look out a window. He fastened his seat belt, then
pulled the other straps over his shoulders and slid them into
their clips in the belt buckle. He shifted to get more comfortable on the black vinyl sheets that supported his back
and his bottom, then pulled the straps a bit tighter.

The crew chief stowed the luggage under a cargo net in
one corner. His assistant slid the door closed, and locked it.
The crew chief came around and checked everyone very
carefully. He pulled Jeffrey's harness straps uncomfortably
tight, then gave a firm tug to the chin strap of his cranial helmet. Jeffrey and the crew chief made quick eye contact. The
Navy didn't salute indoors, but the chief had seen Jeffrey's
ribbons. The chief gave Jeffrey a look of acknowledgment,
and extra respect. Jeffrey, never more rank-conscious than
he needed to be, returned the look and gave a quick nod. The
chief's eyes showed a special hardness that couldn't be
faked, and the gauntness of premature aging that no one
could hide, which proved he'd been in combat in this war. In
comparison, the other passengers looked too fresh-faced,

their eyes were in an indefinable way much too naive, for them to be combat veterans.

Couriers, perhaps, or some other essential administrative jobs.

Jeffrey felt heavy vibrations through the deck and through his backside. The muffled noises getting through his hearing protection grew louder and deeper in pitch. Outside, the ground began to recede quickly, then the Seahawk put its nose down so the main rotors could dig into the air and grab more speed. The helo turned west, inland.

Immediately, two other helos closed in on the Seahawk, one from port and one from starboard. Jeffrey knew these were the shuttle's armed escorts. They were Apache Longbows, two-man army combat choppers. Jeffrey saw the clusters of air-to-ground rockets, in big pods on both sides of each Apache. He watched the chin-mounted Gatling gun each Apache also bore, as the 30mm barrels swiveled around, slaved to sights on the helmets worn by the gunners.

Jeffrey knew these escorted shuttle flights were necessary. The Axis had assassination squads operating inside the U.S.—almost certainly pre-positioned, and pre-equipped, secretly during the long-term conspiracy that led to the war. Some of the teams were former Russian Special Forces, Spetznaz, now in the pay of the Germans and willing to die to accomplish their tasks.

Jeffrey knew this because he'd almost died himself in a bloody ambush on the streets of Washington, D.C., at the hands of one such hit team. It was that brazen attack which made public transportation, or really any ground transportation, too risky for military people with high-value expertise or information. The schedule of the helo shuttles varied randomly, and their flight paths varied as well, to stay unpredictable. The new arrangements were smart, Jeffrey thought, but they couldn't erase the shock the whole nation felt when the Capital was defiled again, with innocent people killed. And it wasn't lost on Jeffrey that these constant escorted military shuttles all around the country were burning up extra precious aviation fuel. Civilian gasoline rationing was already bad enough, with America's overseas shipping lanes—and supplies of foreign oil and natural gas—so insecure due to the U-boat threat.

Slowly, slowly, but surely, the Axis draws the noose around us tighter. . . . Even the battles they lose, they claim for themselves as victories, and half the world believes their shrewd and amoral propaganda.

Jeffrey forced himself to relax. He was well protected now. Depending on the route the helos took, he should be landing at the Pentagon in well under two hours.

Then I'll find out what the heck they want me for.

The passenger compartment smelled of lubricants, plastic, and warm electronics; there was no solid bulkhead between the passengers and where the pilot and copilot sat, and Jeffrey could see the back of their heads if he craned his neck to the right. The compartment was stuffy from the aircraft sitting in the sun before, so the crew chief's assistant slid open a couple of windows. A pleasant, slightly humid breeze came in.

Through his earcups, and above the noises of flight, Jeffrey noticed a strange new sound. He lifted one earcup, and even over the deafening turbine engines mounted not far beyond his head, he heard a nerve-jarring siren noise in the cockpit. The crew chief and the assistant, whose flight helmets—unlike the passengers'—were equipped with intercoms, seemed genuinely agitated. They began to stare very nervously out both flanks of the aircraft.

The Seahawk banked hard left and almost stood on its side, buffeting Jeffrey in his harness. The helo leveled off but kept turning and stood on its other side, wrenching his neck so he almost got whiplash. Both engines were straining now, and the siren noise continued. Jeffrey was afraid they'd had a control failure and would crash. Then Jeffrey heard thumps, and felt bangs. *Oh God. We're disintegrating in mid-air.*

The Seahawk turned hard left, again. It fought for altitude on maximum power. Through the window Jeffrey saw multiple suns, burning hot and almost blinding. Then he saw something much worse.

Two small black dots were approaching the Seahawk fast, riding bright red rocket plumes that left billowing trails of brownish smoke. Jeffrey understood now those little suns were infrared decoy flares. The Seahawk was under attack from shoulder-fired anti-aircraft missiles. There were Axis assassination teams at work somewhere on the ground.

Either they learned my helo's flight plan, which wasn't set till the last minute, or they were camped there for a while, knowing they'd have a shuttle pass within range eventually—and they just got lucky.

Jeffrey felt more thumps and bangs. His heart was pounding and his hands shook badly, even though his mind was crystal clear. The crew chief and his assistant gestured for everyone to fold their arms across their chests and grab the straps of their shoulder harnesses—to steady themselves and avoid arms flailing everywhere, as the pilot and copilot pulled more violent evasive maneuvers. Jeffrey did what he was told, and it helped, but not a lot.

He hated feeling so defenseless. Any second a missile would impact the Seahawk, or its proximity fuze would detonate. The helo's tail would be blown off or its fuel tanks would be hit and explode or shrapnel would shred the unarmored cockpit. Shattered and burning, pilotless, the Seahawk would dive into the earth at high speed.

There was a sharp blast somewhere close, but the Seahawk kept flying. It made another hard turn, and Jeffrey saw one of the missiles had been fooled by the decoy flares: A ragged cloud of black smoke mingled with the heat flares floating on small parachutes. The other missile was rushing off into the distance, with a perfectly straight red beam from nearby seeming to shove it away, like a rod of something solid. Jeffrey realized this was an anti-missile laser, designed to confuse the heat-seeker head and homing software of the inbound enemy weapon. What Jeffrey saw as a magic rod was the laser beam lighting up fine dust and traces of smoke in the air.

Jeffrey remembered the Apaches. The Seahawk jinked, and he caught a glimpse of one of them, unloading a rippling salvo of rockets at the spot where a missile plume still lingered, rising from its launch point on the ground. The rockets streaked like meteors and pulverized an area of trees in a series of flashes and spouts of dirt. But Jeffrey saw no secondary explosions—he was sure the attackers would have more missiles, and they'd relocate themselves quickly after making that initial telltale launch. They probably even had all-terrain trucks, disguised with freshly cut greenery, so they'd be mobile and harder to spot.

The other Apache emitted a different-looking solid red rod from its chin. This, Jeffrey knew, was a burst of cannon tracer rounds from its multi-barreled gatling gun. The thing could fire three thousand rounds per minute. The gunner and pilot were after something. The gatling gun fired again, and this time there was a brilliant, heaving eruption on the ground. Flames and debris shot high into the air.

Scratch one group of bad guys.

But how many other groups are there?

Jeffrey heard the siren alarm again. More missile launches had been detected by the Seahawk's warning radar.

The view outside was confusing. Missile trails and rocket trails and laser beams intertwined in the sky, and fires burned in several places on the ground—including ones from the infrared flares. Jeffrey knew now why the shuttle's flight path had avoided populated areas. Every piece of ordnance fired had to land somewhere or other, and civilians on the ground could be injured or killed.

There was another hard blast from outside, much closer. The Seahawk shuddered, but continued to fly.

The whole thing started to seem unreal. Jeffrey knew this sensation: It was panic taking hold. There was nothing he could do but stay imprisoned in his flight harness, and everyone in the passenger compartment exchanged increasingly desperate looks. Jeffrey felt like he was in some battle simulator gone wild, or immersed in a demonic videogame. The Seahawk pulled another hard maneuver, fighting for altitude. Jeffrey saw an anti-aircraft missile coming at them from the side, but it was easily rising fast enough to stay aimed right at the helo.

At the last possible second, the pilot rolled the Seahawk so its bottom faced toward the missile. The sickening roll continued, until the helo was upside down. The helo dropped like a stone, the heat of its engines shielded from the missile by the bulk of the fuselage. The missile streaked by harmlessly above them, through the spot where the helo flew moments before.

The falling helo started to finish the other half of the barrel roll. Jeffrey was completely disoriented. He looked out the window to try to regain situational awareness. At first he was looking straight down at the ground—more treetops, very close—and then the Seahawk leveled off. It regained speed.

There was another large explosion on the ground. The air was an even more confusing tangle of tracer rounds and laser beams and heat decoys and smoke trails coming up and going down. The ground now had the beginnings of a serious forest fire.

And another missile was coming right at the Seahawk. The Apaches did what they could to divert it with their spoofing low-energy lasers. The Seahawk popped two more heat flares, but then ran out. The Seahawk had lost too much altitude to maneuver aggressively now, and the enemy missile still bore in.

The missile warhead detonated. Jeffrey felt its radiant heat through the windows a split second before the shrapnel from the warhead battered the helo. Jeffrey was sprayed by a liquid, and was frightened it was high-octane fuel or inflammable hydraulic fluid. Then he recognized arterial blood. The crew chief's head was nearly severed by something that punched hard through the fuselage wall. Jeffrey watched the assistant crew chief look on horrified as his boss died quickly; the young and inexperienced kid went into a trance from mental trauma. Some of the other passengers were bleeding from wounds—Jeffrey wasn't sure how bad. Pieces of smashed window Plexiglas covered everyone and everything. The Seahawk kept on flying, but the vibrations were much rougher and ragged.

Jeffrey had to do something.

UNDERSEA ACTION FROM
THE MASTER OF SUB WARFARE
JOE BUFF

Now available in paperback

CRUSH DEPTH

0-06-000965-9/$7.99 US/$10.99 Can

Reactionary enemy regimes have brutally taken command in South Africa and Germany as U.S. and European shipping lanes are suddenly under attack. Captain Jeffrey Fuller must get his damaged boat back in action to match up against a state-of-the-art German submarine.

TIDAL RIP

0-06-000967-5/$7.99 US/$10.99 Can

Commander Jeffrey Fuller of the fast-attack nuclear submarine USS *Challenger* and his crew must protect an Allied convoy en route to Africa from attack by a virtually undetectable German ceramic-hulled killer sub armed with the most advanced tactical nuclear weaponry available.

Coming soon in hardcover

STRAITS OF POWER

0-06-059468-3/$24.95 US/$34.95 Can

Commander Jeffrey Fuller will go head-to-head against his most dangerous adversary yet—his own allies.

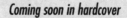